I0664294

Death Stings

Chasing the Dead: *Death Stings* is a stand-alone mystery introducing Sir James Marchant, a recently widowed landowner who is running a sanctuary for retired Police horses. It is also the first of three books featuring Sir James and reveals an ancient vendetta that spans the trilogy.

When an old friend is found murdered, James is drawn into the investigation. Having a brother in the Force proves to be no protection after he discovers a child's body near his land and the only suspects are himself and people he is sure are innocent.

Who else could have a motive?

What is the mystery behind the strange bond between young Holly and the first victim?

Could a child really be the murderer?

Also by E. Bamford under other labels

Death Pledge
Death in Rio
Death Pact

Look out for the next volume soon.

See more on www.EBamford.com
and www.uppbooks.com

First published in Great Britain in 2016
by U P Publications Ltd, Eco Innovation Centre,
PetersCourt, City Rd Peterborough PE1 1SA, UK

Cover design copyright © G. M. Griffin Peers 2016

Copyright © E. Bamford 2016

E. Bamford asserts her moral rights

A CIP Catalogue record of this book is available from the British Library

Paperback Edition ISBN 978-1908135759

eBook Edition ISBN 978-1908135766

FIRST PAPERBACK EDITION

Published by U P Publications
Printed in England by The Lightning Source Group

www.uppbooks.com

www.EBamford.com

Death Stings

E Bamford

U P Publications Ltd
2016

Prologue: Chasing the Dead

Celestine DuPont stood immobilised before her accusers. The year was 1636. It was a time when the Catholic Church was at its most powerful. All France lived in fear of the clerics and none more so than this innocent twelve-year-old.

She had been prepared for the day and was dressed in plain, unbleached muslin, which draped her young, taut body. The sand-coloured cloth had slipped from around her neck revealing white flesh. The girl's dark, wavy hair rested on her shoulders.

Her hands were tightly secured behind her back by a crude plaited rope that cut into her wrists. Her unborn child moved in her distended stomach. Was it as terrified as she was? Her large, brown eyes stared from a deathly, expressionless, white face into a vacant beyond.

Celestine DuPont did not need to hear the verdict. She knew what the verdict would be… guilty as charged. She was living a nightmare. In this nightmare she was the main protagonist. When the nightmare was over she would be dead.

Perhaps she was dead? Her body felt like an empty vessel; maybe her essence had already gone.

Her nostrils flared. There was nothing to negate the

obnoxious stench penetrating her nostrils as it wafted down from the unwashed in the public gallery. Human breath stole what little oxygen there was in the intimidating courtroom.

She surreptitiously raised her eyes to the public gallery. Her accusers were gnawing food with toothless gums then throwing the leftovers over their jiggling, excited shoulders. Liquid was being poured down thirsty throats from dripping leather pouches. Her stomach churned; how could people behave in such a way at time like this?

The men who ruled had intended this day to be a day of reasserting their authority: another day in which to control the masses through fear. In the minds of her countrymen, it was to be a day of entertainment and the best was yet to come.

Celestine DuPont was to be the star attraction.

How had it come to this?

On her first day at the palace, Cardinal Simeon had vowed to her mother that the church would take care of her. Celestine was an eleven-year-old virgin. Before long she had found herself elevated to the Cardinal's bed.

"It is God's wish, my child. We must all do God's work in the best way we know how. I am the instrument of God. Being dutiful in pleasing me you will please God."

Celestine did everything asked of her and now, less than a year later, this man was judging her, accusing her of blasphemy and heresy. She was with child. Her crime was, innocently and proudly, announcing that she was to be the mother of God's child.

His Eminence sat behind an elevated bench. Beneath him four more clergymen, dressed in the cloth, recorded the proceedings on parchment with quill pens. He ignored her as he listened intently to her accusers, his face grave as he waved a little pouch of herbs beneath his long, pinched nose.

He was an impressive man: a man of great intellect. He was dressed in a flowing cassock of cardinal red. His biretta fitted perfectly on his balding head. He was self-righteous and superior: frighteningly so.

His intimidating sermons were repetitive. He was the instrument of God. He was God's right hand. God spoke to him daily. It was God who gave him his instructions. It was God who schooled him in the way to care and protect the people of his province. His sole purpose in life was to guide them along a blameless path. A path that would lead them to the life hereafter and to sit on the right-hand side of God.

Celestine heard testimony after testimony. All lies. She was a child, ingenuous in the ways of the world. Listening to her accusers she now knew it was Cardinal Simeon who was the evil one, not she. She had been far too young to understand.

On entering into the service of the Cardinal she was younger than the other children. She remembered her mother reassuring her as they hugged and said their goodbyes. "I will be thinking of you every minute of every day. I love you Celestine you are a blessed child. His Eminence has promised to take good care of you. Remember to do exactly as you are bid". Her mother had kissed her gently on both cheeks. With tears in her eyes she left Celestine to enter the palace to embark on a cloistered life of serving His Eminence. In return she would be instructed in the sacred teachings of scripture.

Not one person guided her in the ways of the outside world. Not one person explained that what was happening to her was a deadly sin. They whispered and sniggered behind cupped hands, revealing nothing. Cardinal Simeon was "God". Everyone lived in awe of him. If only someone had explained to her, that what was happening was wrong, she would have run back to her mother instead of naively announcing to the people who lived in the palace that she was with child, God's child.

Celestine wasn't listening any more. Her eyes fixed, she held back her tears. The intensifying stench made her feel faint. She was brought out of her reverie by the sound of Cardinal Simeon's gavel hitting the bench. He turned to face her. He placed a black cloth on top of his biretta. In an unwavering, unemotional voice he passed judgement. His spiritless glacier eyes cruelly echoed his words as he pronounced her guilty as charged.

She was to be taken directly to a prepared place, tied to a stake and burned alive. Cheers, along with ear-piercing shrieks of delight, pervaded the room. The rabble in the public gallery, satisfied with the verdict, screamed for her blood. They threw anything to hand at the young girl as she was taken away.

The crowd outside the palace had multiplied as the muttered verdict rippled through the town. A riotous mob had also gathered at the designated place of execution. The words "Whore… Witch," rang in the air.

Keen to see the blasphemer in the flesh the crowd

surged forward, pressing against each other. A woman slipped and fell, then another and another, trodden on and ignored by the wave of stinking humanity, which crushed them to the ground, their screams ignored.

Without emotion the Cardinal later remarked to his aide, "Peasants were trampled on and a few died at the hands of an unruly rabble, clambering to gain a better position, to witness the end of a young girl's life. I hope this has been a lesson to them."

Celestine's heart beat violently. Her feet scraped the ground as she was dragged along until her limp body was hoisted onto a pile of crisp, dry wood and tied to a stake. The young men, who had been thrashed into confessing the possibility that they were the father of her child, were now sheepishly arranging more bracken around her.

Celestine's memory was suddenly pierced with pure insight. Her mind became crystal clear. The meaning of her recurring dreams, her powers of prophesy, her treasured gift of healing, she now understood it all. Her mind clawed at the unfolding scenes in a desperate effort to cling on to her sanity.

She pictured her mama arguing with her grandmamma. It was the same argument she had overheard again and again, "Mama, we have all been blessed with the gift but Celestine's gift is far more evolved than ours. We must protect her. I want her to live. Promise me mama you will not encourage her, not just yet." Her mama, her grandmamma and her aunt were crying.

"Mama, Oh Mama, don't you understand Celestine must live for all of humanity's sake."

Her grandmamma had replied. "I agree with you, Celestine's gift must be developed."

"No mama no, the time is not right."

"We will go away. I will take her away. We will search for a safe place," her grandmamma insisted.

Her mama retorted, "No, no, in these uncertain times we are a lot safer here, we are known here. The villagers will not turn against us, we have helped so many.

"I have made arrangements. She is to go to live in the chateau adjoining the cathedral where she will be instructed in the ways of Catholicism and have the protection of the church. It is the only way to keep her safe. Mama, we are so blessed. Because the Cardinal enjoys our produce he has agreed to take her. In return, we will gift him all the honey he wants. You know how rare it is for people like us to get accepted and to acquire a position in the palace. Celestine's gifts can be developed later."

Her vision began to fade as Cardinal Simeon arrived gripping, a large leather-bound copy of the Holy Bible, to his chest. He stood poker-straight and waited. When his flock had given him their full attention he held the bible high. Shaking it before her he demanded she repent.

With unbelievable strength of mind, the twelve-year-old fixed her eyes on him and screamed, "I, Celestine DuPont, curse you in the name of the Circle of Life and my unborn child. I will pursue you throughout the ages. I will seek you out. I will raze you to the ground. I will have my revenge. As each flame pierces my body so you will die. My baby and I will have our revenge." Celestine spat these, her final words, over and over.

Cardinal Simeon's eyes flashed hatred, his mouth and nostrils taut as he fought for control. With pent-up rage he shook the holy bible and shouted, "Listen to her; hear her admission of guilt. Her own words condemn her. She is a heretic; a blasphemer, a witch who believes in the Circle of Life. It is right, what we do here today. I will destroy this evil and save you all." The crowd roared with delight.

A toothless man smirked as he came forward; his infected body covered in layers of frayed, filthy bandages. A red woollen scarf was draped proudly around his neck. A bribe? A gift? Only he and the giver knew. He shook and danced from foot to foot in excited anticipation. He handed Cardinal Simeon a burning stick of resinous wood. The Cardinal took it, bent and held the stick against the dry bracken until it took hold.

Flames sprang to life, crackling and spitting in rhythm with her words. Shards of bright orange faded into translucent white then darted towards Celestine's feet in ravenous anticipation.

Her tears dried before they fell.

Her intake of breath burned her throat.

Her lungs were about to explode.

She choked her curse one last time… "I will hunt you down …I will have my revenge…I will find you…I will find you…my baby…my baby…my baby…." Her voice faded as it was carried away on clouds of black smoke in their urgency to reach eternity.

The flames touched her long gown and shot upwards. A spark caught her hair and burst into flames.

The people cheered.

The last words Celestine heard were from her adoring mother, her aunt, her grandmother and her sister as they screamed and screamed her name.

The agonizing pain in her once beautiful, brown eyes penetrated her brain like red hot burning arrows. Her sizzling blood stopped flowing. Her fresh, young skin began to bubble, shrink and peel away as the flames ate into her flesh. Her face, no longer young and beautiful, was now a melting twisting picture of distorted horror.

Celestine DuPont was tied to a stake, unable to move. No one could or would help her now. Her head fell forward. The end had come. Her soul along with her baby's soul had departed. She was nothing more than burning flesh: a human torch with which to light the night sky as the people danced.

Cardinal Simeon kissed the Bible. Holding it high for all to see he made the sign of the cross. Without showing any emotion, other than a glimmer of satisfaction in his eyes, he walked away. Celestine and her unborn child – his child, were dead. His reputation and authority remained intact.

Then the celebrations began in earnest.

Three women and Celestine's younger sister slipped away unnoticed to escape the foul stench of burning flesh from the rapidly disintegrating body of their beloved Celestine. With barely a sound they hurried home to their small cottage in the heart of a wood, their plans and dreams for Celestine having ended in an unbelievable and horrific way. The scene they had witnessed and their pain would remain as acute for the rest of their lives.

With heavy hearts the three women were forced to remind themselves of who they were…

They were the women who lived a reclusive life.

They were the women who kept bees.

They were the women who made potions …the women who cured all ills yet no-one would admit to having received such a cure.

Stories were made up about them. Children sang songs about them; adults mocked them behind cupped hands – not for much longer they realised.

They were now in danger.

They would be hunted down like wild animals.

They would be dealt with like wild animals.

They had to leave and leave quickly.

They had to protect their bees, their gifts and their belief in the Circle of Life.

It would only be a matter of hours before the villagers grew bored and turned their attention to new sport. Drunk, they would have the courage to act; they would swarm down on Celestine's family and their crime? They were responsible for bringing the daughter of Satan into their midst.

The three women put their meagre belongings into drawstring cloth bags. They loaded their cart with as many of their beehives as possible. They took one last look at the cottage that had been their home for generations.

Their eyes and faces red with drying tears, they used the darkness of the night along with their instincts to guide them. As they entered the depths of the wood they turned to say one final goodbye to the life they had known. In the distance they saw a procession of burning torches silently and stealthily weaving through the trees towards their cottage. They fled.

In 1638, tired and weary, the three bedraggled women and one young child settled in the Vale of Stourbridge close to the Scottish border. Their hives still intact, their future uncertain, their lore kept safe and their history a dark secret.

Chapter 1 – The year 2012

Bright summer light had morphed into a murky grey. A ghostly quiet engulfed the valley. All that could be heard was the sound of fast-flowing water as it crashed into rocks, in a desperate attempt to reach the North Sea. There was a tang of expectation in the air. Not a leaf flickered, nor did a bird fly and not a creature roamed.

The storm had been forecast and had already arrived on the far side of the valley, it was going to reach the apiary earlier than expected. Eve realised she would be unable to complete the task of fitting or repairing the mouse-guards she had scheduled for today.

There was still plenty of time before autumn set in and, with Holly's help, they would all be done in time. She smiled to herself, as she always did when she thought of the child. From the moment she had set eyes on Holly, Eve knew exactly who Holly was. The child must be protected, receive the best education and be taught to understand the world.

Eve glanced up at the sky. How long did she have? Prancing, black clouds were advancing from the north-east, determined to obliterate all light as they deposited their unwelcome cargo of acid-rain onto the earth below. It was unstoppable. She would finish this hive and then call it a day.

Seconds later the first boom of thunder was heard followed by a resonating rumble, which ebbed away across the valley into the distance. She began to count. She reached ten as forked lightning lit the sky. The storm was ten miles away.

The visitors' centre was closed. Eve guessed that all her staff would be ensconced in their homes by now. She slipped the guard that she was holding back into place as huge drops of rain began to fall. They were slow and spasmodic at first bouncing off the newly-painted white hives, in a graceful sort of way. Plop, plop, plop: it sounded as if someone were plucking strings on a cello: slow and deep then faster and faster and louder and louder until the frantic sound mingled into one.

A voice startled her. "Oh! Hello," Eve said, glancing up to face her unexpected visitor. "You've chosen a bad time to call. Quickly, go inside; the kitchen door is open, I'll be right behind you."

"I won't keep you, I must get back. Have you changed your mind?" The visitor demanded without making a move to leave.

"No, I'm afraid not. It's not possible. I thought I had made myself perfectly clear. Let me finish this, and then we can get in out of the rain. We'll both get drenched standing here."

Eve turned her back on her visitor and returned to the hive she had been working on to check that it was properly closed. She neither saw nor felt the instrument of her death as it hit her. The sickening sound of breaking bones was not heard by anyone as her body made contact with the hive. She fell and lay motionless across the white, wooden structure, her arms dangling on either side. Eve appeared to be hugging the home of her beloved bees, the bees she had lived, loved and cared for, all her life.

The walls of the old farmhouse vibrated with the sound of unceasing screams bringing Becky's concentration to an immediate halt. She threw down the pen she was using …it rolled off her desk and clattered onto the floor. Ignoring it, Becky raced through the office, down the hall, into the kitchen and out into the yard.

She yelled through the rain, "Holly, Holly, where are you." then stopped and listened. The rain was heavier now, beating down, cutting into her face. She tried to wipe away the water that streamed into her eyes with the back of her hand, but more water immediately took its place. Her vision was blurred.

In all ten years of Holly's young life, Becky had never heard her daughter so petrified and screaming so hysterically… Where was she? Listening hard, Becky realised in which direction the screams were coming from and jumped over the low metal chain separating the visitors' centre from the apiary. The swinging sign attached to the chain read '*Private*'. It rattled as it swung to and fro with the force of the wind. Skirting the corner, she raced alongside the building, turned right onto the path leading to the orchard and apiary and came face to face with her little girl.

The screaming child stood shaking from head to toe. Rain dripped from her sodden clothing. Her torso was covered in red …blood? Becky gasped as she fell to her knees and began searching her baby for some kind of wound.

"No, no..." Holly spluttered. Her arm was trembling as she pointed.

Lying a few feet away Becky saw the motionless body of Eve. She was sprawled on the ground facing the heavens. The storm was now directly overhead. Flashes of lightning lit up the sky followed by deafening rumbling thunder as the rain lashed the ground. Eve's blood was rapidly diluting as it filtered into the parched earth.

"I tried, I tried…" Holly sobbed. Becky let go of her and moved in trepidation towards Eve's body. She was no expert but, being unable to locate a pulse, she was sure Eve was dead. Too stunned to do anything other than take her child into her arms to comfort her she stared over Holly's shoulder at the body of the woman who had been the best friend she'd ever had.

"Mummy, mummy," Holly whimpered. "Eve's dead…and…and…"

"It's all right sweetheart, it's all right."

"It's not, mummy, it's not. The bees, it's the bees." Holly's voice quivered. Her body shook as she forced herself to say the words. "They've gone. They've all gone."

Chapter 2 – Sir James

Across the green fertile pastures of the valley, the music of Mozart faded into the ether as Sir James Marchant locked the barn door. The horses were inside safe and secure in their individual stalls, being calmed by the soothing music. His brother had once made a derisive comment when he found out about the music. "I don't believe I am hearing this James, why don't you give them a TV as well?" It never altered James' belief in the fact his horses did like hearing the music.

His beloved horses were never fazed. They had faced rioting hoards, tear gas, explosions along with volleys of gunfire many times, so a storm was nothing for them to be concerned about. Today was different. The storm of all storms had been forecast and they sensed it. Pendragon was the only one still taking it in his stride; he was too old to be daunted, he had seen it all before.

James owned two chestnut stallions, Bolt and Taser; both were purebred French Trotters. The other horses he housed were retired police horses mainly from Maybury Hall.

Maybury Hall was where the horses had been trained

and stabled throughout their working lives in readiness for duty with the North East of England's Mounted Police. Horses were also retired to his sanctuary from forces across the country when the need arose. He had established the sanctuary for two reasons... He was a lover of horses and, additionally, his younger brother Harry had, at one time, been in the mounted section before deciding to become a detective.

Satisfied that there was little else he could do, he pulled up his jacket collar, bent his head and shoulders and, shielding his face from the biting rain, he ran. He crossed the cobbled yard and quivered as he opened the side door to his rambling farmhouse and entered into a storeroom.

The building was a handsome, three-storey stone farmhouse. On the ground floor, was a large, old-fashioned kitchen with an Aga, a walk-in larder, a store room and a wash room, which had been renamed a utility room. The family room, with its cosy feeling and wood-burning stove, was the room they used most. As the name suggests it was used only by family and close friends. A huge sitting-room opened into an equally large, impressive dining room. There was a good-sized cloakroom and, overlooking the front of the property, was James' study: all tastefully furnished, if a little dated.

The first floor had been modernised. It boasted three bedrooms with bathrooms en-suite, along with a small gym. The second floor also had three bedrooms, two of which had en-suite facilities. The third floor mirrored the second floor. Above the third floor was an attic, which went high into the eves. All rooms were aired and kept ready for use by Ella, his cleaner. The property was much too large for one person. Marchant's farm had been in his family for generations. It was the family home and James was determined it would remain so.

The estate was now the second largest in the county. It employed a manager called Reg, who had been with the family since he was a boy; he and his wife lived in the Gate House. Farmhands tended the acreage, fewer these days due to automation. Stable lads took care of the horses.

Although James and his brother Harry came from farming stock, neither wanted to take on the farm as a career choice. Horses yes, they were both obsessed with horses. They each decided to follow a different path. James' father made a stipulation that when the time came, as the elder, James would return to oversee the running of the estate and the twenty-two thousand acres that went with it.

Both boys went to university to study Law, a far removed subject from farm management as one could imagine. While at university James was recruited into the Royal Marines and became a 'secret squirrel' and an expert in covert operations.

He quickly adapted to the life being used to the demanding physical work of a farmer and the bleak weather of the north. He rose to the rank of Major and was awarded the George Cross, which he would never talk about.

Their father died. Reluctantly, James did as he had promised and resigned his commission to take on his inherited role of overseer to the estate. On leaving the

Marines he recommenced his studies and having passed all the necessary exams, he was called to the Bar. James was privileged and only ever worked the cases he was interested in. He only hung up his wig and gown when his beloved wife Jean took ill, although he did keep his seat in chambers. "You never know," he had told Harry "I may want to go back one day."

The horse sanctuary at Marchant's farm grew and grew with horses taken in from other forces. Years later James was knighted by the Queen for his contribution to the care of retired police horses. His brother Harry had continued with his chosen career in the police force and was now a DCI in Meedon Bridge.

"Shit!" James cursed, as he shook the raindrops from his sodden jacket. He hung it on a peg and guessed it would take at least a week to dry out.

"They weren't kidding when they said this was going to be the storm of all storms," he grumbled to no one, for nobody was there to hear. He shuddered. It felt like winter and he wished he were coming home to the loving welcome of his deceased wife, Jean, and the aroma of her cooking. That would never happen again.

It was early September and he was on his own in a cold, empty house. James grunted as he pulled off his boots, which were caked with thick wet mud. He threw them into a corner to be dealt with later.

He poured three fingers of malt whisky and took a large mouthful as he climbed the stairs to take a shower. When done and feeling rejuvenated he eased himself into blue jeans and pulled on a thick, dark, navy-blue, cable-knit, woollen jumper, which Jean had knitted for him years ago. Inexplicably, he was drawn to the window and crossing the room he combed his wet hair.

Rain pelted against the glass. It formed into globules then split and ran in rivulets down the window pane. He strained his eyes to see through the blur into the blackness. Menacing clouds tossed and tumbled in anger as they fought with each other while thunder rumbled away in the distance. There was a thin sheen across the glass about halfway down the window, some sort of reflection he imagined, but he couldn't think where it could be coming from. Perhaps a light had been left on in one of the barns.

James found it hard to believe that the rain could be even heavier than it was when he crossed the yard. The noise it made sounded as if, at any moment, the window would smash, bringing shards of glass into the room. His view was now completely obliterated. As he was about to close the curtains, a flash of forked lightning lit up the inky-black sky and the whole of the valley.

On the other side of the river, Eve's home stood prominent against the dark sky. Electric lights blazed in every room. So, that was the reflection he saw. Very strange; he imagined that someone was going around the property checking that all was in order, but why leave the lights on? He doubted there was any need for concern.

He had known Eve all his life; she was the sister he never had. They had attended the same primary and middle school until James was packed off to boarding school.

They shared the same love for their lush beautiful valley and the bleak rolling moors beyond. Eve loved nothing more than to gallop across the moors with the rain in her face and arrive home laughing, drenched through to the skin. He smiled at the memory and wondered whether she would be out now, if she were younger, riding in this storm; nothing would excite her more.

As much as she loved riding, her greatest passion was her bees. "You'll never love anyone as much as you love your bees," James told her many years ago. She had giggled and with absolute conviction had replied, "You are so right. I have no intention of leaving my bees, ever, not ever."

Eve was six-years-old when she had spoken those words and she had never once wavered in her intent. As far as she was concerned there was no contest with anything or anybody; her bees came first. Eve's family had been Beekeepers for as long as anyone in the valley could remember and the delicious honey the bees produce was now distributed throughout the world.

The whisky running through his veins had warmed him and, as he continued to gaze across at the apiary, he became nostalgic. He realised just how quickly the years had flown by. He began to think about the important part Eve had played in his life and how he owed her and her expertise more than he could ever say, or repay.

Two framed photographs were placed side by side on Jean's bedside table. How he missed her. He picked up the picture, which showed three generations of women, his wife, his daughter Nicky and granddaughter Samantha. He glanced at the other one. It was of his dead daughter, Amanda, Nicky's twin sister and the mother of

Samantha. Amanda had been killed in a road accident when Sam was seven. Jean had intended to have an expert superimpose Amanda into the family snap; she died before she was able to arrange it. It was up to him now.

James decided he would ride over in the morning to see how Eve had weathered the storm. He wondered about her hives, some may have been damaged, or worse – which would break her heart.

In the kitchen, he began to search in the fridge and freezer for something to eat. All he found was a frozen cod in parsley sauce, a four-cheese pizza and a shop-bought lasagne. Not good. Nicky was right he not only needed a cleaner but also a housekeeper.

As the wailing wind swirled and whistled around the old chimney stacks, the rain, lashed at the windows and the temperature dropped. It felt more like winter than the end of summer. James craved comfort food. Chicken liver pate with onion marmalade. Warm home-made bread followed by a rich, beef cobbler. He began to salivate.

He would normally have thought nothing about driving into Meedon Bridge to dine at 'The Fallen Angel', which was his favourite watering hole, but not tonight. He had no intentions of negotiating this storm, so he put the idea out of his mind. He'd have to pay a visit to the supermarket tomorrow, how he hated shopping for food.

He popped the cheese and tomato pizza into the oven and began to read his newspaper. Deep in concentration, he forgot the time until he smelled burning. "Oh no!

Shit," he swore as he rescued a blackened pizza. Mumbling obscenities to himself, he found a tin of beef broth, warmed it and ate it with a chunk of old bread.

The heat coming from the Aga wasn't enough. He was cold. He was miserable, yet it was quite ludicrous to even think about lighting a fire or switching on the central heating, for one person and, for only a few hours. He decided to go bed and read.

The windows rattled, reminding him that they needed replacing. Once again he was drawn to his bedroom window. In the east, the sky was starting to brighten. The storm was moving away. On the other side of the river Honeycombe apiary still had every light burning.

Something was not right.

Perched on the edge of his bed he reached for the phone.

He punched in Eve's number.

It was a while before his call was answered and answered by a man whose voice he didn't recognise who just said, *"Hello"*. James asked to speak to Eve.

"Who's calling?" The man's tone was abrupt.

James never enjoyed using his title; however, it sometimes came in useful and something told him that this was one of those times. "Sir James Marchant."

"How can I help you, Sir James?"

"I've already told you, I'd like to speak to Eve."

"Who exactly are you, Sir James?"

"More to the point, who are you?" This officious guy was starting to annoy.

The man didn't reply for a moment then said, "I need to know your relationship to … Eve."

A chilled shudder slid down James' spine, his chest tightened and his breath stalled.

"I'm a close friend," he managed to say. "I've told you who I am. Who the hell are you? What's going on over there? All the lights have been blazing away for hours."

"Hold the line, please, sir?"

It seemed like an age before someone spoke.

"Officer Cranmore here, sir."

"Officer! What the hell's going on?"

"And you are?"

"How many more times do I have to tell you, Sir James Marchant," he snapped.

"Would you be Nicky Marchant's father, the solicitor?"

"Yes."

"I know Nicky, our paths cross often."

"I expect they do…"

"Sir James, are you a relative of Eve's?"

"I'm the nearest she has to one."

"Sir James, there has been an incident. I can say no more for the moment."

James knew exactly what "incident" implied.

"Officer Cranmore. As I am sure you very well know, my brother is DCI Marchant, I'm fully aware of what incident means. What sort of incident? What has happened? Is Eve all right?"

Silence.

"Eve; speak officer Cranmore, speak." James commanded.

Still the man hesitated. "I suppose no harm can be done, it'll be public knowledge by morning. Sir, I wish I didn't have to tell you this over the telephone."

"Get on with it," James was losing his temper

"Eve is no longer with us…"

James hesitated then yelled, "No longer with us! Are you trying to tell me she's dead?"

"Yes sir."

The reply stunned James. He then asked, "Enlighten me. Some sort of accident?"

"Murder."

"Murder! Ridiculous! Explain!" It was obviously a mistake.

"She received a nasty blow to the head. The doctor who examined her is adamant it couldn't possibly have been an accident."

Silence.

It was as if another person was now in control of his mind and having, over the years, listened to many of Harry's accounts of investigations he unemotionally asked, "Any weapon found?"

"No sir."

"Footprints?"

"No, the rain saw to that. We were limited as to what we were able to do in this storm. We've searched with lights. We found nothing. Almost all traces of blood had been washed away before we could get the scene covered. We'll conduct a grid to grid search tomorrow."

"Where was she found?"

"In the apiary."

"I'm coming over."

"No sir. With respect; she's been taken away and the scene has been secured. Nothing more can be done until daylight. It's like a mud bath out there we're doing more harm than good. The paths between the hives are running streams. No doubt any evidence will have washed down into the river."

"More than likely," James groaned. "Have you any ideas?"

"It's too soon to speculate."

"Who found her?"

"A kid called Holly McGrath."

He had forgotten about Becky and Holly for the moment. "Where is she? Where's her mother?"

"Mother and child are on their way to hospital. They're both in shock. The child won't stop screaming. There's nothing any of us can do until daylight."

There was little point in asking any more questions so James thanked the officer and broke the connection. "My God," he groaned as he fell back against his pillows.

Eve dead?

Murdered?

He touched the side of the bed where Jean should have been; she wasn't there, no one was there. He was quite alone. It was incredible: impossible to believe.

He suddenly sat up as he realised he hadn't time to wallow in grief. Eve's unexpected death had given him a problem, one hell of a problem. There was something he had to do before the police obtained the necessary authority to search her home, and remove whatever they felt required further examination, in the process of finding her killer.

James went into the kitchen and made himself a pot of strong coffee. He would not get any sleep this night. He'd been trained to wait. He reckoned that two-thirty would be about the right time. The neighbours should be sound asleep.

It was two-thirty. He went into his office and opened a wooden cupboard door in his desk. It revealed a safe. The safe had been bolted into the concrete floor. He retrieved what he wanted; unable to remember the last time it had been necessary to use them.

He was ready.

It had stopped raining.

Walking out into a blustery wind he stuffed his hands into his pockets as he glanced up. Swirling black clouds scurried across the sky anxious to move on and create havoc elsewhere. He climbed into his BMW X5.

He took his time driving down the long tarmac drive; water now filled the potholes, which had been created by the weighty farm traffic. The wind pounded the car. He drove between the open decorative-iron gates that flanked the driveway. The gatehouse on his right was in darkness and he imagined that, like all good people, his farm manager, Reg, and his wife were sound asleep.

A sharp left took him onto a narrow country lane. Leaves ripped from branches spiralled along the hedgerows and broken bracken bounced in front of the car. Ancient oaks rocked, precariously.

With each bump in the road and movement of the wheel the BMW's headlights created ghostly shapes and shadowy figures as they danced through the trees. The apiary was only half a mile away from Marchant's farm but on the other side of the river. This added time and distance to his journey. The River Tyne meandered down from the mountains; he could see it in the distance, a raging torrent of water frantically racing towards the unforgiving North Sea.

What could have happened? Eve was a phenomenon, a unique human being. Loved and respected by all who knew her. Who would want to harm her? He quivered. "God almighty, I am going to miss you Eve, first Jean and now you, gone forever." In fury he banged his hands on the steering-wheel and wished he could put the clock back a decade when all his family were here and life was perfect.

He turned into Honey Pot Lane and slowly pulled his BMW to a stop. He killed the lights. He got out. He gripped the car door to steady himself as the wind tore at his clothes, he listened and looked. Only the sounds of the wind and the raging river could be heard, nothing else moved.

Fifty yards ahead on his right was a terrace of six picturesque, stone cottages, built for the farm-workers of old. They boasted small, neat, front gardens and long, narrow, back ones, they were in complete darkness. To his left, a grassy bank, varying in width, sloped down to the river and disappeared from view.

The air was heavy. He savoured the powerful odour of damp earth, which made his nose twitch. It was an honest smell: an exciting smell, the smell of rejuvenation, of life itself. It would be a good day tomorrow; it was cruel that Eve would not see it. Satisfied that it was safe to continue he climbed back into his car. Fighting against the wind he managed to close the door. He then restarted the engine and drove up the lane.

He reached the entrance to Honeycombe Farm and the visitors' centre and pulled the car to a stop. No sign of any police activity. They were hardly ever needed in this part of the valley; a patrol car would occasionally drive by, to check that all was in order at the apiary. However, James realised that Eve's death meant that more officers would be drafted in from other forces.

He counted eight cars in the car park, he knew everyone.

Standing facing the property, Honeycombe farm, Eve's home, was to his right. It had a pretty, floral, front garden and a little-used, stone-flagged path up to the door. He ignored it and walked across the lane to the five-barred gate on his left, which led into a cobbled courtyard.

As he expected the gate was secured with yellow 'scene of crime' tape. He untied it, pushed the gate open then drove his BMW into the yard. He pulled to a stop outside the kitchen door of Eve's sixteenth-century stone-built farmhouse; all the lights were now off.

He sat staring at the dark outline of the visitors' centre and the beehives beyond where Officer Cranmore had told him Eve's body had been found. To his left, across the cobbled yard, a low, chain-link fence was fastened to the wall of the visitors' centre and the other end was attached to a huge oak tree that bordered the lane, prohibiting the public access to the apiary.

The entrance door to the centre opened onto a reception area. To the right a corridor wound around the inner wall of the building. The first door a visitor would come to opened into a screening room, large enough to accommodate thirty people. Framed pictures of the history of bee-keeping adorned the walls. By pressing a large blue button, at the side of a large screen, a short film would automatically spring into motion showing how Eve's family had created the apiary and how it had changed over the years.

The next room had a wall of glass through which visitors could watch the bee-keepers at work. The next room also had a glass wall where visitors could watch the honey being harvested, bottled, labelled and stacked into boxes ready for distribution.

The corridor continued right and led into a café, which provided an extensive range of herb teas, coffees and soft drinks. An array of freshly-made pastries and savoury snacks were also on offer.

Leading from the café, an enticing gift shop displayed locally produced bric-a-brac. Varying merchandise made from honey and its by-product; honey-mustard, beeswax: face creams, balms, candles and polishes.

Eve's home faced the lane and went back to align itself with the end wall of the café, leaving a gap between the two buildings, of approximately one metre. The complex was in the shape of a U. It was all in total darkness.

He had put it off long enough. He hoped he would not have to spend too long in the house. James went back to the gate, closed it and replaced the scene of crime tape as a precaution in case somebody decided to take their dog for a walk now that the storm had passed.

He opened the boot of his BMW and took out two

sturdy boxes along with three strong supermarket 'bags for life'. He had no idea where to start and he had no idea of the amount he would find. He left the boot open. From his pocket James pulled out the set of keys he had taken from his safe. He let himself into Eve's kitchen. The only people who used the front door of the property were Eve's private patients.

He pulled on protective gloves. He would be a fool to take any chances. His fingerprints would be found all over the house, which would be quite understandable, but not necessarily where he intended to search tonight. James made directly for the offices.

Becky and Holly lived with Eve. Becky helped Eve with her research and the daily paperwork relating to The Centre. He knew Becky had her own office. Eve had her office adjacent to her treatment room. He first made for Eve's rooms. It was more than likely that he would find there what he was looking for. He walked across the room and closed the curtains. He switched on the light and began his search.

He didn't think that what he sought would be in her desk drawers but he looked anyway. In the second drawer down he found four memory-sticks and slipped them into his pocket. He opened cupboard after cupboard, they were packed with files or specimen jars, tubs, creams all made from honey.

A low cabinet sat next to the window. It was locked. He smiled, confidently. All he needed was a key. He worked his way through the bunch of Eve's duplicate keys, not one fitted the lock. He dared not force the door open – that would give the investigating team, something to think about. *Key, key, key. Where would Eve keep such an important key? Close to hand. Handbag of course.*

Eve's handbag was lying alongside her desk: no reason for it to be anywhere else. He rummaged through the bag feeling guilty, taking no solace in the fact that what he was doing was for the best. There was no key. To make sure, he tipped the bag upside down and shook out all the contents. He separated the items; there was a purse, he checked inside, no key. There was a packet of tissues, car keys, a small makeup-bag and a pen attached to a small notebook.

He clapped both sides of the soft, red-leather bag together to make sure he hadn't left anything inside and felt something hard. He opened up the bag again, as he did so he noticed a zip running along the left hand side. He slid open the zip and retrieved a small address book. Why would Eve carry an address book when all such information would be on her computer? He flicked through the book and understood. He slipped the small, pretty-flowered, address book into his pocket.

She may have carried the key with her. It was an important key. Important enough for her to want to do that, if she had, then real trouble lay ahead. Eve was now at the morgue and the key would be found. Bedroom? This was his only hope. He was almost running as he made for the stairs. Eve's room was at the back of the property where she could see her precious hives first thing in a morning and last thing at night.

He stood in the doorway and glanced around the room. It was lit by irregular beams of light coming through the window as the dispersing clouds crossed over the shimmering post-storm moon. The original low beams appeared lower than he remembered and barely skimmed the four poster bed, which dominated the room. James had not been in Eve's bedroom for years. The last time was when he'd gone up to fetch Amanda after she had refused to come home. It had changed little; it was still decorated with vibrantly coloured, butterfly-patterned wallpaper: all so 'Eve'.

He first pulled open the drawer to the left-hand bedside cabinet, nothing. He hurried to the right-hand bedside cabinet. He pulled open the top drawer. Bingo. There staring up at him was a key ring with keys attached.

He felt sweat form on his brow and neck. It trickled down his back as he jumped down the stairs two at a time and raced back into Eve's treatment room. By the shape of the lock he knew what size of key was needed. He found it. He opened the cupboard and with relief and urgency he began to pack the boxes with the contents of the cupboard. Only the boxes were needed.

When he was done his prime concern was that there were not as many as he had expected. He then realised it would all depend on supply and demand. He was sure he had emptied the cupboard but, not taking any chances, he got on his knees, bent his head and thoroughly examined the inside. He hadn't missed any. There was something else he had expected to be in there, but it wasn't. The more he considered it, the more he came to the conclusion that Eve would no longer have need for it: not after all these years.

The possibility crossed his mind that there could be more somewhere else, in the house, or maybe, even in

The Centre. He doubted it. Eve would never have taken the chance of someone finding it. He closed the cupboard door leaving it unlocked. He put the keys into Eve's handbag. He then put the boxes along with the unused bags into the boot of his car. He locked the kitchen door, climbed into his BMW and made for home.

Chapter 3 – Becky

Becky sat alongside her daughter's bed and gazed at her. Her plump young face was framed by long, dark hair. She appeared at peace: her breathing shallow and her head motionless on a pristine white pillow. For how long, Becky asked herself.

When Becky had worked as a librarian in Meedon Bridge, meeting Eve had transformed her life and each day she thanked God for all the good things that had happened to her since. Now, those things were going to be taken away.

Eve was dead.

What would they do? Where would they go? She fought back tears. Eve had been the best friend a person could have and Holly adored her, even more than me, she smiled to herself. She could live with that.

Now Eve was dead she would never be able to repay her for all she had done for them. It was beyond belief that someone had murdered her.

She kept telling herself it was early days: asking herself how the police could believe it to be murder so soon. There would be an autopsy, wouldn't there? Only then they would be sure how she died.

Becky had never met anyone who had ever spoken a word against Eve. Eve had spent her life caring for people. It was her whole life. It was her calling. She would help anyone in need, with no exceptions.

Becky realised that Holly would sleep for hours yet; the doctors had sedated her heavily. She wanted her to sleep for as long as possible, the simple reason being that when she awoke she would be reminded of the horrific scene she had witnessed and start screaming again.

Holly loved Eve and she loved the bees. When Eve introduced Holly to the bees she became brim full with excitement to such an extent it baffled Becky and still does. Holly had told her that when she grew up she wanted to be like Eve and be a *keeper of bees*. Such a strange thing for a little girl to say: now both Eve and the bees were gone.

Hundreds of hives were empty. Holly had told her the bees circled Eve's body and then flew away. The police woman didn't believe her, not for one second. She'd said to Holly, "Are you asking me to believe the bees knew Eve was dead and so they flew away." Holly had replied defiantly and with the innocence of a child she simply answered, yes.

If the police woman suspected that Holly was telling a lie, what was the chance she would believe anything else Holly said? Something else was worrying Becky. She had overheard a conversation, between the woman officer and her male colleague when they thought they were out of earshot, which really scared her.

"Do you think she did it?" the woman officer asked.

The man replied, "Shouldn't think so she's only a kid."

"Huh! Been done before."

"I know but I doubt it."

"Why?"

"Just do. Something about the kid …she's sweet."

"Sweet! What planet are you on? No such bloody thing these days. What about the mother? It's possible she did it, ran back to the house, cleaned herself up and waited for her kid to discover the body. She knew it was the first place her kid would go when she came home."

"What mother would do such a thing?" she'd heard the man ask.

"A mother who wanted to get away with murder."

Chapter 4 – Sir James

It was around four in the morning when James returned home. The powerful wind had buffeted his BMW, whipping up fallen branches, bracken and debris. He had watched huge oaks precariously lurch back and forth and he was convinced that many of the ancient trees would not survive the night.

With muddled feelings and adrenalin running wild he realised there was no possibility of sleep so he made a fresh pot of coffee. As he drank he visualised an early morning meeting with the hierarchy at police headquarters followed by a hastily drafted-in team from adjoining forces. Instructions would be given and the application for a search warrant made and only then would the investigation commence in earnest.

Maybe the forensic team would come back? He somehow doubted it. Regardless of the advancement of forensic science it would be a miracle if anything were to be found at the scene after such a storm. The paths were running streams. Debris carried on the wind would be miles away by now. James had lived through many a storm. Last night's storm was the worst for nearly thirty years; he didn't need the BBC weather man to tell him that.

Eve was a prominent member of society. She was a Trustee on the hospital board of the new Meedon Bridge hospital also the local hospice as well as being the president of the Bee Keepers Society of Great Britain. There would be a lot of interest in the case and many influential people would be baying for blood. An early arrest would be most welcome and from what little everyone knew of the newcomers, Becky and Holly, James didn't need to be convinced that they would become the most likely suspects.

He took Eve's handbag-sized, flowered address book from his pocket and placed it on the dining room table. He then fetched the phone, a pen and some paper on which to jot down addresses. Sitting at the dining table he began to flick through the pages of the book. Most of the telephone numbers had been crossed out. There were only numbers under the letters G, J, K, M, R and W making eight telephone numbers in total.

Four hours later, James began to dial the first of the numbers. A woman answered after five rings. She sounded both middle-aged and as if suffering from lack of sleep.

"Mrs Gordon?"

"Yes."

"Mrs Gordon, my name is James Marchant. I'm a friend of Eve Dupton, I have known her all my life; we grew up together."

Silence.

"Hello, are you there? Mrs Gordon, please don't be afraid. I'm referring to Eve from Honeycombe Apiary?"

"Er …yes… Why are you telling me this?"

"Because I want you to trust me. Mrs Gordon, I wish I didn't have to make this call. I am afraid I have some sad news. Eve died yesterday."

The woman caught her breath. Shocked, she cried, "What? died! But, but…"

Without hesitation James continued. "I am working through Eve's private address book to notify her special friends."

He stressed the word special. "My job is to carry out Eve's wishes. I believe Eve gave you and your family a lot of comfort over the past few months. I'd like to help you if I can."

Again silence.

The woman hesitated, obviously uncertain. "I'm not sure. I don't know. I, I …don't know what you mean."

James was quite sure she did know what he meant.

"Mrs Gordon, I have a small amount of the product Eve used to give you and when it's gone, it's gone. Do you need more?"

The woman spoke with uncertainty. "If you have some to spare…"

"It is what Eve would have wanted me to do. I will happily come to see you, just name a time."

The woman said a time. James sensed her apprehension and he pictured her worrying up until the time they met when he would then put her mind at rest.

James repeated the call seven more times.

It was time to go. James put on a pair of trainers and slipped his arms into his jacket, it was still wet so he put it back on the peg and routed around until he found an old anorak. He closed the door behind him. Fresh air greeted him, cleansed after the storm, and James stood a moment and savoured deep breaths before making his way to the yard.

The yard was a hive of activity. Reg, his estate manager, was directing the hands who were collecting huge amounts of debris. It wouldn't have surprised him if the whole of Osbert Wood had been uprooted and transported into the yard.

At the sound of horses' hooves James noticed Carl, one of his stable lads, holding tightly on to the reins of two fractious horses. He was leading them out from the far end of the newly-built stable block.

"Good God," he swore. Reg was his usual calm self. "Did a hurricane hit the place? What a mess. How are the horses?"

"All fine. Don't ask me how," Reg said as he pointed to where the storm had downed a huge tree. One of its branches was sprawled across the roof of the new stable block. "It caught the end of the building. We were lucky. I'm surprised you didn't hear it."

James realised that the tree must have fallen when he was at Eve's.

"It could have been a lot worse. I doubt the insurance will pay up – act of God, they'll say." The sound Reg made reflected clearly his opinion of insurance companies.

"Before you get on to them Reg will you speak to

Barber's and get them up here to see what needs to be done, whatever it is, it has to be fixed and fixed quickly."

"Already done, I got Sid Barber at home; I intended to be the first in line."

James smiled to himself; he could always rely on Reg. "As if I needed to ask. I would normally help out Reg but, unfortunately, I'm expecting to be busy for the next few days, which will mean leaving everything in your capable hands." James hesitated while deciding what to say. There was no easy way and this wouldn't be the last time he would have to say what he was about to. "I guess it's too soon for you to have heard…"

"Heard what?"

"It's Eve – Eve from the apiary."

Reg laughed. "We all know, Eve," he said lovingly. On noticing James' set expression he said, as his face clouded. 'Why what's happened?"

James looked down on the cobbles. "She was murdered late yesterday afternoon sometime during the storm…"

The woman manning the reception desk at the Meedon Bridge Hospital was middle-aged with short, fair hair. Her uniform was pristine and she welcomed him courteously. The badge she wore said her name was Maud.

"Can I help you?" she asked.

"I'm enquiring after Becky and Holly McGrath. They were brought in late last night."

"One moment and I'll check." Maud began to tap on the keyboard of her computer.

"Yes – here it is." The expression on her face altered into a frown. "I'm sorry," she said. "It says here that they are not allowed visitors."

"Who gave those instructions?"

"The police, apparently." Maud replied, screwing up her eyes implying that she didn't understand.

"That should not apply to me, Maud. I'm their solicitor."

Maud relaxed and smiled she had obviously been expecting him to make trouble. "I suppose not. Go up those stairs," – she pointed in the direction he should take – "at the top, take a right and keep going until you come to another reception desk. If you give me your name, I'll tell them to expect you. They'll direct you from there."

"Sir James Marchant," he called as he turned and walked away.

On reaching the second reception desk a nurse glanced up from the computer she was working on. Her badge told him that her name was Betty.

"Hello Sir James. How are the horses this morning?"

Her remark took James by surprise. The young nurse apparently knew exactly who he was.

"They are all well, thank you. Although they were a little fractious until the storm blew itself out."

"I wondered about them. My brother has joined the Mounted section of the police and talks of nothing else so I know all about your horse sanctuary." Her eyes shone and her lips curled proudly as she pictured her younger brother, dressed in a police uniform, riding one of the sections magnificent horses. She pointed. "If you go along that corridor Becky and Holly are in room 9. It is the last one on the left."

Minutes later he was tapping on the door marked with the number 9. He opened it and popped his head around it. Holly was sleeping obviously heavily sedated. Becky flinched as she saw him. He put his fingers to his lips implying that she should be quiet. He closed the door and, lifting a chair from the far corner of the room, he placed it next to hers besides the bed.

Becky's face was puffed and the rims of her eyes were red-raw, having cried so much during the night. On seeing James, the tears began to roll again. She reached for a box of tissues a nurse had left for her.

"Becky, by rights, I shouldn't be here so I must be quick. You are likely to get another visit from the police. In case we are interrupted let me, first of all, say this; be careful how you phrase your words to avoid incriminating yourself. Tell them the truth by all means." James looked directly into her eyes. "However, if they imply that you may want to call a solicitor, think before you speak. Ask them why would you want a solicitor, something like that? If they make you feel uncomfortable and you do want someone to speak for you," James hesitated as he reached in his pocket and produced a card. "Take this, keep it safe all my numbers are on it."

Becky lifted her head and her lips began to tremble. She was no longer on her own.

"They think Holly or I murdered Eve," she sniffed.

"They probably do at the moment."

"Why? Why would they think that?"

"Statistically, murders are often committed by a family member or someone who is known to the victim, also, a lot of murders are committed by the person who discovers the body."

"Don't frighten me James."

"I'm sorry I didn't mean to."

"That doesn't make sense surely, if you murdered someone, you wouldn't go and report it." Becky sounded surprised.

"I'm not a psychologist so I can't answer that one."

"James I don't know what to do. I've sat here all night thinking about where I should go for help. I don't mind admitting it I'm scared to death."

"I'm here now and I'm going to help you. You meant the world to Eve and Eve meant the world to me. She would want me to do everything I can to sort this out. I'm not leaving it entirely up to the police. When we've finished here I'll go and talk to Nicky, she hasn't heard yet and, if it comes to you needing a solicitor then she's it. So stop worrying."

"I thought you were a solicitor?"

"No, I'm a barrister. Between the two of us you have nothing to be concerned about. Now, tell me exactly what happened?"

Becky took another tissue, wiped her nose then began. "The first thing Holly does, if she has been out, is to go to the apiary and check on the bees. Yesterday was no exception although the storm was directly overhead. She was worried about them. I was working in the office and suddenly above the sound of the rain I heard her screams. She sounded terrified.

"I ran as fast as possible and found her standing rigid and still screaming. She was sopping wet and the front of her dress was covered in blood. I immediately imagined some sort of accident that she had cut herself. I looked for the wound. She pushed me away and pointed to Eve."

"Where was Eve?"

"Lying on the ground. Holly told me she found Eve sprawled across one of the hives. Thinking she had slipped and got stuck she tried to lift her off. After a struggle she managed it. Eve wouldn't speak to her and she became frightened. She didn't know what to do. She rocked and rocked Eve, trying to wake her up. Eve still didn't move. Then she saw the blood. Oh James …she was petrified. She lay Eve on the ground and started to run towards the house only she froze. She said her legs wouldn't move. All she could do was stand and scream." Becky stared at him. "She's only a child, James. How can the police possibly think…?"

"They have a job to do. The police will be asking a lot of people a lot of questions and that will include me."

"Who could have done such a thing? Everyone loved her. All she lived for were her bees and to help people. She's healed so many. She's never hurt a single soul. Just think what she has done for us. It doesn't make any sense."

"It's my guess she interrupted an intruder and the guy, for whatever reason panicked. That person must be found." James stood and put the chair back where it was. He then walked back to Becky and touched her shoulder. "Now, I don't want you to worry. Remember to tell the police exactly what you have told me."

"But, I already have…"

"I understand that, but they will ask you again and

again. They will ask you the same questions over and over, only in a slightly different way."

"Trying to trick me, you mean."

James answered with a nod of his head. "The hospital will probably release you later today. When you're home, call me. In the meantime, I'm going to see Nicky. I want her to know what has happened before she hears it from someone else."

Becky nodded.

"Remember what I've told you, don't let them lead you into saying something you will later regret."

"I have nothing else to tell them. What I've told you and what I told the police is the truth. That is what happened. That is all Holly and I know."

"I realise that. We'll talk again later." James opened the door, glanced both ways, and as no one was about he closed the door quietly behind him and left.

He found and knocked on the door of the administration office. He gave his name, heard a buzzing sound and the door clicked open to allow him entry.

An elderly woman was busy behind a desk as James approached. He explained that he was a close friend of one of their Trustees who had sadly and unexpectedly died. He needed the telephone numbers of the other Trustees to enable him to notify them.

It was common knowledge who were the members of the board of Trustees so under the circumstances, the woman called Jenny didn't object.

James left with the information and sitting in his car in the car park James began to make the calls. Relieved when he had finished he drove to Lay Lane Surgery. It was where Eve practiced part-time as a GP and he asked to see Dr Cobb the senior partner. He explained that it was a personal matter of which Dr Cobb should be informed as soon as possible.

He was ushered to a chair in the waiting room amidst young and old with their varying complaints. A woman behind him, somewhere to his left, had an awful cough and he hoped he would not leave with more than he had come in with.

As instructed he sat watching the monitor.

A young man hobbled along the corridor towards him his leg plastered up to his thigh and James felt sorry for his obvious discomfort and the frustration he must be feeling. He hoped he had come from seeing Dr Cobb. He had. Writing appeared at the bottom of the monitor – Sir James Marchant to see Dr Cobb in Room 7.

It took less than three minutes to tell the doctor what had happened and was thankful when the doctor said he would inform all the other doctors including the Meedon Bridge Hospice where Eve spent a lot of her time making the dying as comfortable as possible.

Shortly after James arrived home the doorbell rang. He was sitting in the dining room with his head bent pouring over some of Eve's papers, which were sprawled across the table. He bundled them up and pushed them aside placing, on top, an unopened envelope Eve had given him a few months before.

A man and a woman stood outside and he guessed straight away who they were although he had not expected them quite so soon.

"Sir James Marchant?" The woman asked brusquely.

"Yes."

"I'm Inspector Blackwell and this is Detective Mike Cranmore." The woman gestured towards the younger man. "We'd like to have a word with you. May we come in?"

"I am due to leave in fifteen minutes."

"We won't keep you long."

James led the two officers into the sitting room where they sat at opposite ends of a well-used, green-leather chesterfield and James sat opposite them in a matching chair. James observed the Inspector as her eyes darted around the room. She was about five-feet-five inches tall with bleached, blonde, shoulder-length, straight hair that was twisted and clipped at the nape of her neck. Her eyes were grey, rather large and inclined to protrude. She appeared to be hyperactive and James suspected she might have an overactive thyroid although he was no expert in the matter. By contrast, Cranmore appeared to be a pleasant young man with a much calmer nature. His tongue-in-cheek expression gave the feeling that he permanently harboured a joke.

"How can I help you?" James asked.

"Am I right in thinking it was you who telephoned the deceased last night?"

"Yes and her name is… was… Eve."

"Can you tell me why you did that?"

"As I explained to your officer, I noticed all the lights were on and when, two hour later, they were still on, I became concerned so I telephoned her."

"Why would you do that?"

James frowned and shook his head. He would have to spell it out. "She was a friend. Why would anyone have all their lights blazing away in the height of a storm? I'm rather old-fashioned and I still unplug electrical equipment even the TV although I have been assured that it is not necessary to do so these days."

"I see," she mused.

"Also, as only three people live at Honeycombe Apiary and three people can't be in a dozen rooms at the same time. Impossible, wouldn't you say?"

She didn't answer for a moment. "Would you mind if Cranmore went to see what it was you were able to see last night?"

"It's daylight.'

"Cranmore has a good imagination."

"Then I'll show you the way."

"I think he will be able to find it, if that's all right with you?"

"No problem. Up the stairs and turn right, walk along the corridor and you will come to my room, it's the last one on the left."

The Inspector continued. "What is your relationship to the deceased?"

"I've known her all my life."

"I'm sorry you must be very upset."

"I am."

"I'm new to this area. I get the feeling that it is a close-knit society," she said.

"It is a farming community, everyone knows everyone living here in the valley, except for a few townies, who are a recent addition to the area. As the older generation die off the townies buy up their homes and use them as weekend retreats."

Blackwell nodded. "It's happening all over."

"Since you knew the deceased so well what can you tell me about her? I've have been told she didn't have any living relatives."

"That's right."

"Who would benefit from her death?"

"No one, her estate is in Trust."

"Can I have the names of the Trustees?"

"There's only one…"

The corners of Blackwell's mouth twitched. "And that someone would be you."

"Right again."

"Which means that you are solely responsible for distributing the monies?"

"I am solely responsible for administering her wishes, if that is what you're implying."

"Can I have the name of her solicitors?"

"Of course, it's Lane and Son in the High Street in Meedon Bridge.

"So …there isn't anyone who will gain, other than the trust?"

"That's correct."

"Not even you, her life-long friend." There was sarcasm in her voice.

"Not even me. The trust will start to work after the funeral and ensure that Eve's wishes are carried out to the letter."

"Do you know if Eve had any enemies?" Blackwell

asked.

"Not an enemy in the world."

"She had one," the woman said looking directly into James' eyes.

"Eve was a well-liked and a respected member of our community. I have never heard a bad word spoken about her." James was taking a dislike to this woman. She was about thirty. Her face was expressionless. She was abrasive and humourless.

"How well do you know the people who live in the cottages in Honey Pot Lane?"

"I know them all. I know who drives which car. I know who lives in which cottage their approximate age and so forth. They're all involved with the apiary in one way or another."

"How so?"

"They work in the shop, café, in the grounds. They help Eve attend the hives. At least one member of each family is employed at the apiary. Except for Mr Clark who was retired and he recently died. His cottage is about to be renovated."

"Sold?"

"Definitely not."

"What do you know about Rebecca and Holly McGrath?"

"Delightful people."

Cranmore re-entered the room. Blackwell waited for him to speak.

"It is possible to see Honeycombe farm in the distance, Ma'am. In the dark and with all lights on it would have lit up like a Christmas tree."

Blackwell huffed. "I'm sorry to have to ask all these questions, Sir James. You do understand?"

"Perfectly."

"Since you appear to be the closest thing to a relative would you be prepared to identify the body?"

He felt as if he had been kicked in the stomach by one of his horses and hoped she hadn't noticed him flinch. "Of course, I'll come into town later this morning".

Blackwell stood. "Thank you and thank you for talking to us, if I need to speak with you again…"

"You know where to find me. Don't leave one stone unturned, Inspector. I want Eve's killer found."

"We all do, sir."

James knew it was not to be the last he'd see of the pair and he went back into the dining room. He picked up the envelope he had left lying on the top of Eve's papers was about to open it then decided against it. When Eve had handed it to him she explained that it was the previously discussed codicil to her Will.

James knew what the envelope contained and at the time he had recently lost Joan and didn't want to consider the possibility of Eve dying so he had decided, as there was no urgency, to lock it in his safe. Once again he decided to leave it until later in the day. He bundled up the papers and returned them to his safe. He had people to see, places to go and errands to run.

Chapter 5 – Nicky

With shoulder-length, brown, unruly hair Nicky stood a proud five-foot-eight inches. Both his twins had unruly hair, James vividly remembered. Nicky didn't seem to care. Amanda was always complaining and used instruments of torture in an attempt to straighten hers. Nicky scrunched her hair up and wrapped some sort of band around it. "You remind me of one of Dad's horses" Amanda would say to Nicky. "Why don't you get with it?" Whatever that meant.

Amanda lived life to the full. She married at eighteen giving him the only grandchild he guessed he would have, and doubted he would ever see again. Nicky, although not lacking in Amanda's spunk, was more studious; she loved reading and music. She went on to study Law in London.

When the senior partner of Lane and son died, Lane's only son Peter didn't want to continue with the firm. He had never wanted to be a solicitor. He sold the firm to James who purchased it for Nicky. The younger Mr Lane bought a boat and disappeared to the Caribbean to spend his life sailing from island to island.

Both girls had a good sense of humour and he missed how they used to bounce of each other and make him laugh. Those were the days.

Amanda was the first to die, killed in a road accident. Her husband migrated to Australia taking his only grandchild with him and never made contact again. Joan, his adored wife was the next family member to die, and now Eve, all gone. As he stood in the doorway watching Nicky work he prayed that nothing would ever happen to her.

Nicky sensed a presence and glanced up. "Dad! I didn't hear you come in."

"I won't keep you long sweetheart." He surreptitiously closed the door so as not to be overheard by the other members of her staff.

He took the chair across from her desk.

"You look awful, Dad. Is anything wrong?"

"I haven't had much sleep. Nicky something has happened."

"Oh no, that's all I need right now, I have conferences all day."

"This can't wait I'm afraid," he hesitated. "Nicky… Eve is dead."

With a huge intake of breath her body was flung against the back of her chair. "Oh my g…" she gasped.

James quietly continued. "She was murdered late yesterday afternoon during the storm. She was found in the apiary by Holly when she returned from spending the day with a school friend."

The silence was chilling as Nicky slowly absorbed what he had said. "Dead!" She almost choked on her own words. "Surely you're mistaken. Auntie Eve... dead... there has to be a mistake."

"No mistake."

"I can't believe it..." Grabbing the water bottle besides the papers she was working on Nicky took a gulp from it. Breathing deeply, she then spoke slowly. "Now start again. You did say murdered?"

"Yes."

Tears welled in her eyes as full realisation of her father's words penetrated her numbed brain, she shook her head. "Impossible! Who on earth would want to murder Eve?"

"The only explanation I can think of is that she disturbed an intruder while she was working in the apiary."

"Someone was trying to steal one of her hives, you mean?"

"Her bees are worth a lot of money. I can't think of anything else, can you?"

"No. Everyone loved Eve," Nicky's face scrunched into an expression of disbelief and with elbows placed on her desk she held her head in her hands. "I don't know what to say," she mumbled. "It's ironic; she spent her whole life caring for her bees, and now she has given her own life trying to save them."

"That's not all, something very strange happened."

"Oh..."

"Holly told her mother that as she reached Eve, the bees left the hives, they circled Eve's body, and then flew off."

As Nicky looked up at her father, her expression

changed from disbelief to astonishment. "You are joking? In that storm?" she asked. "Have they come back?"

"I don't know I'll check later."

"That is so weird."

"What you're saying is that Holly was at the scene at the time of the murder."

"No, she arrived shortly after."

"You realise what the police will be thinking, Dad."

"They are. I don't believe for one minute that it had anything to do with the child."

Nicky's eyes widened as she realised something. "Dad, Eve was President of the British Bee Society – of Great Britain," she stressed. "The police will have one hell of a job on their hands if they decide it must be a Bee thief. I bet there was more than one member who was jealous of her."

"No doubt. All I know is that however long it takes I am going to make sure whoever did this will pay."

"Leave it to the police, Dad. You'll upset Uncle Harry."

"Don't care if I do I want this bastard found."

Nicky pulled a face. "I'm not feeling up to work now."

"You've a busy day ahead, it'll keep your mind off things. Can you come over tonight?"

"Yes."

"Bring any papers you have with regard to Eve's affairs and make sure you have everything copied onto your computer. The police will be asking for them soon." James stood and pushed back his chair. "Oh, I'm out of food can you…"

"I'll call in at Waitrose on my way over."

"I have to go and identify Eve's body. Then I've a few calls to make. I should be home around six."

"I'll be there." Nicky hesitated. "Oh dad…" Her voice faded.

"I know, I know."

"You must be devastated."

"I am Nicky. I am…"

After identifying Eve's body James pulled into the first petrol station he came across. He filled up his BMW with diesel. He also bought an egg and cress sandwich and a bottle of water. He ate it on the way to the first address on his list.

The address was in an area he had never explored before and he took a wrong turn and had to double back on himself. Even his sat-nav hadn't heard of this place. All was explained when he arrived, it was a new-build on a garden plot.

The woman who answered the door was probably in her late thirties. She looked tired. He felt sorry for her as James knew from experience what she was going through. He gave her what she had asked for, which she felt would be sufficient for her needs and left. No money changed hands. James was not looking forward to the next couple of hours but what had to be done must be done.

When he had completed these tasks he'd rest, assured in the knowledge that the people he had visited, would never allow it to become public knowledge.

James had planned a circular route that would involve

him driving almost one hundred miles. He hoped to be home around six.

Although he hadn't slept, his adrenalin seemed to be working overtime and he was thankful for his Marine training. His second call was to a Mrs Walker in Mayford. Close to tears, her appreciation was overwhelming. She said she was sure that what he had given her would be sufficient for her needs. He repeated the same operation six more times and was relieved when all the contents of the boxes he had filled the previous night had been delivered and that the boxes were quite empty.

He drove to Honey Pot Lane and parked opposite Eve's home and the visitors' centre. A young officer guarded the gate, which still had the yellow crime-site tape wrapped around it. He introduced himself. Becky and Holly still weren't home. It was obvious they were keeping Holly in hospital for another night.

James explained to the officer what it was he needed to do. "All I want is to check on a few hives. I have no need to go anywhere near the crime scene."

"I'm sorry sir it's not possible."

"It will only take me a few moments," James said trying desperately to convince.

"My orders are not to let anyone on to the property until I hear from H.Q. Why I don't know as forensics said they had finished. However, until I'm told …I'm sorry," he said as he shrugged his shoulders.

"I've seen that bored expression before," James said with a sympathetic smile.

The officer scoffed. "Wasn't exactly what I signed up for? As soon as I get the call saying that the centre can be re-opened the happier I'll be and I can go home."

"Officer …just a few hives, it will only take seconds."

"I'm sorry, sir. It's more than my job's worth."

James wasn't taking no for an answer. "Can you see that gap between the café and the house?" James pointed.

"Yes."

"If I were to go through there it will take me to the back of the property and to the top end of the apiary, which is nowhere near the crime scene. I only need to check on a few hives. It won't take me more than a couple of minutes."

Realising where James wanted to go, which was, as he had said, well away from the crime scene, the officer muttered something then glanced up and down the lane, first right then left. All was clear. "Is it really so important?"

"Very."

"O.K. You'll have to be quick and I'll have to come with you."

"Fine by me."

On reaching the perimeter of the hives at the top end of the apiary James stepped towards the nearest one. The officer stood well back. "Shouldn't we be wearing protective clothing?" he asked.

"I don't think it will be necessary." James slowly lifted the lid, which was still wet from the storm, water ran down the wood and fell onto the ground. He glanced inside. He saw a few stragglers. Dying he guessed. He repeated the operation five more times to convince himself that the bees had actually gone. He'd check on the other hives tomorrow. He was convinced that what Holly had told her mother had happened.

"Why do you want to look inside the hives?" The officer stood looking confused.

"The moment Eve died the bees flew away."

"Shit! No kiddin'."

"I'm not kiddin'," James mimicked. "It was what I'd been told and I needed to check it out. I'll leave the other hives until I am officially allowed to be here."

"The bees flew off? Do you mean to tell me that they knew the woman had died so they just up and went?"

"It looks like it."

"Sounds like something out of a Sci-fi movie."

"There's a lot more to bees than most people realise. Do you know that if the bee population were to be wiped out the human race would quickly follow?"

"Huh, wait until I tell the wife about this."

"At a guess I'd say that if she buys honey she'll probably know."

"She does, she loves it and so do I."

They reached the gate. James realised by the expression on the officer's face that he was thankful there was nobody lurking about and that James with his crazy stories was leaving.

It was around five when James reached home. He opened the boot of his car and took out the empty boxes then his face darkened. Staring up at him was one lonely Blue-topped jar. "Shit!" How did that happen? He picked it up and slammed the boot down and strode into the house.

In the kitchen he held the jar in his hands bouncing it up and down as if it was a hot potato. He wasn't thinking straight. He eventually moved some jars in a top cupboard and tried to hide it at the back; it would have to do for now, he would decide what to do with it later.

He then opened the lid on the wood burning stove and dropped Eve's address book inside and watched until it caught alight and began to burn.

He decided on a shower.

When James returned to the kitchen, Nicky had finished unpacking a shopping bag full of groceries and was about to put chicken breasts, stuffed with garlic and herbs, into the oven.

Her sad eyes pleaded. "Please tell me that when you got to the morgue there had been a terrible mistake and it wasn't Eve."

"I only wish," he said and quickly changed the subject. "Did you bring all the papers?"

"Yes and I also checked that we have everything that we need on the computer along with another hard copy."

"I called in at Eve's on the way. Becky and Holly are still not home. They must be keeping Holly in hospital for another night. The child has had a nasty shock I only hope she can come to terms with what happened; she adored Eve."

"I know." Nicky breathed in deeply and exhaling slowly she continued. "Dad, I've been thinking, it is quite remarkable how they met and also how they instantaneously bonded."

"Hmm…they became the family Eve never had."

"They must be devastated."

"Becky certainly is; Holly was still asleep when I went to the hospital."

"Dinner will take thirty-five minutes, according to the packet," Nicky said grinning. They seemed to live on nothing other than pre-prepared meals these days.

"Fine by me."

"Would you like some wine?"

"Yes please," he replied.

"Fancy anything in particular?"

"A Rioja would be nice." He walked out of the kitchen and made for his office. He unlocked his safe and took out the papers he had been working on earlier in the day. He went into the dining room and placed them on the table. His intention was that, over their meal, they'd flick through them, refresh their memories and discuss anything that might have to be dealt with as a matter of urgency.

The letter he hadn't opened lay on top of the pile. He opened it and began to read as Nicky walked through the door carrying two plates.

"Dinner's up," she called.

"Hmm…."

"What's that you're reading?"

"It's a codicil to Eve's Will."

"Codicil! When did you get that? I've not seen it."

"She gave it to me shortly after your mother died. I was too upset to think about it at the time so I locked it away and forgot about it."

Nicky's faced paled fearing a problem. "Well… what's in it?"

"Nothing to worry about. She has only put in writing

the things we discussed regarding Becky and Holly."

He handed the codicil to her and poured two glasses of his favourite Rioja placing one alongside Nicky's meal and taking a sip of the other as he sat down opposite her. A bowl of soup with bread the previous night; coffee for breakfast and a day old egg and cress sandwich for lunch. He didn't realise how hungry he was until the first piece of chicken touched his stomach.

"You gave me a fright for a moment but I remember the discussion now." Nicky looked across at her father. "You seem preoccupied, Dad. Is there a problem?"

"I didn't expect this to happen so soon. In fact, I honestly expected Eve to outlive me. She was so healthy."

"I don't think any of us could have envisaged such a thing happening. Thank God Eve put this in writing," she touched the codicil. "If she hadn't who would ever have believed it?"

"You're quite right."

"I didn't have chance to re-read her Will this afternoon, remind me."

James picked up Eve's Will and glancing at it and said, "Nothing has changed. All monies are governed by the Trust; I am the only Trustee, at the moment. I am to supervise the renovations and when the *Retreat* is operational I am to appoint a board and CEO to oversee the running of it. The Apiary will be kept separate from the Retreat and, that's about it."

"Eve never lived to even see the start of the renovations," Nicky said sadly. "When do you think you'll be able to start?

"As soon as can be arranged, after her funeral. It will take a good six months, maybe longer. It should run smoothly. Eve didn't want any holdups while people squabbled over idiosyncrasies. I know exactly what Eve wanted and I am going to deliver, stone by stone."

"Dad, do you think Eve knew she wasn't going to live to see her dream come true."

"I've no idea. Knowing Eve, it wouldn't surprise me. At least all her affairs are in order. She's left nothing to chance."

"It's amazing, what sort of person would have all their affairs in order by the age of fifty-four?"

"A sensible person," he said nodding at her in a warning away. "Anyway, there is nothing to hold up the work now that General Milton has died."

"Ooooh – it makes me so mad." Nicky growled as she shook her head. James was in no doubt about it judging from her tight lips and flushed cheeks. "The lease on the Manor had ended almost twelve months ago yet Eve let him stay on when he became terminally ill. She had to put back the project she'd been planning all her life. There isn't another person in the world who would have done such a thing and where did it get her? Murdered. It is not fair, Dad. It's just not fair."

"Life isn't fair and you being a solicitor must have learnt that by now. Eve was being Eve and knowing you I doubt you would have asked him to leave either. She was a healer and people's health and happiness came first, no matter what. That was her belief it was her calling."

"It's still hard to take."

James slapped the codicil of Eve's will with the back of his fingers to bring the conversation back to its contents.

"When Eve wrote this it was all in the future. This piece of paper says that, in the event of her death she wants Becky to join the board of Trustees when it's fully operational.

"She wants her to continue with her research into the authentication of her reincarnation cases and to continue putting these cases into book form for which she will be well remunerated.

"She would also like Becky to continue to oversee the administration of the Apiary and Visitors' Centre.

"Eve has also given Becky and Holly permission to live in her house for as long as they wish.

"She hopes that Holly will accept responsibility for caring for her bees. If at a later date she is unable to do so, then advice on employing a qualified beekeeper to oversee the apiary can be obtained from the Bee Society. That's basically it."

"Dad, Holly is only a child she can't make such a decision, at what age? Twelve?"

"Ten and she already has."

"She has!"

"I've spoken with her often about it and she has told me that if anything happened to Eve she would take care of the bees."

"When did she say that?"

"One day when she came to exercise Pippa."

"Sam's pony?" Nicky was surprised. "I'd forgotten about Pippa I thought you would have sold her years go."

"Not on your life, your mother wouldn't hear of it. She always hoped Sam would be allowed to come back to England one day and Pippa must be here waiting."

"Sounds like Mum." Nicky pictured her mother and smiled. "What exactly did Holly say to you?"

"She said she loved the bees and was going to care for them until the day she died. I tried to make it clear that she mustn't make promises she may not be able to keep. I reminded her that one day she would marry and maybe move away. She said. Oh no, I'm going to be a doctor and care for the bees, just like Eve."

"That's child's talk, Dad."

"Maybe, have I told you that Eve said a similar thing to me and she was only six at the time. It's quite uncanny?"

"I didn't know that. There must be a lot I don't know – after all, you were practically brought up together."

"That's true," he laughed. "Picture it, Eve and me crawling around on a carpet while our mums drank tea."

"Sorry Dad, can't picture it."

"James chuckled. "As you're aware a Trust Fund has been set up for Holly's education. I think Eve knew that, one day, Holly would follow in her footsteps."

"So why are you concerned? I can tell you are, Dad."

"I'm not concerned. I was wondering, what if Becky knew about this codicil? How would the police view that?"

"Oh I see, then we are talking motive."

"Exactly. I've known Becky and Holly for about eighteen months. Eve knew them for a lot longer. I think I'm a pretty good judge of character and I am sure that they're not involved in any way. More importantly, I trust Eve's judgment. Eve was too astute to be fooled by a young woman out for profit. However, I only wish I could shake the feeling."

"So, what are you going to do?" Nicky asked as she placed her knife and fork on her empty plate.

"My duty and find out. At a guess the police will ask for the Will tomorrow. I think we should hold on to this codicil until I've spoken to her."

"Will you tell her about it?"

"Certainly not. The less she knows the better. If the police confront her then her expression of complete confusion and ignorance will be obvious to even the simplest of minds."

Clearing the plates Nicky hesitated.

"What's on your mind?" James asked.

"How do you know?"

"The same way that you knew something was on my mind. Nicky you're my daughter, I also know when something is troubling you."

Nicky sat down again. "It's that we don't really know Becky and Holly, eighteen months is not a long time. Eve has told us about Becky's deprived background. We know how she was raised in a variety of foster homes and she had Holly when she was fifteen.

"What we don't know Dad is what type of people she mixed with back then and if she kept in touch with any of them?"

"Nicky, you only have to consider what she has achieved since becoming pregnant. She continued with her studies, she kept the baby and became a single hard-working mother. To my knowledge she put her past behind her when she was given the job at the library in Meedon Bridge."

"There's something else. Are you sure you're not deluding yourself into thinking that Holly is Sam. As much as I feel you would like her to be, she isn't."

"No I am not," James snapped. Her suggestion horrified him. "I would love Sam to be here with us now. I would love to ride with you Sam and Amanda across the valley the way we used to. Nicky, that is not going to happen. Amanda, along with your mother have gone forever. I can't do anything to help Sam but I sure as hell can do something to stop the life of this other little girl being ruined."

"I'm sorry dad I had to say it because they're about the same age."

"I understand." He patted her hand as she stood and began to collect the plates.

"I bought some strawberries, imported of course. Would you like some?

"Hmm…please." He mumbled and again began to reread the codicil to Eve's Will.

Nicky kissed the top of her father's head as she passed him on the way to the kitchen. "Okay dad, I'm right behind you on this."

Chapter 6 – Holly

Sitting on the edge of his bed James ruffled his hair with his fingers while staring at the floor. Memories of the last thirty-six hours slowly returned. Had it really happened? Eve, murdered? People die; of course they do, but murder, and so close to home.

Glancing at his bed-side clock he was astonished to see how long he'd slept. He had missed a whole eight hours of sleep on the night Eve had died. He was no longer a Marine and a lot older. He needed to spend more time in his gym or maybe take some sort of retraining.

He showered, dressed and made his way to the kitchen. Having stayed over, which Nicky frequently did after a bottle of wine, she had written James a note saying she had left for the office and hadn't wanted to disturb him.

A pot of coffee was still hot on top of the wood-burning stove, so he poured himself a mug and popped a slice of bread into the toaster. When it was done he spread it with butter and a dollop of Eve's famous honey. It crossed his mind …with the bees gone, would there ever be any more? He flicked through the Telegraph then The

Times both papers having arrived first thing.

Nothing had been reported about Eve's death. Were the police keeping a lid on the story because of the possible involvement of a child? If that were the reason, then the police must be trying to make a case against Becky or Holly. He needed to speak to his brother Harold.

James decided to check on the yard first to see if all was back to normal after the storm. It was and he heard the lads as they did their daily chore of mucking out the stables. He found Reg in his office ordering feed for the animals.

"You've done a good job Reg. You'd never believe it was the same place."

"Thanks."

"Any other problems," he asked.

"Not a problem as such. I'm expecting the Vet. One of the pregnant Blue Greys appears to be uncomfortable and I am trying to avoid her losing her foal. Also, Barbers have assured me that they will finish repairing the roof this morning."

"Fine: where are the horses now?"

"Out on the south west pasture."

"That's good grass."

"Even better after the rain. James, have you heard any more about Eve?"

"No. I expect they're waiting until they have a better understanding of the situation before making it public." James didn't want to say anymore.

"It'll whip around soon enough you know how tongues wag here – country folk." Reg laughed. "I'll tell you something they had better make sure that they get it right and quickly or they'll have a lynch mob sweeping down on the police station. Eve was much loved in these parts."

"Don't I know it. I'm going to have a word with Harry see if I can come up with anything."

"Will he tell you?"

"He'd better, if he doesn't I'll beat it out of him, after all, I am the big brother."

Reg laughed. "That would be worth seeing."

"I'll keep you informed, Reg," James said as he turned and began to walk away.

"I'd appreciate that."

"Call me if you need me."

"Will do."

The parking area on the opposite side of the road to Honeycombe Apiary James counted four cars apart from the six he knew. He crossed the lane and walked into the yard. The visitors' centre was on his left and he counted four adults along with two excited children about to enter the centre? Directly ahead and through the glass window of the gift shop he counted three more adult's searching through trinkets and locally produced produce.

On his right was Eve's farmhouse and he saw that the door to her kitchen was open and he hoped that Becky was home and that it was not the police laying an assault on the place.

"Hello Becky," James called cheerfully as he walked into the kitchen. He felt a sense of relief when he saw her sitting at the kitchen table staring into space. "How are you feeling today," he asked.

"Terrible. The police have been."

"Already!"

"Yes, they've taken Eve's computer and some other stuff. I was in no position to stop them."

"What about your computer?"

"They didn't ask and I didn't say. They only asked where Eve's office and consulting rooms where."

"Sloppy," James said.

"Why would they want my computer?"

"They'll want to examine it, I'm sure. I think someone has been negligent, they'll be back. I suggest you make sure you have everything backed up on a memory stick."

"They weren't the same officers who came the night Eve died. They didn't speak much just ignored me." Her body jolted and she stared at James. "What's the matter with me? Why didn't I think of that?"

James frowned. "What?"

"Checking that I had everything on a memory stick, I'll do it as soon as you've gone."

"It's called stress, Becky. How is Holly, where is she?"

"She's down by the river. She has a special place where she goes when she wants to be alone. It is where she does her homework and sometimes she takes her sketch pad she is forever sketching Moxley Manor."

James remembered how his two little girls loved to have a secret place. "Do you know where this secret place is," he asked, more out of curiosity than on a need to know.

"Yes, it's where the river bends there is a clump of

rocks that jut out into the river. I didn't object to her going today I'm not much company at the moment."

"James laughed, "It's not secret then."

"What?"

"Her secret place."

She giggled. "I suppose not. Can I make you a cup of tea?"

"There's no need."

"Please let me it will give me something to do."

Becky filled the kettle, placed two mugs on the table and popped a tea bag in each one as there was a knock at the door. Becky stopped what she was doing and went to answer it.

"Becky, is Holly in? Can she come out to play?" A young voice called. A boy of about eight, straddling his bike and wiggling its front wheel, was outside the kitchen door.

"She's not here Billy she's gone down to the river. I'd leave her alone if I were you she has a lot on her mind."

"I know where she is; she will want to see me," he called confidently as he twirled the front wheel of his bike around and pointed it in the direction of the open gate to the lane and peddled away like fury.

"Oh dear, what have I done I shouldn't have told him where she was. She'll not be pleased."

"I've seen him out playing he seems like a nice boy."

"He is, in fact he's adorable. It's a shame about his step-father. He's not his real step-father. I've come to learn about country folk since coming to live here. They are so old fashioned, they pretend things are legal and above board when they're not."

"You have learned quickly, Becky." James became thoughtful "What exactly is the problem with the step-father?"

"Apparently, he gives the boy a hard time so Billy is always out playing, wanting to be with Holly. He follows her around like a little lamb."

"It's a shame there aren't any other children living in the lane. He must be lonely." James understood. When he was brought up living miles away from civilization at least he had Harry to play with.

"He is lonely. Holly is good with him although there is an age gap. Sometimes Holly has a lot of homework and she can't always play with him."

James nodded. "Tell me, what did the police have to say to you today?"

Becky bit her lip then began to speak. "They came back to the hospital as you said they would and asked the same questions. I couldn't add to what I'd already told them. I am worried James; I don't think they believe me."

"It's their way, I'm afraid. I see you have been able to open the visitors' centre?"

"Yes, thank goodness. It all seems to be under control and no one is asking awkward questions only the girls are subdued. I told them not to say anything to anyone until we have more information. I don't think they liked taking instructions from me; it was different when Eve was here."

"You did the right thing, Becky. It won't be long now before all the valley knows."

"That's what I'm worried about. When the whole valley has heard we will be inundated with sight-seers and even worse if they think Becky or I had something to do with it."

"You must be prepared for that. Any problems don't hesitate to call me."

Becky nodded then pulled a tissue out of a box which lay on the table appearing reluctant to speak. "There is something else and you did say you would help me…"

"Yes I did."

She lowered her head and twiddled with the tissue she was holding. "It's that I don't know what to do."

"About what?"

"Now that Eve has died Holly and I can't stay here. The police said I mustn't go anywhere until they have completed their enquiries. I will have to look for somewhere else to live. I don't have any money and I now I don't have a job. If the police want me to stay in the area, will they provide me with somewhere to live? I'll also have to start looking for a new school for Holly."

Becky had answered his all his questions without him having to lead or ask her outright. She knew nothing about the codicil. He felt immense relief

"Becky, now listen to me, I am the trustee of Eve's will."

"Will? I didn't think anyone so young would have made a will."

"She didn't have any family remember. Anyway, it will take weeks if not months to have everything legally sorted. In the meantime, there is nothing for you to worry about. I will honour the contract you made with Eve…"

"Contract!" Becky's voice rose and her eyes flashed in sudden panic. "But…but…I never signed a contract."

"You made a verbal contract with Eve, so as far as I am concerned, it is legal and binding."

"It is!"

"You can continue to live here until I inform you otherwise. If it should become necessary for you to leave we will work out what is best for you and Holly and I will help you in any way I can. It is what Eve would have wanted."

He sensed Becky's relief. She began to laugh. "I can't believe it, I can't believe it," she repeated over and over. "Oh James thank you so much. I have never been as happy as I have been living here with Eve." Tears rolled down her cheeks and she sniffed then blew her already red nose. "I can't believe it's over. I'll never forget Eve, never. At least I now have time to sort things out. Gosh, what a relief. You have no idea how grateful I am."

"All I ask is for you to continue on as usual. I know this will be hard. Try to imagine that Eve has gone on holiday for a few weeks and you have been left in charge. Remember the apiary was not only Eve's business, it was her life. Her legacy must be maintained."

Tears of relief began to trickle down Becky's cheeks as she giggled and sniffed at the same time. "I think I can do that. Eve has gone on holiday," she repeated almost to herself. "Oh...James I only wish she had."

"So do I," he said pushing back his chair. "I must go, I'm off to the police station to see what else I can find out."

As James pulled his BMW to a stop outside police headquarters he noticed a small red-headed woman wearing a flowing, dark-brown, woollen coat. She appeared to float down the steps, she was quickly followed by a man in a dark suit. It was the newly elected leader of the opposition. What was she doing here?

The custody officer manning the reception desk looked up from what he was working on. "Good morning, Sir James. DCI Marchant is in if you'd like to come through. He has already had one illustrious visitor this morning I'm sure he can cope with another."

"Sarcasm is the lowest form of wit, so I've been told, Wesley." James said with a grin knowing whom his brother's first visitor was having just seen the leader of the opposition leave.

James knocked and entered his brother's office.

"Hello Harry."

"Oh no, you're all I need."

"Huh, what a way to greet your only brother."

"I'm up to my eyes in it James, please be quick." Harry's manner then softened as he stood and held out his hand. "Sorry brother. Nasty business," he waved James to a chair opposite him.

"You can say that again."

"Before you say anything James I know how close you were to Eve, we all were, however, as much as you are tempted…"

James raised his eyebrows in a pretend confused manner. "What are you trying to say?"

"You know very well what I'm trying to say I want you to keep out of it. This is police business. I know you knew Eve better than I did but I'm still devastated and Gillian well ...she's in shock."

"She'll not be the last, Harry. I only wanted to know…"

"Where we are up to," Harry interrupted. "You know as well as I do that it is too premature to speculate, however, our new Inspector Blackwell is confident of as early arrest."

"I bet she is."

James' sly grin did not go unnoticed by his brother. "By the expression on your face I guess she's already paid you a visit."

"Sure has…" James didn't elaborate. "I've never seen her before. How long has she been here?"

"About two months."

"And already she's made enemies."

"Astute thinking, James. I'm afraid so, she doesn't gel with us rural folk."

"Put someone else on the case?"

Harry groaned and leaned back in his chair. "This isn't the Met James. She was the only qualified Inspector I had available at the time. I don't know who is pulling her strings, all I know she is on the up. An early arrest is what we both won't and if she can bring that in …it will be promotion for her and I hope then I can wave her good-bye."

"She's barking up the wrong tree."

"Why did I think you would say that?"

"I understand how you want me to keep out of it, Harry but I can't I'm the Trustee of Eve's estate and Nicky is her solicitor. If it should become necessary Lane and Son will act for Becky and Holly. If Blackwell continues to pursue this line of enquiry she has me to deal with and

I'll not be gentle."

"Shit – James. If you make waves, I'll never get rid of her."

"I can't see why not. You are making it sound as if you are scared of her."

"Don't be ridiculous. I repeat I don't know who is pulling her strings. Until I do I have to tread carefully. If I try to get rid of her without a promotion, imagine what she would say – that she was victimised."

"Victimised! Don't make me laugh."

"I'm deadly serious. I can see the complaint now. In the course of doing her job she happened to upset DCI Marchant's brother so he put her up for a transfer that she didn't request."

"That's childish. You honestly think she would?"

"Damn sure she would."

Silence.

"Then we will not have to put a foot wrong. Now, tell me Harry what was in her first report?"

Harry groaned then spoke rapidly. "Verbal report – she said that Eve was a much loved and respected member of the community. She had no known enemies.

Becky was brought up in homes and foster homes. Always in trouble. Gave birth to Holly when she was fifteen. Lived hand to mouth ever since until she met Eve where, to quote Blackwell verbatim, 'they were given a meal ticket for life'."

"Bitch!"

"Holly found the body within minutes of Eve's death. Both Holly and her mother were covered in blood. The storm was raging so no sensible person would have been out. The visitor's centre was closed. She thinks the case is open and shut. Not good, James."

"Motive?"

"Eve was about to throw them out."

"Never!" James remembered the codicil to Eve's will. If that had been remotely Eve's intention she would have immediately instructed him to destroy the codicil? Blackwell was wrong. James stood. "Keep me informed Harry, on or off the record. I need to get to the truth."

"Oh God," Harry complained, "isn't it the younger brother who is supposed to be 'the pain in the neck'?"

"Your time will come," James goaded.

"This has to work both ways; you keep me informed. Anything you unearth that is relevant to this enquiry I want to know about it. The last thing I need is a case of wrongful arrest. James, I know you miss the Marines and are bored out of your skull but I repeat, this is police work, why can't you leave it to us."

"As I see it, Blackwell seems to have tunnel vision. All I intend to do is to keep my eyes and ears open. This is too close to home, Harry. She has made it blatantly obvious that either Becky or Holly murdered Eve and all she has to do is to decide which one.

"Tread with care little brother. Holly is only a child. Blackwell will bring herself down and take you with her if you're not careful." With a knowing nod of his head he put both hands on the arms of his chair and pushing on them he stood. As he reached the door he suddenly remembered something and asked, "I saw Sarah Milton as I was coming in. What did she want?"

Harry rolled his eyes. "You've got a nerve James."

Leaning back in his chair he huffed. "As if I haven't enough to do? She is throwing a celebration bash on Saturday to mark her elevation to leader of the opposition and to show off Moxley Manor, no doubt." Harry's voice oozed sarcasm.

"Little does she know," James said grinning.

Harry ignored James' remark. "Apparently, there will be important guests, the rich and famous – you get the gist. These will include members of the government and she wants me to attend along with a significant police presence to insure their safety. How am I going to explain the overtime budget? Where am I going to get the men? This is the valley for God's sake. There is hardly any crime here."

James' laugh was more of a snort. "Rather you than me. Give my love to Gillian and the boys." As he closed the door behind him he heard his brother call "You're no longer in Special Ops James and don't you forget it."

James re-opened the door and poked his head back into the room. "Forgot to ask, Cranmore…"

Harry groaned as he shook his head. "Will you never give up?" He took a deep breath. "Got potential – and I mean what I say James. Don't even think about playing detective, that's my job."

James was driving up his driveway when he was forced to swerve, then stop, to allow a black Daimler to pass him. The driver nodded as he drove on. On entering his house he saw an official envelope lying on the black and white tiles of his entrance hall. He picked it up. It was addressed to him and on the left-hand corner of the envelope was written, *By Hand.*

It was a pre-printed invitation to a reception with the date and time handwritten, and scribbled at the top was, *I apologise for such short notice.* The invitation read: Sarah Milton MP requests the pleasure of the company of Sir James Marchant at a reception to be held at Moxley Manor this coming Saturday at 7p.m. She works fast James mumbled to himself then he realised how time was running out for her so she had been given little choice if she wanted to impress her peers.

Chapter 7 – Blackwell

Nicky sounded cross when she eventually got through to James. "Did you leave the phone off the hook? You've been engaged for hours?"

"I've had a lot of calls to make and, believe it or not, I've also been trying to reach you."

The tension in Nicky's shoulders eased. She always worried when she couldn't contact her father, and particularly now with all that had been happening. "Probably dialling each other at the same time," she laughed. "What I wanted to tell you was that the police had a warrant and have removed Eve's papers along with her will."

"Only to be expected."

"True, what was it you wanted to tell me?"

"I went to see Becky."

"Oh, and…?"

"She doesn't know anything about a will and certainly doesn't know about a codicil."

"Are you quite sure?"

"Yes, she was in a terrible state. The police had told her not to leave town and she said she didn't know what to do. She realised she would have to leave Honeycombe farm now that Eve was dead. She hasn't any money to speak of and said she will have to look for another job. She asked me if the police would give her somewhere to live since they insist she stay in the area. She felt that the chances of her getting a job locally would be difficult and almost impossible a job with accommodation. She would probably have to move back to the city, which she didn't want to do."

"Phew …that's a relief. What did you tell her?"

"I told her I was the Executor of Eve's will. I told her it will take a while for everything to be legally sorted. In the meantime, I asked her to continue doing what she has up to now, and if it should become necessary, we would then discuss what was best for her and Holly."

"Clever."

"Not just a pretty face," he laughed. "However, it's not all roses. I went to see Harry."

"And…?"

"Inspector Blackwell."

"You mean the new girl. I've met her briefly. Can't quite make her out."

"That's the one. She's desperately trying to build a case against mother or child I don't think she cares which. Apparently she's on the fast track and a result such as this would clinch her career."

"What can you do about it?"

"Not a lot. First of all I'll hand over the codicil to the police and after that I'm not sure – start my own inquiry. Where to start? That's the question… Shit!"

"What is it, Dad?"

"The woman herself has pulled up. Damn. I'll have to hand over the codicil. I would rather have taken it in to headquarters in my own time and given it to Harry."

"Don't Dad! Don't give it to them. Another few days won't make any difference it will give us more time. You haven't found it yet. You forgot you had it, that's all."

"Makes sense, talk later." James replaced the receiver and hurried to the door and opened it before Blackwell and Cranmore had time to knock.

"Going somewhere?"

"No, I noticed you arrive."

"That was very considerate of you, Sir James." She said in a patronising way as he held the door open for her. She stepped inside followed by a tight-lipped grinning Cranmore.

The two officers followed James into the living room. "Can I get you anything, tea, coffee?"

"No thank you. I'll come straight to the point. Sir James, you didn't tell us that the firm of solicitors, Lane and Son, is your daughter's firm."

"Didn't I? I must have thought it irrelevant."

"I wish I could believe that."

James suppressed a smile and glared at the woman. "I hope you are not insinuating that I was deliberately thwarting your investigation."

"No not at all," she replied sheepishly.

"If you would like me to clarify, Mr Lane died and his son, who was a reluctant solicitor, wanted out. I bought the firm for my daughter. We decided not to change the name as it was a well-known and well-respected firm."

"So the firm has nothing to do with you?"

"I thought I just said that. It was bought for my daughter."

"Someone told me you were also a solicitor, Sir James."

"No, I'm a Barrister." Blackwell threw a questioning glance at Cranmore. "You play your cards close to your chest, Sir James."

James ignored her remark. "I believe you have already obtained a search warrant and removed items from Eve's home. Inspector, this is not the inner city where bully-boy tactics might be necessary." He looked her firmly in the eyes. "I'd like to explain to you that the relationship between the police and the public living here in the valley is second to none. I would hate that relationship to change.

"Being the only trustee responsible for Eve's Estate I think a telephone call informing me of your intentions would have been in order."

Blackwell's cheeks flushed. "I meant no disrespect, Sir James. I'm new to the area and country ways. Please forgive my lack of consideration."

"Hmm... Tell me, how are you progressing with your enquiries?"

"It will be solved before long, it has to be. I have a politician breathing down my neck."

"Politician?" James feigned innocence.

"Sarah Milton,"

"Ah yes."

"She owns Moxley Manor, you know?" Her voice went up an octave. "She's hosting a reception this Saturday and a lot of dignitaries have been invited. She insists the case is solved before then."

This woman has to be joking. "I'm sure you will be able to manage that, Inspector." James forced himself to say.

Blackwell sensed sarcasm in his voice and clenched her teeth. "She doesn't want her guests to be aware that a murder has taken place on *her* doorstep and that a culprit is lurking about and could attack again at any moment."

"No one does. Sarah Milton, now you mention her I had heard," he said nodding his head.

"Heard, how?"

"I saw her leaving headquarters this morning."

"Oh and why were you at headquarters?"

"I was visiting my brother."

"Your brother?"

"DCI Harold Marchant."

Blackwell's jaw dropped as her mouth opened. Her nostrils flared and her lips tightened into a long thin line as she realised the connection. James guessed that the woman had imagined Marchant was a common local name. The glare she threw at Cranmore would have killed if it had been able. There was a lot Blackwell had to learn and it was clear to James that none of her colleagues were of a mind to enlighten her.

He felt for his brother who'd had Blackwell forced upon him. As soon as she moved on the better it would be for everyone. This was a rural community and the likes of Blackwell did not fit well.

"I may not necessarily agree with Sarah Milton's politics Inspector, however, in this case I have to agree with her, I also want the case to be solved quickly. Do you have a suspect?"

"Sir James – I think you know we do – in fact we have a choice of two."

"I wouldn't be so sure about that."

"Oh, and do you know something that I don't?"

"I know Becky and Holly McGrath."

"Sir James, there was a storm raging overhead every sensible person would have been behind closed doors. The child found the body within minutes of your friend's death. We know what time the bus from Upper Meedon Bridge dropped Holly off at the end of the lane. We know how long it takes to walk that lane. Both mother and child were covered in blood, diluted by the rain maybe, but more than enough for forensics to work on. I am waiting for them to tell me which one touched the body first." Blackwell hesitated. "As a lawyer you will understand perpetrators of crimes, do you have a scenario?"

James mused a moment, not sure she really wanted an answer. "I think it's an outsider. The storm was overhead. The visitors' centre was closed. Eve went to check on the hives and discovered someone, perhaps looking for shelter. Panic ensued and Eve was hit. I believe it was not premeditated."

Blackwell tried hard not to laugh. "So what you are saying is that someone was trying to get into one of the hives to shelter from the rain."

"Inspector Blackwell, I'm not impressed by your sarcasm. At the far end of the apiary there is a tool shed large enough to shelter more than one person. I suggest you go and study the area before you come here again with your know-it-all attitude.

"If you continue to insist that either Becky or Holly have committed Eve's murder then I'm informing you now, that Lane and Son will be representing them."

Silence followed as Blackwell absorbed that remark.

Blackwell rose. "It looks as if we are going to be seeing a lot more of each other so I apologise Sir James if I have upset you." Blackwell was visibly agitated as she strode towards the door followed by a grinning Cranmore, who winked at James as he passed. James left them to find their own way out.

James glanced at his watch. Maybe he could catch the end of the news. He found the remote and switched on the television. The screen was filled with a mop of red hair. Sarah Milton stood at the despatch box. "Damn I've missed it," he groaned. It was now Prime Minister's question time.

"Would the Prime Minister explain to the house the rapidly increasing number of unemployed and what he intends to do about it?" Her voice echoed around the chamber.

The Prime Minister was smiling. "Mr Speaker, if the Rt. Hon. Lady had checked the figures before she entered the chamber she would have seen that unemployment is down by one-hundred-thousand this month."

"Mr Speaker, yet again the Prime Minister has not answered the question."

Good God! I can't cope with this lunacy. James reached for the remote control and switched off the television.

Nicky had been right. Holding on to the codicil would give him time to decide on some sort of strategy. He lifted the telephone receiver and pressed in Philip Cook's number. No reply. Where was the man? There wasn't much he could do until he had spoken to him so he buzzed Reg on the intercom and asked him to saddle up a horse, one in need of exercising.

He changed and went down to the yard. It was late in the afternoon and all was quiet. The lads were finishing up and most of the horses were out to grass.

Reg had Pilgrim saddled and waiting for him when he arrived. Pilgrim was stamping and raring to go.

"He's looking forward to this, James. The storm has thrown out our schedule. We will be back on track by tomorrow."

"A good blow will do us both the world of good," James replied as he mounted. He pulled on the horse's right rein and as he turned he said, "Reg, will you do something for me. Have the lads search the outbuildings to see if we have had any uninvited guests staying here in the last few days."

"Will do," Reg replied.

James carried on and rode Pilgrim out of the yard and before long he was galloping across open countryside and down the sloping land to the footbridge that crossed the River Tyne. On the other side he almost took the bridle path that would take him to the apiary. He stopped short. Those days had gone. He would get used to it in time.

Instead, he continued galloping along the riverbank until he emerged from beneath overhanging trees and into bright, early-autumnal sunshine and sprawling countryside. On his left the river meandered north and to his right he saw Moxley Manor. He brought Pilgrim to a stop and stared at the stately building.

Moxley Manor stood in an elevated position, majestically viewing the valley and the river. If it was the last thing he did he would bring Eve's dream into fruition.

Kicking Pilgrim in the flanks, he took the steady climb up to the Manor and made his way to the rear of the building, where he dismounted. He tied Pilgrim to a post outside the gate to an unused paddock. General Milton had given up riding years ago.

The door to the kitchen was open and he called, "Helen, are you in?"

Helen, a divorcee in her middle forties, was a spritely woman with a quick wit.

She had been housekeeper to the late General Robert Milton and had rattled around this great house with him for the last ten years. Her dress was always immaculate and James had never seen her without makeup no matter what time of day he called.

She was a remarkably attractive woman. Her thick, dark, wavy, shoulder-length hair was her crowning glory. She had two boys in their twenties who had left the valley; one now lived in Birmingham and the other in London.

Helen appeared through the door at the far end of the kitchen. "Oh, hello James. I thought I heard someone."

Today, she looked stressed. "Is your new boss giving you a hard time, you look tired?"

She scoffed before answering. "You have no idea. Twenty-four hours to organize an, *aren't I the greatest* bash."

"I saw her an hour ago on the box, Prime Minister's questions; she must have caught the first flight after I saw her leaving police headquarters first thing this morning."

"Oh, I can't watch that programme, it's like watching a load of ignorant, overgrown schoolboys. Her brother is still here. He is supposed to be supervising the arrangements. That's a laugh he is always out. God only knows where he gets to. Can I get you a drink?"

"Love a beer, thanks."

Helen took the position of housekeeper when General Robert Milton resigned from the military and took over the remainder of the lease on Moxley Manor. Before he became ill he was a great one for entertaining. He loved a good party. He would host one at least every month. James and Jean were always invited. As James was a retired Marine they had a lot in common.

Helen went to the fridge and retrieved a beer. As she was about to get a glass James stopped her. "I'll take it from the can, save on the washing up you have enough to do."

"Oh no you won't. People have died drinking from cans."

"Died! You are joking?"

"I'm not. There was a case recently of a whole family being wiped out from drinking from a can."

James frowned and looked perplexed not being sure if he should believe her or not.

"It's true. The warehouse where the cans had been

stored was infested by rats and they had urinated on the cans. They were infected with…" She thought a moment, her mind scanning her memory banks, before she spoke. "Hantavirus, that's it, and they died."

"Good God! What's Hantavirus?"

"It's rare I grant you. Apparently the symptoms are flu-like. Because of the similarity it was not diagnosed until it was too late. It happened about a month ago. I can't stop thinking about it. I'll never drink from a can or bottle again."

"In that case I'll take a glass."

Helen giggled as she poured the beer into a glass. "Perhaps I should boil all bottles and cans…"

"Now you are joking?"

"Yes, I've got enough to do."

"I expect you've heard about Eve?"

Helen lowered her eyes and she stared at the table. "I don't want to talk about it. It is too horrid for words."

She quickly changed the subject. "You would not believe how things have changed here, James. I adored the General. Since her ladyship arrived on the scene – well – it's not the same and anyway if she thinks I'm going to be at her beck and call she can think again. I'm leaving; it shouldn't be too difficult to find another position."

This was music to James' ears. He refrained from saying anything for the moment.

"James you will find who did this wicked thing, won't you?"

"I'll not rest until I have."

She smiled comforted; she knew he was telling the

truth. Helen then reverted to her own predicament.

"The General was such a sweetie. How he produced such an awful daughter I will never know. She's as hard as nails, James. She must take after her mother no wonder the marriage failed."

"Maybe you're right."

"I miss the General. To think he has not been dead three weeks and she's throwing a party. She never knew her father was alive until he became terminally ill."

"What do you mean?"

"When the General's condition became terminal he told me about his two children."

"I didn't even know he had any children."

"Neither did I, until he asked me to find them. Can you believe it he hadn't seen them in almost forty years?"

"Sarah was four and Michael was almost two when his wife left him for a bank clerk. Imagine what a shock it was when I discovered who his daughter was. Well, I didn't find them, a detective did. She wasn't leader of the opposition then. I don't quite know what Michael does. He seems to be her gofer. They make a good team."

"I sense a touch of sarcasm."

"You most certainly do," Helen snapped. "James …I suspect the old rogue knew who and where his children were. He took an active interest in politics; remember the heated discussions we used to have on a card night? Also, he would never miss question time."

James laughed. "Knowing the General I'd say you're right, he knew exactly were his children where."

"Michael was the first to come and that was two months after I'd contacted him. Then he brought Sarah.

You should have seen the expression on her face when she saw the old place. Lit up like a Christmas tree, it did. She spent hardly any time with her father. She was mainly routing through his papers. She said it was her responsibility to get his affairs in order. I bet she was searching for a will and the Deeds to this house."

"Probably. Any papers relating to the General's affairs are kept at Lane and Son, Nicky deals with it all."

"I know," Helen giggled, "but she didn't. I often wondered why the General never told her. James, the only people who really cared about him were you and Jean and Eve and me. The rest only came for his social evenings.

"Did you know that Eve would visit twice a week …more nearing the end, she would give him healing and she would always bring him his favourite honey – don't like the stuff myself."

"That sounds like Eve."

"She never charged for any of her healing sessions. The General came to rely on them he felt so much better afterwards."

"Most people did." James stood. "I mustn't keep you. You have a lot to do." He reached into his pocket and pulled out an envelope and handed it to her. "I only called to give you this – my acceptance to the *lady's* kind invitation."

"You're coming!" Helen's eyes widened and she began to laugh.

"Wouldn't miss it for the world. It's surprising where a title will get you."

"The best table in a restaurant, so I've been told,"

Helen giggled.

"Something like that – thanks for the beer, Helen. See you Saturday."

He recognised the man's frame from the back, solid build, five-foot-ten with short brown hair and wearing a ridiculously garish shirt. He was talking to Reg.

James walked Pilgrim towards them. The man turned at the sound of the horse's hooves. "James, good to see you," he called.

"Hmm …not sure about the shirt, Philip."

The man was Philip Cook who had first met Eve when they both studied general medicine in Edinburgh. After Edinburgh, he diversified into psychiatry/ psychology and had a thriving practice in Amston, in the Lake District.

"Can't I go on holiday without all hell letting loose? Reg has told me what happened. Shit! I don't know what to say."

James dismounted. "Then don't. He's rather hot Reg," James patted the horse's" neck and handed over the reins to his estate manager.

"Leave him to me," Reg said as he led Pilgrim back to the stable block for one of the lads to wipe him down.

James and Philip began to walk towards the house. "I've been trying to contact you for the last couple of days."

"So I gather. You didn't leave a message. Okay, okay stupid remark. It's not the sort of message you would want to leave on an answer phone."

"Exactly."

"I didn't pick up any messages until I landed and when there were so many missed calls from you I knew something was up. My cell wasn't working in Cuba for some reason so I used the hotel phone occasionally to touch base."

"I felt I should speak to you in person," James said.

They had reached the house. James opened the door to the storeroom and let Philip pass. Inside James sat, as usual, on an upturned box and pulled off his boots. Philip walked on through into the utility room and on into the main part of the house.

"What are you having, James?"

"Whisky," James called after him.

Divorced and single Philip had been a regular visitor to Marchant's farm and more so since Jeans death. He was quite used to helping himself. Philip handed James his whisky as he came into the family sitting-room and took one of the leather armchairs.

James shivered and glanced at the log-burning fire. "I think I'll light it. It goes cool so quickly these days I can't believe it's still September."

Philip laughed, "You're getting old. It has never bothered you before."

"I wouldn't call 'fifty-four' old."

"When you've stop fiddling with that fire could you please tell me what happened and don't leave anything out." Philip demanded.

James watched as the logs burst into flames and he began to tell Philip what had happened. Philip's face became increasingly taut and when James had finished he asked, "So, that's where we are up to. Phew …what conclusions have you come to?"

"I think we can write off anyone she knew. At a guess I'd say she disturbed someone, probably a tramp, looking for a place to shelter from the storm."

"And so you think he panicked."

"It has to be. There are plenty of large stones bordering the paths, he could have picked one up and hit her with it. Or, he hit her with something he carried for his own protection. He was probably high on cheap cider. Anyway she fell across a hive and didn't move, so he ran off."

"All the stones bordering the paths are painted white. I clearly remember coming one day and she had a big trestle table outside the kitchen door and that is what she was doing, painting stones. If she was hit by one, then he either had to take it with him or drop it, it would be covered in blood."

"Or throw it in the river," James added, as he rested his elbow on the arm of his chair and his chin on the palm of his hand, picturing the scene.

"If that's what happened they'll never find it. The river is merciless at present. I was quite shocked at the force of the water as I drove across the bridge. What weapon do the police think the killer used?"

"They have yet to say. I can't see what else can have been so readily to hand. You should have been here, Philip, it was one hell of a storm. All signs of blood had been washed away before they had a chance to search the area."

"Forensics will find something,"

"I suppose so,"

"An intruder makes more sense than accusing either Becky or Holly. I've got to know Becky quite well since she moved in with Eve. She makes one hell of a casserole, you know." Philip said with a grin as he recalled.

"Seriously, what's your professional opinion?" James asked.

"Becky is a perfectly rational human being, I am quite sure of that. As far as Holly is concerned, Eve used to bring her to the Lakes on occasions. She is a normal ten-year-old. To think that either of them could have committed such a crime is irrational. Anyway, anyone who can make a casserole as good as Becky can't be all bad."

James laughed, "Thanks for that."

"What?"

"Making me laugh. I haven't done that in days. Another scenario could be that it was a patient."

"That is equally unrealistic. Unless the patient had severe psychological problems and Eve wouldn't have even tried to deal with those, she would have brought me in."

James got up from his chair, walked across the room to the sideboard and picked up the cut-glass decanter half-full of whisky. "Top up Philip?" he asked, waving it in the air.

"No thanks. I'm pretty wacked and I still have an hour's drive ahead. James, did you ever think it odd when Eve took Becky and Holly in?"

"Yes and no. Eve wouldn't do anything without careful consideration. I remember asking if she was quite sure it was the right thing to do. She answered, *quite sure* firmly, and that was good enough for me."

"Did Eve ever discuss her work with you?"

"Not these days."

"Did she ever discuss reincarnation with you?"

James swallowed a laugh. "Not since we were children. That sort of trivia ceased when we went to separate universities. What are you getting at?"

Philip became pensive again then said, "I'm not sure. You do know I'm contributing to Eve's book about my patients experiences of reincarnation."

"I had heard."

"Well, I have a few recordings I think you should hear. They're very interesting. I'll edit them, pick out the parts I think are relevant and send them over to you."

"Recordings?"

"Eve's regression sessions: as she's deceased, and under the circumstances, I don't think I am breaking any confidences. I'd like to think she would want me to do everything possible to help find her killer." Philip groaned and clenched his teeth. "I can't believe I've said that word."

James ignored his remark. He too found it a difficult word to say. "You have me intrigued, what recordings?"

"I'll get them delivered to you by courier tomorrow. When you've listened to them give me a call and I'll come over."

"Are you telling me that my theory of an intruder is wrong?"

"Not necessarily. Listen to the recordings and then we'll discuss it."

Nicky Marchant lived in a flat above Lane and Son Solicitors, in the town of Meedon Bridge. If she wasn't working she spent most of her time with her father up at the family home. It was at the farm they discussed cases in quietude. It was also where she gleaned information.

Although the horses at the sanctuary were retired, their ex-handlers were frequent visitors. The bond between man and horse was difficult to break. On these occasions, Nicky gained information that often helped her in representing her clients.

Nicky decided to spend more time at the sanctuary in the hope of hearing something that might help Becky and Holly avoid the pain of being arrested for a crime, she believed, they did not commit.

This evening she had called to see her father, who told her about Philip's visit.

"What do you make of Philip's remarks about reincarnation? He asked. "What can reincarnation have to do with anything?"

"Dad, I don't know. You grew up with Eve. I remember Mum telling me that you saw each other practically every day. After Amanda and I were born she would come over and help Mum look after us. She wasn't married and didn't have children of her own. If anyone knew anything I would have thought it would have been you."

"We did see a lot of Eve. Maybe she talked to your Mother. It's more women's talk than men's."

"Well, we can't ask either of them now. All I know is Amanda and I adored her and if we ever had a pain she'd take it away in a flash. The heat that came from her hands was unbelievable and then, like magic, the pain vanished."

James chuckled as he remembered "All I know is that she helped many, many people and in particular, the dying. She was a Godsend to me when your mother became terminally ill."

The pain of her mother's death was still raw. "I never thanked her enough, in fact, I know I didn't. And now she's dead and I can't."

"Did Eve ever suggest having a regression section with you?"

"No, but I bet Amanda did. It was the sort of thing she would do."

"You're probably right. Nicky, I'm wondering, if the recordings where made thirty or more years ago they would have been put on tape. I don't have anything on which to play a tape, I binned such equipment years ago."

An expression of quiet disbelief crossed over Nicky's face. "Dad, really ...he would have had everything transferred onto a DVD or memory stick by now."

"Oh sure, yes, yes," he laughed feeling more than a little ignorant.

Chapter 8 – Paul Biggs

It would be afternoon, at the earliest, before the courier arrived with Philip's package, giving him plenty of time, so James left the farm and drove across the valley to Lower Maybury, which was situated on the west side of the River Tyne. The village boasted two thousand inhabitants. It had a quaint C of E church with its overpopulated graveyard and crumbling headstones. It had three pubs, a small shop brim-full of stock, and a primary school for the children of the village and surrounding smallholdings.

He drove along the High Street until he came to the last building on his right. The building was a converted Methodist Church. The church was inconspicuous now, melting into its surroundings, and appeared little different from the adjoining residential homes.

A low gate led onto the property and a narrow path meandered between well-attended flower beds up to the front door. The sign above the door read, *Carvers Mission for the Homeless*. He knocked. No one answered so he walked around the property to the rear. A covered terrace spread along the entire breadth of the building, which was a new addition. Outside the back door eight shoes were placed in a neat line – four pairs. Very tidy. He knocked at the door.

A casually-dressed man in his early sixties answered his knock. He looked surprised. It was apparent the man was not expecting anyone.

"Yes…" The man hesitated, "How can I help you?"

"If you have a moment I'd like to talk to you about your guests."

"Why! What's happened?"

"Nothing to be concerned about. If I may come in, I'll explain."

The man led James through a small vestibule and on into the main building. The large room was laid out as a dining room. He noticed four bedraggled men sitting at a table at the far end, the owners of the shoes.

"Stragglers, I'm afraid. Please take a seat," the man said gesturing towards the nearest table.

"I'll not keep you long. It's quite a place you have here," he said glancing around the room. I've heard all about your work. I have to be honest I didn't know exactly where you were. It's easy to miss."

"We purposely keep a low profile. Well, Mr…."

"I'm sorry, Sir James Marchant."

"Paul Biggs."

They shook hands and the two men sat, Paul Biggs looking indecisive and apprehensive.

"What can I do for you Sir James?"

"I have a farm on the other side of the valley and from time to time some of your residents have used a derelict outbuilding of mine."

"Jeez, I might have guessed," the man groaned. "A complaint."

"No, no not a complaint," James said quickly. "If I had objected I would have done something about it years ago. I was glad to have been able to help if only in a small way, in fact my farm manager makes sure that there are a few tins and bottles of water in there, the ring-pull kind, on the off-chance someone was hungry.

"What I need to know is, have you heard of any strangers in the vicinity or, maybe, you might have overheard your guests talking about one."

Biggs, now slightly more relaxed, pondered. It was obvious to James that the man was apprehensive about saying anything. James also didn't want to disclose too much at this stage. It was an awkward situation.

"Not recently. The men who use this facility are regulars, unlike in a city where you could see a person once and perhaps never set eyes on them again."

"I can believe that," James nodded.

"Occasionally we have a new guest and, occasionally, we lose one when they get their lives back together. They come and they go.

"Sir James, I am baffled as to what you want from me," he said. "Our guests arrive after dark and most leave after breakfast. We then have the day to clean up and prepare for the following night.

"In extreme weather they can be here during the day. They use the track at the rear of the property and come in through the back door. We are considerate of our neighbours. Our guests have never been any bother to the community and we do not get complaints. When we first set up the hostel people objected. Now we live together in complete harmony."

"So I've heard."

"Would you like me to show you around?"

"That won't be necessary I can see you run an excellent facility."

"Then let me explain a little about our operation. We can comfortably sleep twenty-five. We have mattresses stored in the loft in case of emergencies. As you know we get a lot of snow in these parts. We will not turn anyone away. We give them a hot meal. We have shower facilities and people donate clothes, which we desperately need." He sounded frustrated and then hesitated. "Sir James, what is this all about?"

"Clutching at straws, Mr Biggs."

"Let me make one thing clear our guests are homeless they are not criminals."

"I wasn't thinking any such thing."

"Then what are you thinking?"

"I am thinking of strangers loitering in the area that is all."

Paul Biggs shook his head obviously confused by his unexpected visitor and his inane questions.

"The night of the storm did one of your guests arrive in a distressed state?"

Paul Biggs began to laugh. "You must be joking they knew the storm was on its way. We were fit to bursting at around three thirty and I knew every one of them. Homeless people develop a nose for the weather. I am sorry Sir James, I can't help you. If you'd like to come back in the evening, when everyone is here, you can speak to whoever you like."

James left, he had learned enough, no stranger had been seen in the area and, if there had been one, then he had yet to hear about the Mission. Also, all of Paul Biggs' regular guests were inside the Mission when the storm broke.

On reaching home James made for the kitchen where he popped a tea bag into a mug. He poured boiling water into the mug, gave it a swirl with a spoon, then poured in a drop of milk and sipping the hot tea he went into his study. He didn't think there would be anything of interest on the memory sticks he had taken from Eve's office but as he had nothing to do until Philip's package arrived he decided to take a look.

He sat staring at the screen and flicked through page after page of patients' notes, which were of no interest to him. He wasn't sure what he hoped to find. However, he was certain he would know when he saw it.

He ejected the stick and replaced it with another one, it was empty. He tried the third stick and found it to contain information on the Bee Society and minutes of meetings Eve had chaired.

He clicked onto names and addresses and found there were hundreds of members. James never realised that there were so many beekeepers in the country ranging from one hive in a back garden to commercial ventures like Eve's apiary. What he was interested in were the members of the executive committee.

He found a number for the secretary and punched it into his landline. After four rings he heard a woman's voice.

"Bee Keepers Society." It was a rich cheery voice that of a happy middle-aged woman. "Felicity speaking, how may I help you?"

"My name is James Marchant and I would like to speak to the secretary."

"Speaking."

"May I call you, Felicity?"

There was a slight hesitation then the woman said, "Of course."

"Felicity, I wish I didn't have to tell you this over the telephone. I have some rather distressing news…"

He paused as he heard her gulp.

He guessed that the woman was imagining that something terrible had happened to a member of her family. He quickly continued. "It's about Eve, the president of your society."

"Yes…" she said, hesitantly. James sensed caution along with relief in her voice.

"I'm afraid she died on Monday afternoon."

"Died! You can't be serious," she babbled. "Thank God I'm sitting down. How? What happened? Was it an accident?"

"It wasn't an accident, Felicity. She was murdered."

"Murdered! That's ridiculous. Who are you? Is this some sort of a joke, if it is I'm not amused?"

"It is no joke. As I explained I'm Sir James Marchant a neighbour and lifelong friend of Eve's."

Nobody spoke for a moment and in a quiet voice Felicity continued. "Oh, I know who you are. Eve has spoken of you often, Sir James. You created the sanctuary for retired police horses, didn't you?"

"That's right."

"Oh dear." There was silence for a moment. "Then it's true?"

"I'm afraid so."

"I can't take this in. I don't know what to say. So many people are going to be awfully upset. Have you any details?"

"Not at the moment I felt you should know as soon as possible. Felicity, do you know of anyone in the society who may have wished Eve harm?"

"That is a preposterous idea," she spluttered. "I'll admit many were envious of her expertise and the quality of her product. Members used to joke saying that Eve talked to her bees. That she instructed them to collect only the nectar she required from blossoms. It was silly talk. Her honey was consistently of the highest quality it was sold worldwide. She won every accolade possible and many may have envied her, but murder... I don't think so."

"Felicity, if there is anything you can think of that could help the police discover what happened to Eve, I wish you would tell me."

"Sir James, I don't know what to say. All I can do is to contact all our members and see what transpires. If I hear of anything that I think is a bit suspicious I will let you know, I promise."

"That's all I can hope for, thank you."

"Oh dear, you do realise Sir James that Eve has been our President for over twenty-years she will be sadly missed."

"I understand."

"Will you please let me know as soon as you can about the arrangement for her funeral? Our members will also want to know."

"I will." James gave her his various telephone numbers and ended the call.

The envy of many?

Was there a Bee Keeper who wanted to topple the Queen?

At around one, the courier arrived. James signed for the package and as soon as he was alone he opened it.

He retrieved a disk and slipped it into the computer on his desk in his study.

He then went into the kitchen, made himself a ham and pickle sandwich and a mug of tea, then returned to his study, where he sat and read the note that Philip had enclosed with the disk.

James,

As arranged I enclose the disk.

This is the first recording of Eve's regression session. It was made when we were both studying medicine at Edinburgh. When you reach the end of the disk I hope things will be a little clearer. I will explain further when we meet.

The second half of the disk was made recently and it is of me regressing Holly. Becky doesn't know anything about it. I think we should keep it that way for the time being.

I have edited the disk so that all you have to listen to are the relevant parts.

When you have listened to it please call me and I'll drive over.

Regards,

Philip.

James pressed start and settled back in his brown, button-backed, leather, office chair and waited. He heard Philip's voice loud and clear. "Are you ready?" he asked.

"Quite ready," James jolted on hearing Eve's young light voice. Although he was expecting it, it still came as a shock.

In a monotone voice Philip began. "I want you to imagine the colour red. I want you to see it with your inner eyes. Maybe think of a red dress or a red apple, imagine the colour red enveloping the whole of your mind and body. Nod when you can do this."

Silence.

Philip continued. "I now want you to see with your inner eyes the colour orange, picture an orange or an orange pumpkin or perhaps an orange sunset. Nod when you have done this."

Silence.

"Now, I want you to see with your inner eyes the colour yellow, picture a banana or perhaps a yellow sun. Nod when you have accomplished this."

Silence.

"Again I want you to see with your inner eyes the

colour green, picture a green golf course, or a green wood. Nod when you have done this."

Silence.

"Now, I want you to see with your inner eyes the colour purple, perhaps picture plums or the regal robes of kings or clergy."

Silence.

"Lastly Eve I want you to see with your inner eyes the colour indigo, the shade between dark blue and dark purple. Let the colour indigo, which symbolizes, meditation, deep contemplation and intuition, envelope you and become part of your whole being and help you on your journey." Silence. Philip continued. "You are standing before a door, do you see the door? Nod if you do?"

Silence.

"Open the door and step through. Where are you?" Philip asked.

"I'm standing in a long corridor with doors on either side."

"How many doors are there?"

"I don't know I can't see to the end."

"Walk along the corridor and stop at any door you choose. …Have you stopped outside a door?"

"Yes."

"Open that door."

"I'm opening a door on my left."

"Where are you?"

"I'm in a big room. Like a barn. I'm sorting vegetables. I'm putting them into boxes. My mother is working alongside of me."

"Where is this barn?"

"I don't know. It's very cold."

"How old are you?"

"I think I'm 10."

"Are you a girl or a boy?"

"I am a girl," she giggled. "I am not very pretty."

"Are you with other people?"

"Yes there are lots of us – all women."

"Do you recognise anyone from that life who is alive in your current life-time?"

"No."

"Does anything happen in that life-time that helped to improve the life you are now living?"

"No, all I do is pack boxes. I am always cold. I am frustrated. I want to leave. I have to search."

"What are you searching for?"

"I don't know. Forgiveness, must forgive."

"What or whom do you have to forgive?"

"I don't know. I can't leave this place." Eve unexpectedly let out a ghastly scream. "I'm having a baby. Help me, please help me, I'm dying." Her breathing became restricted.

"Eve, come out of that life and return to the corridor."

Eve's breathing returned to normal. "Now mark that door with a number."

"I've marked it number one."

"Do you want to go through another door?"

"Yes."

"Choose one Eve …have you found one?"

"Yes. I am opening the next door on my left."

"Go on through… Where are you now?"

"By the ocean. It's evening and I'm about to go out to sea. I'm a fisherman. I am big and very strong. My wife and two children are standing on the quayside waving me off. I am happy except for this desperation I have to search…"

"What are you searching for?"

"I don't know."

"Is it a good life?"

"I have a good life but I must find. It's imperative to forgive. Must find."

"Do you find the answer in that life?"

"No."

"Come out of that life and mark the door with the number 2. Do you want to try another door?"

"Yes."

"Do you want to go forwards or backwards?"

There was a break in the tape and James guessed that Philip had done some editing to speed up the process.

Eve continued.

"I'm walking along the corridor I am going to choose a door on my right."

"Open it, where are you now?"

"I don't think I'm in England. It looks a bit like somewhere on the continent. It's similar to a place we went on holiday one winter while the bees slept. It's nice and warm. Lots of people, poor people. The buildings look ancient. I've seen pictures in storybooks. I'm now in a noisy room surrounded by babbling people."

"What sort of people?"

"Horrible, dirty, smelly people. I'm frightened. There are priests. One is dressed in red robes he is sitting high up behind a desk. He picks up something black. It is a piece of cloth and he is putting it on his head, Oh my God! He has pronounced the death penalty.

"People are all around me I'm being smothered. I'm being pushed and shoved by stinking bodies to outside the building. I see a stake and a pile of wood. I'm being pushed closer.

"People are jeering and shouting. I hear screams of delight. People are dancing and stamping on my feet. The fire is lit. Black smoke curls upwards – so much smoke. I can't see. I can't breathe. I hear a curse – it consumes my brain." James heard Eve take a deep shuddering breath then, in a sobbing voice, she continued. "I will hunt you down – I will find you – my baby and I will have our revenge. You will die by a thousand cuts…" Oh no the flames are getting higher. The crowd is jubilant. It is so hot. So much smoke I can't see, I can't breathe."

Eve began fighting for breath.

Then he heard Philip's voice. "Eve I want you to come out of that life. It is over. Go through the door and mark it no 3. Where are you now?"

A calmer Eve answered. "I'm back in the corridor."

"I want you to walk through the door by which you entered the corridor, take a deep breath and rest."

Silence.

"How do you feel now?" Philip asked.

"Drained."

"Shit Eve …that was scary. I had to get you out. I'd love to have found out more about what happened and what led up to the burning. I dared not leave you in there. I'm no expert. I had no idea what effect it could have on you. Shit Eve, how horrible."

Eve giggled. "I'm fine, honestly Philip. I now understand why I have such a fear of fire."

"That's enough for one day I think I deserve a drink."

Eve shrieked! "You deserve a drink?" Then James heard them both laugh.

He listened to Eve's infectious laughter and felt a warm glow inside his chest. It was a laugh that he would never hear again. It brought back many happy memories.

Silence.

Was that it or was there more?

What was it he was supposed to learn from the recording?

What he had heard was pretty horrendous and he decided that he would never be regressed. He didn't want to know, what if he had once been Charles 1st. He had no wish to experience his own execution again. He heard Philip's voice and this time there were no preliminaries.

"Are you ready, Holly?"

Holly! My God! Philip really had regressed Holly! James heard Holly's soft reply, "Yes."

"Do you see a door in front of you?" Philip asked.

"Yes."

"Open the door and walk through."

"Where are you?"

"There are lots of people. They are dressed funny. I am in the middle of them. They are laughing and dancing and there is loud music. People are eating and drinking. Whatever they are drinking is making them silly. What are they doing? I can't stop them. Smoke." Holly's voice faltered. "I can't breathe."

James heard Eve's voice. "I've heard enough. Bring her out Philip"

"Holly I want you to come out of that life now. Please make for the door."

Holly continued speaking. "I can't move. He is evil. I will seek you out – I will have my revenge – my baby and I will have our revenge. I will hunt you down…"

"Holly I want you to leave that life now," Philip stressed firmly but calmly.

Although Philip's voice appeared calm, James sensed panic. Holly continued speaking.

"The fire is getting closer. Everything is a blur. I can't see anyone anymore." Then Holly's unexpected howl was the most sickening sound James had ever heard.

"Holly, I insist you walk back through the door."

Silence.

"Where are you now?" Philip's voice still remained firm and calm.

"In the corridor."

"Good, now come out through the door by which you entered the corridor."

Silence.

It was the end of the disk. James groaned as he reflected on what he had heard. What the hell was that all about? Was it to prove to him that Eve and Holly were somehow connected?

Perhaps that was the reason Eve had taken such an interest in Holly. She had an instant affinity with the child, a sort of sixth sense.

Eve believed that she and Holly had both known each other in a previous lifetime or, as James suspected, it was something buried deep in their minds from confused images or tales told. Or maybe Eve had told Holly about her own past life regression sessions. He was sure Holly would know a little about Eve's work. He was certain, however, that Eve would never have gone into such horrific detail. Holly is only a child with a child's vivid imagination, yes, that's it – vivid imagination.

His problem was, why did Philip think that any of this was relevant to Eve's death and why did he think it acceptable to regress a child?

He reached for his telephone, lifted the receiver and punched in Philip's number.

"Hi James, how did it go?" Philip spoke before James had a chance.

"It needs more than a bit of explaining," he snapped.

"Just thought I'd give you something to think about. When do you want to get together?"

"The sooner the better."

"I'm on my way," Philip answered.

"Fine. I have to talk to the staff at the apiary around five. It shouldn't take long. I'll be back about six."

"I'll be there."

James had only just replaced the receiver when it rang again. It was Nicky.

"Are you in tonight I was thinking of coming over I don't want to be on my own."

"I think you mean you don't want me to be on my own."

Nicky laughed.

"In that case will you bring dinner with you? Philip is

coming. He sent across some recordings he'd made of Eve's regression sessions. I think you should listen to them."

"Oh! Very intriguing. Anything interesting in them?"

"All Double-Dutch to me."

"Not sure I'll be much help but it'll be good to see Philip, I haven't seen him in ages. I may be a little late. I have a conference at five. It shouldn't take more than twenty to thirty minutes. I can't cancel as we're in court first thing tomorrow."

"Anything exciting?"

"Divorce. Trying to fight a plausible, manipulating bully. Everyone who doesn't know him thinks butter wouldn't melt in his mouth."

"Will you be able to get that over to the judge?"

"I doubt it. Men rule here and this guy Gareth Jenkins is one hell of an act."

"Any children involved?"

"One."

"I see your problem. You can only do your best, Nicky."

"True... I'll pick up a Thai on the way home."

"Perfect."

Philip's recordings had made James think about another inexplicable event. The strange behaviour of the bees. Regardless of appearing foolish he dialled Felicity at the Bee Society. Felicity answered, she didn't sound as cheerful as she had earlier.

"Felicity it's James Marchant again."

"Have you any more news," she asked, rapidly.

"No, I'm sorry, not yet"

James heard Felicity tut. "Felicity, something I failed to mention, something strange happened the moment Eve died."

"Oh…"

"When Holly found Eve's body…"

"Holly! You mean the little girl who lives with Eve…?"

"Yes."

"Goodness gracious me! What a dreadful thing for a child to have to see. She is such a delightful little girl. Eve often brought her to meetings."

"Yes, she is. What I'm about to say, Felicity, may sound a little odd but I'm hoping you will be able to explain it to me." James faltered. "Holly told me that when she found Eve's body, the bees left, they swarmed out of their hives and disappeared."

Silence.

"I'm not sure I understand, you mean they have left the hives and they haven't returned?"

"Yes all of them, over a hundred colonies gone. Thousands of bees flying who knows where." James hesitated, he couldn't believe he was having this conversation.

"Thousands Sir James! Each hive can house up to sixty thousand bees multiply that by one hundred and, in fact, I know Eve had more hives that that. We are talking of six million bees at the very least," Felicity groaned.

"I didn't realise. I've always taken the bees for granted they were part of Eve's life and also part of country life."

"That's true. A lot of people take the humble bee for

granted. With you it was horses, with Eve it was bees. Are you quite sure they've not returned?"

"Quite sure. Holly checks on them daily. Have you any idea why they did that?"

Felicity was fidgeting he could tell. "Spooky," she eventually said. "Sir James I've been keeping bees for fifteen years now and I have never come across anything like it, however, many of our members have been keeping bees for a lot longer. If you like, I'll send out an e-mail to all our members and see if someone has any ideas."

"I'd appreciate that."

"In the meantime I suggest you Google Bee-Keeping. There are plenty of sites from basic bee-keeping to bee mythology. I think you'll find the mythology sites interesting reading, but keep in mind it is mythology.

"Although it's very strange the bees flying off like that. I don't know how much you know about bees?"

"Not a lot."

"They're highly intelligent insects. Did you know that bees communicate to each other by doing an elaborate and complex dance? For an example, if a bee returns from a successful gathering of nectar it will perform a dance and using its tail will indicate the direction of where the food is to be found. The intensity of the waggle will tell the other bees how far away the food is."

"Well I never…"

"There have been scientific studies," Felicity continued. "These studies have proved that bees are also good at maths, they can tell the time and, wait for it, can also recognise letters."

"Now you have got to be joking."

Felicity chuckled. "No joke. There's a lot people don't know about bees. Most people think they blindly make honey and that's all there is to the humble honey-bee." Felicity spoke with pride. It was obvious to James that, like Eve, she adored her bees. "I'm a bit concerned, Sir James. Have there been any reports of swarms or of people being stung? There are millions of bees out there. Surely someone would have seen something."

"I haven't heard of anything, so far." James sensed that Felicity was thinking.

"Scientists call a bee swarm "a cognitive entity" this means that it can think. What this swarm is thinking right now I have no idea. They will eventually settle and create nests, the question is where. Have you reported this to the authorities?"

"No."

"Leave it to me Sir James, I'll contact them. Keep me informed, and if a situation should arise our members will be only too willing to help. We will be able to work faster than the authorities."

"You've already been a great help, thank you. I'll be in touch as soon as I have news of Eve's funeral."

Chapter 9 – Becky

Becky opened the door. Her eyes were shining. Her skin glowed and she was smiling …such a transformation since the previous time they had met. James suspected it was the relief in knowing she did not have to leave Eve's home, the home and the life she had come to love, at least, not for the time being.

He wished he could tell her about the codicil to Eve's will and put her mind at rest. Unfortunately, it would not be prudent at this time, particularly with a murder charge hanging over them all, including him.

It was obvious that Blackwell had taken an immediate dislike to him. Wouldn't it be a catch for her if she arrested Superintendent Marchant's brother for murder?

"Holly not in?" James asked.

"No, she has been backwards and forwards checking to see if the bees have returned all day. She's so upset, James. I imagine she's now at her special place on the river bank."

"I wish there was something I could do to help. Perhaps when she gets back you will ask her to give me a call I'd like to have a chat with her?"

Becky looked sceptical. "You won't frighten her will you? She has been through enough with that Blackwell woman. She hasn't actually accused her outright, of killing Eve, she only implies it."

"I've become very fond of Holly I would never do anything to upset her. All I want is to hear what happened from her."

Becky understood.

"How did the staff take it when you told them it was business as usual?" James asked.

"Relieved but I'm not sure they believed me."

"I half-expected it, that's why I'm here." James glanced at his watch; it was four fifty. "They'll be starting to close up now, I'd better go across to the centre and reaffirm what you have already told them, and then you shouldn't have any problems."

"I'd appreciate it, thank you."

"When I'm done I'll get straight off. I'm expecting a visitor."

Becky nodded and walked James to the door. He felt her eyes burning into his back as he crossed the yard. He wished there was more he could do for them both but at the moment there was nothing. He glanced back as he entered the centre. She had returned indoors.

The four members of Eve's staff were waiting for him in the café. James re-affirmed everything Becky had told them. The apiary would continue to operate as it always had and all their jobs were secure.

"We have a business to run and we will run it exactly as Eve would have wanted."

A perplexed Penny was the first to speak. "But the bees have gone, Sir James."

"I know. They will have to be replaced. We have enough products in store to keep us going for a long time. Now that the winter months are upon us it will give us an opportunity to prepare for next season. Have you all been interviewed by the police?"

"Yes," Maureen answered with a glint in her eyes. "Some woman asked if we had seen any strangers loitering about."

Instantaneously, the staff burst out laughing. Gina said, "We told her, only about a hundred a day, more when we have coach-trippers."

James' lips curled into a grin. "What did she say to that?"

"Nothing, she was too mad to speak," Penny added. "She also asked if Eve had any enemies, well, we all know Eve, who could possibly have had a reason to harm her? The thought is preposterous."

"I agree." He hesitated. "There may have been someone or something that happened recently that was out of order or out of character. Can any of you think of anything?"

"No," they replied shaking their heads.

"Mary, you're in charge of the day-to-day running of the centre. Are you quite prepared to continue to do that?"

"Of course," Mary replied. "I'm relieved that the centre is not going to close. I love working here."

James was pleased to hear it. He knew he would have to rely on her a lot in the coming few weeks. "I am sure

I don't have to ask for you to continue to support Becky, she is going to need your help," James scrutinized the women's faces and was satisfied with what he saw.

"We all get on with Becky, I can't see that there would be a problem."

"Good, then I'll leave you to finish packing up. If you have any problems, or if you think of anything that would help me, or the police, do not hesitate to get in touch." James put his hand in his pocket pulled out his wallet and handed a couple of his name cards to Mary. "I don't think you have my telephone numbers. Perhaps you will pin these on the notice board."

As James left the centre he glanced through the plate glass window of the viewing room and, in the distance, saw Holly wandering around the apiary re-checking the hives. She was pale, and appeared thinner than she had a few days earlier, if only he could do something to help the child.

Dusk was upon the valley and a red and amber sky streaked the horizon to the north-west promising a fair day tomorrow. Philip had already arrived and was sitting in his car when James drove up to the front of his property.

"Been here long?" he asked as he closed the door of his BMW.

"No, I'm sitting enjoying the sunset. I gather you've had a busy day."

"You can say that again. Come on in I'm dying for a drink. We have to wait for dinner. Nicky is bringing in a Thai take-away."

"Sounds good to me I'm starving."

"You're always hungry, you need to lose weight."

"Never."

Philip was dressed in casual creams and browns very different from the loud colours of his Cuban holiday clothes he had been wearing the previous day. Taking their drinks, they settled in chairs opposite each other in the family room.

"What did you think of the recordings?" Philip asked.

"Confusing to say the least. The first part I could understand but I felt very uncomfortable with the second part. You did say that the first recording was made when you and Eve were at university."

"That's right."

"That's a lifetime ago."

Philip nodded.

"And, the second half was recorded only a short while ago and yet they both tell practically the same story, how come?"

Taking a sip of his drink Philip began. "What I think it explains is why Eve had this powerful affinity towards Holly."

James shook his head. He was not *getting* any of this. "I'm trying to be pragmatic Philip. I wasn't convinced that the tapes were proof of a previous life if that is what you are suggesting. There was nothing tangible in them, names places, streets etc. They both probably watched the same movie."

"As I explained, Eve's regression was a university exercise. It was the first time I had tried to regress anyone. I didn't know what I was doing. Eve was a natural subject. I doubt I'd have made it work on someone else. It has taken years of study and practice for me to be competent in this type of therapy. I chose those recordings because, as you pointed out, of the similarity."

James nodded. "I realised that and, I reiterate, they are not proof."

"Eve told me she had known for some time about Holly's aversion to fire and she had considered long and hard before she came to me and we discussed regression therapy, was it ethical as Holly was only ten etc."

"Did Becky agree?"

"No, she knew nothing about it."

"I thought not."

"Hmm... Although Becky is interested and excited about working on Eve's case histories and was compiling information for the book Eve and I were writing. Eve knew that Becky didn't want Holly to know too much about it. Holly being a child, Becky felt that she wouldn't be able to understand fully what Eve was doing. She felt it could give her nightmares."

"Quite right," James mumbled and took a sip of gin then removed the slice of lemon which insisted in getting stuck between his lips.

"After deciding to go ahead I devised a sort of game. Eve was with me throughout the session. The short session was enough to convince Eve that Holly had been part of her past life. Were you aware that both Eve and Holly were afraid of fire?"

"Eve yes, I didn't know about Holly."

"This is where regression helps heal irrational fears such as phobias or behavioural problems. Eve learned that in a past life there had been a fire and that she was involved in that fire. Remember how she disliked heat of any kind, she never ever sunbathed."

"I remember how she preferred to ride across the valley when the mist was down and how she preferred to holiday in the winter in Canada."

Philip nodded in agreement. "By bringing the horrific event to life under regression, this type of issue can be dealt with. During that session Eve was able to understand and put her fear of fire behind her. This is what she hoped to do with Holly. It was after that session that Eve added the codicil to her will."

"You know about the codicil?"

"She felt that I should as I would be joining the board of Trustees when the Retreat was up and running."

James lowered his head and stared into his drink. "None of it makes sense to me. They appear to be one and the same person. It was difficult to determine."

"I've come to the conclusion that Eve continued to develop her abilities and learned to regress herself. As with any scientific experiment Eve will have made notes or recordings. Do you know of any?"

"No, I've no idea," James answered. He made a feeble attempt to laugh, and then shaking his head said, "Eve has never ceased to amaze me."

"I know you find it hard to believe James, but how could two people who hardly knew each other have similar memories if there wasn't an element of truth in it?"

"I don't know. I'm trying to think of a movie or perhaps making one."

"Don't be so flippant, James," Philip snapped.

"Sorry."

"Do you think Becky would have let a ten-year-old child watch such a movie? Remember Holly is also scared of fire."

"Hmm …did you ever regress Holly again?"

"No, Eve wouldn't hear of it. She felt guilty about the whole thing and wished she had followed her own instincts in the first place instead of requiring proof."

"Perhaps Holly listened to some of Eve's tapes without her knowing?" James mused.

Philip stood and began to walk around the room. "For sceptics like you, let us say it's all mumbo-jumbo, what harm has been done. It made Eve happy and Becky and Holly are going to benefit from the codicil to her will."

"You called me a sceptic, well I suppose I am. Healing hands I can accept. Eve has proved it to me time and time again. God only knows how it works but it does. Reincarnation? I'm not so sure."

"James, you only have to read the papers to see that, almost daily, scientists are discovering things that a year or two ago seemed to be little more than fantasy. That is what Eve and I were trying to do, get some proof."

"Then explain this to me, Philip. I watched a few seconds of a programme a while back until I switched off in disgust, convinced it was all in the mind …crazy people's imagination. There were women all around the world claiming that they had been Cleopatra in a previous life?"

Philip spluttered and coughed as he almost choked on a mouthful of his gin and tonic. "That's a classic example and an easy one to answer."

"Oh?"

"When a patient is in deep relaxation they can often misconstrue the events they are seeing. In some recorded cases what the patient sees is Cleopatra riding in a golden chariot, the operative word here is, sees.

"It is they who are seeing Cleopatra. It is not them as Cleopatra. Multitudes of her subjects would crowd on to the streets to catch a glimpse of their queen so, transposition takes place, hence thousands of Cleopatra's."

"Oh shit, Philip, you have an answer for everything."

"I do my best."

James glanced at his watch. "Nicky should be here at any moment. I think we've time for a top-up."

"Wouldn't say no..." Philip grinned as he handed James his glass.

"When was the last time you saw Eve?" James asked as he poured tonic into Philip's gin.

"About three weeks ago."

"Did anything appear to be bothering her?"

"No. Have *you* noticed anything odd in her behaviour recently? You saw more of her than I did."

"I saw her the day before she died and she was her usual self, which brings me back to the opinion that she disturbed an intruder."

"What about the recordings?"

"What about the recordings? I can't see how they tell us anything, or have anything to do with her murder. It's all gobbledegook to me," James said matter-of-factly.

"I'm not so sure..." Philip murmured.

Chapter 10 – Nicky

"Only me, Dad," Nicky called from the hallway as she opened the door. "Will someone please get some plates? We need to eat this before it gets cold." Nicky began opening the packages and placed them one by one onto the dining table. She had bought – Spicy Beef Salad, Green Chicken Curry, and Chicken with Cashew Nuts, Thai Style Fried Noodles, Fried Rice and a Spicy Green Papaya Salad.

"Wow! A veritable feast," Philip declared as he began to tuck in while James pulled the cork from a bottle of Tempranillo, Cabernet Sauvignon.

Eve's death made no sense to any of them. They talked through their meal going over and over every possible eventuality. In particular, how the police were working on the theory that either Becky or Holly was involved.

"It's laughable," Nicky said defiantly.

Philip agreed.

"I still think it was an intruder," James mumbled.

Philip was getting agitated. "Let's assume you are right, James. Tell me, what do you think could have happened to have sent someone flying off into such an uncontrolled rage, a rage so intense that they were forced to kill?"

"Hmm… That's a tough one."

"Dad, something has been bothering me …I've never given it a thought before. Why didn't Eve marry and have children?"

"I can answer that, Nicky. When we were leaving university to go our separate ways I asked Eve to marry me."

"Wow! It's all coming out now."

Philip smiled. "She turned me down. She said it was not possible for her to have children. I said it didn't matter. She said that it would at some point. So we went our separate ways and remained good friends."

"I'm sorry Philip, I didn't know." Pushing her chair away from the table she said, "I'll make coffee and then I'm off duty."

The two men had left the table and were once again ensconced in chairs opposite each other in the family room.

Nicky arrived carrying a tray. On the tray she had placed three mugs, a cream jug and a pot of coffee, no one took sugar.

She placed it on a low table between the two men. She then went to the cocktail cabinet and poured two large Brandies.

"There you are you can help yourself. I'm going to listen to the recordings."

"The disk is still in the machine," James called after her.

Ten minutes later Nicky returned and sighed, "Phew …that was heavy stuff. Not sure what it all means."

"Tell us your thoughts?" Philip asked.

She sat on the sofa, pulled her legs up and tucked them beneath a cushion. "I'm guessing that Dad thinks it's a load of bunkum."

"Quite right," James nodded. He then pondered for a moment. "That's not exactly true. Eve was a remarkable lady and often seemed to belong in another world, a world that you or I could never begin to understand. So I'll correct you, Nicky, not bunkum. My cynicism may be due to ignorance but, more important to me, is the lack of evidence.

James pulled himself up in his chair and slapped its arms with the palms of his hands. "Back to the recordings, we're both listening Philip."

"Tell me, how much do you know about Eve's family?" Philip began.

"Ah, now I do know about that. Eve's family came to the valley around the time our family did. We go back a long way."

"Go one," Philip urged.

James forehead creased as it took him a moment to recall the almost forgotten history. "It was in the early seventeenth century. King Charles was trying to quell a rebellion on the Scottish borders known as…"

"The Bishops War," Nicky interrupted. "It is local history. We studied it at school along with the Border Reivers."

"That's right, it had to do with him trying to force one religion on the Scots and they were having none of it. He had a lot of casualties including his best general who he didn't expect to survive.

"Eve's family lived on a small-holding close to the border and became embroiled in the fighting.

"The men in the family fought for the king and the women healed the wounded by using their knowledge of herbs and honey. No one in those days fully understood that pure honey was an antiseptic. To cut a long story short the general survived and a grateful king gave the family Moxley Manor, which he had acquired as spoils of war."

Nicky chuckled. "Wouldn't it be great if that sort of thing happened today?"

"What?"

"The realm bestowing conquered estates on their devotees."

"You wouldn't even get a beef burger these days." Philip, not being a royalist, scoffed.

"We've enough land to look after. That war and subsequent wars left many prominent families destitute. Tired of death and destruction many families were only too willing to relieve themselves of the responsibility of land management, many went abroad. That's how our family came to expand this estate."

"This is all very interesting." Philip took a deep breath. "What I want to know is what happened before that."

"Before what? Was there a before?" James asked, mischievously.

"I assume there was."

"I don't know, Philip. I don't know where they

originally came from."

Philip shifted his position and made a move to get up. Nicky jumped off the sofa. "I'll do it," she said as she took his glass. "Dad, another one for you?"

Philip laughed. "I thought you were off duty."

"I am, so after this, you're on your own."

"Thank you, Nicky," James handed her his empty Brandy glass. "Go on Philip."

"You told me that these thought provoking subjects were never discussed after you had both reached adulthood."

"That's right. We had passed the age of frightening each other with ghost stories."

"Okay, well, after our university session Eve became curious and asked questions at home. Her mother showed her a trunk, which had been stored for years in the attic. Inside was a wealth of old documents and in particular a journal written by a Francine Du Pont. The journal was written in French; the story had been handed down generation to generation. Eve had the journal translated to make sure that what her mother had told her was correct.

"Apparently, in the early sixteen-hundreds this Francine Du Pont had lived in France, in a cottage, with her ageing mother, her sister, and her young daughter, Celestine. The men in the family having died or disappeared. The women were believers in the Circle of Life."

"Never heard of it," Nicky chipped in.

"I imagine it is what we would call a cult these days. Moving on, all the women were psychic. The child

Celestine was exceptionally gifted."

"How?" James queried thinking of Eve's abilities.

"They had the gift of second sight. They prophesied and healed. They healed with herbs and honey."

"We know Eve had healing hands," Nicky said. "Go on…"

"At that time, across Europe including here, the burning of witches was a frequent occurrence and Francine was concerned for her family's safety, in particular that of Celestine. Against family opposition she was able to secure a place for her child in the Cardinal's palace.

"There she would live and work and be instructed in Catholicism. She would be taught ways that would guarantee her daughters safety. In private they continued with their own beliefs."

"Having listened to the disk I don't think I want to hear the rest." Nicky shuddered as she spoke.

"Well I do, so shush. Go on Philip."

"I think you can guess the rest. She was twelve-years-old. She became pregnant. The father of her child was the Cardinal. She was tried on trumped up charges and burned at the stake."

"Oh my God! He even killed his own child."

"Hmm… After the burning the three remaining women left France and made their way to England, and guess what they took with them – their precious bees."

"This has given me goose pimples," Nicky quivered and rubbed her hands up and down her arms as she struggled to her feet. "I'm off to bed I'm due in Court first thing. I'll probably have nightmares now."

"I'm sure you won't," James said smiling at her as she bent and kissed him goodnight on his forehead. She blew a kiss towards Philip and took herself off to bed.

As Nicky closed the door behind her James said. "Well I'll be damned. What a story, however, it is a story and nothing more. I think you are getting carried away with yourself, Philip."

"Is that what you believe? Do you think Eve would have left it at that?"

"I'm not following you."

"Eve researched the event and found that a child named Celestine Dupont was burned at the stake in 1636 in a cathedral town on the outskirts of Paris."

"What! I had no idea. I have to confess, it's all very strange. I guess you're trying to convince me that reincarnation is a reality."

"We're a long way from scientifically proving anything, one way or the other. Eve told me the story because it was relevant to the work we were doing."

"I wonder," James mused. "Did Eve ever confide in you that the Cardinal was living in this time-line?" James burst out laughing. "See what you've done you've got me taking this seriously."

"Keep an open mind James, keep an open mind."

"I am and I have been doing a lot of thinking. Tell me, who was Eve in that first time-line? Was she Celestine or was she her mother, her aunt or her grandmother?"

"I don't know. Since listening to the recording again I've cast my mind back to the session with Holly. When it was over Eve became pensive. I was getting Holly a glass of water and noticed Eve shaking her head and she mumbled something."

"What?" James demanded.

"I didn't take much notice of it at the time but it sounded like forgive or forgiveness will end it. I never spoke to her about it again."

"Am I right in thinking that you believe Eve is Celestine and somehow the Cardinal has caught up with her and somehow initiated history into repeating itself. I don't think so, Philip." James stressed. "What would be his reason for wanting to kill her again in this lifetime?"

"I can't answer that."

"None as far as I can see so, it boils down to my theory, that she was disturbed by a complete stranger. It has nothing to do with anything that happened centuries ago."

"I agree with you up to a point. I'm the expert here, and yet even I can't imagine what could have aroused so much passion in a complete stranger, to make him kill so violently. Eve was a healer. She cared for man and beast alike, if it were a stranger, Eve would have taken kindly to him and offered hospitality."

"True; very true." James nodded in agreement.

"If you're right James; think about the number of visitors to the centre each day. Or, perhaps it was a fellow jealous bee-keeper? Tradesman? Someone who lives in her cottages? Any number of people. Tracing such a person would be an impossible task."

James leaned forward and resting his elbows on the arms of his chair he cupped his glass. "I agree with you and that's my worry. It's also why Blackwell will never believe the intruder scenario. It will take too much time. Too much work. As well as the costs involved, she is after a quick conviction. It means she won't stop trying to pin the blame on either Becky or Holly."

Chapter 11 – Philip

"We'll take my car." James said to Philip as he locked the door behind them. Walking towards his BMW he zipped up his anorak. The air had a bite to it; an early autumn was on its way and James was still waiting for summer. However, it was, and not before time, going to be a dry day. The expected sun should warm the air around lunchtime.

The lane was still littered with broken debris left by Monday's storm. As far as the council was concerned the clearing of country lanes was not a priority.

Ten minutes later they parked in the car park of the visitors' centre, crossed the lane and opened the five-bar gate and entered. Water glistened between the cobbles as they stepped carefully on the slippery stones.

"I'd like to see where it happened before calling on Becky?"

"No problem, the centre doesn't open until eleven."

"Will the police be there?"

"I didn't notice a car. However, I expect the scene is still cordoned off."

"What do they hope to find now."

James shrugged his shoulders. "Who knows?"

They had reached the twelve-foot gap, which separated the centre from the trees lining the lane. They stepped over the chain-link fence with its hanging sign clearly marked 'Private' and made their way around the back of the building to the apiary.

White beehives stretched before them like a regimented army on the march. On and on, up and up only to disappear over the rise into an orchard.

On their right a yellow crime-of-scene tape flapped in the breeze. The shape of the crime scene was oblong, about fifty-feet by forty-feet surrounding a number of hives. The hive they were looking for was covered by a tent.

James and Philip stood silent, deep in their own thoughts. Then James untied a tape and pulled back a flap.

"It is so hard to believe. Eve, why Eve?" Philip said, as his face creased in pain. "She had so much work still to do in her life." He breathed in heavily. "You said she was found lying over this hive."

"That's right. Holly said she looked as if she was hugging the bees. She managed to lift her off the hive and lay her on the ground, when she didn't move she began to scream."

"That explains the blood."

"You said Becky hugged her, which would also explain the blood on Becky."

"I agree. Apparently, by the time Becky arrived the storm was directly overhead and the paths between the hives had been transposed into torrents of running water."

Philip began to consider the situation. "How would someone get to here without being noticed? And why would they want to?"

James shrugged his shoulders. "Possibly through the trees from the lane, or…" James pointed north, "maybe over there where the river bends. It's possible someone came from that direction having climbed the wire fence, it wouldn't be too difficult."

"Hmm…" Philip murmured.

"Or, if they were energetic, they might have walked across the fields from Upper Meedon Bridge."

"Doubt it, if they knew a storm was brewing."

"I think that's what's troubling Inspector Blackwell and why she feels she doesn't have to extend her enquiries any farther than the immediate vicinity."

"How many properties are near here?" Philip asked.

"In the lane there are six cottages and at the top of the lane, as you very well know, is Moxley Manor. After that, the nearest dwelling is about half-a-mile to the south. Across the Tyne there's a smallholding and then you come onto my land. We're quite isolated here."

"I've seen enough. There isn't anything we can learn from being here." Both men began to retrace their footsteps. Philip suddenly stopped and lifted the lid to one of the hives. He grunted. "Nothing, only a few dead or dying bees. It's incredulous. You said you have checked all the hives."

"I have and believe me, Holly checks them at least twice a day. She is desperate for them to come home."

"It's strange how she became so obsessed with the

bees. Surely you must agree, James."

"I suppose so but what else is there for her to do living in these parts."

They arrived at Eve's kitchen door and James knocked. Within seconds Becky answered. She was dressed in fresh, blue jeans and a dark blue, perfectly pressed, long-sleeved jumper.

"Hello James, Philip!" she said with surprise in her voice. "How nice to see you both." She sounded a lot perkier today. "Come on in."

"Becky, I've been dreaming about your scrumptious casseroles for so long I decided not to stay away a moment longer," Philip said, with his tongue firmly entrenched in his cheek.

Becky flushed a little then scoffed. "You embarrass me, Philip. They're all I can make and you know it."

"I would be happy to live on them for the rest of my life. You should write a casserole cookbook."

Becky pursed and curled her lips, raised her eyebrows and tutted. "I'll put coffee on. Holly is in the dining room."

Holly was intently pouring over a set of building plans. She heard the sound of heavy footsteps and looked up. "Uncle James!"

James loved hearing her call him Uncle it reminded him of when his granddaughter Sam used to run to him after she'd fallen over crying, "Grandad, Grandad." Like so many things those days were gone, never to return.

The uncle business had all started when Becky and Holly came to live with Eve. Becky had insisted Holly call him Sir James. He was not comfortable with being called Sir James and certainly not by a child. Although on occasions, he did use his title, when it was to his advantage.

Becky explained to Holly it was a question of respect for one's elders. James said he didn't mind being called James, most people did, whether he liked it or not.

It was Holly who came up with the idea. "You love Eve as much as mummy and I don't you, Sir James. So, in a way, we are like a family." He remembered how she had cast her eyes down looking a little embarrassed. "I haven't any real Uncles or Aunties or any Grandparents. I did call Mr & Mrs Grimshaw, Uncle Jim and Auntie Clare when we used to live with them but Uncle Jim died." She stopped abruptly. "Perhaps I could call you Uncle James? I would like you to be my Uncle." And so it was done and everyone was happy.

"Are you looking at the plans for the Retreat?" James asked although he knew exactly what they were. "Can you understand them?"

"Oh yes, Eve and I have looked at them lots of times. Eve explained them to me. I know where everything is supposed to go. I've been so worried Uncle James that's why I'm looking at them."

"Worried, a little girl like you should not be worried."

"Well I am. Uncle James, will the Retreat still be built, I mean, now that Eve has died and the bees have gone?"

His eyes widened in horror and staring at her said, "Most definitely, and, young lady, I am going to need your help."

"Oh I'd love that but..." Her face turned sad. "I don't

know how long we will be living here. Mummy did tell me that we don't have to move just yet..." She hesitated before speaking again. "I suppose if we did move, well, will I be able to come and visit."

James turned towards Philip and mouthed, *later*.

"Not only can you come and visit, you can come and stay with me, if you'd like to."

Holly's eyes widened. "That means I can still ride Pippa."

"You certainly can."

"Oh Uncle James you are the best," she cried. Jumping up from the table she flung her arms around his waist and reached up to kiss him. James laughed as he desperately tried to disentangle strands of her long, dark hair from his mouth.

Becky arrived and placed a coffee percolator, cream jug and mugs on the table. "That smells good," Philip remarked as his nose twitched.

It was then James noticed the inglenook fireplace "Good God! I'd forgotten all about that."

It was six feet high, seven feet wide and three feet deep. It now had a large wood-burning stove in the centre. In the alcove and on either side were benches. In the olden days, people would sit keeping warm around an open fire and perhaps the cook would sit to one side stirring a pot of something, which bubbled away for hours over the flames. The bench on the right-hand side was up and a concealed door was open. A Priest hole. It was a small room where, in days gone by, fugitives would hide from their enemies.

"Did you tell the police about *that*?" James said rather

abruptly and he strode towards the open door.

"No, I never gave it a thought. I was in such a state I didn't know what to do. This isn't my house, so I kept quiet and let them go wherever they wanted to go, and take whatever they wanted to take."

"Now, now it's alright, Becky. It's perfectly understandable, you were under a lot of pressure," Philip comforted.

Becky tried to smile but couldn't. "I still feel as though I am walking in a dream. I'm not thinking clearly."

"I can help with that. I'll bring a couple of tablets over on my way home. Take them before you go to bed and you will feel better after a proper night's sleep."

She shook her head and mused. "I had genuinely forgotten about the Priest Hole until Holly opened it this morning." With a bit of an embarrassed giggle she said. "Even if I had remembered, I was pretty pissed-off by then. I wasn't in the mood to be helpful."

"I'm glad you did forget, Becky," James said.

Ignoring James's baffling remark Becky began to rip open the packaging on a box of delicious chocolate squares.

"Coming Philip?" James called as he disappeared inside the hiding place.

"Coffee is ready," Becky mumbled.

Philip followed James into the small room. Lying on a shelf directly in front of him was the piece of equipment James had been searching for the night Eve was murdered. It was a relief, as he hadn't realised how, unconsciously, it had played on his mind.

Philip's faced creased in confusion.

"What's all this about?" he whispered.

"I'll explain later. We need to pack this stuff up and get it out of here."

Philip was more than confused now. With a shrug of his shoulders, "Anything you say," he grumbled.

"Becky," James called. "Do you have a box or something? There are one or two things of mine in here. I may as well take them as I'm here."

"I've a couple of boxes you can have, I bought some plants yesterday. They're outside I'll go and fetch them."

Hanging on hooks fixed into the ceiling herbs were drying and more herbs were in jars lining a narrow shelf. Sitting alongside the jars was the highly sensitive piece of equipment he had been looking for on the night Eve died. Next to it stood a pestle and mortar followed by a neat stack of sterile, blue, jar-tops wrapped in transparent, individual packs. The shelves on the far wall were crammed with books, all medical.

Becky passed the boxes to James. He began to pack them with the jars of dried herbs, jar tops, and the all-important piece of equipment.

When one box was full, Philip took it without a word and put it in the boot of the BMW while James continued to fill the second box. The last item he found was an airtight tin. James took off the lid. It was full of biscuits. He replaced the lid and put the tin into the box.

When he was satisfied, all that remained in the Priest Hole were Eve's medical books. "I think that's the lot, it's time for coffee."

Philip was very subdued as they sat drinking. "I don't think there is anything in there that would be of any interest to the police Becky," James said. "I'd forget all about it if I was you." He hesitated. "It might be an idea if you wiped the shelves down with disinfectant or something like that. Get rid of the overpowering smell of herbs."

Philip was even more confused.

Holly appeared a lot happier as they talked about the plans for the Retreat so James decided not to question her about what happened the day Eve died.

Becky flinched on hearing a confident knock on the door. She glanced at her watch and pulled a face. "I can't think who that could be."

When she opened the door James immediately recognised the voice and glanced across at Philip and mouthed *police*. He heard Blackwell ask to come in."

"Of course," Becky replied.

Blackwell's face crumpled as she entered the room.

"Sir James, I wasn't expecting to see you here."

"Nor I you. Let me introduce you, this is Dr Philip Cook."

"Dr Cook." Blackwell nodded towards Philip. "I've only come to return Eve's tool box. I felt you may have need of it. Forensics have finished with it." She looked at Cranmore who obediently placed the box on top of the table.

"That was quick," James said.

"We don't mess about when we're dealing with murder, Sir James."

James noticed Blackwell's lips curl. He pondered on how extraordinary it was that human beings' unspoken thoughts and feelings can smother a room. The atmosphere was repressive. Holly stood and, without a word, hurried from the room.

"Holly," Becky called after her.

"It's quite all right I have no need to talk to her," Blackwell said.

"Do you have the autopsy results," Philip asked.

"Not yet Doctor."

"Why the delay?"

"I can't answer that. I honestly don't know. You can rest assured that as soon as I hear anything I'll let you all know."

"We'd appreciate it. We do have a funeral to arrange and a lot of people need to be informed."

"Good grief what's that?" Blackwell's eyes widened and giving an astonished laugh made for the fireplace.

"It's the library," James answered in a rush.

"May I…"

Becky couldn't bring herself to answer.

James reached the Priest Hole before her and entered. Blackwell bent her head and followed him inside. "As you can see it's where Eve kept all her reference books. Some of them are very old. So old that she kept them in here. The room has the perfect atmosphere to protect them."

She stepped closer. "It's all right I won't touch them." Her eyes scanned the books on the shelves. "It's quite wonderful. Eve was a G.P. wasn't she?" Blackwell muttered as she peered at the spine of a book which read, "The Anatomy of Plants."

"Yes, and she was a good one."

"So I've heard."

Satisfied, Blackwell bent her head and walked out through the fireplace and back into the room.

She only glanced at the books and not at the floor, sprinkled in dust from the hanging dried herbs. With the door being open, the smell of herbs has dissipated and mingled with the strong aroma of coffee. "I've read about such rooms in historical novels," she said in quite a cheery tone. "I won't keep you any longer." With a slight nod of her head she made for the door and Cranmore, like a little lamb, followed.

"What was that all about? I don't believe she has nothing better to do than return a tool box, which now that the bees have flown would not be needed." Philip remarked.

"I agree. I can only guess that it's something she didn't want to say in front of us. It was also odd she didn't question you as to exactly who you were."

"I'm glad she didn't. If I'd told her I was a psychiatrist, she would have assumed I'd been brought in to prep the girls."

James agreed. Becky was in the kitchen and James called to her. "We'll get off now, thanks for the coffee, Becky. Any problems give me a call."

Becky reappeared wiping her hands on a towel. "You don't have to go. I could make you some lunch."

"That sounds good, any chance of a casserole?" Philip said quickly, his eyes wide with anticipation; then he winked at her.

"Not today Becky, thank you all the same we still have a lot to do,"

Philip pulled a disappointed face.

"I understand. Don't you be such a stranger, Philip?"

Philip winked at her again and they left.

"How about lunch at The Pigs Trotters? You look as if you need a drink."

"I don't need a drink I'd like an explanation as to your bizarre behaviour back there. What was so special about a few jars and dried herbs and what overpowering smell? There's nothing nicer than the smell of herbs."

"Let's get rid of these boxes, we can drop them off at my place and then I'll explain everything over lunch."

Nicky's car was parked outside when they arrived. "I thought Nicky said that she was in court this morning?"

"She did, I wonder if this is a good or bad sign."

They carried the boxes into the house and stacked them in the utility room. They found Nicky in the kitchen. She was about to spread honey on a piece of toast when James yelled, "Noooooh....," as he rushed towards her and grabbed the jar of honey.

Nicky appeared to leave the ground as her body flinched. "Dad! Whatever has got into you?"

James breathed fast as he tried to composed himself.

"Dad, if you don't mind I'd like to know why I can't have some honey on my toast? I haven't time for anything else Court resumes at two. I only called to collect some papers I left here last night."

"Buttered toast is better for you."

"Since when...," she snapped as she began to spread butter on the piece of toast and hurriedly took a bite. "I think I deserve an explanation, come on Dad, I'm waiting," she glared at him in a threatening way.

"I think we both do," Philip nodded in agreement. "Your father has been behaving in a bizarre way all morning."

James bit his lower lip wondering how to begin. "Oh dear, I suppose I had better tell you. What I'm about to say must not go any farther than these four walls."

Philip and Nicky glanced at each other, totally confused.

"We all agree that Eve's calling in life was to heal the sick, right?"

They nodded in agreement. Nicky murmured something as she wiped melting butter off her chin.

"When a terminally ill patient is near to the end, yet death is not quite imminent, depression can set in. Eve concocted a selection of herbs that had properties to relax and enlighten the mood. She baked a kind of biscuit then, using a pestle and mortar, she ground them and mixed the fine powder into the honey."

Nicky scrunched her face as she thought. "I remember now; Mum always had a jar of honey along with a packet of water-biscuits by the side of her bed." She hesitated then continued slowly. "If my memory is correct that jar was different from the usual ones we buy, it also had a blue top. I didn't think anything of it at the time."

Nicky picked up the jar James had taken from her and placed on the table. "This has a blue top." She raised her eyebrows and, with wide eyes, stared directly into her father's expressionless face. "Dad, what are you trying to tell us?"

"I think I know," Philip chortled. "Come on tell, what kind of herbs, James?"

"Didn't you recognise any that were hanging up to dry?"

"No I didn't. I was too concerned with what was going on with you."

"As I said, there was a variety of herbs all legal, except for one."

"Cannabis!" Philip snorted.

"Exactly."

"Mum and Eve were the best of friends. She did whatever it took to help control your mother's pain and I backed her one-hundred-per-cent."

"So you knew about it," Nicky accused.

"Yes, but I only became aware of it when your mother's health deteriorated and she became too mentally-ill to manage her disease. It was then that Eve suggested the special honey. The cannabis was in a low dosage, enough to lift the spirits and to give your mother the strength to get through the day. It also gave your mother a little hope. Patients needed to feel that they could and would conquer their illness."

"Mum died months ago. Why the hell did you keep the stuff?"

"I didn't."

"You didn't! Oh my God!" Her spontaneous laugh interrupted her flow. "It wasn't only Mum she gave it to, was it? "I can't believe what I'm hearing," she spluttered. "Our Eve. To think she was growing Cannabis. Of course! It would never be noticed dotted amongst the plants in her heated greenhouse, and let's be honest nobody ever went in there except Eve." Nicky began to laugh again. "The sheer guts of it."

"Judging from the expression on your face I'd say she's shot up in your estimation, Nicky," Philip said grinning.

"She has."

"Eve would do everything and anything possible to alleviate suffering; she was an expert on herbs, she knew what she was doing."

"Steady on," Philip cut in. "I can see a problem here; Cannabis is still illegal."

"I know that. I think I have it covered. It was only when Jean took sick that I learned about the special honey. As I've already said, when Eve felt it was time, she explained to me exactly what the ingredients were and what each ingredient was supposed to do. I didn't care what was in the stuff as long as it relieved your mother's suffering and that is how each and every one of Eve's patients felt."

"Phew …she was quite a lady, Dad."

"She was. She also explained to me how she operated. As you know she was very active at the Hospice. If a patient was terminally ill and Eve felt that the honey could relieve some of their suffering, she would explain everything to the carer then leave it up to them to decide. No one had ever refused her help. If they were in their own home she would visit them and administer hands-on healing and then leave a jar of blue-topped honey. And, before you ask, there was no charge."

"Knowing Eve, I didn't expect there would be. I only wish I'd married her," Philip reminisced. "I did ask, you know, years ago."

"I did too, when I was twelve." The two men laughed.

"Dear me, Dad. Tut, tut, did Mum know?"

"I did say I was twelve. When Eve died, it gave me a problem. I knew the police would get a warrant to search the premises. They would undoubtable have found her store of special honey.

"I waited until the middle of the night then drove to Eve's. Becky and Holly were in hospital. Cranmore had told me that they were not leaving an officer on duty and that they would be back at first light.

"I have a key so I let myself in. I searched and eventually found the blue-topped jars of honey. I also found an address book, which Eve kept in her handbag.

"The book contained names and telephone numbers of her special patients. She couldn't trust such knowledge to a computer. The majority of names in the book had been crossed out. I assumed they had all died.

"I counted eight names. It was too late to go to bed so I waited until it was a respectable time before making the calls. I informed the carers of these patients what had happened, and told them I had a limited supply of honey.

"I don't know who was more scared, them or me. They were very brave to trust me."

"They could have thought you were the police," Nicky said.

"Exactly. Anyway, I took the honey and gave them as much as they felt they would need, keeping in mind I only had a limited amount.

"The last of Eve's patients was a Mrs Evans and her daughter was adamant that her mother would only need one more jar. The doctor had told her that her mother would be on the strongest drugs possible by the end of the week. I put the other jar back in the boot, drove home, and forgot about it. Next time I opened the boot there it was, like a phoenix rising up from the dead. I realised I had to get rid of it. I put it at the back of a cupboard in the kitchen intending to dispose of it later."

"And I found it. Oh Dad, I'm so sorry I shouted at you. That also explains your appearance when you came to see me on Tuesday; death warmed up is how I'd describe it."

"That bad eh?"

Nicky began to laugh. "Think about it, Dad, it's quite funny, really. What if you hadn't come home when you did? I'd have been dancing on the desks in the court room."

"And, carried off to the cells, no doubt."

Philip was contemplating. "Just to clarify, James – when we went to see Becky had you genuinely forgotten about the Priest Hole?"

"Yes, and believe me, I was so relieved when I saw those scales sitting there. I'd searched for them on Monday night but couldn't find them. I decided that, as Eve had been making the stuff for so many years, she no longer needed to use them. If the police had stumbled across them, it might have set off alarm bells. They weigh precisely and are not the sort of scales you would come across in a family kitchen."

Nicky gasped and jumped up from the table. "Goodness is that the time? I was supposed to have read through these papers before court resumed." She snatched up the papers and almost flew out of the room.

"Nicky, not beyond these four walls, remember," James called after her.

"I'm a solicitor, Dad. I'm no fool," and they heard the door slam.

"What's with the forlorn expression, Philip?"

"Hum …I was thinking. Why didn't Eve tell me about the Cannabis?"

James grinned as he leaned back against the table. "And I was wondering why Eve never confided in me, about Holly being regressed."

"Maybe she felt you wouldn't understand?"

"I don't believe that was the reason. As far as we were both concerned, it was on a, *need to know basis.*"

Chapter 12 – Moxley Manor

Against a backdrop of ebony, moonless, night sky, a dazzling snake of car headlights moved closer and closer to Moxley Manor. Light's blazed from every window of the great house. It was a magical and luring sight; "Will you step into my parlour?" said the spider to the fly;

James ignored the person directing the cars to a hastily created parking area and continued up the long drive. A moving shadow to his right caught his eye. A man dressed in dark clothing. James spotted the *earwig* and shoulder holster before the man ducked back into the bushes. He continued on and drove around to the rear of the building where he parked. Normally, he would have entered through the kitchen, but not tonight. Tonight he was an invited guest at this prodigious event. He made his way to the front door.

Sarah Milton and her brother Michael were standing inside the entrance to the Manor greeting their guests. He took his place in line and observed. Sarah was small, slimmer than he had imagined when he had seen her rushing down the steps of police HQ. Then, she had been wearing a loose brown coat, which flapped wildly in the wind. Tonight she was wearing an emerald green dress, and with her massive head of auburn hair, both dress, and hair, distracted attention from her plain face.

Her brother, Michael, was taller than Sarah, maybe six feet or a little over. He had the same full head of auburn hair, which was combed up and back, accentuating his large, broad nose and thick lips. The two moving heads reminded James of flashing beacons. James also noticed Michael's long, orang-utan arms that flopped back into place after he shook hands with his guests.

He had reached Sarah.

"Delighted you could come," she purred like a teenager responding to the attention of a new boyfriend.

"Sir James Marchant," he answered with a slight nod of his head. "Thank you for inviting me." It was obvious to James that she hadn't a clue as to who he was. This was one of those, *get the locals on side do's, they may come in useful one day.*

James was handed a glass of mediocre champagne and he walked on, leaving the next guest to shake the hand of the Prime-Minister-in-waiting.

He now stood in the once-impressive reception hall and glanced up the sweeping staircase to the gallery.

The lights had been turned low to distract from the decaying affluence of what once was. The heavy, burgundy, brocaded, ceiling-to-floor drapes had lost their lustre. The rugs covering the polished-oak floor were the worse for wear. Yet, in the subdued lighting it was still impressive and, judging from the expression on some of the guests faces, they thought so too.

He stood a moment. How different the interior of the building would be in another twelve months. There was a lot of work to do and James intended that it be carried out to the highest of standards. Moxley Manor would be restored to its former glory and known throughout the world, all in memory of his life-long friend, Eve.

After the manor house was almost destroyed by fire in the late 1700's it was rebuilt in the early 1800's. Over the years it grew into the truly magnificent building it was today. It wasn't the largest manor house in the county but it's 360 degree spectacular views made it the most enviable. James understood how Sarah Milton had become enamoured with the property yet, not for the first time, he wondered why she had bothered to hold this event.

Casting his eyes around the room he reached for a canapé from the tray carried by a passing waitress. He recognised a couple of MPs who had travelled up from London for this auspicious occasion.

He spotted members from the Chamber of Commerce, Clive Broadbottom from the local Farmers' Union, and then he saw Dr Cobb talking with a small group from Meedon Bridge Hospital and the Meedon Bridge Hospice. He joined them.

"Ah, Sir James we were just talking about Eve. Tragic, quite tragic," Dr Cobb said. "Have you any further news?"

"I wish I had. It's still early days."

"She will be sadly missed." A woman, whom he knew to be Sister Riley from Meedon Bridge hospital added, "I can't take it in. It has shocked the whole county."

Another woman in her mid-thirties who he didn't know said, "Will this mean that the apiary will close?"

"Of course not." James retorted. "The apiary will continue for as long as we eat honey."

"Who will run it? Everyone knew it was Eve's project."

Dr Steele shot her a withering glance. "Oh Jenny …the apiary will have been set up in some sort of a company or trust."

"Oh, yes, of course," she giggled. "You can tell I'm a doctor and not a business woman."

Not wanting to discuss the subject further James excused himself and moved on. He continued to nod at acquaintances and, as he nodded at Councillor Smart, a movement through the window caught his eye. He moved closer. Sarah Milton's auburn hair shone beneath one of the lamps lighting the footpath that encircled the Manor. She was talking earnestly with someone, rubbing that person's right arm with her left hand, as if to comfort. He surreptitiously moved closer to the window.

He still couldn't make out the identity of the person she was talking to. Unexpectedly, Sarah leaned forward and kissed the person on the lips then she quickly turned and re-entered the building. The person Sarah had been talking to remained still for a moment with their back facing him. He failed to stem a smile. James was one-hundred-per-cent sure he recognised the person as they moved stealthily away and disappeared into the shrubbery.

"Very interesting," he mused.

He noticed Harry arrive and he weaved through the

jabbering throng until he reached him.

"I see you were also summoned, Harry."

"Hmm …rather be at home watching TV."

"Me too."

"Sarah has started working the room so I guess we can leave after we've spoken to her."

"That's the procedure. Anything new to tell me?"

"No."

"Come on you must have something."

"James, I have asked you to keep out of it. Please let us do our job."

"Don't play games Harry, you know how important this is to me. What has Blackwell been saying?"

Harry moved from one foot to the other and faced James square on. "All I will tell you is that she is still convinced that her first suspects are the right ones. We're waiting for the final autopsy result and forensic are having a tough time. The storm made gathering evidence almost impossible. A word of warning, Blackwell has started to take more of an interest in Eve."

"Eve! Why would she do that?"

"Her exact words were, "I can't believe such a woman has ever existed, she is whiter than white. Someone is hiding something and I intend to find out what it is."

"Bitch," James swore beneath his breath.

"Sir James, Harry." A practiced disingenuous voice reached them through the murmurings of the throng.

To James' left he saw a mop of curly auburn hair.

"I do hope you are enjoying yourselves." Sarah Milton cooed. "This is my first attempt at organising a reception. I hope I haven't made too many mistakes as I intend to host many more in the future. If you have any advice, I'm always listening."

The three forced a laugh. James did wonder if there was ever a politician in the world that would listen to any advice let alone take it.

"I'm sure you have enough people to help you, Sarah. I think it would be impossible to add anything to enhance tonight's excellent soirée."

"You're such a charmer, Harry. Sir James, I've been informed of the tragic incident at the end of our lane. The lady who runs the apiary, murdered they say."

"That's true."

"Sad so very sad. I believe you're connected to the apiary."

"I am."

"Must be dreadful for you. Have you any idea what happened?"

"Harry is the one to answer that."

"Harry?" She tilted her head and, with her eyes fixed on his, she waited for an answer. Her expression was similar to a teacher trying to get the truth out of a pupil. We've all seen the expression – *I'm waiting.*

"It's early days and everything that can be done is being done. We will find the culprit."

"Of that I am in no doubt. You have quite a reputation, Harry. Your result record is quite impressive."

"Did you ever meet Eve?" James asked interrupting this admiration society.

Sarah slowly shook her head. "I only wish I had. Every time I pass the visitors' centre I tell myself that I must go in and take a look, it appears intriguing." She sighed, "I really do need more spare time."

"You should try to make time, you'll be impressed. They also make the best afternoon tea in the valley."

Sarah forced a smile.

"I'd like to congratulate you on being elected leader of your party." James said, nearly chocking on his words. He was not a member of her party and did not agree with their policies.

"Why thank you, Sir James. More work I'm afraid but I do love it." Their time was up. She glanced around. "Please excuse me I must mingle. "Keep up the good work, Harry."

"Harry?" James raised an eyebrow. With a twinkle of mischief in his eyes he grinned at his brother as he watched Sarah Milton become dwarfed by her guests.

"Oh yes, she's my new best friend," Harry said playfully.

"She'd be the last person I'd want to be my friend, or invite to dinner," James murmured. "What I've seen of her at the ballot box she'd freeze the food."

"She gets thing done that's why she was given the job. Anyway since we've had our little chat and you know more about these things than I do, can we leave?"

"Yes."

"Thank God for that."

"Love to Gillian. I'm going to find Helen I have something I want to ask her."

As James began to make his way to the rear of the house he remembered something he should have asked Harry. He looked through the crowd for him. Harry had gone. He retraced his steps and caught up with his brother as he was about to leave.

"Harry, one moment… I see you managed to get a last-minute security team together for tonight. Who's running the show?"

"Sergeant Littleton and officers brought in from High Bridge. Why do you ask?"

"Not important. Enjoy the rest of your evening." James waved and disappeared back into the throng.

"James…" Harry raised his shoulders then let them drop with a groan. What was his brother up to?

Helen was where James had expected her to be, in the kitchen finishing up. She was smartly dressed in a long-sleeved, blue dress, which set off her short, blonde hair, which today was flicked out at the ends. As usual her makeup was impeccable. "Still at it I see."

"Hello James, no, it's all done."

"What about the washing up?"

"You must be joking. That's the caterer's job. Didn't you notice their field kitchen?"

"No I didn't."

"It's quite incredible. They have sinks, cookers, fridges and freezers in it. My kitchen, although big, can't cope with tonight's numbers."

James laughed. "Reminds me of when I was in the Royal Marines."

"Ah well, I wasn't in the Marines so it's all new to me." A girlish, cheeky grin spread wide, implying to James that it wouldn't be cooking that would attract her to the Marines.

"Since you've finished perhaps you have time for a

chat?"

"Love to. Is it so boring in there that you have to come below stairs, for entertainment?"

"These events are always boring."

Helen mischievously scrunched her nose like a naughty little schoolgirl. "How about a nice glass of wine. Some decent stuff?" she whispered, conspiratorially.

"Now you're talking."

"Come with me." Helen led him into an adjacent storeroom. As she entered she picked up a pair of filthy wellington boots and moved them to one side and, as she did so, she complained, "Just look at them, filthy. I wouldn't mind, but I've never worn the damned things. The wine is up there," she said pointing. "The best ones are in the top racks. You remember how the General liked his drop of wine."

"I remember."

"The hours he would spend searching through catalogues before making a decision to buy. He was like an excited schoolboy while he waited for them to be delivered." she spoke with fondness. "I miss the evenings we all spent together."

"I also miss those evenings. Jean loved our card evenings."

Helen looked to the floor. "James, he was such a nice man. I know I've said it before but I can't believe he fathered that woman and …and her brother, well …he's even worse."

"From what little I've seen of her I'm inclined to agree with you. Have you ever watched her at the ballot box?"

"Not likely. I see enough of her here."

"She's ferocious. That's why the newspapers refer to her as the red-headed tornado. Anything in particular?" James asked gesturing towards the racks of wine.

"You choose, I've tasted them all, they're all good. The General gave me all his wines that's why I've hid them in here so her ladyship can't get her hands on them. He said to me, 'Every time you open a bottle Helen, think of me'."

"Then that's what we'll do." James reached up and began to search through the bottles reading the labels. "I like this." He turned the bottle towards her so she could see the label. "It's a Rioja?"

"Fine by me. I hope you don't mind drinking it in the kitchen."

"Not at all." James pulled a sad face, "Oh dear, Cinderella never got to go to the Ball."

"Afraid not," she replied as she placed two glasses on the table and passed James a corkscrew. "You open it I'm going thieving."

She had disappeared before he had a chance to enquire what she was up to. Out, like a whirlwind, through the kitchen door and seconds later arrived back with a plate of mouth-watering canapés.

"Wow, hope we don't get caught."

"No chance, madam wouldn't deign to come into the kitchen."

They raised and touched their glasses. "To the General."

"To the General."

"Also, to Jean and Eve."

"Yes, to Jean and Eve." They chinked glasses again. "Thank you for that. Helen …I've been doing some thinking lately."

"Did it hurt?" she teased. Now that her work was done she had relaxed.

"Helen…"

"I'm sorry, I shouldn't be factitious, do go on."

"I'm not sure this is the right time, however, I'd like to be serious for a moment."

Her head bent to one side and her mouth dropped as her shoulders slumped. His remark intrigued her. "I'm listening, she said."

"You're leaving at the end of the month, right."

"Right," she scrunched her eyes as she concentrated, wondering what he was about to say.

"Are you fixed up yet, with a job I mean?"

She shook her head. "No, I haven't even started to look for one. In my mind, I was planning to stay with one of my boys for a while, although, I haven't told either of them yet," she giggled. "When the work starts on the Manor I'll leave and then I'll make appointments with a few agencies. There's still a lot to do here, I can't be bothered thinking about anything else. The furniture has to be made ready for auction, remember. This means clearing out drawers, making sure I don't inadvertently give away any family secrets."

"Helen, what I wanted to say is this…"

She viewed him with trepidation.

"Since Jean died, Nicky has been an angel, looking after things." He hesitated. "I'm sure you'll agree with me that she has her own life to lead. The problem is that she thinks I need help. I have a cleaner, so there aren't any worries with that side of things. It's the other chores such as, cooking and shopping. It's not that I can't, after all, I am navy-trained. I can polish my own shoes, sew on a button and iron," he boasted with a smile. "The truth is I don't want to do any of these things. Jean took care of everything; I'm beginning to think I must have taken her for granted."

"Nonsense."

"I have enough to do with the construction of the restaurant, and the opening up of the estate to visitors. I've come to accept the fact that Nicky's right. What I was wondering is, now that you are soon to be unemployed, would you consider being my live-in housekeeper, or have you had enough of taking care of old men?"

Helen's jaw dropped and he caught a spark of excitement flash through her eyes.

"James, you're not old! Good God you're only just in your fifties. In today's way of thinking that puts you in your thirties."

"Wow, how about that," he laughed, and then said, "You know what I mean."

"I …I don't know what to say." She choked back a tear. "If we are telling each other the truth, I haven't done anything about looking for a position, because I've been in denial. I've been so happy here in the valley, and I just didn't want to leave. I love it here."

"That's good."

"You're being serious?"

"Of course I am."

"Would we have the same arrangement as I had here with the General?"

"Exactly, only I've no intentions of being ill."

"I don't know what to say."

"So you've said, twice. A yes would be a good place to start. I've been giving it some thought. You can have one of the bedrooms en suite on the second floor and the adjoining bedroom can be made into a sitting-room, to give you a little privacy, what do you think?"

"Oh dear, oh dear... My heart is beating so fast, it feels as if it's going to explode, it can't, can it?"

"I doubt it. Am I reading your response as a positive?"

"Oh yes, yes, James you have no idea how I've been feeling, I really didn't want to leave the valley."

"So you said. Then it's settled. Let's drink to it." James raised his glass. "Here's to sampling many more bottles like this one," he took a mouthful of his wine. "Pretty good," he said. "Now, all we need to do is discuss salary."

"Plenty of time to talk about that. I'm perfectly happy with what The General paid me."

"Done, plus ten per cent."

Again they chinked glasses.

Chapter 13 – James

A gust of wind whipped across his head as James left the Manor. He pulled up his coat collar to protect his ears. Cold wind attacked his eardrums, not good. The damage to his eardrums occurred when he was in the Marines. It probably had something to do with the sound of gunfire. The temperature had dropped considerably, probably down to around four centigrade. He started the engine of his BMW. He made sure the heater was working and began the drive home. As he reached the apiary he noticed four police cars parked in the apiary car park and James felt for the men who must have been instructed to walk the rest of the way up to the manor. Their orders, no doubt, were to keep a low profile.

The lights were on, in what had once been Eve's home. He ignored them and drove on. He unlocked the door to his own home, took off his coat and threw it at a row of pegs attached to the wall alongside the door. Passing his study, he glanced in and noticed the green light flashing on his land line. He crossed the room, picked up the receiver, and checked his messages.

There were two messages; both were from Becky.

"James, Billy Bradshaw has gone missing and it appears that Holly was the last person to see him. Call me when you get this message."

Her next message was, "James, as soon as you hear this please call me. I've also left a message on your cell phone." James had switched off his cell phone while he was at the reception. "I'm calling Nicky now. I'm worried stiff. The police are at the Bradshaw's as I speak and I know it is only a matter of time before they come here I'm not sure how much more of this I can take."

James swore as he slammed the receiver back into its cradle. He rushed to the door and snatched his coat off its peg. He strode towards his car and drove as fast as he dared to Honey Pot Lane and the apiary.

The door to cottage Number 2 was wide open and the light from inside lit the path as two officers were leaving. James didn't recognise either of them. He parked in the apiary car park next to the police cars he'd noticed earlier, crossed the lane then knocked at the kitchen door. Becky answered immediately.

"Thank God you're here," she gasped.

"I'm so sorry I was up at the manor. There's a big reception on tonight."

"I know. I guessed that's where you might be."

"Where's Holly?"

"Holly, Nicky, Inspector Blackwell and another officer are in the dining room."

"Did Nicky get here before Blackwell?"

"Yes."

"Good."

"I've made some coffee. I fancy something a lot

stronger but I daren't, not until they've gone. Come into the kitchen." Becky's hands were shaking as she poured coffee into two patterned, porcelain mugs. James pulled a chair away from the table and sat opposite her. "Law of nature, I guess. Everything comes at once." Taking a sip of the hot coffee James then asked. "Tell me what happened?"

Becky scrunched her shoulders as she moved her head from side to side. "Holly went out to check the hives and got back as the light was fading. It must have been about six when Mrs Bradshaw knocked on the door to say that Billy's tea was ready. I told her that Billy wasn't here. She was confused and mumbled, '*I thought, I thought...*' Then she snapped, '*Where is he?*' She was trembling and visibly shocked. Her eyes were searching in all directions. She began to sob as she told me that when she called for him to come in, she noticed his bike propped up outside the gate. It had a buckled front wheel, and she had assumed that he had come here to see Holly, being too afraid to come home. Her partner is not the most tolerant of men, James. He has little patience with Billy. She was sobbing hard by then."

"What are you saying that Billy is frightened of him?"

"I don't know. Since that man moved in with Carol, Billy spends a lot of his time up here with Holly, a lot more than he used to. That's why she gets a little impatient with him sometimes."

"When did the man move in?"

Becky tried to remember. "Probably about six months ago," she said.

"What's his name? I don't think I've ever seen him."

"David somebody, I don't know. Yes I do, I remember now, it's Green, Dan, yes that's it, Daniel Green."

"Then what happened?"

"I called Holly. I asked her if she'd seen Billy." She pulled a face as if she was annoyed. "Yes, she answered. He was being a nuisance. I asked her how? She told him she was busy checking the hives and told him to go away."

"And did he?" James asked, urgently.

"He wouldn't go at first, but eventually he did."

"Do you know why he was being a nuisance?"

"Holly said he was being silly. He was riding his bike in circles and saying in a sing-song voice that he knew who had murdered Eve. Holly told him not to tell lies. That was when he decided to leave and rode away calling, '*See if I care, see if I care.*'"

"Holly didn't believe him?"

"Of course not."

"Was that all there was to it?"

"Not quite. It was getting dark so Holly came home. Along the path she found his bike with its buckled front wheel." Becky gave a naughty little giggle. "Holly said she felt like leaving it but decided against it. So she struggled with it and left it outside Billy's gate and came home."

"And she said nothing about it?"

"No, it was only when Mrs Bradshaw arrived that she told us what had happened. She assumed that Billy had bumped into a tree and left the bike. Boys are like that was what she said.

"I reminded her that he was only eight and she

mumbled, '*I suppose so.*'"

"Then what happened?" James asked.

"I told Mrs Bradshaw that we would come with her to search for him. We knocked on all the doors to the cottages; he wasn't in any one of them. We then began to search the likeliest of places where Billy could hide. It was pitch black, with no moon, and it had started to rain. It was quite impossible to see anything. As it had gone half-past-seven we came back and 'phoned the police. I didn't know what else to do. Mrs Bradshaw was crying hysterically by then.

"The police said they would send someone. That was when I phoned you. When you didn't call me back, I realised you must have gone out for the evening, so I called Nicky. I was pretty certain the police would be here before long wanting to talk to Holly, since it was she who had found the bike, and after what had happened to Eve…" Becky's voiced trailed off.

"You did the right thing to call Nicky. Have the police returned Eve's laptop?"

"Yes."

"I'd like to use it if it's all right with you."

"Of course it is."

James had an idea and he needed some information. The idea had come to him on the drive over.

"You know where it is."

"Does she have a password?"

"It's honey."

James laughed. "Oh, very secure. No one would ever guess that one."

James went into Eve's consulting rooms, booted up

the computer and waited. He opened up Eve's address book, found the name he wanted and copied it, along with the address and telephone number, onto a piece of paper.

He was back in the kitchen seconds before the dining room door opened and Blackwell, followed by Cranmore, came out. James saw Holly being comforted by Nicky in the room behind them. He felt his blood rise and noticed Blackwell's face turn thunderous when she saw him.

"Why, Sir James, small world."

What was it about this woman that annoyed people so much? "Isn't it," he replied, coldly.

"I thought you would be attending the reception at the manor house."

"I did."

"Uncle James," Holly cried, as she ran to him clasping her arms around his waist and burying her head in the firm flesh of his stomach. Blackwell faced Becky. "We'll be off now. I have a lot of things to arrange."

"Like what?" James asked, knowing full well what she meant so more for something to say than anything else.

The glare she threw at James read *it's none of your damned business* but she answered anyway.

"A search party," she retorted as she passed him, but not before James noticed her changed expression of satisfaction.

She had won that round.

"If we can be of any help?"

"I'll let you know, Sir James," she replied briskly as Becky closed the door behind them.

"Mummy, why do they keep asking me the same

questions over and over again? Do they think I'm lying?"

"I shouldn't think so, darling."

"It's their way," Nicky shrugged dismissing it as trivial. "Don't let it worry you."

"Why don't you go get ready for bed and I'll be up shortly," Becky tried to sound unconcerned.

"I don't feel like going to bed," she sulked. "I won't be able to sleep."

"You're probably right. Get ready and then we'll think of something to do to take our mind off things."

"Can I come down again?"

"Sure, it's not too late and it is Saturday. Say Goodnight to Nicky and Uncle James." After hugs and various *Goodnights,* Holly thumped up the stairs to her bedroom.

"Well..." Nicky shook her head in an uncomprehending sort of way. Her disapproval showed also in the tone of her voice. "You're quite right, Dad. She is some woman. I bet she'd make the Queen confess to being Jack the Ripper. It's not what she says it's how she says it and how she looks at you. She implies without accusing."

"She hasn't inspired you into wanting to become her next very best friend."

"Very funny, Dad."

"Tell me what happened?" Becky pleaded.

"It was as Holly said, she asked the same question over and over in a slightly different way. I frequently interrupted saying that she had already answered that question and there was nothing more to say. She sat, saying nothing, with a smug, disbelieving expression on her face. It was difficult for me to tell her to leave as it wasn't my house."

"You should have thrown her out." Becky was furious her face was flushed and her eyes flashed distain.

"I doubt it would have helped the situation. In the end I repeated that it was enough for tonight and if, and I stressed the *if,* she needed to speak with Holly again, I said, 'you wouldn't mind would you Holly?' Holly said, 'no', and it was then that she decided to leave."

"You can tell she hasn't any children. I bet she never does. No man in his right mind would have her."

"You have a point, Becky." James smiled to himself knowing that it was probably true and that Blackwell wouldn't want children anyway. "We'll be off now. Try not to worry too much, Becky. Nicky and I will work things out."

Chapter 14 – Billy

The phone rang. James hurried into his study. "James Marchant," he answered, quickly.

"Sir James, Felicity here from the Bee Association."

"Hello, Felicity."

"I'm calling to ask if you have a date for Eve's funeral. I'm inundated with people wanting to know."

"I wish I had. The police are still refusing to say when they'll release her body."

"I guess that means they're no nearer to finding out who killed her."

"So it would seem. Have you been able to glean anything from your members?"

"No, everyone is as shocked as I am. James, do you remember asking me about the intelligence of bees? How you thought it strange that when Eve died her bees took flight?"

"Yes..."

"I remember suggesting that if you Google 'Bees' you will discover lots of information and many a weird story." There a slight hesitation before Felicity continued. "But ...there is none weirder than the story I was told yesterday."

"Oh?"

"One of our members from Somerset telephoned me after hearing I was enquiring about odd bee behaviour. He told me of a lady beekeeper who died in his area. She kept bees in her back garden, and had done so all her life.

"When the funeral directors brought the coffin out of the house the neighbours opposite came out to pay their respects. It was then that they noticed her name written on the roof, it was clearly written. The bees had formed themselves into letters that spelled out the word, *Sally*."

"Are you joshing, Felicity?"

Felicity laughed. "I thought that would make you smile. Apparently, it's quite true. This man has the picture and newspaper cutting. He's going to scan it and send it to me. I'll forward a copy to you as soon as I receive it."

"I'm not sure I believe that story, however, I would be interested to read the report, thank you. I'll let you have details of Eve's funeral as soon as I have them. We'll talk again." James was smiling as he replaced the receiver.

He then dialled another number.

Having ended the twenty-minute telephone conversation he locked up the farmhouse, climbed into his BMW, checked his watch, and began his journey. It was relatively easy and one hour and sixteen minutes later he pulled up outside 26 Maybury Crescent, Wallington, which was north of the city. The door to the house opened before he had a chance to get out of the car.

A woman in her late fifties stood in the doorway. She was wearing a bright red woollen coat, something black showed beneath, it was impossible to tell, black shoes, black bag and a black floppy hat. She was pleasantly rounded and about five-feet-six-inches tall. She turned and locked the door to her home, then bent to pick up a suitcase and began to walk down the path. James met her before she had reached the gate and taking her case said, "Hello Clare, I'm James."

"I guessed as much," she teased. "I wasn't expecting anyone else."

James put her case into the boot of his car. With seatbelts fastened he checked his watch.

"Well James," she sighed. "This is quite a to-do. I find it so hard to believe. Eve was a wonderful woman, it doesn't make sense."

"I agree." He turned his head to look at her. "Thank you for coming, Becky needs you right now, more than ever. From what she has told me you were the stabilising influence in her life."

"I'd like to think that Jim and I played some small part, but the truth is Becky did it all on her own. It was having the baby that gave her a purpose in life. Jim and I loved all our foster children but Becky was our favourite, shouldn't say that, should I?" An embarrassed and guilty smiled crossed her face.

"Well, I'm not so sure, she's a lovely young woman with a pleasing personality and her optimism is refreshing. We have all taken to her."

"That's good to hear. Do you know that when she got pregnant we almost lost them both?"

James glanced at her, his frown questioned, why.

"It's true. The social wanted her to have an abortion.

Then they wanted her to have Holly adopted – boy, did we have a fight on our hands. Holly was born on Christmas Day that's why she was called, Holly. January the 6th is her official birthday."

James laughed. "I didn't know," he said. "Like the Queen she has two birthdays."

"Well, it's never fair for a child born on Christmas Day, is it?"

"You're right of course."

"Anyway the hospital was short-staffed and the social had closed down for Christmas Day and Boxing Day leaving only emergency numbers. Both mother and baby were fine so we took them home. It made it more difficult for the social to take the baby when Jim and I were registered foster-parents.

"We've been fostering since our late twenties. Jim was very forceful and told the social that they were welcome to live with us for as long as they wanted." Her lips smiled and her eyes shone with pride. "Jim and I always believed in Becky. We knew she would make a good mother and, given the right opportunity, she would do well for herself one day."

"She has certainly done that. Do you know before she came to live and work with Eve, she was a librarian in Meedon Bridge? That was where she met Eve."

"Yes, I do know," Clare said, proudly. "James, are you quite sure Becky will want to see me? She may be embarrassed about the whole affair. Being questioned over and over about the murder of a woman she admired so much, it must be so hurtful." She hesitated before continuing. "What about the little boy who has gone missing? The police can't think it has anything to do with Becky or Holly. Oh dear, she may feel she would rather wait until things settle down before telling me. I can't begin to imagine how she must be feeling."

"I guarantee she will be thrilled when she sees you and right now she needs you." James glanced at the woman sitting beside him who appeared to have wandered off into private thoughts so he kept quiet, kept his eyes on the road, and continued to drive.

A few miles on Clare spoke again, "Becky had a troubled childhood but to think that she could commit murder is preposterous. I know for a fact she adored Eve, and little Holly took to Eve the moment they set eyes on each other. There was an immediate rapport, strange in a child so young."

"As I explained on the phone we have a new overzealous Inspector who, I believe has her own agenda. The woman craves an early arrest. She has made up her mind that either Becky or Holly is responsible for Eve's death."

Eyes wide and lips tight Clare then said, "I repeat: it's preposterous. Did you know that before Jim died Eve came all this way every other week to give him healing? That was what Becky called it. After she had gone Jim felt so much better for days. My friend Rosa was convinced Eve was a psychic."

"Yes, she was."

"My friend also said that Holly was psychic."

"Did she? Why would she say that?"

"It was after I told her what happened when Holly was four."

"Oh…" James glanced at her waiting for her to continue. "Tell me?" He had to know.

Clare slipped her arms out of her coat lifted her bottom off the seat a couple of times as she pulled the coat from beneath her.

"I'll stop if you like."

"No need, I've done this more times than I care to remember."

Coat off, she threw it onto the seat behind her revealing a black fitted dress with a high cowl collar and like every woman of a certain age she kept her hat on. She shuffled back in her seat and made herself comfortable and began her story.

"Holly was four, coming up to five. Becky and I were in the kitchen one morning discussing their futures. Becky decided that she wanted to get out of the city, make a new life for herself in the country where nobody knew her. I was upset, of course, but I had no intention of letting her know, or stopping her. She was twenty and having a young child to take care of we were concerned. Anyway, as Holly was due to start school Becky felt that it was the right time to make the move. I'm sure you understand."

"I do, I've had two daughters."

"Well, as we were chatting the door was flung open and Holly stood there and she said, *Mummy, who is that nice man playing with me in the sitting room?* You don't need me to tell you what happened next, Becky shot through the door. I picked up Holly and hurried after her. There was no one in the sitting-room. Becky then searched the whole house checked in wardrobes under beds, you get the picture. There was no one in the house.

"For some unexplainable reason the incident made Becky think about Holly's father. She wondered what it would be like for Holly when she started school. Maybe the other children would ask her where her daddy was, and such like? She wanted Holly to be able to answer any questions with a believable story even if it was not the whole truth. Becky then decided to trace him. One of her old school friends put her in touch with friend after friend."

"I get the gist," James said with a smile.

"Eventually, she spoke to a boy who had been on the same school trip to France with her and unbeknown to Becky had kept in touch with Holly's father."

James was confused. "Oh, so Holly's father was not a classmate?"

"Oh no, he was French. He was a young boy from the village near the centre where the school was staying."

"I didn't know..."

"This class mate of Becky's told her that Holly's father had been killed in a motor-bike accident four weeks earlier. On the exact day, would you believe; that Holly had been playing with her imaginary man in the sitting-room?"

James felt a cold shiver trickle down his spine. "Good grief! Did Holly's father know he had a daughter?"

"Apparently he did, the boy told Becky he had sent him a photograph of Holly when she was born. Remember, Becky was still at school and all her class mates wanted to see her baby and take pictures. Lots of them came to the house around that time."

James scratched the back of his head. "The boy never got in touch?"

"He was only a boy himself, James. It was not doable, even if he had wanted to. He was probably too scared to tell his parents, sad really, they don't know that they have a grandchild here in England."

Moving his head from side to side James spoke in a heavy tone, "Kid's…" He turned to face Clare. "Well, well what a remarkable story," he said.

"I don't expect you believe in stuff like that?"

"I'm learning daily about *stuff like that*. When Eve died, I feel as if I went to bed, and woke up the next morning in a parallel universe. Nothing surprises me now."

It was lunch-time and the crowd was increasing in Honey Pot Lane. Word had spread about the disappearance of Billy Bradshaw late the night before. An eight-year-old boy had vanished while out playing, which he did daily, in an area where he had lived all his life, and only days after the murder of a neighbour. Put the two events together, and it had more than aroused the public's curiosity.

Officers were trying to control the people who had volunteered to help search for Billy. Sad to say, they had been doing more harm than good, trampling along the tow path and stamping through the undergrowth, possibly destroying evidence. Blackwell had eventually managed to get the whole area cordoned off and was giving the volunteers instructions as James and Clare arrived. It was clear that little Billy Bradshaw was still missing.

Disorderly trees ran along the east side of the lane bordering the apiary. The west side of the lane shrub land sloped down to the towpath and the fast-flowing river. Two scene-of-crime tapes had been strung across the lane and towpath, one at each end. Holly had found Billy's bike somewhere in the middle before lugging it to Billy's cottage.

 No way in, no way out.

The boy lived in one of the old, stone-workers' cottages on Honey Pot Lane, all of which were owned by Eve, and now by the Trust. They had small front-gardens and long, narrow back-gardens, which bordered onto fields that gently rose to the top of a brow.

The family Yates lived in No 1.

The Bradshaw family lived in No 2.

The Coleman family lived in number 3.

The Wicks family lived in number 4.

The Henshaws lived in number 5.

The 6th cottage was empty due to the premature death of old Mr Clark.

James glanced to his right and saw officers working door to door along the little row of cottages.

Another group of people was milling around the centre and a few policemen were desperately trying to move them back. He had to beep his horn to make them stand aside to enable him to get into the car park.

He parked. He glanced below at the angry river. Upstream, inside the secured area he noticed men in protective clothing working the shrubbery. Downstream and across the river he saw more people swarming across the fields coming from the direction of Meedon Bridge. They were making for the foot-bridge to cross the river, and no doubt with the intentions of helping with the search.

He should have anticipated this but he had honestly believed that Billy would have been found by now, and if not, it would have taken a lot longer for the word to get about. Last night he hadn't been unduly worried, he had reasoned that once Billy became hungry he would pluck up the courage and return home.

Now he was becoming concerned it was obvious that something untoward had happened to him.

Where was the most likely place for a child to hide? There were ten dairy farms spread across the valley some sadly in need of repair, plenty of places to hide. Many of the fields had a central spinney and then there was the dense Osbert Wood which ran through his land. The rocks at Kirk Crag were also a possibility.

There were many affluent properties with outbuildings built on huge plots, including his brother's, which had outbuildings still waiting to be renovated. Kilnpit Quarry was on the outskirts of Barnsfield. James was sure Billy would not have ventured so far. The question that baffled James was, why would Billy run off?

James carried Clare's case as they crossed the lane and walked towards the centre.

A cry of "Auntie Clare, Auntie Clare," came from Holly as she broke away from her mother and came running towards them. "Mum it's Auntie Clare," she shouted over her shoulder to her mother. James saw the delight on Becky's face and knew he had made the right decision in contacting Becky's foster mother.

Holly reached them and flung herself into the arms of her adopted Aunt. "What are you doing here?" Becky panted as she reached them. Her elated expression quickly changed to one of concern. Becky suddenly understood the reason for Clare's unexpected appearance. "James, have you…?"

"Yes, she knows what has happened."

Becky struggled with the word as her eyes began to fill with tears and she asked, "Everything?"

"Everything. Now I suggest you all go inside, you must have a lot to talk about."

"I've come to support my favourite girl and I won't let you send me away."

"I'll not do that Clare. I'm so glad you're here."

"So am I," Holly said as she took Clare's hand and began to pull her towards the kitchen door.

"James, the police are not hopeful they'll find any useful clues. It poured down again during the night and the paths are, once again, like mires. They hadn't even begun to dry out after the storm on Monday. Blackwell is complaining, the other officers are moaning as they keep getting stuck in the mud."

"All I hope is that Billy found shelter and fell asleep somewhere."

"Let's hope so. We'll catch up later. I need to check on a few things," he called as he walked away. He reached into his pocket and took out his cell phone.

"Harry, have you heard about Billy Bradshaw?"

"Minutes ago. Gillian and I went out for a meal after last night's shindig and overslept this morning, only just made church. A couple of officers were waiting for me when we got home. What can you tell me that I don't already know?"

"Probably nothing. Blackwell interviewed Holly last night, Nicky was present."

"Why?"

"Because Holly found the bike and pushed it to Billy's home."

"I know that. Why was Nicky there? Did Blackwell suggest it?"

"No, Becky tried to contact me. My phone was off. I was at the reception. She anticipated a visit from Blackwell and needed support so she called Nicky."

"I don't need to spell it out to you what Blackwell is thinking, James."

"I know damned well what she's thinking, and my advice to you little brother is to tread carefully, there is more to that woman than meets the eye."

"James, your tone implies that you know something and are not telling…"

James had already cleared the line.

His next call was to Philip Cook.

"Shit! This is getting farcical. The boy's not dead, he's missing. Is Blackwell treating Holly as some sort of suspect?" Philip snapped.

"She sure is, and you're quite right, it is getting farcical."

"What's up with this woman?"

"A lot more than we know at present. I've got some checking to do and when I have a clearer picture I'll let you know."

"If I can be of any help call me. Try to give me as much notice as you can, I'm back at work now so I'll need time to rearrange appointments."

James made his way to the visitors' centre which was a hive of activity. It was unusual for this time on a Sunday morning. Coffees and teas were being served at an alarming rate. Not many people were interested in anything to do with the apiary they were too busy speculating on the murder and disappearance of Billy Bradshaw.

The ground was squelchy under foot. Nevertheless, he decided to examine the immediate area and, after checking on a few hives to confirm, yet again, that the bees had not returned, he trudged higher. Perhaps he might see someone lurking about watching the scene unfold below. He was beginning to think that something bad had befallen Billy Bradshaw.

On reaching the brow, James savoured the clean, fresh air. He stood observing the 360-degree view. The sun was breaking through the clouds. After yet another night of rain the green grass of the valley shimmered and the heather that survived between the rocks on the crag glistened dark purple.

In the distance, his own land was at peace where his cattle and sheep munched methodically, and across the river to the south, his horses grazed in the pastures.

People milled around the visitors' centre and in the distance a few cars meandered down the lanes. People returning from Church, people going out for Sunday lunch, otherwise there was nothing out of the ordinary. God was in his heaven and all was well with the world, if only.

He remembered the storeroom on the north side of the apiary, it was a long shot but he'd give it a try. He made his way to the wooden store-room. It was locked. He peered through the two windows. He called Billy's name there was no reply. Convinced he was not in the store-room he began to leave. But, to be sure, maybe he should inspect inside.

It didn't take him long to pick the lock with the mini set of tools he had attached to his key ring and always carried with him. It was remarkable the number of times he had found the need for then, such as, when finding an animal caught in packaging wire brought across the fields on the wind. Or, plastic bags casually thrown away and stuck in fencing, always a danger to the animals. Other uses he found for his tool set he had acquired when serving in the Marines.

Although the sky was heavy with threatening clouds he didn't need to switch on the light as the natural light was quite sufficient.

The shed was six feet by eight feet and used to store tools, new and old hives, along with gallons of sugar syrup that Eve had made to supplement the bees winter feed. There was a bench stretching along one side of the shed on which repairs were carried out.

He called the boy's name again. "It's James Marchant here Billy. No need to be afraid." There was no reply. He walked to the back of the shed and searched behind hives, boxes, sacks of seed, tools. There wasn't any place suitable for a person to hide, so James left. He fiddled with the lock until it clicked back into place and mentally reminded himself that it needed to be replaced with a more robust one.

It didn't make sense. Where was Billy? Was he really so afraid of his mother's partner that he was too scared to go home. He had crashed his bike. It had a buckled front wheel. It wasn't the end of the world. Why hadn't Eve ever spoken of this man? He appeared to be a nasty piece of work. Could Eve have confronted him? Maybe they had a row. Maybe this man knew more about her death than he was letting on.

Billy boasted that he knew who had killed Eve. Maybe someone had overheard him. Maybe he knew who that someone was. Maybe that was the reason he didn't want to go home. Maybe he felt he would be the next to die. Maybe that was why he ran away. Rather a lot of *maybe's*. However, James was not ready to dismiss any wild scenario just yet.

Weaving through the apiary on his way back down to his car he lifted the roof of a few more hives, no change, still no bees. In the distance he could see Blackwell followed by two other officers coming down the path from where Billy's bike was found. He quickened his pace as an idea came to him. He took out his cell phone and switched it to camera. He pointed the lens in the direction of Blackwell. He took a few pictures of her without her noticing.

Chapter 15 – Sunday

James punched in the number for his friend and old colleague, Colonel Martin Webster, in his cell-phone. After six rings his wife Coleen answered and after a few niceties she handed the phone to her husband.

"James, good to hear from you. How are things?"

"Fine."

"I'm sorry I was unable to make Jean's funeral."

"Martin, I know what your workload is like. I was delighted Coleen came."

"I still feel bad about it; I was fond of Jean."

James quickly changed the subject. "Martin, do you remember Eve?"

"You mean the honey lady?" Martin began to laugh. "It's impossible to forget such a fascinating woman?"

"True… She was murdered about a week ago." James spoke in a rush.

"What! Murdered! Shit! Are you having me on?"

"You know me better than that, Martin."

"How? Why?"

"That's what everyone is asking."

"Tell me from the beginning?"

"She was working in the apiary. She must have been interrupted by an intruder, no one knows. It's still early days."

"Why are they calling it murder?" Martin was obviously shocked.

"She had a nasty wound on her head. The doctor who examined her concluded that it wasn't possible to have been caused by an accidental fall."

"Weapon?"

"None found."

"The examiner is quite sure that she didn't fall?"

"Yes. I'm still waiting for the full autopsy report. I'm hoping they'll come up with something to prove it was an accident. I wondered about a heart attack, and then a fall. I think I'm kidding myself. I've seen the wound. It had obviously been caused by coming into contact with something heavy."

"Hmm… What can I do to help? I gather that's why you're calling."

"Yes Martin, do you still have any contacts in the Met?"

"One or two, maybe, why?"

"About a month ago, an Inspector Blackwell was transferred to this neck of the woods. I want to know more about her. Is this something you can help me with?"

"What about Harry?"

"I don't want Harry to know anything about it, not yet."

"I see…"

"As much as possible, Martin. What she was working on, reputation, that sort of thing."

"I see. So she's not fitting in with country life, eh?"

"You can say that again."

"Let me have her details. I gather this Blackwell woman is working the case."

"Yes, and she's desperate to make an arrest but she's barking up the wrong tree."

James heard Martin rummaging for what he imagined was a pen and paper. "No need to write anything down. I've got a couple of photo's I'll e-mail them along with the information that I have. Must make sure we get the right Blackwell. God help the Met if there are two of them."

Martin chuckled. "I'll not be able to do anything until tomorrow. It might take some time; I'll probably have to jump through a few hoops before I get to the right person. As soon as I hear anything I'll let you know. Fine woman Eve …hmm …fine woman," he murmured.

"Thanks Martin, I owe you one."

Sunday was a day James loved. Reg was off and the two stable lads on the Sunday morning shift had long gone. James had the place to himself. The yard was quiet except for the snuffling and occasional stamp of Pascal or Pendragon. Hooves on a concrete floor. They remained in their stalls. The other horses were out enjoying the refreshed pastures after the recent rains.

Reg had kept the two elderly horses indoors in readiness for the vet who was calling first thing Monday morning.

He felt the vibration in his jacket pocket before he heard the ring-tone of his cell.

"Hi Dad I'm back at Eve's, Blackwell has been here again questioning Holly."

"Doesn't that woman ever rest? Good God it's Sunday afternoon. What did she want this time?"

"You tell me. The woman is a piranha, she won't let go. She seems to think Holly is not telling her the whole truth. She keeps asking her where they went to play, where Billy could be hiding, you know the drill.

"She has also told Holly to stay indoors for the rest of the day. According to her, people are muttering, she thinks it would be best for the child if she kept out of sight.

"Holly is very upset. In fact, she's not upset, she's heartbroken. *'Why is everyone blaming me?'* she screamed at her mother. Clare tried to comfort her but it wasn't easy. This is all too much for a child to take. I'm going to be making an official complaint."

"Good. What did Blackwell mean by muttering?"

"I wonder... Did she? Could she have killed Eve? Could she have killed Billy? The usual innuendoes made by the chattering classes. Who are these people? They're not from around here. I'm going to stay a while longer. Too many people hanging around, I feel uncomfortable, reminds me of a lynch-mob in the old westerns. I'll leave when they've all gone."

"Should I come over?"

"Don't think it's necessary, Clare's here, remember."

"Of course, then tell Becky I'll call tomorrow. Are you coming up to the farm when you're done?"

"Not tonight Dad, I've got papers to go over. I have an important conference first thing tomorrow."

"Oh Nicky, before you go, I've something to tell you, it might as well be now. As you know Helen is leaving Moxley Manor at the end of the month."

"Yes…"

"I've asked her if she would like to work for me, be my housekeeper."

Nicky gave an excited shriek. "That's wonderful, Dad and...?"

"She has agreed," he laughed. "I thought you'd be pleased. You can get on with your own life now, without having to worry about me."

"Huh, who are you kidding, I'll never stop worrying about you."

Chapter 16 – No. 2

Following his morning meeting with Reg, James drove to the apiary. He pulled his car to a stop outside cottage Number 2. After opening the gate, he walked up the path. Carol Bradshaw's exotic double-headed Dahlias, the envy of all who had seen them, had been buffeted by the storm.

Their bent stems brushed the muddied ground. The vibrant pink, purple and white petals were spotted and bruised beyond salvation. They all looked desperately sad.

Carol opened her door. It was obvious that she hadn't slept. She was wearing the same clothes she had worn the day before. The whites of her eyes were as red as her flushed face and she appeared even sadder than her garden.

"Hello, I hope I haven't called at a bad time," he asked. "I only came to see if you've had any news?"

"No, Sir James."

"Please drop the Sir, Carol."

She nodded and blinked telling him she understood. "The police have begun to search again. I wanted to go with them but the Inspector told me to stay here in case Billy came home."

"That makes sense. I expect Billy's step-father is out searching. I'm sorry I don't know his name."

"Huh!" She shook her head in disgust and took a step backwards. "Would you like to come in?" she asked.

"No thank you, I won't keep you."

She took a step towards him. "Dan is not Billy's stepfather. Dan is probably at one of his mates sleeping off last night's drinking session. We were giving our relationship a try before committing ourselves, and now, I don't mind telling you, it's not going to happen, not now and not ever. Friends tried to warn me he was only after a meal ticket, well I'm not keeping him. He can starve as far as I'm concerned."

James decided not to take the conversation any further. He was out of his depth. "I've spoken to Holly," he said quickly changing the subject. "She has told the police of all the places she used to go exploring with Billy. I know this is a long shot, as I live on the other side of the river. This morning I have instructed all my workers to search any likely places on my land where Billy may be hiding."

Carol Bradshaw hesitated then asked, "Did Billy ever ride his bike over to your farm?"

"Maybe, I don't honestly know, I never saw him. According to Holly he didn't like horses he said they were smelly." James noticed Carol Bradshaw's attempt at a smile.

"I can't see why he would run off like that. All he did was *buckle* the front wheel of his bike, it's not the end of the world," she said with a rush.

"He's young, who knows what goes on in a child's mind."

"It's the first time he's been out since the storm, and to run away like that…"

"Did anything happen at home to upset him?" James asked not sure if he should and wary of her reply.

"Not as far as I know." Her voice faded. "He was bored with being cooped up. Dan flew into a rage after I'd allowed him out." She looked earnestly into his face asking for confirmation that she did the right thing. "The boy needed to get some fresh air."

"Cooped up, why?"

"He got drenched the day of the storm and caught an awful cold, which went to his chest," she sniffed and took out her handkerchief and blew her already red nose.

"Ah, now that explains it. He was still not quite himself. When we're not well we are inclined to be a little irrational. Try not to worry I'm sure the police will find him anytime now." James forced himself to sound cheerful. "Cold and hungry like all boys, they're all the same."

"I hope so. I've made a pan of soup with vegetables I rescued from my garden."

"That will do the trick, he'll be starving. We'll all keep searching, and don't worry about the Centre everyone is managing fine."

"That's good to hear James. Now that Eve has died, what's going to happen to the Centre?"

"Business as usual, nothing will change." He turned to leave. "If there is anything else you can think of that I can do to help, please, do not hesitate to get in touch." James left, pleased that the question he had wanted to ask Carol had been answered. Billy had been out the day the storm broke and it was quite possible that he did see something. As soon as the child returned home he would do his best to prise it out of him.

The café in the visitors' centre was busier than normal. Human nature being what it is James was sure it was due to the disappearance of Billy, and the murder of the Honeybee Lady, as Eve was fondly called.

He realised it would be necessary to check on the Centre daily to see that things were running smoothly, until Becky and the other staff were competent in their extra allotted tasks. He hoped it wouldn't take long as work was scheduled to start on Moxley Manor in early October.

He left the Centre feeling he was more of a nuisance than a help so he crossed the cobbled square courtyard and knocked on Becky's kitchen door. Clare answered. She was smartly dressed in a blue skirt, a darker blue, V-necked jumper and a pretty sparkly necklace adorned her throat. Her face was made up and James noticed for the first time that her short hair was wavy and brown.

"Do come on in."

"Have I come at a bad time? Are you about to go out?" James asked.

"All dressed up, you mean?" Clare giggled. "No, we're having a quick coffee and then Becky is going to take me across to the Centre to show me what goes on over there to see if I can be of any help. The visitors appear to have doubled in the last hour and Becky thinks there will be more to come."

"She's quite right. It's going to be a busy day."

Clare led James into the kitchen and Becky held up a mug giving it a little knowing shake. "Usual?" she asked.

"Please. Where is Holly?"

Becky laughed. "Where do you think, she's checking on the hives," she said as she poured him coffee.

"I see. I decided to call as Nicky told me Holly was upset last night. I gather she's back to normal this morning?"

Clare glanced sharply at Becky, then lowering her eyes she stared into her coffee mug. She picked up a teaspoon and began to stir the hot liquid; round and around the spoon went. "I think we should tell him," she said, quietly.

"I know that," Becky snapped. Moisture filled her eyes and throwing her arms up into the air she choked back tears. "But how? I don't understand it myself."

"Tell me what?"

Clare looked at Becky and then at James holding eye contact for longer than was necessary.

This was the second time in only a few minutes that someone has pleaded with him for help and assurance. He moved back into his seat waiting for someone to speak.

Clare began, "Nicky was quite right, Holly was very upset last night, she kept saying that the police think she killed Eve, and now they think she's made Billy run away."

"I gave her one of the sedatives Philip had left for her

and she eventually cried herself to sleep," Becky interrupted. "Later when I went in to check on her she was still snuffling in her sleep. I sat with her stroking her forehead until she slipped into a deeper sleep. Then I went to bed."

Taking a mouthful of coffee in an effort to play for time, Clare continued. "It was what happened this morning that was odd."

"Oh…"

"Holly woke up about ten minutes ago. She breezed into the kitchen and when I say breezed, I do mean breezed," she stressed. "She had a happy smiling face and appeared not to have a care in the world. It was as if what had happened last night hadn't happened. I asked her if she wanted some breakfast, she replied '*not hungry*' and grabbed her coat. I asked her where she was going and she practically sang out, '*to check on the hives.*' It was most odd. I didn't know what to say so I said '*you're not going to join in the search?*' She calmly replied, oh dear, James, I don't want to say it…"

"Do go on."

"She said, *'No, he's not coming back.'* She then skipped out of the door. Clare and I just stared at each other. It was as if we had been struck by lightning. I made a pot of coffee while we tried to work out what she had meant by the remark and then you arrived."

"We can't make any sense of it, James."

"Very strange," he mused. "You're quite sure you heard correctly?"

"James …we both heard," Becky sighed in slight annoyance.

"Of course," he said. He put his empty mug down on the table and stood. "I'll think on it. I have an appointment with the auctioneers up at the Manor. Ask Holly what she meant by 'not coming back' it sounds to me as if she's remembered something. I'll call in later. If you haven't been able to get her to tell you what she meant, then I'll give it a try. Or Clare, perhaps you stand a better chance of finding out."

Clare nodded. "You might be right."

"I must go, I'm running late. I'll probably be a couple of hours. In the meantime, if you come up with an explanation, call me."

Business with the auctioneer at the Manor was completed. Both James and the representative from the auction house were happy with the estimated value of the furniture. A house of this size and the amount of antique furniture would warrant a whole day's auction. The furniture would be collected in the last week of September. It would be stored and the odd repair done and the furniture would be put on show, ready for the sale, which was scheduled for the end of October. The type of brochure had been agreed upon and it was felt that a lot of money would be raised.

Helen followed them around each room labelling the furniture that was going to auction and the furniture that was going to stay in the Manor. The auctioneer left and James joined Helen for a sandwich lunch.

It was around four when he reached the apiary. He hadn't heard from Becky and he still hadn't been able to make any sense of Holly's throwaway remark.

Maybe that was not what she intended to say. Her words came out just plain wrong. After all, only, moments earlier, she had woken from a deep sleep. He reworked Holly's words in his head rephrasing them in a variety of ways trying to come up with a different interpretation. Nothing made any sense.

There were still a lot of people milling about the entrance to the apiary. He noticed Becky and Clare through the patio window of the café and doubted that they'd had a chance to talk to Holly. He knocked at the kitchen door, opened it and went in calling Holly's name. He found her sitting alone at the dining-room table, reading.

"Ah, there you are. How are you feeling today, Holly?"

"I'm fine thank you, Uncle James," she jauntily flicked her hair back over her shoulder."

"I'm glad to hear it. Nicky told me you were upset last night."

"I'm better now."

Oh, and what has happened to cheer you up?"

She tightened her lips then smiled, as if she knew something that nobody else knew.

"Do tell me. Whenever I feel down I'd like to know a fast way of cheering myself up."

"Oh no," she laughed. "I couldn't – I couldn't tell you."

"And why not?"

"Because you wouldn't understand."

"Try me…"

"I've told the police everything I know."

"Then what happened to cheer you up?" Her face was radiant and James was certain that something had happened.

"Oh, all right," she said sheepishly. Only if you promise me you won't laugh." She narrowed her eyes as she looked sternly at him.

"I promise, he said. "Cross my heart."

"In that case I'll tell you." She took in a deep breath and leaned back in her chair. Her eyes were darting around the room, checking to ensure that no one else was listening. Confident that they were alone she began in a whisper. "I woke up in the middle of the night. I remembered what had happened yesterday and I became scared again. I was about to go and get into mummy's bed when I saw her."

"Saw her! Who?"

"Eve of course," she retorted. "She was sitting on the end of my bed and she was smiling at me."

The back of James' neck prickled. "Perhaps you were dreaming?" he suggested. Then he recalled the incident Clare had recited. When Holly was only four she had been playing with a man in the sitting-room. No man was found. Later it came to light that, at exactly the same time, Holly's natural father had been killed in a motorbike accident, in France.

"I was not dreaming," she snapped. "She was there. I saw her as plain as I am seeing you."

"Did she say anything?"

"Now you're laughing at me," she sulked, and she began to get up from her chair. James guessed she was about to run.

"Stop Holly, I'm not laughing at you, I'm very interested. Please go one."

"Well…" she hesitated and shuffled back into her chair. "She didn't talk, like we are talking, I sort of heard her in my head. When I asked her a question she answered in my head …in my brain, no …in my mind. Anyway, I could hear her answer. She didn't move much. Sometimes she would blink and sometimes nod her head."

"What did you ask her?"

Holly beamed. "I asked her if she was happy."

"And…?" He watched her face, intensely.

"She nodded and said, *yes*. I told her I missed her and I heard her say she missed me." She stopped abruptly and stared at him as if he was a bit dumb. "I told you she spoke in my head."

"I heard you, go on."

"Well, I asked her if she knew where Billy was. She blinked and I heard a yes. I asked her if he was coming back. She told me *no*. I became frightened for Billy and so I asked her if he was with her, and she blinked and told me, *yes*. I asked her if he was happy and she said, *yes*. I was about to say something else but it was then she faded. Please Uncle James," she pleaded. "Please, don't tell anyone. Eve said I had a gift. She also told me, never to mention it to anyone, as people who didn't have such a gift wouldn't believe or understand."

"I'm sure your mother would believe you. Was that why you told your mother Billy wasn't coming back?"

"I didn't mean to say anything, it just slipped out. I was so happy knowing that Eve and Billy are together, not here, but in another dimension."

James raised his eyebrows. "Dimension?" he said.

"That's what Eve called it. Eve came to see me, which means she is watching over me and now she's looking after Billy, she always did like Billy. So you see Uncle James, everything is going to be all right. I'm not frightened anymore."

"Aren't you upset that Billy is dead?"

Holly frowned. "Yes …but that's being selfish. All it means is we won't be seeing him for a while. He's fine now, he's with Eve. His mum's boyfriend can't beat him anymore."

"You know about that?"

"Yes, Billy told me, we were friends." She began to twiddle with her jumper as her face became crestfallen. "I wish I could be with Eve."

It was hard watching the child and James found it difficult to rationalize his thoughts. He was talking to Holly as if she were an adult and every word she spoke was fact. "You have things to do here," he said. "You have to help me rebuild the colony of bees. You have to help me continue with Eve's work. We have to get the Retreat up and running. That's what we must do, and by doing that, it will please Eve more than anything else. Holly, did Eve ever take you up to the Manor?"

"Oh yes, I've been all over it and I've seen all the plans for the renovation. I used to go every week with her until those horrible people came. Then Eve only took me when they weren't there."

"Which people?"

"I don't know. They only started coming a few months

ago, which made me cross."

"Oh why?"

"Because Eve said that they were the General's children. The General had been ill for a long time so if they were his children, why hadn't they come sooner? They interfered with our games."

James leaned back in his chair, smiling, and asked, "What sort of games?"

"We played Dominos, Drafts and …don't tell Mum," she glanced quickly around the room and whispered. "He was teaching me to play Poker."

James found it hard to refrain from laughing. "Oh, I know the General and his Poker, he loved the game."

Holly looked pensive. "You do believe me don't you? I mean about Eve coming to see me." Her pleading young eyes stared into his.

"Yes I do, Holly. I really do." James couldn't believe the words he had just uttered.

"I'm happy now I know that Eve is happy. Billy is with her, lucky Billy." She kept smiling and James added, "If Billy is dead; do you know how he died?"

"He *is* dead," she snapped, "and I don't know what happened."

James was thankful that Blackwell wasn't hearing this. She would probably have Holly committed. However, James felt that there was an up-side; Holly was not frightened anymore and it appeared that she was not at all disturbed by death or by dying. He then asked.

"Has this sort of thing happened to you before, Holly?"

"Seeing dead people, you mean?"

"Oh yes," she said matter-of-factly.

She told him about the first time it had happened when she was little. "Other times when I'm upset I see people, well not people, they are always women. They don't say anything either, all they do is smile. When they've gone I feel better."

"Who do you think these women are?"

"I don't know."

"Who do you think the man was?"

With the confidence only of a child, Holly said. "He was my father. I heard Auntie Clare and mum talking once. When I started school mum told me that my father was in heaven. She explained it to me in case the other children wanted to know why my father never came to the school. I knew then that the man I played with, that day when I was little, was my father. He came to see me, like Eve did last night."

"How can you be so sure?"

"I just know."

"I see. Why do you think he came to see you?"

"To say good-bye, of course," she said with irritation in her voice.

"Did you tell Eve about this?"

"Oh yes, we talked a lot, she knew all about these sort of things." Holly straightened in her chair. "Did you know Eve told me that in the next life it's possible to be in three places at once? Not the real you, it's a mind thing, it's possible, in the next life, to project an image of yourself. Like a hologram, I think that's what she called it, it must be such fun. And, did you know that they don't sleep or have clocks, they just know stuff."

"No I didn't. I obviously have a lot to learn."

Holly giggled. "Uncle James …spirits are not flesh and blood they can do things we can't. When we die we leave our bodies behind because, where we go we no longer need them.

It was obvious that Holly thought him to be a simpleton. How much of Holly's story did he believe? It was more in Philip's line of work and he wished he were here now listening to what she was saying. He could not comprehend this mumbo-jumbo as he called it; he was a down-to-earth northern farmer, a marine and a legal man, not a philosopher, dreamer or scientist. Yet here he was taking this child seriously.

"Holly, I think it would be a good idea if you tell your mother what you have just told me. She needs to know why you suddenly changed from sad to happy. Last night you cried yourself to sleep and she was very worried about you."

"Do I have to?"

"I think you do. It is all to do with trust, Holly. We all need the help and support of each other. We need to be truthful if we're going to discover what happened to Eve, and also Billy."

She nodded, she understood. "Now, you're a mature young lady."

"Too old for my age, I've been told that many times," she laughed. "Mum says it is because I'm an only child and have spent most of my time with adults. It's true Uncle James, I find children so boring?"

"Hmm …so, will you speak to your mother and tell her what happened? Do it for me, Holly."

"I suppose so, but…"

"No buts Holly, your mother will believe you so don't worry."

"I've remembered something else, Uncle James. As Eve faded," Holly's eyes had a far-away expression in them as if organising her thoughts. "I suppose it's a time thing," she said.

"A time thing?"

"How long you can project your image. Anyway, what she told me didn't make any sense."

"Tell me all the same?"

She hesitated, then stood. She'd had enough.

"I'm not sure. It sounded like *…forgive …must forgive,*" she murmured as she left the room.

The visitors' centre reminded James of a railway station in rush hour with people coming and going. He saw Becky and Clare dealing with customers in the shop so he decided to leave them to it and go home.

At the bottom of Honey Pot Lane, he took a right turn. As he came to the bridge crossing the River Tyne, he came face to face with a police road-block. He waited in line. On the officer's instructions he wound down his window.

"I'm sorry to bother you, sir. Do you use this road often?"

"I do, I live on the other side of the river."

"Your name is…?

"Sir James Marchant."

"Any relation to…" The officer asked knowing full well who he was.

"He's my brother." The officer nodded. "Sorry sir, orders are we have to stop and search every car."

"I've no problem with that," James popped the boot and got out of the car. He joined the officer at the back of his vehicle and pulled up the door. He stepped back and let the officer do his duty.

"Do you know Billy Bradshaw?" The officer asked.

"Yes very well."

"Have you heard that he is missing?"

"Yes. Does this searching of cars mean you are working on the theory that he may have been abducted?"

"We are considering all possibilities."

"Have you seen any strangers loitering around here lately?"

That was the futile question James had been asking people for a week now. "We get a lot of people walking along the bank of the river. None of them stop long enough to be identified or remembered. Also, we get a huge amount of visitors at the apiary. Coach loads to be exact, from all over the county," he grinned.

The officer groaned. "I fell into that trap, didn't I?"

"It had to be asked."

"Thank you. You may go Sir James."

While James was waiting his turn to continue his journey he called Reg. "Can you get someone to saddle up Bolt or Taser for me I need to get some fresh air to clear my head."

"Will do." Reg then told James that Bolt had been exercised. Taser was still waiting to go so he would have Taser saddled and ready by the time he arrived. James reached the farm without further interruption. He quickly changed into suitable clothes, pulled on his well-worn, brown leather boots, and was in the yard within fifteen minutes.

Glancing skywards he guessed he had a good hour before dusk fell. The sun was low in the sky. Its dying rays danced across the fields drying the remnants of wet grass. At least the sun was there. It came and went quickly these days so he was pleased to see it. For the past few weeks, all it had done was rain.

He patted Taser on the neck and mounted. He walked his horse out of the yard then kicked him in the flank. Taser responded and began to trot sedately around the outside of the exercise paddock. He came to a five-bar gate leading into one of his fields where ewes busily stripped the grass. They had been brought down off the moor for late lambing. He leaned over his horse's neck, opened the gate and rode through.

After closing the gate behind him he gave Taser his head and Taser, knowing what was expected of him, happily galloped across the field with his mane and tail flying. They came to another gate, which led onto a rutted track. Ahead and to his left, lush pasture rolled on and on, into the distance. To his right was the unruly Osbert Wood, which ran along the eastern side of the estate. All was quiet; it was too early to bring the Blue Greys down from the moors, and into the wood.

In the distance and behind a fence he recognised the dyed spiky hair and muscular tattooed arms of Damian Crab. Those muscular arms had got Damian into trouble on more than one occasion. The last time had put him inside for six months following a drunken brawl.

After being approached by Damian's parole officer, James had given the young man a job and since then he had proved to be an asset, willing and hard-working. Damian was born and bred on a council estate in the city and was initiated into a gang – not good. He'd had little contact with the countryside or animals before he came to the valley. Watching him James doubted he would ever leave. He hoped not, anyway.

He decided not to interrupt him; instead, for a brief moment he observed him making ready the diet feeders used for additional winter feed for the Blue Grey's. *'They're hardy beasts, like me.'* Damian had once said with a laugh as he flexed his muscles, and he was right. The breed called Blue Greys, certainly are hardy beasts. They thrive on rough terrain and are not fussy or pampered like other cattle. The animals eat practically anything and they produce an abundance of good quality meat. However, when the winter snows arrive they are brought down from the rough-grazing in the north to the relative shelter of Osbert wood where their diet is supplemented.

James had often overheard ramblers remark on the colour of their coat, which is as the name suggests, blue grey. *'Blue grey cows, never heard of them. They're probably diseased. I'm keeping away'*. Apart from their colour these animals lived in a wood… *'You gotta be kiddin' me'*. It was because of these overheard remarks that James had pinned notices on the gate to the wood explaining all about the breed. It also gave him the idea to open the estate to the public; this would stop the occasional trespasser causing havoc by leaving gates open and dropping litter. It was the first stage of his plan. The second was to build a restaurant. This was well underway. The restaurant would be provided with organic produce grown on the estate.

The landscape changed from the lush fertile fields of the valley to barren rocky moorland. Taser negotiated sparse clumps of gorse, rocks and purple heather as he climbed upwards.

The ground between the rocks was soft with thick mud in places. James began to wonder if this was such a good idea. It was a long shot. Billy would never have made it this far even if he had known of the place. The area was too remote.

He then reminded himself that he and his friends had frequently climbed up to the Crag at his age. Regardless, he felt the need to check. It would satisfy him that he had done everything possible in the hunt for the child. He didn't think the police would consider searching this far afield. If they ever got around to it, it would be far too late for Billy.

Taser was starting to sweat as he pulled himself up to the clumps of vicious-looking rocks known locally as Kirk Crag. He dismounted. James could see for miles …his horses in the pastures below …his Cheviot sheep grazing and his favourite Blue Grey cattle as they roamed freely on the moor: no people.

It was a lonely deserted place. The terrain was such that only the intrepid walker would dare negotiate the Crag. He dismounted and left Taser, knowing his horse would not go far as there was nothing to tempt him away.

He scrambled down a rocky slope until he saw the entrance to the small cave he knew to be there.

He took out his knife. The bracken, which overhung the entrance, looked untouched. He wondered if he were wasting his time, no one had been here in years. Billy was only small; maybe he had scrambled beneath the bracken and not disturbed it. With his back against the rock he held on with his left arm and put his left foot on the protruding ledge. Once he felt secure he swung his right leg, arm and the rest of his body around and launched himself into the cave.

James didn't remember it being so difficult. The last time he'd negotiated the Crag he had been half his height and half his weight. He leaned over the edge. The drop, which as a lad had seemed enormous, was now only a drop of about a metre before the land gently sloped away.

Billy was not inside. If Billy had made it to the Crag and spent the night here he would have died of hypothermia. He felt that no human had been in the cave for years; probably not since he was a lad. There were bird droppings, rabbit droppings, rotting bracken, there were traces of snails and a snake had found its way in and shed its skin. He noticed a pile of empty, rusted beer cans blown into a corner by the wind. He should have got rid of them.

Along with his four mates they would negotiate the Crag before dusk. They would sit on the ledge dangling their legs in thin air. It was there that they sampled their first cigarette and drank their first can of beer. They felt like Gods as they surveyed their domain below.

Years later, his father told him that one evening he had

noticed strange tiny specks of alternating light up on the Crag. He had taken his binoculars and honed in on them and watched as the boys passed around a cigarette.

He was wasting time. He had seen enough and went back to Taser. He was confident that no one had recently been on the Crag so he mounted his beloved horse and began the trek down into the valley.

The sun had disappeared and, glancing up, he saw threatening, black clouds fast approaching, he was about to ride into a belt of rain. Seconds later he felt the first drop.

He decided that the quickest way back was to take the narrow mud-track, which ran along his side of the River Tyne. He gave Taser his head, knowing that he would not slow until he reached a fork in the path where they would turn right and climb back up to the farm. They had gone about one mile when Taser stopped dead and James nearly went over his head.

He couldn't fathom out why Taser had behaved in such a way. Perhaps it was a rabbit or possibly a stoat that had scurried across the path. Strange, he hadn't noticed any movement. With Taser's experience with animals that should not have distressed him either. Something obviously had, but what? Then he saw it and was in no doubt as to what it was.

Over the years the force of the river had cut into the bank creating a small inlet. Half submerged and wedged was what appeared to be a discarded bag of rubbish. James instinctively knew he had found Billy.

Strands of soft, child-hair now caked with mud swayed back and forth like the tentacles of a jellyfish, each time the river entered and re-entered the cut on its rush to reach the North Sea.

One arm floated in front of the head and a tiny, rigid, white hand peeped from beneath the sleeve of an anorak now blackened with silt, the other arm was wedged beneath the body.

James dismounted and Taser backed a few steps. He had a decision to make should he leave the body where it was? Or, should he pull it out? He doubted there would be any sign of life. What if? He slid down the bank before he had answered his own questions. He grabbed hold of Billy, yanked him off the reeds and pulled him up onto the bank. Filthy water seeped from the clothes and bubbled from the orifices of the tiny body. Little Billy Bradshaw was dead.

The rain was heavier now, coming down with such force that it cut into his exposed flesh. He hadn't anticipated this. He managed to get a signal on his cell, his fingers slipping off the numbers. He was told to wait where he was.

He sat on the edge of a stone barely large enough to take one cheek of his backside. It, at least, kept him off the ground and Taser needed a rest. He sat in silence next to the body and waited. The rain penetrated his clothing, not an inch of his skin was dry. He was cold, wet and miserable as he stared at the tiny body. At least in an hour or so he would be warm and wearing fresh clothes. That was not to be for Billy, never again, Holly was right, Billy was not coming back.

As he waited his mind revisited the pain he had felt when he was told of his daughter Amanda's death. He was with Jean when she died, watching, feeling inadequate as she slipped away. Then just days ago the shock of Eve's death.

Now, before him lay this child whose life had barely begun. He thought of Carol and her pain, which was yet to come.

Listening to the ever-rising, roaring river, as it cascaded down from the mountains, James knew he had made the right decision. The last thing he would have wanted was that a rogue surge took the body of little Billy Bradshaw downriver and out into the North Sea, never to be seen again.

The sound of blaring sirens penetrated the rain. One, two, three cars followed by a heavier vehicle sped across the bridge and parked in the small car-park. A line of officers scurried along the path towards James, Blackwell in the lead. He was cold, wet and irritable and not in the mood for a conversation with the officious Inspector.

He waited.

The sour-faced woman and an officer called Whitman were the first to reach him, the rain already soaking into their clothing. She was mumbling and swearing under her breath about the weather. James guessed she had realised that once again there would be little evidence left due to it having been washed away.

Two more officers arrived, then a team from forensics along with the duty doctor. The police photographer was trying his best to protect his camera with a waterproof sheet he kept in his car for such an occasion. There was little to photograph.

"This is a repeat of what happened on the day your friend Eve was killed. The bloody rain took away all the evidence," she snarled. Her hair looked like long, curly sausages as it dripped rainwater. She tried to wipe her face with her wet hand to no avail. James stemmed a smile. She would soon be as drenched as he was.

"I doubt there would be any evidence to find," James said.

She glared at him. In a clipped, grating voice she answered. "What makes you the expert?" Not waiting for an answer she turned to the doctor who was examining Billy's body. "How long?" she snapped. The doctor did not reply.

Blackwell turned back to James; her mascara was trickling down her cheeks making her look like a clown. There was no denying the anger that lay beneath.

"Anyway, what made you come up with that ingenious conclusion?"

James answered her in a calm fashion. "To be on this side of the river he would have had to have left his bike, which we know he did, walk down the lane, cross over the bridge, walk along this path, slip into the river and drown. Almost a two-mile walk, I'd say."

"That, Sir James, is the silliest thing I have heard today. It is obvious that he entered the river on the other side and was dragged downstream and the current pushed him into these reeds."

"Exactly, so even if it wasn't raining there would be no evidence to be found here. As you said, this is not where he entered the water."

Blackwell glared at him as if he were an idiot. "Sir

James, it is raining on both sides of the river."

"It doesn't always," James said, knowingly.

Blackwell went quiet.

"Inspector, I am pretty sure that death was due to drowning. I'd say that he has been in the water probably forty-eight hours. The pathologist will be able to tell you more when he does the PM. Having said that there are one or two marks on the body I'm a little concerned about. I couldn't begin to speculate on those in these conditions." The doctor picked up his belongings and started to walk away, leaving two paramedics to carry Billy Bradshaw's body on a stretcher along the path towards the waiting ambulance and then on to the morgue.

James sensed that Blackwell was out of her depth here in the valley or was it because she was now so wet she was unable to think straight.

"I've never seen such mist and rain. Is it always like this in the valley?"

"I'm afraid so."

James was quite sure he heard her mumble the words *Moron to live here*. "I'll need you to give a statement," she said again trying to wipe the rain from her face.

"Sure," James said. "No problem. If you don't mind, I'd like to get out of these wet clothes first."

"9.30am tomorrow morning. I have to be somewhere else now. You know, Sir James, I'm thinking it strange that you happened upon the body."

The officer who had arrived with Blackwell was obviously embarrassed. He began to clean off the mud from his shoes on a clump of grass.

"What you're saying is that you don't think it was an accident, you think he was murdered. You heard what the doctor said. He drowned." James' eyes widened in disbelief, as he stared at her.

"He also said that there was bruising, so the question is, did he fall or was he pushed?"

James found her remark to be so incredulous he began to laugh. "So you think…" The lines around his eyes deepened as his mouth set. "That the person who stumbles upon the body is often the murderer, yes?"

Unexpectedly, Reg was standing in the doorway beneath an overhang to the estate office. "What are you doing here, thought you would have left by now." James called as he drew closer.

"Weather turned nasty again, just thought I'd come back and double-check on things," he shouted through the rain.

The sound of Taser's hooves on the cobbles grew louder as he approached Reg.

"Good God! What happened to you? Fall in the Tyne?" Reg laughed as he drew alongside.

"Not quite," James said, dismounting and handed the reins to Reg.

"Couldn't you have found any shelter?"

"No, although I did find something else …little Billy Bradshaw. I had to wait until the police arrived."

"You what!"

"You heard, I found Billy. If it hadn't been for Taser, I would have missed the body?"

"How?"

"Taser spooked. He saw the body before I did."

"Good God, poor kid. What happened?"

"Too soon to say. I think he slipped and fell in the river. The current must have taken him across to our side and he was lodged in a small cut a couple of miles downstream. There is no letting up, the river is still raging."

"Well thank God you found him, if he had reached the sea he would have been lost for good."

"That was my thought exactly."

"Are you going to tell Mrs Bradshaw?"

"That's Blackwell's job. I noticed Damian working on the diet feeders I hope he had the sense to come in?"

"Made it before the worst downpour."

"How did he get on?"

"Two are past repair so will have to be replaced, the others only need minor repairs. No problem. We'll be ready for whatever the winter has to throw at us."

"Good, I'm going to take a shower. I'll be over first thing tomorrow I have to give a statement to Blackwell at nine-thirty sharp. She thinks I murdered Billy."

Reg gasped at the ridiculous accusation. Stunned into silence his mouth tightened and his eyes darted from side to side as the full extent of James' words registered. "You can't be serious."

"Quite serious."

"Is this woman for real?"

"I don't know, you tell me."

"You said he fell in the river."

"That's what I imagine happened. Her problem now is – did he fall or was he pushed?"

"And why would you want to kill, Billy?"

"I was giving it some thought on my way back. It may have something to do with Holly saying that Billy kept repeating that he knew who killed Eve. She is probably working on the premise that Holly or I killed Eve. In either case I did it to protect myself, or I did it to protect Holly."

Reg found it difficult to keep his face straight. "Okay, then what's your motive for killing Eve?"

"I haven't worked that one out yet," James laughed. "I'll see you tomorrow. I need to get out of these clothes, I'm drenched." James waved as he sauntered off.

Reg called after him. "I'll get Sylvia to start baking cakes. Big enough to put tools inside to help you break out." Reg turned and, still tittering, he began to walk Taser beneath the overhang, back to the stable block and his stall.

"Thanks for that, Reg." James replied with a wave over his shoulder.

Chapter 17 – Holly

The news of Billy Bradshaw's body being found had ricocheted around the community at an alarming rate. The five-bar gate was closed when James arrived at the apiary, and a rowdy group of noisy onlookers, had congregated outside in the lane. He drove into the packed car park opposite and double parked. He didn't care if anyone wanted him to move his car; hard luck, they'd have to find him. Most of them had no right to be parked there.

He realised why these people were here. They had, without proof, become judge jury and executioner. They shuffled from foot to foot, building up steam in readiness to attack. Their prey was a child and even worse, a newcomer. Holly's crimes: she had found Eve's body and was the last person to see little Billy alive.

As he struggled to negotiate the crowd he overheard mutterings. *Do you think she did it? Nar, she's only a kid. What about the mother? Yeah, I'd put my money on the mother. Still think it's the kid. Kids are evil nowadays. Can't trust kids. They're all on drugs.*

He'd had enough; there was only one way through this

mob and that was to use brute force, an art in which he was well schooled. A booming voice broke through the smouldering air. "Police. Clear the way, clear the way." An officer was opening the gate and James was being pushed back when he wanted to go forward. Body against body. He saw through the crowd. The five-bar gate was now open and two unmarked police cars swished out and down the lane.

James swore as he began again to force his way to the front. A man told him to get lost. James put his hand on his shoulder and pressed, he knew how and where to press. They locked eyes.

The man gave way and shrank back, allowing James to go forward. He had to repeat this tactic twice until he finally reached the gate as the officer on duty was struggling to close it against the force of the crowd trying to get into the court-yard.

"Let me through. I'm a member of the family," he told the officer.

"Have you any identification, sir?" The officer was clearly agitated.

James groaned. No time for niceties he put his foot on the bottom bar of the gate and hauled his body up and over landing in the courtyard. He then charged towards the kitchen door as the officer still struggling to secure the gate shouted after him, "Sir, sir stop sir…" James ignored the officer's demands.

The court-yard was deserted and the visitors' centre was deserted. He reached Clare who was standing in the kitchen doorway staring at the crowd behind the gate. Her face was a picture of fear.

"James, thank God you're here. They've taken Becky and Holly. Billy Bradshaw has been found. He's dead."

"I know Clare, I found him."

Clare allowed James to pass then she closed the door and James heard her lock and bolt it.

"First things first Clare, does Nicky know?"

"Yes, she's meeting them at the police station."

"Good. We now know that Billy drowned."

"It was an accident, James."

"More than likely. Whatever it was that happened, it had nothing to do with Holly, I'm quite sure of that, so put it right out of your mind."

Settled in chairs opposite each other, across the kitchen table, Clare said, "The police arrived about half-an-hour ago and began asking Holly the same old questions, then they said they wanted her to come to the station.

They told Becky it was because they wanted to talk to her with a child psychiatrist present. They mumbled something about it being the Law. Becky was demented and there was nothing either of us could do. I stood and watched them being taken away like common criminals. It was awful James, all those people standing there gawping and shouting horrid things." Pent up tears filled her eyes, she had tried so hard to remain strong, but it had become impossible.

"Those people are not from around here. I didn't recognise anyone of them. You did everything you could possibly have done. How was Holly?"

"She was fine; she has this renewed confidence, which, I believe, didn't help her. Steely-eyed Blackwell kept watching her every move."

"Steely-eyed," James smiled. "Very apt Clare. Did they say what they believed to have happened?"

"Oh yes, remember Holly had already told them that Billy had come into the apiary while she was checking on the hives, boasting that he knew who had killed Eve."

"I remember."

"Blackwell said to Holly that they understood how it happened, and she had nothing to worry about. They just needed to be sure of the truth.

They believed that Holly had followed him, caught up with him along the path, there was a scuffle, the front wheel of his bike got buckled and Billy fell into the river. It was an accident."

James huffed, "That's clever, lulling the child into a false sense of security. If Holly admitted to that, which she won't, because it's not true, then Blackwell will work on the assumption that she also killed Eve. It would only be a matter of time before she got a confession. Holly is far too young to understand any of this and the game the woman is playing."

Clare scrunched her lips and frowned. "That can't happen, can it? I mean, cajole a confession out of her?"

"Over my dead body."

"There's something about that woman. I just can't put my finger on it."

"You're not alone. They must be thinking that Holly, having watched Billy fall into the water, picked up his bike, pulled it along the path, and left it propped up against the wall of his house.

"She went home, calmly ate her meal and said nothing.

Mrs Bradshaw called to see if Billy was with them. When he wasn't, she put on her coat and went out searching for him. I don't think so."

"Neither do I."

James decided to wait with Clare until he heard from Nicky. Her call came at around six-thirty.

"Dad, it's not good. They're taking Becky and Holly to a remand centre, saying that they will be more comfortable there than spending the night at the station."

"Have they been charged?"

"*Helping them with their enquiries* was how Blackwell phrased it. As the child psychiatrist was not expected until morning, it would be better if they 'put them up'. I told her to charge them or let them go. I would bring them back in the morning. She became irate and charged them both on suspicion of murder."

"She did what!"

"You heard."

"What the hell has got into her? Is she out of her mind?"

Groaning, Nicky said, "Why is Harry putting up with her? This is not the Uncle Harry I know."

"He had no choice. He's obeying orders. Apparently she's being pushed from above."

"Did you mention Philip to her?"

"I called him as soon as the police took them in for questioning. After all he is a psychiatrist. When I mentioned him she laughed at me and said, '*a friend of the family, I don't think so.*"

"Anyway, Philip is on his way."

"Good. Is Harry there?"

"I asked to see Harry, Blackwell took great pleasure in telling me he was not on duty."

"Call him Nicky."

"I have. His phone is switched off."

"Try calling Gillian, see if she can find him."

"Already done and when I do speak to him, I'm going insist he take Blackwell off the case. If he doesn't, I'm going to make such a stink, which he'll regret for the rest of his career, uncle or no uncle."

"Calm down Nicky. I think he'd like to, but he has no one to replace her. I warned him about this. Unless Blackwell has positive proof I'll also make a stink that will hit the press big time."

Nicky laughed. "Together we'll win."

"That's my girl we'll fight to the bitter end."

"Clare, since Becky and Holly will not be home tonight, perhaps you would like to join us for a bite to eat? You haven't met Philip; he was a close friend of Eve's and a good friend to Becky. He's a psychiatrist and he's on his way here. We can all meet up at The Fallen Angel."

"That would be nice James if I hadn't already put dinner in the oven. Why don't you both stay here and share it with me. I do need the company and we can talk."

He thought a moment. "That would probably be a better idea, if you're quite sure."

"I'm sure, I'll lay the table."

"Clare, I'd like to go up into the attic. I've had an idea. Have you a torch? I can't remember if there is any electricity up there."

"I'll take a look in the kitchen." She was back minutes later. "You're in luck. It's quite a powerful one too," she said as she handed him a shiny, silver torch about nine inches long with a diameter of two inches.

James switched it on. It almost blinded him. "Perfect, thank you."

"Shout if you should want me, I'll be in the kitchen."

James took the stairs two at a time it was hard to believe he was doing this. Was he starting to believe all this crazy stuff? As he reached Holly's bedroom he stopped. He stood in the doorway and pictured Eve sitting on the end of the bed, as Holly claimed she had the previous night.

Only Eve was dead…

Standing on his toes, he reached up and pulled open the door to the attic. He unhooked the ladder and let it slide down until its lower rung rested on the landing floor. He switched on the torch and climbed up and pulled himself through the three by three-foot gap.

A large skylight, in about what James knew to be in the middle of the room, cast an eerie light. Shining his torch, first on the wall to the left of him, and then to the right, he found a pull-switch. He pulled and hey presto there was light.

Two naked bulbs dimly lit the long, narrow room. One was almost directly over his head and another was at the far end of the room. The attic stretched across the entire length of the building. He began to work from left to right leaving footprints in the dust; it had been a long time since anyone had been in the attic.

Stacks of boxes lined the walls. James began to peer

in box after box. Some were crammed with Christmas decorations, spare bedding, toys, and ornaments. There was a stack of empty suitcases an old hammock, a spare carpet cleaner, an old dresser and a broken antique chair, which, if repaired, James knew would be worth a fortune.

It was difficult to stand up straight; his neck had begun to ache. He had about another six-feet to examine. It was then he saw it. An ancient, battered, leather, brass-studded trunk, half-covered with a greyish blanket.

Intricate symbols adorned the leather, which meant nothing to James. Attached to its lid and hanging loose, was a sturdy black leather strap also edged with brass studs. A weighty metal lock hung loose. The person who had last looked inside the trunk had not bothered to relock it; why would they? It was not going anywhere.

He lifted the lid and found it to be full of books and scrolls. He hadn't felt such excitement since he was a child and his hands began to shake. The contents of this trunk were hundreds of years old.

James sat on the floor and tentatively lifted out book after book and placed them reverently on the floor. Stunningly beautiful, carved leather-bound, ancient books and ledgers. The sight sent a shiver of delight down James' spine.

There were medical books, books about herbs all lovingly illustrated with precision. They were written in the French language. It had been a long time since he'd had the need to use his French. Maybe he'd remember a few words.

He continued to empty the trunk. He knew what he was searching for.

An idea came to him. When the new library in the retreat was completed he decided that these books should be displayed in glass cases for visitors to appreciate. These books represented the family history of the founder of the retreat, namely, Eve.

The next book he picked up was smaller than the rest. Roughly eight-inches by six, it was bound in faded, brown leather. As he was about to take a peek inside it a voice called, "You up there, James?"

Shocked out of his reverie, he answered, "Yes, come on up you're not going to believe what I've found."

Philip, being plumper than James, groaned as he pulled himself through the gap. "You've found it!" He caught his breath and croaked with excitement. Bending his head, he shuffled towards James. His eyes widened as he stared at the books lining the floor and then he saw the book James was holding. "Is that the journal?"

"I'm pretty sure it is."

"Phew… These books must be worth a fortune. What are you intending to do with them, we can't keep these hidden in an attic, they should be in a museum." Philip made a move to pick up one of the books petrified that it might disintegrate before his eyes.

"Careful, remember some of them must be about six-hundred-years-old," James said. "I suggest we put them back. Keep them airtight. We need them examined by an expert. As for keeping them hidden, I was thinking about putting them in a display case in the 'soon to be' library, at the retreat."

"Splendid idea. I'd like to take a closer look at the journal now if you think it's wise."

"So would I. We need more light. Let's go," James said making a move to go back down from the attic.

Having brushed the dust off their clothing they sat at the dining table. James suddenly had a thought. "We'd better use gloves," he said as he carefully placed the book on the dining table. "I don't want to mark anything. Eve should have some in her surgery."

He found two pairs of lightweight surgical gloves and sat alongside Philip placing the journal on the table in front of them. With great care he opened it.

"Can you read it?" Philip asked.

"It's difficult, this was written hundreds of years ago. It's like us trying to read Shakespeare for the first time and English is our mother tongue. I think we'll have to have it translated."

"We could try the universities, or perhaps the British Museum would be a better idea."

"I don't believe this! It's not the journal, after all. Shit! It looks like a recipe book. See here?" He pointed to the left hand page. "It's a list of ingredients," James said moving the book closer to Philip. "I'm sure that's French for ginger and that word, basilica, must be French for basil."

"Shit! Hold on..." Philip sank back in his chair. "We'll take another look in the trunk. It's got to be in there, somewhere."

James had fallen silent and continued to turn the pages one by one. "Sorry Philip, this is honestly nothing more than a recipe book. How disappointing. It was the size of it that made it look like a journal." He turned over a few more pages. "Wait a minute… I don't think it's an ordinary recipe book." What began as disappointment turned into excitement.

"What do you mean?" Philip asked.

"At a guess I'd say that these are recipes for potions."

"Potions! Now that is interesting," Philip's eyes widened. "It hasn't been a waste of time after all. They knew the penalty for witchcraft; obviously they had to keep them hidden. But, wouldn't you have thought that they'd have known all the recipes off by heart?"

"Maybe, but they would need them to be passed down from generation to generation, so some sort of record would have been required. The journal must still be in the trunk."

"You mean you can feel it in your water?"

"Something like that. Shush…"

"Why, what is it?" Philip leaned closer to see what had grabbed James' attention.

"I'm trying to decipher this ancient French." He turned the page and stared. "Listen to this." Clearly written was the date, 1636. Beneath it James read out slowly as he tried to make sense of the words, "I Francoise DuPont and here lower down is the word Celestine." James carefully turned to the next page. "This is it," he exclaimed. "It is the journal. Francoise DuPont wrote her journal starting in the middle of a recipe book."

"You're joking! Now that *is* clever. At first glance it would seem innocuous enough," Philip regained his enthusiasm.

"Remember, they didn't have safes in those days."

Philip tilted his head and raised his shoulders and

nodded to the walk-in fireplace. "They would have had Priest Holes or similar."

"Didn't you say Eve had the journal translated when she was at University?"

"Yes, but I never saw it."

"Then where is it?"

They tore off their disposable gloves and made for the hall both men took the stairs two at a time, James arriving first at the attic. Having hauled themselves up through the opening they scurried towards the trunk. There sitting on top of one of the books at the bottom of the trunk, in plain sight, was a dust streaked envelope and inside was the neatly folded translation.

"It must have slipped out when we lifted up the journal. If that was the case, why didn't we notice it?"

"Too thrilled at finding the journal, I expect."

Philip had a mischievous expression on his face. "It was staring up at us, we should have seen it. I say Eve put it there when we went downstairs."

James shook his head and grunted in despair. "Don't go there Philip, there's only so much I can take."

"Okay, I'm only joshing."

James glanced across at Philip. He wasn't so sure Philip was joshing. "Let's close up here; I want to see what this journal has to say."

"We know what it will say, it will confirm Eve's story. This journal is going to revolutionise our scientific research. In fact, I believe it's going to shake the world." Philip gave a little chuckle and muttered, chasing the dead.

"What was that?"

"Err …nothing."

"I suggest we take the trunk back to my place. It needs to be thoroughly examined and we haven't begun to look at the scrolls. Blackwell thinks she's solved the case so she may decide to rip this place apart and I don't want her getting her hands on these."

"I agree, you're the trustee, you have every right to take it."

After repacking the books James closed the lid and the two men began to drag the trunk to the opening of the attic.

"I'll go first. You slide it down to me."

"Be careful Philip I don't know how strong the strap is, it's perished in parts."

The leather straps wrapped around the trunk prevented it from slipping. Slowly it slid down the ladder then with a thump it dropped onto the landing.

"Shit!" Philip yelped.

"What's wrong?"

"Caught my little toe, it's nothing, I'll live."

Having put the journal back into it, the two men managed to lift the trunk into the back of James' BMW and close the boot. Clare watched them in confusion as Nicky's car pulled up. Becky and Holly got out. Clare rushed towards them and threw her arms around her two charges. "Thank God," she gushed.

"What happened?"

James stood proud. "How did you manage it, Nicky?"

"You're going to love this one, Dad. Good old Uncle Harry."

James couldn't refrain from smiling. "Come on tell…"

"Gillian had managed to contact Harry. He arrived and marched Blackwell into his office. I'm surprised the whole valley didn't hear him yelling. And you should have heard the sniggering from the duty officer," she was laughing as she recalled. "That was all there was to it. Apparently a call was made to the officer here at the gate. When he said that the crowd had dispersed her excuse for protecting them '*only thinking of their safety*', had gone up in smoke and we were allowed to come home. We have to go back in the morning." With wide eyes and with a jaunty tip of her head she said, "So… here we are."

"That's just great. I think we should leave you three alone now. I'll see you all tomorrow."

"What about dinner?" Clare worried.

"Some other time, you have a lot to talk about. We'll get something at the pub."

Philip touched Becky's arm as he bent and kissed her cheek. James noticed Becky flush.

Nicky had also noticed Becky's face change colour and she whispered to her father as they walked away. "I know what you are thinking Dad, too big an age gap."

James was about to get into his car when he heard Clare say, "Where are your shoes? Didn't they give them back to you?"

"No, they need them for testing," Becky replied."

Something that had been niggling away at the back of James' mind suddenly came to the fore.

Why did he keep thinking about shoes, the shoes neatly placed outside of the Mission door?

His own dirty boots, which still needed cleaning, and

the dirty wellingtons, which Helen had never worn. "What's all this about shoes?" he shouted back over his shoulder.

Clare returned to the doorway, "I'm sorry, should I have mentioned it? I didn't think it was important." She hesitated for a moment. "When they took Becky and Holly to the police station they also took all their shoes."

That's interesting. The only possible explanation was that the police had found a foot print. "Thanks Clare I just wondered, good night." James caught up with Philip. "I gather you'll be staying over."

"Might as well, I don't feel like driving back, it's a bit late. I'll get off first thing."

"Then I want to do a detour. Will you follow me up to the Manor, I've had a thought."

"Sounds ominous."

"I'm going home. We'll talk tomorrow, Dad." Nicky interrupted, turned, and then walked towards her car. There was a clunk and a flash of bright orange light.

"Fine. Goodnight sweetheart."

"Goodnight, Nicky," Philip called as she was closing her car door. She started the engine then drove away.

"Ominous you say, I'd say more like crazy. I want to ask Helen a couple of questions and I want you to pay close attention to her reactions. You're the psychiatrist."

"Sure, I've never met Helen, and it's years since I've been inside the Manor."

"I want you to keep something in mind. I have asked Helen to be my housekeeper, so it's important that I don't upset her."

"Can she cook?"

"Philip…"

There were more clunks and more flashes of orange light. Then the two men drove away.

Instead of turning left to go to Marchant's farm they turned right and continued on up the lane towards Moxley Manor.

Chapter 18 – DuPont

When they reached the Manor, the building appeared quite sinister, framed against the backdrop of a night sky. A sliver of a silver moon and a few stars, peeping out from behind the clouds were the only light.

James drove to the rear of the building and parked. Helen's car was in its usual place.

Noticing a light burning on the third floor, he hoped that she had not retired for the night. He took out his cellphone and called her. She answered immediately.

"Sorry to bother you this late, Helen. I'm outside. If you're not in bed could I have a quick word? It's rather important."

Her giggle was childlike. "It's only nine. I'm not exactly in bed. I'll be right down," she said.

They heard the bolts being drawn back and then the door opened. Helen stood wrapped in a long, green satin dressing gown. She might not have been in bed but she was certainly ready for it. She stepped aside to let them in.

"You've brought company. I'm not dressed for visitors; you should have said…"

"You look fine. This is Philip Cook who is joining the Board of Trustees and will be in charge of the Retreat, when it's up and running."

"Oh I see …then I'm pleased to meet you Philip." They shook hands. "I guess we'll be seeing a lot of each other. Can I get you both a drink?"

"No thank you, we'll not keep you."

"Sit down anyway."

Three chairs were pulled away from the large refectory kitchen table and they sat.

There was a moment's silence. Helen lifted her shoulders and then let them drop. "What's this all about?"

"I'd like you to cast your mind back to Saturday night, when you moved a pair of wellingtons? They were in the way of my getting to the wine," James said.

"I remember…"

"What can you tell me about them?"

Helen put her hand to her mouth to prevent herself from laughing. "I don't think they will suit you, James. They're a bit too flowery and fluorescent, even for you."

"I wasn't looking to borrow them. I want to know if you've cleaned them."

"My giddy aunt!" she chuckled. "Is this some sort of test as to how efficient I am?"

"My giddy aunt! It's been many years since I've heard that expression," Philip laughed.

James shook his head. "No, I'm being serious. This is important. Have you cleaned them?"

She leaned back in her chair and eyed him with suspicion. "To be honest, I haven't," she appeared slightly embarrassed.

"Good."

"What's this all about?"

"I'd like you to tell us the story of the wellingtons," James said leaning forward and looking directly into her face trying to convey the message that he was being serious.

Helen frowned. "This is all very mysterious. I bought the wellingtons when I came to work for the General as his housekeeper. Not having ever lived in the country I thought I might need them, although I'm not one for traipsing around muddy fields. When I arrived I discovered that there was a stone-slab path around the building. It also has a stone-slab court yard and stone paths leading to the fountain and around the formal garden. Consequently, I've never had an occasion to wear them. They have lain in the storeroom from the day I bought them."

"Until Saturday," James confirmed.

"Yes."

"What happened on Saturday?"

Helen stared at the table as if getting her thoughts in order, then she spoke in a measured tone. "Saturday was hectic. The caterers were installing the field kitchen. Deliveries came throughout the day. It was very busy." She looked directly at James as if waiting for him to question.

"I can imagine …and then what happened."

She gave a little disgusted snort. "Later in the day I found my wellingtons outside the kitchen door and they were filthy. I was so cross. I picked them up and practically threw them into the storeroom out of sight. I hadn't time to deal with them, and anyway why should I? I hadn't worn them but I intended to find out who had."

"Do you now know who borrowed them?" Philip interrupted.

"No, I don't. Things began to happen. I had more important jobs to do other than clean dirty wellies. If I'd known who took them I'd have given them a piece of my mind."

"Where were the Miltons?"

"Oh dear, it was bedlam here..."

"Think Helen, it's important."

"I don't know I didn't see either of them until she summoned me to check that all was running to plan. That must have been about six."

"What time was it when you found the wellingtons?"

"It was before that."

"Before six?" James clarified.

"Yes, I remember the florist had delivered the flowers. They arrived at four, and they were here for almost two hours. I noticed the boots as they were leaving. That must have been somewhere around five-thirty, five forty-five. Honestly James, I don't know. I had no reason to remember."

"That's good enough. Are the Miltons here?"

"No, they're in London. What's this all about, you're scaring me."

"It's nothing to worry about. Can I show Philip the wellingtons?"

"Of course, you know where they are. I'm going to have a brandy are you quite sure you won't join me?"

Philip smiled, "I'll join you, since I've decided to stay over."

"Are you having one, James?"

"All right, just a small one."

Helen took down three glasses and began to pour three brandies from her personal reserve while James took Philip into the storeroom.

"There they are," James pointed to the wellingtons.

"She's not lying, James," Philip whispered. "If that's what you wanted to ascertain. Talk about scaring the poor woman. If I'm thinking what you're thinking, then you are scaring me. You'll never prove it, and you need a motive."

"I know, and I've a good idea what it is. I need to talk to Harry."

"I'll cancel my appointments for tomorrow."

"Not tomorrow, maybe the day after, I want to take this slowly. If I show my hand too soon I might blow it."

"See your point."

When they got back to the kitchen Helen was already sipping brandy, her face now flushed with its warmth.

"Helen, I want you to do something for me."

"If I can."

"Don't touch those Wellingtons. I'll have them removed tomorrow."

"What's this all about? Can't you take them now?"

"I'm afraid not, I don't…"

"You don't want your fingerprints found on them."

"You could say that."

She let out a little gasp. "Is this about Eve or that little boy?"

"I'm not sure it's about anything yet."

"What about my fingerprints? They're all over them." Her voice was now raised in panic. "Perhaps the person who used them left them at my kitchen door to implicate me."

"I don't think so. You'll not be implicated in anyway. There's no need to be concerned. I have a theory and I want to test it, that's all."

"Perhaps someone just borrowed them. You were busy so they didn't mention it. Nothing more sinister than that," Philip added.

"You're probably right." Realising it could have happened that way she sat bolt upright. "Huh! The cheek of it," she exclaimed. "They could have at least washed the bloody things and not left them for me to do."

Chapter 19 - Dupton

After they had managed to get the trunk into James' study, Philip stood grinning as he rubbed his hands together. "Here goes, the moment of truth. All our questions are about to be answered," he said as he lifted the lid.

"Oh, very droll…"

They sat on the floor alongside each other, and began to lift out book after book. With trepidation they turned the pages, this time examining them in greater detail.

Time passed quickly. Some were written in French and others in calligraphy. It was a slow and painful task trying to decipher the writing and the language. Most books appeared to be ancient medical reference books.

Nearing the bottom of the trunk James came across a large, heavy ledger. It was a book of accounts dating back to when Moxley Manor was built. In it were lists of materials used and alongside were the prices. The cost of labour and the time it took to complete each task was also meticulously recorded. The building had taken three years and seven months to complete. That was eighty years before the King bestowed it on the women called

Dupton.

"This trunk is an historical gold mine," Philip remarked closing a book. "I'm going to take a look at the scrolls."

"Take care, they're fragile and could easily disintegrate. The last thing we want is to be left with a pile of dust."

"They look strong enough."

"Looks can be deceiving."

"You're quite right," Philip said as he helped himself to a roll of paper secured by a pink ribbon. He opened it. James did the same with another. "What's yours about?" he asked.

"Haven't a clue. I can't make any sense of it." James retied it and unwound another one. Philip continued doing the same.

"I don't think we're going to learn anything tonight. We need an expert to examine these."

"I agree." Philip said, but he was reluctant to stop, and continued working his way through the scrolls. He came to one that felt heavier than the others. He slowly began to unwind it. His eyes widened, he caught his breath, which made him cough.

"You okay?" James asked.

"Yes," he gasped. "You're not going to believe this..."

The scroll was written in calligraphy, a priceless work of art. After the text, it revealed witness signatures and a prominent wax seal. "James, this is a seal of some importance, I wonder..."

James leaned across and took a closer look. "It looks very official." Philip laid it on the floor and carefully secured each corner with a book to stop it from rolling back. Such a force could cause the scroll to rip. "Can you understand it? You're the Lawyer. You're used to reading legal documents."

"Hum…"

"Look!" Philip pointed to the word, Dupton.

James was deep in concentration. "You're right and look here, Moxley Manor, and here the word, feminine. I recognise the words 'in perpetuity' and 'gratitude'. There's a lot of legal jargon. The document is signed Charles, followed by the Kings seal. I need time to decipher it." James read a little more, and then looking across at Philip said, "This, my good friend, is a document signed by the King, giving Moxley Manor to the women named, Dupton, and this," James said with an uncontrollable grin as he pointed to the red seal, "is the King's very own seal."

Philip burst out laughing. "I don't believe it, it's incredible, this proves the journal."

"It certainly does." James leaned against the trunk and smiled a smile of satisfaction. "Phew – this calls for a drink," he said.

"You can say that again."

"Come, I think we'd better leave it to the experts. There's nothing more we can do tonight."

They returned the books and scrolls to the trunk and retired to the sitting-room where Philip accepted a large brandy.

"It's been quite an evening. So …where do we go from here?" Philip asked.

"I'll get in touch with the British Museum. If they

can't do the translation, they'll certainly know someone who can."

"What about Northumbria University?"

"Possibly – they are local." James stretched his legs and took a sip of his drink. "You've given me quite a problem, Philip."

"Oh…"

"All this reincarnation stuff. I was trying not to take any of it seriously. Having said that, tonight one question I wrestled with, has been answered."

"Oh, what was that?"

"Eve's name."

The creases on Philip's forehead deepened. "What do you mean, Eve's name?"

"It's the Law. I don't remember when it was changed. In the past, when a woman married, she took her husband's surname."

"They still do."

"Not all women, they're not legally bound to these days."

"So …what are you saying?" Philip asked.

"Celestine DuPont, Eve Dupton, we know that the women came to England from France in 1636. DuPont is notably a French name. Reluctant to sever their ties with France, they altered it to Dupton. Simple change and it sounded more English, wouldn't you agree?"

"Yes, so how come after all these centuries, they still carry the same name."

"Never gave it a thought."

"Well I had."

"Go on…"

"The answer is in the document. The King gave the property to the women Dupton, in perpetuity. In the past, when a woman married, she promised to obey. She not only lost her own will to her husband, she also lost control of her wealth. The husband took over all aspects of her life."

"To spend her money as he liked."

"Exactly. They kept their name and any future husband had to accept the terms, or the women would lose the property. No doubt we'll find other legal documents saying that the husbands waived all rights."

Philip laughed. "The King was certainly grateful to those women."

"He was and he protected them from money-grasping men."

"It certainly makes sense. Maybe there weren't any husbands, only lovers."

"Maybe, their nearest neighbour was miles away. They could behave as they liked. In those days, any sort of employment, would have been a gift from God, so I doubt any of their staff would gossip."

They drank in silence. Philip was the first to speak.

"I got carried away with the contents of the trunk I forgot to ask. Tell me about Helen's wellingtons. Why were you so interested in them? Have they found a print?"

"I'm pretty sure they have. Why else would Blackwell take their shoes?"

"Hmm… What can you do about it? The police are not going to confide in you. You're one of their suspects, remember."

James chuckled. "Reg has already put me in prison. He told me he'd find a way to smuggle in tools, so I could escape."

Philip laughed. "Maybe a spade, then you could dig your way out."

James gave Philip *the look.* "Helen's wellingtons are for elimination purposes, or not, as the case may be."

"What if they did match, it would send the investigation in an entirely different direction. Hmm... I see where you're going with this – interesting."

"Exactly, I'm also waiting to hear from an old friend. I'm hoping it'll prove something else I've been pondering on."

"Would you like to share it with me?"

James cast his eyes away. "Not just yet." Philip drained his drink and stood. "In that case I'm off to bed. I have to leave early in the morning. I'm a patient man. I can wait. I spend my whole life waiting for my patients to open up and talk."

"As soon as I make any sense of it Philip, you'll be the first to know. Deal?"

"Deal."

"I'm only sorry you had to come all this way for nothing. I should have known Blackwell would never have agreed to your interviewing Holly. Anyway, they're both home and that's the main thing."

"I wouldn't have missed going through those scrolls for the world. I've learned a lot tonight."

"We both have."

"Keep me in touch and don't do anything stupid. We need you to work on the Retreat. You can't do that from behind bars." Philip was grinning at the thought as he went off to bed.

"I'll try not to. Good night."

Chapter 20 – The Police

James walked into Police Headquarters at nine-thirty.

The officer manning the desk was called Metcalf who he knew well.

"Good morning Sir James. Inspector Blackwell is not here at present. She's instructed me to ask you to wait in interview room 3."

"I'm here to give a statement, can't you take it?" James noticed the expression on Metcalf's face. "I know, I understand, you're only following orders. I'll make my own way."

Metcalf nodded. "Would you like a cup of tea?" He called after him.

"What! You know you can't make tea, I'll have a coffee: milk, no sugar." Knowing the lay-out of the station James went into interview room 3. No change. No window, one table and three uncomfortable chairs. James groaned and sat down. Metcalf arrived with his coffee.

"How long is Her Highness going to be?"

"I don't know. She doesn't confide in me."

James glanced at his watch, it was nine-thirty-two. Ten minutes and no longer, that's all he would give her.

Five minutes had past when James decided he was wasting time. He went to the reception desk and asked officer Metcalf for a pad on which to write his statement. Metcalf bit his lip.

"Come on, hand one over, someone can type it up later. I can also sign it later there's no panic."

Metcalf shrugged and reluctantly gave James what he asked for. James returned to the interview room and began to write. Almost immediately there was a knock at the door. It opened and James was expecting to see Blackwell, it was Metcalf.

"There's someone asking for you," he said.

"Oh?"

"A Reg Atkinson. If you want to see him, I'll send him down."

"Yes please." James had concluded his daily meeting with Reg only an hour ago. What could have happened, in the meantime, to warrant his coming to the station?

Moments later Reg walked into the room. "What's the problem?" James asked.

"No problem. I was coming into Meedon Bridge anyway. This fax came through shortly after you left. I guessed you'd want to see it, as soon as possible."

"Then I gather you have…" James said with a grin.

"Pretty juicy reading."

James knew who the fax was from and the timing couldn't have been better. "I appreciate it Reg, thanks."

"See you back at the ranch." He joked as James began to absorb the information. The fax was, as he guessed, from Colonel Martin Webster. "Where would we be without contacts?" James mumbled.

It was interesting reading.

Having worked her way up the ranks, Blackwell became assigned to the diplomatic protection squad. During that period, she gained all the qualifications necessary to enable her to advance to the rank of Inspector. She was disliked by many, but especially by those male officers prejudiced against what some still referred to as Dykes.

Being in the diplomatic protection group she came in contact with Sarah Milton, who at that time, was an MP. Later, she was assigned to Sarah, after she became the leader of the opposition. One month ago, she unexpectedly asked for a transfer, to the Vale of Stourbridge, for what she called personal reasons. This was granted without question and she left the Met almost immediately.

Her record showed that she was on the fast track. Great things were expected of her. The blurry picture Martin had attached was also interesting. There was no way either of them could ever deny their relationship. It was obvious why the Met didn't object to her transfer, they anticipated trouble.

"Well I never," James mused. He placed the fax on the table, looked again at the photograph then returned to writing his statement. When he was satisfied with it, he signed it, knowing he'd have to sign the typed copy later. He left the room.

"Is Harry in," he asked Metcalf as he handed the pad to him.

"No, he was in early this morning, and then he left in a hurry."

James was disappointed. However, there was nothing he could do about it. "Tell Blackwell, that I waited half-an-hour, giving her twenty more minutes than I would have given anyone else. If she wants me, she knows where to find me."

"Not too sure I'll say that but I get the gist," Metcalf couldn't refrain from grinning.

The outer door was flung back and Harry stormed into the station. "Ah, the man himself…" James said before Harry cut him off.

"Not now James." He growled as he continued down the corridor. James took no notice and followed him into his office.

"What's up with you today?"

"Too much. I haven't got time for this now, James."

"I suggest you make time."

Harry made a guttural sound as he flopped into his chair. "Make it quick," he groaned.

James took the chair on the opposite side of his brother's desk. "I want you to do something for me."

Harry's lips tightened as he glared at his brother over glasses that he didn't wear.

"I'm guessing that Blackwell has found a footprint where Billy Bradshaw entered the river." Harry didn't reply, making it obvious to James that it was true. "I want you to go up to Moxley Manor and collect a pair of wellington boots from Helen, she is expecting you."

"What the hell are you talking about? I've got better things to do than collect your boots."

"Just listen, will you. Helen has a pair of wellingtons, which she has never worn since the day she bought them, a decade ago."

"So…?"

"On the evening of Sarah Milton's reception, they appeared outside the kitchen door, caked in mud. This was around 6pm."

"My, my, what do we have here, the crime of the century? What do you expect me to do about it? Clean them."

"Harry, you're embarrassing yourself." James chastised. "Billy went missing around that time. Someone borrowed those wellingtons. I think you should see if it matches the print Blackwell found. Also, if forensics finds any traces of clay it will prove in which direction the person who borrowed them went. There's only one vein of clay running down to the river within a mile of Moxley Manor and that is between Moxley Manor and the apiary. It will tell you if the wearer went to the apiary."

"Must I keep reminding you, this is a police investigation? We don't need any do-gooders interfering. For God's sake keep out of it and let Blackwell do her job."

"Do I have to remind you that I was recommended for a knighthood by the Northumberland Police, and – I was made an honorary member of the police force? A rare accolade. I'm not trying to interfere. Like any good citizen, I'm helping the police with their enquiries."

Harry leaned forward and with his elbows on his desk held his head in his hands. "You drive me insane," with his lips tight he stared across the desk at his brother.

James rolled his eyes and tutted. "I'm trying to help

here…"

"I know that." Harry began to shake his head as he stared at his brother. "Do you realise what you're saying?"

"Yes, I'm saying that someone from the Manor could have been at the scene when Billy entered the water. The only people at the Manor at that time were Helen, who never went out that day, the caterers, a couple of gardeners, Sarah Milton and her brother and two florists. You see where I'm going with this? If the heel print matches, Blackwell will be forced to extend her investigation. There's no way, she'll have the wellingtons tested, on a theory of mine, because she'll not want to take the investigation to Moxley Manor."

Harry glared at his brother in sheer frustration. "I'll put someone on it."

"No Harry, it must be you. I don't think we should mention this to anyone, not yet."

The room fell silent, the air still. Harry then spoke. "James, I can't help you."

"For God's sake Harry. These wellingtons need to be examined and these people need to be interviewed. Are you going to ignore this and let Blackwell ruin a little girl's life. She's trying to incriminate Becky or Holly. You know damned well that's her intention."

Leaning back in his chair with his eyes darting from side to side and with his lips pressed firmly together Harry sat, thinking. He eventually spoke. "Why would Blackwell want to incriminate either one of them?"

"She wants a quick result."

"She's not that desperate, and she's anything but

stupid."

"Holly found Eve's body, she was covered in blood, and it was Holly who was the last person to see Billy alive."

Harry nodded in agreement. "It's not that I don't want to help you, I can't."

"Of course you can. What the hell do you mean by, can't…?"

"I'm to have nothing to do with the case."

"What!"

"Do I have to repeat myself? I'm to have nothing to do with the case. It's entirely Blackwell's case and she is to report directly to the Super. That's why I wasn't in earlier, I was summoned."

"You have got to be joking," James emphasised every word. He found it difficult to believe what he was hearing.

"I wish I were."

"This doesn't make sense. What happened?"

"The Super thinks I'm too close to the case, and it would be better for all concerned if I left Blackwell to it. She's new to the area; she's come from the Met, and will deal with the case sympathetically and more importantly, objectively."

"That's a laugh – she hasn't so far."

"Maybe not."

"He's been got at," James growled.

"Don't be so ridiculous. You're sounding as if there's some sort of conspiracy going on. Anyway I'm going to take a few days off."

"That's crazy! Do you think for one minute that the

rest of your officers won't put two and two together? They'll never believe it. You: taking a holiday during such a high profile case. The first murder we've had in the valley for years?"

"I've no choice and it's not a holiday. I have to read a paper at a conference in Leeds on Tuesday. It was arranged last year. It's been decided that I take tomorrow and Friday off to prepare my paper. Monday, I travel to Leeds. Tuesday is the conference, followed by a big dinner. I'll stay over, and come back on Wednesday."

"I see. Perhaps the Super is hoping that, if she's given enough rope, she'll hang herself?" James was seeing another side to this.

"Maybe, or perhaps the Super is the one pushing her. I have every intention of looking into her connections, someone, somewhere, must know something James. I have to take this slowly."

"I understand." James began to laugh. "And you talk to me about imagining a conspiracy. The difference is, I'm not thinking there's a conspiracy, Harry, I know. Here, read this." James handed over the fax that Reg had brought to the station only minutes earlier.

"Where did you get this?"

"From an old friend."

"Huh, you've got it in for Blackwell, haven't you?"

"I don't recall your being thrilled at the prospect of working with her until you retire. I recall you wishing her gone. If you want another opinion of the woman, ask Nicky."

"How did your *old friend* get this information?"

"Policing, security it's the same all over. He has

contacts at the highest level in most political and security organisations."

Harry was shaking his head as he read. "I still don't know what the problem is. So, she's a lesbian; she has friends in high places. We all know she's on the fast track."

"Fast track, Harry, come on now? Then why come to the Valley?"

"To broaden her experience and to become proficient in all aspects of policing," Harry said in a patronizing, superior, tone while trying to keep a straight face. "That's what the Super told me the day before she arrived."

"Think about it, Harry. If you were on the fast track, would you want to come and work in the Valley? No, you'd want to be where the action was, and that's in the Met.

"When Sarah Milton first set eyes on the Manor she made up her mind to settle here. In her naivety, I believe she thought that by living here they could keep their affair a secret. It was Milton who was behind Blackwell's transfer."

"Are you saying, Sarah Milton and …Blackwell?"

"I am."

"Phew… I wasn't expecting that. Times have changed James, whether you like it or not. Anyway you have no proof. It's all hearsay – rumour, gossip, call it whatever you like."

In frustration James leaned back in his chair. After a moment he shot forward and banged the palm of his hands on the edge of Harry's desk and stared across at his brother. "On the night of Sarah Milton's reception, I was making my way around the room talking to various people. A shadow shot across the window, it was someone in a hurry. It was cold and dark out. Being the inquisitive person that I am, I moved closer to the window. This was shortly before Sarah made her appearance in the Hall and began working the room.

"There are lamps at intervals lighting the footpath around the perimeter of the building. I saw Sarah talking to someone. She was gently rubbing that person's arm as if to comfort them. Seconds later she kissed that person on the lips, rubbed the arm again, then left and made her way back inside, to start courting the likes of you and me. The person she was talking to had their back to me. I watched that person hurry away. I recognised that back. It was Blackwell."

"You actually saw Blackwell and our *prime minster in waiting*, kissing. You have to be joking." Harry was now laughing.

"You can laugh. I don't think her private life matters a jot, but I'm not sure the people of the United Kingdom are quite ready to vote for a lesbian prime minster. If she wins the next election and does a good job, then I believe the nation won't give a damn what she is. She will then be free to introduce her partner to the public. In the meantime, she's keeping it very quiet."

"It sounds like a plan. You should have become a detective instead of a marine?"

"Too boring," James laughed. "If it's proof you needed, well now you have it. If you want more proof take a look at this…" He handed over the photograph. "It's a bit grainy because it was taken on a rainy night, through a window. Imagine if one of the tabloids got a hold of it. It's called deception, Harry. She should come out of the closet and take her chances."

"Single sex partnerships are acceptable these days." Harry's tone portrayed his own personal doubt.

"Are they? Not with a lot of people, whether they admit it or not. What I saw through the window on Saturday night happened. I believe that after Blackwell had spoken with Carol Bradshaw, and learned that Holly was the last person to see her son, she came up to Moxley Manor. She came to report to her real Boss to get instructions before going to see Becky and Holly."

"I still can't do anything, James. If the Super thinks I've ignored him and am continuing to involve myself in the case well – it's not going to go down too well for me."

"I don't think you should, not for the moment. What you can do is get those wellingtons now and take them to forensics, before people find out you're off on holiday."

"I've explained that," Harry snapped. "I'm going to a conference."

James ignored his brother and continued. "Tell forensics they were forgotten and put them with Holly and Becky's shoes. We need to match that print. We need a soil analysis and fingerprints. Fingerprints found on the wellingtons are important. No one needs to know anything about this, until the results are back."

"For God's sake stop telling me what to do," Harry glared at his brother and then groaned. "I could lose my job over this."

"From where I'm sitting I think you already have."

"Great, thanks for that."

"Don't worry about your career. You'll get promotion if what's happening is what I think is happening."

"Really… Are you sure you don't have anything else you'd like to tell me?" Harry tipped his head to one side and gave James the same glare he had earlier, when he peered over the rim of a pair of glasses he didn't wear.

"I think you've had enough for one day."

"You had better be right about this. If not, I suggest you emigrate and take with you those thrillers you enjoy reading so much."

James grinned. "Once a big brother, always a big brother."

"I'm forty-six. I can look after myself," Harry barked emphatically as he stormed across the room. "I'm going to need Helen's fingerprints for elimination," he said as he opened the door.

"She won't object," James replied, following his brother out of the room and down the corridor.

The sound of Blackwell's footsteps resonated towards him and her voice was getting louder as she shouted instructions to an officer who was obviously following her. Their heavy footsteps were coming from his left proceeding in the direction of interview room 3.

Harry had reached a side door, which led to the car park, and he held it open for his brother. James took it from him, and quietly closed the door behind them. Without a word and only a brief wave of an arm both men made for their respective cars.

Chapter 21 – The Rat's Hole

The Rat's Hole, on the outskirts of the village of Meedon Bridge, was his nearest watering hole. The landlady, Mona, was a great cook and he wondered what was on today's menu. Maybe a roast, or steak and kidney pie, or maybe it would be grilled salmon, whatever it was, it would be good.

It was a small, typically cosy, country pub, with ivy covering the two storey building. The décor gleamed with polished brass. Adorning the walls were photographs of farm animals, taken at various country shows and sepia photographs of farmers and their families taken alongside ancient machinery, depicting times gone by,

Since Mona and Jim had taken over the pub little had altered. The chairs and tables were made of dark wood with spindly legs and backs. The only noticeable changes were the curtains and cushions. Mona had kept to the same theme, only using brighter and more modern colours.

One thing they had refrained from doing was to paint the walls or smoke-stained ceiling, as it kept the old ambiance. The changes were subtle and this pleased some of the regulars, but it was still not to everyone's taste. The locals objected to change of any kind.

The grassy garden, with its benches and colourful umbrella's, sloped down to the river. In the summer months The Rat's Hole was inundated with day trippers and holiday makers, this also, didn't go down too well with the regular clientele.

He parked his car and went inside. The entrance was in the centre of the property. To his right was a small bar seating about twenty people. It had an open fire, which today was not lit. He noticed one man perched on a stool at the bar, and four men drinking beer and playing cards at a round table. A man and a woman were eating a sandwich and drinking lager at another table.

The bar to his left was slightly larger and more comfortable. A middle-aged couple sat in the corner and a young couple sat on the window seat, admiring the view across the river. An elderly man sat alone, in what was obviously his usual chair, besides the unlit fire. Jim would be lighting it in a day or two, as the days were getting colder, and the nights were drawing in. The fires in both bars would stay lit throughout the winter until the following spring. A central bar served both rooms. He chose to turn left.

James pulled himself onto a high stool at the bar. Mona beamed when she saw him. She was small and slim, around five-three he imagined. She had short, curly, brown hair and hazel eyes and, as always, her face was made up to perfection. Today she wore black slacks with a red jumper, looked relaxed and very pretty.

"Hello James, it's been a while," she spoke with a delicate Highland-Scottish accent.

"I've been rather…"

Mona cut him off. "We know. It must have been a terrible shock for you. Jim and I couldn't believe it when we heard. Eve was such a lovely lady and so young."

James nodded.

"What can I get for you?"

"A half, please. I've a lot to do this afternoon. What's on the menu today?"

"Today's special is braised shoulder of lamb."

"Perfect. What sort of potatoes?"

"Roast," Mona said as she picked up a glass, pulled half a pint of bitter, and handed it to James.

"Even better, I love your roast potatoes."

"Jim does too, that's how I've managed to keep him all these years." She giggled as she spoke. "I'll be as fast as I can. Are you eating it here or in the restaurant?" Without waiting for an answer she had disappeared into the kitchen.

"Here will do fine," he called after her.

James leaned across and reached for a complimentary newspaper that was hanging from a rack on the side of the bar, and he began to read.

He heard the entrance door open and two men walked in. They went into the bar on the right and leaned on the counter. Jim appeared from nowhere and began to pour two pints of bitter.

James glanced across the bar at the two men; he hadn't seen either of them before. It appeared that this was not their first pint of the day.

Jim was a huge man, twice the size of his petite wife Mona. He was about the same age as James. He'd been a rugby player in his youth and still kept himself in shape. Muscles bulged beneath his bright-green shirt. No one in their right mind would dare to tackle Jim.

Mona arrived with his food. He unrolled his knife and fork from the paper napkin, and began to eat. Home cooking, how he missed Jean's cooking.

Jim was talking to the two men and James overheard the word, *Billy*.

He looked again at the men who were in their thirties. He wondered what they were doing drinking, in a pub, at this time of day.

He had to accept that the main topic of conversation in the Valley, over the past week, would have been about Eve's murder, and now little Billy Bradshaw's death.

One of the men leaned to his left, to peer across at him from the other room and then, before James realised, he had walked through into the bar, where James was eating, and leaned casually on the end of the counter.

"So," he snarled. "You're the bloke."

"I'm sorry, do I know you?"

"You're the bloke that done in my little Billy."

"Excuse me?"

"You done in Billy, good kid were our Billy. Just because ye posh and we ain't – don't think ye goin' to gerr away with it."

The man's face had darkened, his thick, bushy eyebrows had bunched together and a tiny sliver of spittle trickled from the corner of his taut mouth.

"What the hell do you think you're doing?" Jim

demanded.

"You said he found Billy."

"Yes I did, and I imagined you might like to thank him. If it were not for him, Billy would be in the North Sea by now."

"I'll thank him, all right," the man slurred as he stealthily slid closer to James, his teeth clenched. "It was you, you done him in," he repeated.

Ignoring the man, James piled another forkful of lamb, smothered in mint gravy, into his mouth. He didn't see the man tighten his fist and pull his right arm back. Within a split second the man let it fly. His fist caught James on the left side of his head forcing him off his stool, which tipped over and fell to the floor.

As James reached out to steady himself, his right arm collided with his plate and sent it skidding along the counter top. It fell to the floor and smashed into pieces. Lamb, peas, beans, carrots and potatoes flew in all directions. Blobs of gravy covered the front of the bar and the thick brown liquid bounced off the floor.

Quickly composing himself, James shot to his right avoiding another fist as it flew towards his head. He blocked the attempt with his right arm. This made the man even madder. He took another swing at James and missed.

"That's enough, Green." Jim shouted.

When the man tried to strike a fourth time, James caught his wrist and twisted it up behind his back, making pain shoot up his arm. Green yelped like an animal caught in a trap. He had not anticipated such a response, or strength from an older man.

James frogmarched him across the room knocking over more chairs as his captive fought for release,

The events of the past week had caught up with James and he was not in the mood to take any more nonsense. In retaliation, with his free hand, he took hold of the man's head and crashed it against the wall. "Gerr off... Gerr off. You broke my nose," he yelped. "I'll sue. I will. I'll sue..." His voice trailed off as his nose and throat filled fast with blood.

Not forgetting the rules of engagement, James knew that the drunk couldn't take any more. He kept the snivelling man pinned against the wall, where blood dripped onto the floor, while he waited for help.

Jim had lifted the hinged top of the bar, and was charging across the room to reach them. His face was red, his eyes were narrowed and lips taut. He began to yell. "That's it, Dan Green! Out! You're barred, and this time it's for life. I made excuses for you on Saturday. No more my lad. Out!"

Jim relieved James of his attacker and, holding both Green's arms tightly behind his back, he frog-marched him towards the door.

The door to the Rat's Hole opened, and Inspector Blackwell walked through, followed by an officer who neither James nor Jim had seen before.

"What the hell's going on here?" she demanded.

Hands on hips, she surveyed the room. Food strewn over the floor, tables and chairs overturned. She strode towards the three men. "Sir James, I repeat, what is going on?" Turning to Jim she said, "Mr erm... Let that man go."

"He assaulted me," Dan Green whimpered looking at James.

Jim let go of Dan Green and stepped back. "That's not true, Inspector." Jim was shaking his head in disgust and said, "You really are a piece of shit. Lying now, something else you're good at."

"It's true Inspector, he assaulted me, this guy…" Green snorted as he pointed to James. "See, my nose, it's broken," he mumbled pathetically, wiping blood away from his face, with the back of his hand. "They're sticking together; it's like that in these God forsaken parts."

Mona arrived stony faced. She carried a mop and bucket and a bundle of old newspapers along with a roll of cleaning cloths and began to clean up the mess. "I'll help you with that Mona," James offered.

"No you won't," Blackwell barked. "You were supposed to give me a statement this morning."

Mona raised her eyes in disgust at the woman's tone. "It's quite all right, James. I can manage. In this line of business, I've had to clean up far worse."

Blackwell raised her eyebrows, cocked her head, she was waiting for an answer from James.

"I did."

"You did?"

"As you ordered, I was at HQ at nine-thirty, precisely. I waited until ten. Since you had obviously forgotten our appointment, I gave my statement to the officer manning the desk and left."

"I… I've not had the chance…"

James knew she was lying. He'd heard her walk down

the corridor towards interview room '3'. Did she expect him to believe that she hadn't demanded an explanation from the officer at the desk?

An inebriated Dan Green, slurred, "Arrest him, why don't you arrest him?"

"Oh my God," Jim groaned as he waved his arms around the lounge gesturing to the young couple sitting on the window bench, then to the other couple in the corner, who looked as if they were stuck to their seats. He also indicated the old man sitting by the fire, with his pint in front of him, taking it all in, and enjoying every moment. "There are enough independent witnesses here to tell you exactly what happened, Inspector.

"I'd be grateful if you'd leave so we can clear up. Please take this scum-bag with you. I don't want to see him in my pub again."

Blackwell stared at the rapidly, materialising bruise, on the side of James' face. "If it's true, and this man here did assault you, do you wish to place charges?"

"Not under the circumstances, he's obviously distraught over the death of his step-son."

"That's very gracious of you," she said, her voice riddled with sarcasm. "It looks as if I arrived in the nick of time before things really got out of hand." She'd made a joke and she didn't realise. "I was on my way to see you when I recognised your BMW in the car park."

"Oh…"

"Forensics have completed their work. Your friend's body can now be released."

"Best news I've heard in days, thank you."

Inspector Blackwell and the other officer left The

Rat's Hole taking Dan Green with them. She mumbled something about having wanted to talk to him. James wasn't interested and also decided to leave.

"I'm so sorry about this, Mona."

"Don't go James, go into the restaurant and I'll plate you up another portion," she said as she replaced the mop in her bucket.

"I've lost my appetite, thanks anyway. I've got things to arrange now."

Mona understood. "Will you let us know when you have a date for the funeral?"

"I will." He placed a couple of twenties on the bar and walked towards the door.

"I don't want those, James." Her eyes widened.

"Oh yes you do. You have a business to run, and now you have to buy more crockery."

Chapter 22 — Honey Pot Lane

The sky was overcast. There was a distinct chill in the air as James drove to Honey Pot Lane; at least it was not raining.

He reached the row of six cottages as Carol Bradshaw was walking down her path lugging a huge suitcase. He pulled to a stop as she opened the gate and threw the case out into the lane. It came to rest against the low wall bordering her cottage. James wound down the window.

"Going somewhere, Carol?"

"No."

"How are you feeling today?"

She had the same clothes on as she had on the day before, and the day before that. She'd probably slept in them. Her unmade-up face was blotchy and swollen; the whites of her eyes remained red. How much crying can one person do?

"It doesn't get any better, James. If it's not one thing it's another." He glanced at the case. "They're Dan's things?" she said. "I don't want to set eyes on the man again for as long as I live."

"I gather he's not being supportive?"

"Huh! Inspector Blackwell came to see me earlier. They've found a lot of marks on Billy's body. Bruises. They appear to have been administered over a period of time. About the time Dan moved in. Now I know why he insisted in helping him at bath time, male bonding is what he called it. What he was doing was stopping me from seeing them."

James' hands gripped the steering wheel as he pictured the man whose nose he had just broken.

"I realise now why Billy has been acting strangely, staying out longer than usual. All sorts of little things have added up to one big one. God love my child."

James showed Carol the manifesting bruise on the left side of his face. "He did this to me about half an hour ago."

"He did what! I don't believe it... Why?"

"He was told that I found Billy's body and he decided that I'd killed him."

"The fool."

"He was drunk, Carol."

"He's always drunk." She took in a shuddering breath. "I've been such a fool. What if Billy's death wasn't an accident and he, he…"

"Now now, don't go jumping to conclusions, we'll know soon enough. The police have him at the station as we speak. They'll get to the truth. Does Dan have a key?"

Before Carol could answer, a small, white van pulled to a stop behind him. There was a picture of a lock and key on its side and the words beneath it read, 'Craymore

Locksmith' followed by a telephone number, a mobile number and a website address.

"I know what you're thinking." She nodded towards the van.

James smiled. "Good. I'll leave you to it, just remember, if you need anything."

"I know, I'll call."

He parked opposite the apiary and crossed the lane, entering the yard through the open five-bar-gate. He hesitated before continuing to the visitors' entrance.

It was very quiet.

There wasn't anyone manning the reception desk, so he walked along the corridor and into the café. It was lunch-time; busy with people eating soup, quiches and salads or baked potatoes with various toppings, that sort of thing.

All appeared to be in order.

Neither Becky nor Clare was there.

Joan sidled past him carrying a plate of honeyed scones. "They've been out. Got back about fifteen minutes ago," she said.

After putting the scones down on table '5' she returned to behind the counter and busily began to pour mugs of coffee.

James followed her, "How's it going?" he asked.

"No problems."

"Call me if..."

"I will."

He nodded, smiled at her, and left.

He crossed the courtyard and knocked on the familiar kitchen door.

"Hello James, it's a good thing you didn't come earlier, we've only just got in. We went to Butts Farm to get some meat." Becky said as she began to fill the kettle.

"Joan told me you'd been out. For a change, I'm the bearer of good news," he said, as he pulled a chair away from the kitchen table and sat.

"What's this? Did I hear you say, good news?" Clare remarked as she entered the kitchen. On seeing James her jaw dropped and her eyes widened. "Good grief! James, what have you done to your face? You look awful."

"Thanks for that, Clare. I had an altercation with Dan Green."

"Dan Green! What about?"

"He accused me of murdering Billy."

"You're joking! What gave him that idea?" Clare began to laugh at the thought.

"You found the body," Becky interjected. "Now we know for certain, he's an idiot."

"He was drunk."

"Isn't he always…"

"We were in The Rat's Hole. Blackwell arrived in the middle of it."

"That woman seems to be everywhere."

"She has a job to do. You will, however, be pleased to hear that we can go ahead and make arrangement for Eve's funeral."

Becky flopped down in the chair next to James. "At last. For the past week I've had the most awful nightmares." James grinned.

"It's no joke, James. They're horrible. I was beginning to think that there was a message in them."

"Which was…"

"That Eve was trying to tell me to hurry up and get her funeral over and done with, so she can move on."

"It hasn't been very pleasant for any of us."

"I bet you haven't had nightmares."

"No, not exactly. Perhaps you'd like to tell me about them, if you think it'll help. That way they might stop."

Becky smiled. "Oh …I've heard that from someone else, a long time ago. If you talk about a recurring dream it will stop." She laughed. "Let's give it a try. I warn you, this one isn't very nice. It begins with Eve lying in the middle of rows and rows of dead bodies. They stretched way out into infinity. It was impossible to reach her. I wanted to get to her to bring her home. It was horrible, pale faces and staring eyes and then hands rose up trying to stop me," she shuddered.

"There's more than one body needing to be dealt with – rising hands, the police delaying the funeral – you could be right. The sooner we have the funeral, the better."

The kettle had boiled. "Tea James?" Clare asked.

"Not for me I've a lot to do. I came because I need to know if there is any day next week, that's not convenient for you. I don't want to clash with anything going on here. I'd like to close the apiary on that day."

"I can answer that without checking. We have nothing booked at all. The schools have only just reopened after the summer holidays. It'll take a week or so before they start planning their outdoor adventures."

"Good. Do you have a preferred day?"

"No, surely it will depend on the availability of St Mark's."

"You're probably right. I'll let you know as soon as I've spoken with Reverend Broadbent."

James left.

Chapter 23 – Broadbent

Reverend Arthur Broadbent answered the door chewing a mouthful of food. "Hello James."

"Have I arrived at a bad time? I can call back if it's not convenient," James replied.

"Nonsense, I've just finished lunch – do come in."

Loud footsteps disturbed the quiet as the two men walked on old, highly polished, oak floorboards. James followed the clergyman into a bright sitting-room at the rear of the rectory. Through the patio window a large well-manicured garden could be seen, now, sadly, the worse for wear after the vicious storm of over a week ago.

The room was light and airy with colourful chintz-covered armchairs that James had often sat on, drinking an aperitif with Jean, after the Sunday morning service and before a splendid lunch cooked by Maureen, his housekeeper. He took the chair by the window.

"Can I offer you something, a drink?"

"No thank you," James replied.

"How about a coffee."

"I'm fine, honestly. I won't keep you."

"Then how can I be of help?"

"The police are releasing Eve's body."

"That's good news. So – we've a funeral to plan?"

"Yes, I don't have a date or time in mind. Whatever is convenient for you?"

"The sooner the better, I'd say," Arthur mumbled. "Maureen," he called. "Please bring me my diary I think it's on my desk."

James heard Maureen's unsteady footsteps and within seconds she had entered the room carrying the book. She was an elderly, grey-haired lady and had been housekeeper to the Reverend since he arrived fifteen years ago and also to his predecessor, Charles Wagstaff.

"Hello James, I overheard, you must be so relieved?"

"You can say that again."

"Does this mean they know what happened?" Maureen asked.

"I'm afraid not."

"Oh dear. The members of the Mothers' Union are quite disturbed; you wouldn't believe the stories that are circulating."

"I had heard."

"With a serial killer on the loose, people can't sleep. It's most worrying."

"I don't think the Mothers' Union has anything to be concerned about." James had heard about the wave of public panic; it was slowly engulfing the valley.

"Thank you for trying to put our minds at rest, James. I'm afraid that's not how they see it. If such a terrible thing can happen to people like Eve and little Billy, then it could happen to any one of us." With a weak smile she handed the diary to the Reverend and left the room.

He opened the book at the current week and, mumbling to himself, he turned the pages. "Next week," he said as he gave a little snort. "I'm afraid to ask. How many people are you expecting?"

"I have absolutely no idea," James shook his head. "Eve was well-known and well-loved, and when I think of the Bee Society, and the other organisations she was involved in," James groaned. "I can't begin to imagine."

"That's exactly what's going through my mind. It'll be standing room only. Never mind, we'll manage somehow, no one must be left out."

"I would never do that. I'll not restrict numbers. I'll inform people, and then it's entirely up to them whether or not they wish to attend."

"Will you be serving refreshments?"

"Yes, Eve would want me to. A lot of people will be coming from far afield. When we've agreed on a day, I'll call in at The Fallen Angel, it has the largest banqueting room in Meedon Bridge and it is within walking distance of the church."

"Good choice," Arthur said, nodding his head. Maureen entered carrying a tray. "Now you will have to join me," he said on noticing the two china cups Maureen had placed alongside a pot of coffee.

James thanked her as she poured and handed him a cup. He helped himself to cream.

"You implied that the police aren't any nearer to finding her killer?"

"That's right."

"Nasty business. Who'd have thought such a wicked thing could have happened to such a wonderful woman, and in our sleepy little valley. Do you have any idea as to the motive?"

"The only scenario that makes any sense is that she disturbed an intruder. For reasons we have yet to determine someone, passing through, panicked."

"If Eve had disturbed an intruder, don't you think that person would just have made a run for it?"

"Yes, that's something I don't understand. Why was it necessary to resort to violence? Eve was a tiny little thing. She couldn't possibly have looked threatening even if she had tried."

"What if someone was trying to steal her bees?" Arthur asked.

"If that had been the case, then and only then, Eve would have fought like a wild-cat to protect them. There was no evidence of a scuffle or fight.

"I've spoken to the secretary of the Bee society. Eve's honey consistently won prizes and I wondered if there was any jealously amongst their members. She said she would make discreet enquiries but I doubt anything will come of it."

"It may not have been a registered bee keeper."

"That's a thought. If that were the case, it could take an eternity to get to the truth."

"James – did Eve ever mention having a premonition of an early death?"

"Not that I know of." James' eyebrows knitted together as he contemplated the remark. "What do you mean? Did she say anything to you?"

"No, but I got the distinct feeling she was putting her house in order."

The codicil to Eve's will, filtered into James' mind.

"In all the years I've known Eve, she never once mentioned the family mausoleum, that was, until a few weeks ago."

"Good grief! I'd forgotten about the mausoleum. I've had so much on my mind, I've automatically been thinking of a grave and gravestones. What did she say?"

"Not a lot. It was more what she didn't say. I was on my way out, about a month ago now. I was making my way along the path towards the East gate when Eve caught up with me. We stood talking and she kept glancing across at the mausoleum. It's quite an impressive structure, if a little spooky. I'm not a fan of mausoleums, unlike the Scots. Suddenly she changed the subject and said, *'It needs a jolly good clean, it's quite frightening, no one should be frightened by death'.* Her remark took me by surprise."

"Then what?"

"That was all. When she'd gone I went back into the church and looked up our records. The last person to be entombed in the mausoleum was Eve's mother and that was before my time."

James nodded. "I remember. It was a month after Eve celebrated her twenty-first birthday. She said to me, thank God I'm an adult, if I'd been any younger I would have been put in a children's home, and then what would have happened to my bees?"

Reverend Broadbent laughed. "Ah, her bees, nothing could come between Eve and her bees. The strange thing is, James…" Arthur rested his elbow on the arm of his chair and rubbed his chin, as if deciding whether or not to continue.

"Go on," James urged.

"I took a more detailed look at the church records. Eve never married, nor had any children, which means that she was the last of her blood line. I found it strange that there was only one place left. When Eve takes that place, the mausoleum will be permanently sealed. Another thing I found to be strange was that all the people interned were women … and they all had the surname of Dupton. Generation after generation of women called Dupton, interesting wouldn't you say?"

James took a deep shaky breath and quickly said, "That's a story for another day, Arthur. What I do know is that everything to do with Eve was strange, wonderfully strange. Are you saying that she may have had a premonition about her death?"

"It was the expression on her face, as she looked at the mausoleum. I find it hard to explain, it was all very curious." Arthur pondered a moment. "There's a saying, I'm not sure of the exact wording, something like, someone just walked over my grave. That was how I felt as I looked at her."

James didn't want to continue this line of conversation. "Whatever it was, it's in the past. Now, you've given me a problem. How do I go about cleaning the stone? Preferably yesterday."

"Rather a tall order. I can give you the telephone number of a stonemason, if he can't help you, he should be able point you in the direction of someone who can."

"Thank you. I think it might have to be sandblasted," James mumbled.

"That's a specialist's job, it will be costly."

"I realise that. I'd still like it done. I'm going to have it done," he stressed, "…and, I've got one whole week."

When he was back, seated in his car, he called the number that the clergyman had given him. The man who answered didn't sound hopeful, that the cleaning of the mausoleum could be done in time. He did suggest that as it was so urgent, he might be able to bring men in from another part of the country, but that would be costly. James said that expense was no object.

His next call was to the local funeral parlour, the only funeral parlour within a radius of twenty miles. He made arrangements for them to collect Eve's body from the police forensic laboratory. He promised to call in to the funeral parlour the following day to choose a casket.

The date and time for the funeral was fixed for the next Thursday at 11a.m. He called Reverend Broadbent who agreed that Thursday was the best of the three choices he had been given. He called Becky and gave her the information.

He then drove to The Fallen Angel to make arrangements for refreshments to be served after the service.

Greg Renshaw, the manager, was a lithe young man full of enthusiasm. Although not knowing if he was to cater for one or five hundred was an enormous challenge, as James and Eve used to patronise The Fallen Angel on a regular basis, he was only too willing to take it on.

Greg opened the diary, which was lying on a lectern. He turned the pages to the following week. "You're in luck. Nothing is booked for next Thursday either for lunch or dinner. I'll close the banqueting suite. He drew two pencil lines across the page and wrote Sir James Marchant across the top. I imagine people will come and go so I'm sure we'll be able to manage."

"That's great, many thanks." With those few words, satisfied with the outcome, James left.

Chapter 24 — Sir James

Back at the farm James changed his clothes, took off his shoes, pulled on his riding boots then went down to the yard.

No one was about.

He saddled Taser and rode out, around the paddock, down the track and after forking right continued to ride up onto the moors.

A weak sun shone between thinly-scattered clouds.

The higher he rode the cooler it got and James kicked Taser into a gallop. The fresh air brushing his face cleared his head and he felt refreshed and ready to take on his next task. He still had to put a notice in the local paper, and `phone as many people as he could, to notify them of the time and place of Eve's funeral.

Reg was in the yard when he returned.

"Sorry I missed you, I was checking the last of the fences."

"Much to do?" James asked as he dismounted.

"Very little left to do. They stood up to the storm remarkably well." Reg took hold of Taser's reins. "I'll have someone attend to Taser."

"Thanks. The police are releasing Eve's body. The funeral will be next Thursday morning. I've arranged with The Fallen Angel to supply refreshments after the service."

Reg nodded. "At last things are moving. Have the police told you anything else?" Taser began to move impatiently. "Steady boy, steady,"

Reg comforted the animal as he tightened his hold on the reins.

"No, Blackwell is still treading the same old path."

"By now she should be taking her investigation farther afield. What does Harry have to say about it? I thought he would have got to the bottom of this by now."

"The problem is that there's so little to go on. Also, it's not Harry's case. He's off duty preparing for a conference in Leeds next week."

"You're joking …talk about priorities."

"It was arranged last year, apparently."

"The valley police are not experienced in solving murders. Don't you think they should have brought in CID, or whatever they're called these days?

"Oh, and Blackwell has been here questioning the lads. I'd say she's building a profile on you."

James laughed. "I'm not surprised, I'm still in the frame, remember? Reg, feel free to tell anyone you think who may be interested in the arrangements. I'm going to telephone now and see if I'm not too late to put an announcement in this week's Meedon Bridge News. Oh, and before I forget, next Thursday, all staff can have the day off, full pay and no strings."

"Thank you. I know one or two people who would

definitely like to go. Eve has helped a lot of families here in the valley. Is there anything I can do?"

"Thanks, but no thanks, I think I have everything covered."

It was five-thirty.

James held his head between his hands, ruffled his hair and scratched his scalp. His throat was dry, and his voice hoarse from talking. He again examined the list of V.I.P's names and hoped he hadn't left anyone out. From the positive responses he'd received so far he wondered if the church would be able to accommodate everyone.

He also wondered how Greg Renshaw would cope with the estimated numbers.

He pushed the chair away from his desk, stood and stretched. It was a moment or two before he could feel his legs. He stamped each foot on the floor then shook each leg in turn. Is the seizing up of one's extremities the first signs of ageing, he wondered?

Ella had left the daily newspapers on the hall table. He picked them up and stuffed them under his arm as he went into the family-room, which was warm. He poured himself a large brandy, topped it up with ginger and took a handful of cashew nuts from a small dish on the drinks tray. He popped them into his mouth and made himself comfortable in his favourite, leather, high-backed chair.

What a day?

Taking a large gulp of his drink he slowly began to unwind. He opened *The Times*, and had just begun to read when his mobile vibrated in his trouser pocket. He had half a mind to let it go to answerphone but decided against it. It was his brother.

"Hi. Harry."

"Are you at home?"

"Yes."

"Anyone with you?"

"No."

"Okay if I come over?"

"Fine by me."

"I'll be with you in fifteen."

Chapter 25 – Harry

Harry arrived exactly fifteen minutes after his phone call.

"I guess you're finished for the day," James said on opening the door. He led his brother into the family sitting-room.

"Yes, and what a day," Harry complained.

"Drink," James asked, as his brother flopped into the winged chair opposite the chair he was sitting on.

"Please… whatever you're having."

James poured another brandy and topped it up with ginger. He handed it to his younger brother saying, "I hope this is about the wellingtons?"

Harry gave a little snort of pleasure. "After leaving you I went to collect them from Helen, as you ordered." He said with sarcasm in his voice. "I took them to forensics. I put them alongside the other shoes, which luckily, still hadn't been worked on.

"I told Greenwood that they had been left in the boot of the officers' car, and swore, *Bloody rookies*. I explained to him that the matter was urgent. I needed to be the first to know. He agreed and said he would work on them after lunch. He said it shouldn't take too long.

"About an hour ago he called to let me know that he had a preliminary report."

"What do you mean preliminary?"

"He had yet to put it in writing."

James nodded, "I see."

"There was a partial print discovered where Billy's bike was found, and where we think he entered the water. It was a heel print. All other prints had been mulched up. There had definitely been a scuffle. Consequently, the rain had added to the problem."

"How did one heel print survive?" James asked.

"In Greenwood's opinion the person wearing the wellingtons had stepped back into some bracken, and one heel had left a deep imprint. When that person stepped forward, the bracken had sprung back into place. Protected the bracken and the overhead trees, the imprint survived the ensuing rain, which as we know, was heavy, but nowhere near as heavy, as the night of the storm."

James nodded. "I can see how that could have happened. Will you stop keeping me in suspense? Who did the print belong to?"

"It was a perfect match to the heel print of one of Helen's wellington's."

The smile on James' face grew, along with the rogue notions bouncing around in his head.

"Does Blackwell know?"

"Not yet. I asked Greenwood not to say anything about the wellingtons being added later. He appeared amused, he shrugged his shoulders implying, *I know nothing.* He's another person Blackwell has rubbed up the wrong way. He insisted I buy him a pint."

James laughed, "Cheap at half the price..."

"Yes, well you owe me."

No one spoke for a moment, until James eventually asked, "Who else knows about this?"

"No one, at present. What do you make of it? I mean Helen; it can't be. It doesn't make sense. What could possibly be her motive?" Harry said in a heavy tone.

"No, no, it has nothing to do with, Helen. I don't want to put my thoughts into words, just yet."

"Oh..."

"Harry, I want you to read something, and listen to a CD, and more importantly, keep an open mind."

James jumped from his chair with renewed enthusiasm. "Be back in a minute." James went into his study.

He returned moments later carrying a book along with a pair of surgical gloves. "Here, put these on, this book is priceless, so please be careful with it."

Harry took the book and began to turn the pages. "This is written in French – I left school a long time ago. I can't make head or tail of it. It looks, to me, like lists of ingredients."

"There's something interesting about halfway through the book."

Harry tentatively turned the pages until he came to where the contents of the book changed into some sort of a journal. "This is all well and good, James, but it doesn't make any sense to me." He scrunched his eyes, peering harder, trying to decipher the writing. "My French always was pretty basic. At a guess I'd say this is written in a local dialect, not the French I was taught."

He sighed, feeling defeated. "It could be Chinese for all I know."

"I think you'd be able to tell the difference between Chinese and French. It's okay. I only wanted you to see it." James reached for the book, took it back into his study, and relocked it in his safe.

He was taking sheets of paper out of an envelope as he walked back into the sitting-room and handed them to Harry. "This translation is not all of it – just the section relevant to us. It was Philip who told me about the journal."

"Philip?"

"Yes, when Philip and Eve were studying medicine, one lecture touched on reincarnation. They decided to study the subject in greater depth and give it a try."

"As you would…" Harry raised his eyebrows, and grinned.

"At the time it was only an exercise, a bit of student fun. What transpired led them both to take a serious interest in the subject. As you know they both used regression therapy in their healing."

"I do know that they were working on some sort of book together. Eve mentioned it the last time she was up at our place."

"Anyway, when Eve came home for the vacation, she told her mother what had happened during those sessions. She wanted to know more about the origins of their family. Her mother showed Eve the journal. Like you, Eve wasn't able to read it. She had the journal translated. Philip had forgotten all about it until Eve's death, when he started to think over old times, as you and I know only too well."

Harry was referring to the day their mother died. They had sat talking about their mother and their childhood, well into the night, and got horribly drunk.

"After Philip told me the story I decided to search for the journal. In Eve's attic I found a chest full of priceless ancient books and manuscripts. Amongst them, I found the journal." James heard the front door open.

"Only me, Dad," Nicky called.

"I'll leave you to read it. I'll go check on, Nicky."

"Hi Dad," Nicky sang as she saw him. She had a mischievous gleam in her eye as she blew him a pretend kiss. She had put a shopping bag on the kitchen table and was unpacking it.

James walked towards the table.

"Anything good?" he asked peering inside the bag.

She replied teasingly. "I don't think I'll tell you, it's a treat."

"Harry's here."

"Really? He hasn't been here in weeks." Nicky walked to the door and called. "Hi Uncle Harry, are you staying for dinner."

"Thanks, but no thanks, Nicky. Gillian is expecting me."

Nicky grinned. "More for us," she whispered to her father.

"Okay, so tell, what have you bought?"

She laughed, "I've bought a beautiful piece of fillet steak."

James' eyes widened. "Fantastic! I happen to be starving. You have no idea where my lunch went." He pictured his lunch splattered all over the floor of The Rats Hole. Chuckling to himself he left her to unpack the shopping and went into his study. He retrieved a portable Sony CD player along with headphones from his desk drawer and joined Harry in the sitting room. Harry had almost finished reading the last page.

"Finished." Harry said. "Fascinating, I'm sure some historian would love to get his hands on this. I don't mean to appear stupid, James. What's this got to do with anything?"

"I now want you to listen to this CD. It is the recording Philip and Eve made whilst they were at university." Harry was now totally confused, but did as he was bid and put the headphones on as Nicky came into the room.

"What's with the letter?" she asked.

"It's not a letter." James began to explain how he and Philip had found the journal along with the translation. He handed her the loose sheets of paper. "I think you'll find it rather interesting reading. Can I get you a drink? I'm having a top-up."

"Yes please, I'll have a G&T."

"What about you Harry?" James asked, waving his own empty glass at him. Harry shook his head and mouthed, driving. He closed his eyes as his attention returned to the tape.

Nicky handed the papers back to James and, raising her eyebrows, gave her father *the look*, which implied, I don't understand. "What do you make of it, Dad? I gather you think it's all somehow connected."

"Don't you?"

"Reincarnation is one thing. Carrying a vendetta

through life after life is scary. I'm surprised at you, Dad."

"I'm surprising myself. How else can you explain it, the tapes, the journal, they're practically identical."

"I admit it's spooky but it has to be a coincidence, retained memories, perhaps. …Oh, I don't know," she snapped.

Harry ripped off his headphones. Moving the machine this way and that, he finally admitted defeat. "How…"

"Top button on the right side," James pointed.

Harry switched off the player. "It's just a coincidence."

"That's what Nicky thinks."

"It's interesting, but how any of it is relevant to Eve's murder beats me. Nicky's right, you surprise me, James. You've always been of the opinion that people who believe in such things should be locked away."

"I wouldn't have put it quite like that."

Harry rolled his eyes. This was so unlike his brother.

"Will you both humour me? Perhaps we can work this through. I believe that someone had a grudge against Eve."

"You mean a curse made in 1636, give me a break…" Harry interrupted.

"Okay, let's get back to reality," James said jumping back in. "We have a little boy, who shouted to Holly that he knew the name of Eve's killer, and shortly afterwards, he *accidently* slips into the river. Because of the heel print and signs of a scuffle, that theory no longer stands up."

Harry made an indefinable sound.

"I think someone was close-by at the time, and whoever it was heard every word."

"You're saying Billy's death wasn't an accident. Am I missing something here?" Nicky said frowning.

"I haven't had a chance to tell you, Nicky. A heel print was found where Billy entered the water."

"A heel print?"

"Yes – and the heel print came from one of Helen's wellingtons."

"Helen! You have got to be joking," Nicky burst out laughing.

James shook his head. "It doesn't have anything to do with Helen."

"Then will someone tell me who, or what, it has to do with?"

James spoke slowly and decisively. "Let's examine my theory for a minute."

"I think I'll leave you to it. I've things to do. I'm having nothing to do with the case for the next week, so you don't need me. I hope that when I get back from Leeds, Sherlock Holmes here will have solved the crime – crimes." Harry corrected himself and, smiling, he stood to leave.

"Harry, I need your input on this, I'm sure you can indulge your, rapidly becoming senile, older brother for a little while longer, can't you?"

Harry groaned and flopped back into his chair. "Well, if you put it like that, five minutes that's all. I'm getting hungry."

"Agreed. The more I discovered, the more fascinating it became as to how Eve's family came to England. The journal states that a young girl called Celestine DuPont, who was carrying Cardinal Simeon's child, was sentenced to death by him. With her dying breath she cursed the Cardinal. She threatened to track him down, even if it took many life-times. No matter how long it took, she would have her revenge.

"The child's mother, grandmother and her aunt fled and came to England and settled on the Scottish-English Border before coming to Meedon Bridge. The family were predominantly women."

"Dad… there must have been men in the family. Have you forgotten about the birds and the bees?" Nicky said with her tongue entrenched in her cheek.

"I'll not answer that. There isn't a mention of a husband anywhere. Also, all children born were female. They were all born with *the gift* and they believed in the *Circle of Life.*

"Many religions today believe in reincarnation. These women were *healers.* They kept bees, they sold honey, and they used their honey in their healing. Honey, as it has been proved, is an effective antiseptic. In those days, no one other than the DuPont women understood this."

"I think that's highly possible, Dad."

"Good. Centuries later little had changed. The family still kept bees and they still made honey, which Eve used in her healing."

"The family has gone now; Eve was the last of the line." The creases on Nicky's forehead deepened. "Of course, the belief is that you're not necessarily reincarnated into the same family, country or even the same sex.

"I remember Eve telling Amanda and me when we were children. "Dad, I think I know where you're going with this." The creases melted away on her forehead as she became more interested.

"That's right. Becky lived north of the city and had never been to this area. Holly was conceived in France, on a school holiday, her father was a French village boy – no connection to Eve or her family."

Harry began to twitch. Only moments ago he had listened to the recordings, and listening now to his level-headed brother, he was beginning to feel very uncomfortable.

"I don't think the saga has played itself out yet," James said.

"How Dad? This is getting complicated."

"I only wish I knew. I started to think about Eve's regression sessions, and throughout each lifetime, she repeated words such as searching and forgiveness. She was always searching. Man or woman she was always searching. Who was she searching for? Let's not forget, Celestine Du Pont vowed to have her revenge."

Harry remained quiet but James noticed he was listening intently.

James continued. "A couple of years ago Eve met Becky at Meedon Bridge library. Becky began doing research for Eve. When Holly was about eight, she was old enough not to have to go to the after-school club. Someone would bring her to the library, where she'd read, do her homework, and wait for her mother to finish work.

"It was there that Eve first set eyes on Holly. The attraction was immediate and a bond was formed and – you all know the rest."

"Dad, if any of this is to be believed, what are you implying? That Holly is the Cardinal, and Eve was the reincarnation of Celestine. Eve's searching was over she had found the Cardinal. That meant that Eve would have to wait until Holly grew up before being able to tell her that she had forgiven him."

"It's a theory," said James. "However, I think you're wrong. You are both well aware that all of Eve's assets are in Trust. I grew up knowing about the plans for The Moxley Holistic Centre. As soon as the lease ran out the plan would be put into operation. What you don't know Harry, is that Eve added a codicil to her will.

"She has given Becky the right to live in her house for as long as she wishes, or until her death. She has set up a trust for Holly to go to University. She has endowed her precious bees to Holly. Do you honestly think that Eve would have done such a thing if she suspected that Holly was the Cardinal?

"Would she have given The Cardinal the responsibility of caring for her Bees, which meant more to her than her own life? I don't think so."

"So James, if you insist on going down this ridiculous path. Who is the reincarnation of the Cardinal?"

"I'm not sure. I was hoping that, as I've put things in some sort of order, one of you may have some ideas."

"Do you think Eve knew?"

"What? Who the Cardinal is? I think there's a strong possibility. That's why she wanted Holly close by so she could control events."

"What you're saying is, that Eve wasn't Celestine," Nicky added.

"No: I think that Eve was Celestine's mother. Holly is Celestine."

Nicky gulped and Harry's eyes widened as his jaw dropped.

James continued.

"Eve's tapes, along with the journal, confirm the events that happened at that time. At the burning, people were stomping on Eve's feet. If Eve was Celestine and tied to a stake in the process of being burned, that could not possibly have happened?"

"My God! You're right. I think we need to bring Philip in on this, Dad."

"It was Philip who sent me the tapes, remember."

"Do you think this Cardinal is local? Is he living on my patch?" That's what I'd like to know," Harry said with his tongue firmly entrenched in his cheek. He was still sceptical.

James ignored his remark.

"What about Helen's wellingtons?" Nicky interrupted. "How come a print from her wellington was found on our side of the river?"

"Remember when Blackwell took Holly and Becky to H.Q. They also took all their shoes. I knew then that Blackwell must have a print. I also knew on the Saturday night Billy disappeared, someone had taken and used Helen's wellingtons and returned them caked in mud. I asked Harry to collect the wellingtons from Helen."

"Why not you?" Nicky interrupted.

"Are you, or are you not, a solicitor?" James groaned.

"I'm tired, that's what I am."

"I didn't want my fingerprints to be found on them.

Harry was to take them to forensics and say that they had been left behind by mistake and to put them with Becky's and Holly's shoes.

"Greenwood carried out the necessary tests. He told Harry that the heel print they had found on the river bank, where it's believed Billy went into the water, came from one of Helen's wellingtons."

"It couldn't be Helen."

"No not, Helen."

"Does Blackwell know about this?"

"Not yet," Harry replied.

"So, she'll think that the wellingtons belong to Becky."

"She will when she gets Greenwood's report."

"Okay Dad, you're doing fine so far so – if the wellingtons were taken from the manor then who took them?"

"Remember Sarah Milton's reception? How she was determined to make a good impression on her guests."

Nicky nodded.

"She'd engaged a cleaning team. They were there all day. Remember, most of the room hadn't been used in years and her London friends were staying over. A catering company was at the manor all day.

"She had employed extra gardeners. Florists were working on arrangements throughout the house. Lots of strangers were in and out of The Manor, on the Saturday Billy disappeared.

"Helen told me it was around five when most of the workers, except the catering staff, finished and left. Someone with an ulterior motive, or plain nosey, must have noticed the wellingtons and decided to borrow them. Whoever borrowed them knew where they were going and how muddy it would be.

"I believe that they slipped away unnoticed, to try to find out how the investigation into Eve's murder was progressing. That person stumbled upon Holly and Billy and heard every word Billy said ...including that he knew who had killed Eve!"

"It's possible, I suppose. Then it shouldn't be too much of a problem to get the names of all the workers through their respective companies."

"That's what I'm planning to do."

"Jeez!" Harry groaned. "Why did you have to bring me into this?"

"Because you're the policeman in the family and you're in charge of the case."

"It's Blackwell's case, now." Harry snapped.

"For the moment. You're still in a position to influence the woman and point her in another direction."

"James, as you know I'll be away until next Wednesday I can't do anything until I get back. Shit! Collect those names and addresses big brother, you will anyway, just remember I need my job." Harry gave a snort, "I doubt any of the firms will cooperate with you particularly, when they know you're trying to pin a murder on one of their staff, and bring their company into disrepute"

James raised his eyebrows. "Oh, so they won't cooperate, like to bet on that? This is where a title comes in very handy. James Marchant may not get the answers he wants, however, Sir James Marchant usually does."

"Dad! How condescending."

"Condescending or not, it works."

"I'd rather believe that this journal has nothing to do with Eve's death. This French woman was trying to write a novel, and she was too embarrassed to let anyone know, so she hid it in the middle of a recipe book."

"Very few people could read or write in those days so I don't think there would be much demand for novels. Although, I confess, that was what I originally believed until I gave it more thought. Philip and I have managed to make sense of one of the scrolls, which says how Moxley Manor was given to the family by King Charles.

"Over the years the Manor became too big and too expensive to run so, rather than sell it, they leased it and the family moved into a small farm on the estate, which they renamed, Honeycombe farm.

"The money from the sale of the lease enabled them to expand the apiary. It was then that they began to make serious money. I'll fetch the document."

Minutes later he was unrolling the scroll and held it for Harry and Nicky to see. Harry peered closer at the seal. "It appears to be genuine. What are you going to do with it?"

"I've been in touch with the British Museum and I'm waiting for them to get back to me. They're going to send someone to authenticate it."

"You've given me something to think about, James."

"It's given us all a lot to think about."

A muffled phone sounded. "That's mine," Nicky said, frantically looking for her bag. "Damn, it's in the kitchen." She raced from the room. She was speaking as she got back. She sounded anxious. She snapped her phone shut and stared blankly at her father and uncle.

"Becky has been arrested."

Chapter 26 – Dan Green

James slipped on his jacket, locked the door, and drove his BMW as fast as possible to the apiary. He reached the row of six cottages in Honeycombe lane and saw Carol and Dan Green standing at her gate. They appeared to be arguing. He pulled to a stop and got out.

"Everything all right, Carol?"

Carol's face was ashen; she was so frightened that her whole body was shaking. Her knuckles showed white as she held onto the gate, in an effort to stop Green from entering.

Dan Green noticed James and slurred, "You, you…"

James was certain that, after the police had released him, Dan had made for the nearest pub, eventually reeling back to the place he thought of as home.

The suitcase was still where Carol had left it earlier.

"You put her up to this – you…"

"Up to what?"

Green's glazed eyes fell to the case. "She's thrown me out," he whimpered.

"Too true I threw him out! My baby's body was covered in bruises," she screamed. "He did it." She began to choke on her words as her voice faded.

Green was wobbling. "Not me, not me – never, not me," he slurred shaking his head in fervent denial.

Carol lifted her sweater to reveal a massive bruise below the left rib. "And I suppose that got there all by itself?"

"It's a lie. You're havin' it off with someone else –you bitch." Green snarled and pulled his right arm back in readiness to take a swing at Carol. James caught it in time and held onto it.

Green's legs gave way and he slipped to the ground spewing abuse. He sat slumped forward, one leg bent to his right and the other twisted behind him. Unable to move, he was almost pathetic. James grabbed him with both hands, lifted him to his feet and steadied him.

"It's obvious to me, and to all the neighbours watching, that your relationship with Carol is over. I advise you to go. If I ever see you around these parts again, I'll give you more than a broken nose. Hear me?" James pulled out the handle of the suitcase and placed it in Greens hand. He twisted him about, pointed him in the direction of the end of the lane and, with a gentle push, said, "Now go."

"I'll gerr ye. I'll gerr ye," Dan Green mumbled, trying to sound threatening as he waddled down the lane tugging his see-sawing suitcase behind him.

Carol stood behind the low gate, white with shock. "I don't know how to thank you. If you hadn't come along, I dread to think what would have happened. Most of the neighbours are out." Her tears were flowing in earnest now and she wiped them away with the sleeve of her jumper.

"I guessed as much. I think you should get away from here for a while. Do you have somewhere you can go?"

"My mother lives in the Lakes."

"You have a mobile?"

"Yes."

"Do the police have the number?"

"Yes."

"Then I suggest you go. You can return when the police are ready to release Billy's body. Don't worry about your job, it'll be here when you get back."

Carol sniffed and nodded.

"Now go and pack a few things and – don't forget to lock up."

A faint smile crossed Carol's face. "I won't be away long."

"As long as it takes, Carol." James left, wondering if he had seen the last of Dan Green.

Clare looked grave when she answered the door. "James! Am I glad to see you, come in, come in. I guess you've heard?"

"That's why I'm here."

"I don't know what to make of it."

Trying hard to remain calm she led James into the kitchen. James noticed her quivering hands as she filled the kettle with water. Only moments ago he had left one shaking woman and now replaced her with another.

"What exactly did the police say?"

"It was such a shock I'm not sure I took it all in. That Inspector, what's her name, appeared smug. She asked if

Becky would accompany her to the police station to answer some questions."

"You're obviously talking about Blackwell."

"Yes. Becky wanted to know why she couldn't answer her questions here. Apparently she needed Becky to identify something."

James knew exactly what it was that Blackwell needed identifying. The door burst open and a white faced Holly rushed in. "Uncle James," she cried, as she flung her arms around his waist. "They've taken my mummy. They've arrested her. Will she go to prison?"

"No, she will not, Holly." James comforted the child as best he could, by rocking her back and forth. Over Holly's head he asked Clare. "They actually arrested her?"

"Yes, she was formally arrested. They read her rights to her."

"Uncle James, my mummy has done nothing wrong."

James bent his head to the level of Holly's. "I know she hasn't, she will be home shortly. There has been a bad mistake. Nicky is at the police station now and will sort it out. I know what Inspector Blackwell is thinking, and the silly lady has got it all wrong."

"Are you sure?" Holly sounded unsure.

"Quite, quite sure," he stressed.

Holly didn't look convinced. "I'm glad you came, Uncle," and with her arms still clamped around his waist she squeezed him hard.

A feeling of warmth spread over him, he always got pleasure out of hearing himself being called, Uncle. Yet with it came pain, reminding him once again that his daughter Amanda was dead, and that his own granddaughter was in Australia living with her father.

He had long ago, reluctantly, accepted the fact that he would never see her again.

They sat at the table in the generous kitchen-dining room. Clare poured and passed James a mug of tea then placed a plate of biscuits in front of him. Holly, having brightened a little, said, "May I have one, please?"

"As long as you leave the chocolate one for me," Clare scrunched her eyes in a threatening way. Holly giggled, and helped herself to the only chocolate biscuit on the plate.

"Holly, I came to see you as I need your help."

Holly eyed James over the top of her biscuit and asked in a very adult tone, "What is it you want me to do?"

"Your Mother will have told you that Eve is being interred next Thursday."

"Yes…"

"I have such a lot of things to arrange, including the service. We want it to be very, very special, don't we?"

"Yes we do."

"Would you like to help me?"

Holly's eyes widened. "Cool," she exclaimed.

"I'd like you to help me choose some hymns and music?"

"Cool," she exclaimed again. "I know all her favourite hymns." Holly jumped up so excited. "I've got my own prayer book. It has hymns at the back." And she was gone.

"Make a list Holly," James called after her.

Clare and James smiled at each other, pleased with the

child's response, although they had expected little else.

"Thank you for that, it'll help keep her mind off things. Will they really release Becky?" she asked.

"They will, I promise." James then began to relate the saga of the wellingtons whereupon Clare burst out laughing. "Oh James – will you get into trouble? I almost feel sorry for Inspector Blackwell."

"I'm not one little bit sorry for her. She'll be furious when she finds out," he chuckled. "It's a good job Harry is off to a conference. Maybe she'll have calmed down by the time he gets back. I don't think he's going to stand for much more of her nonsense, connected or not."

There was a noise in the hallway. The door opened and in walked a beaming Becky. She had on a pretty yellow and white, short-sleeved dress and her hair had been gently teased. Her movements were jaunty, her cheeks were rosy and her eyes sparkled. It was as if she had been given a permanent, *get out of jail free* card. Nicky followed, also unable to stop herself from smiling.

"Went well, I see," James said, giving Nicky one of his knowing looks.

"I couldn't have wished for better. Becky told her that she had never seen the wellingtons before and when she tried them on they were far too big. I wouldn't like to be working with her over the next couple of days, although I did get the impression that the officer with her was as pleased as we were."

"They're a tough lot at H.Q. they'll be able to take whatever she doles out." James bit his bottom lip and smiled as images of future scenes at H.Q., flashed through his mind.

"We'd better get off now, Dad.

As they walked toward the door, Holly came into the room, carrying her prayer book. She ran towards Becky crying "Mummy, mummy you're back."

Chapter 27 – Eve

The following morning James left to complete the arrangements for Eve's funeral. The church was booked, the undertaker booked, the Fallen Angel booked and an announcement had been placed in the newspaper. No flowers: instead the announcement suggested a donation to the Meedon Bridge Hospice.

Palliative care was what Eve's life had been all about, for her, pain was a *no-no*. A more practical reason for this decision was that Eve was being interned in the family mausoleum. It wasn't quite the same as piling flowers on top of a grave for all to gossip about later.

Eve's wish had been to cover her coffin with a variety of flowers from her two-acre natural garden. It was the garden that for years had supplied the precious nectar for her bees to make their delicious honey. Although the storm had done a great deal of damage, the florist was confident she would be able to find sufficient unspoiled blooms for the task.

His cell-phone rang. "James Marchant," he answered.

The voice replied. "Michael Milton here. I'm calling on behalf of my sister Sarah. She'd be obliged if you would come up to the Manor as soon as possible." His voice was officious.

Summoned rather. "I'm sorry but I don't have time today."

There was a moment's pause. "Sarah is a very busy woman, Sir James. Can you rearrange your schedule? She only has a few hours before having to return to London?"

"I'm afraid not. Could you give me an idea as to what this is about?"

"She would rather speak with you, face to face."

"Then why didn't she call me."

"I'm trying to save her time."

James wanted to tell him to get stuffed but thought better of it. 'I can give her a few minutes around two, if Sarah would like to call on me then, I will be only too happy to see her. I'm sorry, I really must go. Good bye." James switched off his cell-phone and swore.

He had a pretty good idea what the woman wanted to discuss with him.

He pictured her prancing about the Manor complaining and shouting orders as the auctioneers collected furniture. The auctioneers had been warned about a possible confrontation and had been instructed not to take any notice of her tantrums or demands.

What was she doing here?

Shouldn't she still be in Westminster?

Michael must have told her about the furniture being taken, hence the flying visit.

She had been aware what was about to happen up at Moxley Manor.

It had been confirmed, again, on the death of her father. She had been given plenty of notice.

It suddenly occurred to him, that perhaps her intended discussion with him would not be the first time she had discussed the matter.

Now that Eve was dead, maybe she thought things would change: that the project would be scrapped. Anticipating such a thing would explain the lavish reception. The object of which, was to impress the important people living in the valley preparatory to her moving here permanently. He'd thought a lot about that recently. Why else would she want to talk to him?

Sarah Milton arrived at two-o'clock precisely. James answered the door and ushered her into the sitting room. She refused his offer of refreshments. Taking a seat opposite her he asked, "How can I help you, Sarah?"

Her eyes were downcast and her lips were tight and she appeared to be fighting to keep in control.

"I can't begin to tell you how upset I am. I arrive home to be greeted with the sight of my furniture being loaded onto a van and taken away for auction. Helen tells me that it's your doing and she, of course, doesn't know anything about it."

"Sarah, it is not your furniture. You have been notified of everything that is happening, and about to happen up at The Manor. As trustee of Eve's estate I have copies of every letter Lane and Son sent you."

"I don't deal with that side of things, my solicitor does. All I know is that he told me not to worry, that your letters meant nothing and that he would sort it out."

"Then he's let you down. He should have told you there was no chance of getting the lease renewed."

"James," she said putting on the charm. "I'm sure you can do something. The Manor was my father's home; it holds memories of him. I'm entitled to keep it. I know the lease has expired but I don't see why it can't be renewed.

"You attended my reception, I'm sure you realise that having such a property is advantageous for my position. I want to make it my family home. I have a lot to offer the area." James bit his tongue to stop himself interrupting. "I distinctly remember telling you that I hoped to have many more such evenings."

"Yes, you did, Sarah."

She was asking for this, and she's damned well going to get it. Having to deal with Blackwell, and now this woman, James had just about enough.

He bit his lip. He was not going to lose his temper. He spoke clearly and distinctly. "It's a great house, Sarah. I can understand how you would like to live in it. Unfortunately, you are not entitled to. As for its being your family home, with sentimental value, I don't think so. Your father lived in Moxley Manor for ten years, during which time you never came to see him.

"The only explanation I can think of is that you had no interest in him. I never knew of you or your brother's existence, because your father never talked about you, until he was near death. It took two months before your brother made an appearance and you made yours about a month later.

"Things changed when your greedy little eyes saw the

great house." Sarah gasped. James took no notice and continued. "You imagined yourself being Prime Minister and also Lady of the Manor. I've been told that, when you did come, you spent little time with your father; you apparently spent it searching through the house. What were you looking for? Would it have been a Will?"

"How dare you speak to me like that," Sarah screeched as she jumped up out of the chair.

"Sit." James' base voice resounded around the room. "I have not finished." He was surprised when a sheepish Sarah Milton sat back down. "How disappointing for you when, on his death, Nicky produced his Will.

"It was then you found out that the lease had expired six months earlier, and through Eve's kindness, she had allowed your father to stay on, putting her own project on hold, her dream of a lifetime.

"She knew he had little time left, and the last thing a dying person needs, is to be uprooted or disturbed by builders traipsing around the place. Eve always put other people before herself."

James watched Sarah Milton's irritation, not shame or regret. "You may, or may not know this, but the previous owners of the lease went to live abroad." He paused and waited until he had eye to eye contact with her making sure he had her full attention.

"In Iraq your father saved the life of their son, who unfortunately died later of his wounds. A ten-year lease on such a property is not worth a penny, not in these parts. Your father was due to retire. They gave him the remainder of the lease as a thank you for what he did for their son. Your father, Sarah, was a remarkable man. You should be proud of him."

Her mouth opened as if to speak. James cut her off.

"It was here at the Manor that he enjoyed his retirement, he lived well and he played hard. I will never forget his weekend house-parties. You missed out, Sarah. What else did he have to do with his money? We now know he fathered two children who didn't give a damn about him. When he died he had twenty-five-thousand pounds in his bank account. And twenty-thousand pounds of that he left to Helen, his housekeeper. She had taken care of him in sickness and in health. In case you are wondering, the Will was signed and witnessed a long time ago. The remaining five thousand was to pay for his funeral expenses. All that is left for you and your brother are your father's few personal possessions."

"This is outrageous! I'll not stand for this! How dare you? How dare you?"

"It's all legal and binding, Sarah."

She paused, looked at him and saw the expression on his face.

Changing her tone to a voice oozing charm she said, "I'm sure we can come to some arrangement." She came pretty close to fluttering her eyelashes.

James spoke, defiantly. "I'm afraid not."

Knowing when she was beaten, Sarah stood and, like a whirlwind, stormed out of the room muttering, "You're just as stubborn as…" Next, he heard the stomping of her small footsteps down the hallway, followed by the slamming of his front door.

James didn't move. "Very interesting…" he mused.

Nicky had a date, or something; whatever it was, she was busy. He was bored and desperately in need of some sort of social sustenance. The last eleven days had been a living hell. He decided to phone Philip. If he was free, spending the weekend with him in the Lakes sounded like a good plan.

There was a loud banging on the door. He recognised the dum-d-dum knock. "Hello Reg. Come in?" he called as he walked towards the door.

"No time. I'm running late, I've come to tell you that I'm off. There are no problems and there's nothing outstanding that needs doing. I've written up the day's log. Everyone has had their instructions. There's nothing for you to do. I'll be back late Sunday."

"Thanks Reg, have a good weekend."

James closed the door. He had forgotten all about Reg going to Scotland for his mother-in-law's eightieth birthday. He decided to phone Philip anyway, he needed to give him an update; a lot had happened in the last two days.

No one answered the Practice phone. No one answered the house phone. It was just after four. He was always reluctant to call Philip's mobile during the day in case he had a patient with him; he decided to take a chance. He answered immediately, sounding in a good mood.

"Can't talk," he said. "I'm driving. I'm on my way to you. That Okay?"

James was taken aback. "Sure. Any particular reason?"

"No, see you in about forty-five minutes. I'll meet you

at The Fallen Angel. We can have an early dinner."

"Sounds good to me."

Philip had switched off.

It was nine-thirty when James and Philip arrived back at the farm after an excellent meal at The Fallen Angel.

James was pouring coffee and Philip, making himself at home by pouring two extra-large cognacs, insisted, "Perhaps you'll now bring me up to date?"

"I'm sorry about that… I can't believe the place was so busy. There were too many people close-by. I couldn't chance being overheard."

"We're home now so don't keep me in suspense." Philip was shuffling in his chair making himself comfortable and ready to listen when there was a loud banging on the door, it wasn't an ordinary bang. It was two consecutive, commanding thumps.

"Who the hell is that?" James swore. He knew Nicky had a date so it wouldn't be her, and she had her own key, anyway. Reg was away. He wasn't expecting anyone. Grumbling he made his way along the hall to the front door.

He opened it. Standing before him was Blackwell with Cranmore close behind. "Can we come in? I'd like a word," she demanded, already stepping over the threshold and pushing her way in.

"Please do…" James said, with sarcasm in his voice.

Cranmore was thankful she didn't see the expression on James' face. She knew the way, so James and Cranmore followed her along the hallway into the sitting room. "Ah, Mr Cross, nice to see you again." Her tone implied something very different.

"How can I be of help to you, Inspector?" James said, as he caught up with her. "I hope this won't take long."

She didn't answer. No one spoke. James inwardly was fuming. He tried his best not to show it. "Please, do sit down?"

The two officers walked to the sofa and sat. Not even a thank you. Something was obviously bothering the woman.

"If you would rather…" Blackwell glanced across at Philip indicating *not in front of…* "We could go down to the station."

"Here will do fine," he said as he picked up his brandy. Then facing her he raised his glass towards the woman. "Can I tempt you?"

She ignored his remark. "Sir James. How well do you know Dan Green?"

James scrunched his eyebrows confused by the question. "I don't know him. I met him for the first time yesterday lunch-time, you were there."

"Are you sure that was the first time?"

"Quite sure."

"It's come to my notice that after we took Dan Green into custody and shortly after his release, you had another altercation with him, outside Carol Bradshaw's cottage."

James huffed. "That's correct. Altercation: whatever. If you know that much you will also know he was threatening Carol. He wanted to get into the house after Carol had thrown him out."

"I believe there was a scuffle?"

"Not exactly. He took a swing at Carol and I caught

his arm whereupon he, being as drunk as a skunk, slumped to the floor. I hauled him up, put the handle of his pull-a-long in his hand, and sent him on his way. That was all that happened."

"Which way?"

"Towards the end of the lane. The other way leads to Moxley Manor, but you, having been there, would know that." James was referring to Saturday night's reception when he'd witnessed the scene between her and Sarah Milton.

She stared at him her eyes darting from side to side as she was obviously wondering how he knew. Had she been seen? She realised she had. She was silent a moment longer. Her lips tightened and her eyes narrowed as blood rose in her cheeks. "Then what did you do?" she asked.

"I suggested to Carol that it would be advisable for her to go away for a few days until you released Billy's body. She agreed, and told me she would go to stay with her mother who lives in the Lake District. I then continued on to the apiary."

"And you never saw Dan Green again."

"No."

Philip sat in silence his eyes moving from Blackwell to Cranmore then to James. He hadn't a clue as to what was going on. No one spoke.

Blackwell decided to come out of her reverie. "Sir James …Dan Green was found hanging from an oak tree alongside the river. Odd as it may seem, in the exact same spot where Billy Bradshaw entered the water." The temperature seemed to drop as her words registered. James was the first to speak.

"Good God! Suicide?"

Blackwell shrugged. "We don't know yet."

Philip continued to sit quietly, his eyes taking in everyone's reactions.

"On second thoughts, I doubt it would be suicide. He was too drunk," James mused.

"What do you mean?" Blackwell demanded.

"As I said, he was too drunk. He would have to have found something to use with which to hang himself. He would have had to go back to the lane, find a suitable tree, climb it, secure whatever it was, tie it around his neck, and jump. I'll say again, it's not possible, he was too drunk."

Blackwell had her elbow on the arm of the sofa and rested her chin in the palm of her hand her fingers scrunched into her cheek. She stayed like that for a moment while she stared at James.

"You seem to know a lot about such things, Sir James."

"I'm a fan of NCIS." He bit his bottom lip hard as he tried to refrain from grinning. Blackwell was not amused. He then said. "In another life I was a major in the Marine Corps, special ops. I know what I'm talking about; I've seen a lot worse than a dead man hanging from a tree."

"Where were you this afternoon?"

"I was here."

"Can anyone vouch for that?"

"Sarah Milton was here at two." He noticed her flinch. "My cleaner left at five and I met Philip at the Fallen Angel at around six."

Blackwell didn't reply. She stood and Cranmore

followed her move. "Thank you for your time, Sir James."

James followed the two officers down the hall towards the front door unable to believe what had just happened. The woman must think he was born yesterday, he knew what she was trying to do. Dan Green had been murdered, and he was her best suspect. Nicky was right, she had a way of implying things without actually saying a word, and James had to admit she was pretty good at it. *Eve, Billy and now Dan Green: my, my, who's been a busy boy then?* He laughed out aloud at his thoughts, it was impossible not to.

 Philip was topping up his brandy when he came back into the room. "Do you get the feeling that you're her number-one suspect?"

James huffed and in a scornful way said. "I most certainly do. I've murdered three people in little over a week. It's unbelievable. I'd be down at the station by now if you hadn't been here. What you don't know is that Harry is off duty. He's attending a conference in Leeds, he'll be there until Wednesday. Blackwell is completely in charge of the case."

"So it's gone to her head, and don't you mean cases, Eve, Billy and now this guy Green. I'm glad I came over, if only to keep you out of more trouble."

"She's in over her head, Philip."

Chapter 28 – Updates

"Please, now will you bring me up to date? Who is this guy Green and what does he have to do with anything?"

James began to recap what had happened at The Rat's Hole and later outside Carol's cottage.

"I gather you don't think it was a distressed step-father committing suicide?"

"I do not."

"He wasn't Billy's step-father. He was a guy who moved in on a trial basis, it's the in-thing to do these days. If it had worked out, they would have made it a permanent arrangement. Apparently, once he'd moved in he used the place as a hotel, spending most of his time with his mates, usually in a pub getting drunk."

"Carol needs a lesson on how to choose a man, is she attractive?"

It's the first question Philip asks these days now that he's a single man. "She is actually," James laughed. "Green was a nasty piece of work. He beat the crap out of them both."

"He what!"

"You'll be interested in this, Philip. He never hit Carol

in front of Billy and vice versa. Carol kept quiet about it, and so did Billy. It wasn't obvious to anyone as he hit where it wouldn't show."

"Classic. Bullying cowards. The courts are far too lenient with them." Philip huffed in disgust. "I'm the one who has to put their victims back together, and believe me it's not easy."

James was shaking his head. "I'll never understand how you can sit and listen to such stuff, day in and day out."

"With difficulty."

"I'm not sorry he's gone. He was a drunken lout. I wonder, is it possible for such men to be cured?"

"It's possible, but they'd have to kill someone first to get treatment. Do you think he murdered, Billy?"

James sat staring into his drink as he swirled the golden liquid round and around in his glass. "Billy had been in the house all week with a bad cold; apparently Green told Carol that he shouldn't go out. Billy hated being cooped up. After a lot of badgering from Billy, Carol allowed him out."

"Could Green have come home drunk, hit the roof when he found Carol had disobeyed him, and then went to find Billy, and that's how Billy ended up in the river."

"It's possible but I don't believe so. No, Green was not responsible for Billy's death."

"Then who is? Has it anything to do with the wellingtons? Have you heard any more?"

James brought Philip up to date regarding, the said wellingtons, and Becky's subsequent arrest. Philip was not amused. He showed his annoyance with James for not calling him earlier.

"She was gone for less than two hours. Nicky sorted it and after the day I'd had, and by the time I'd had something to eat, I was so wacked that I went to bed. It was all over so there was nothing you could do to help."

"How is Becky?" The over-concern in Philips voice once again betrayed hidden feelings.

"She's fine. Having been exonerated, when she arrived home, she was the happiest I'd seen her in days."

"I'm pleased about that," Philip stood holding his empty brandy glass in his right hand as he took James' glass with his left and then refilled them both.

"Early today wasn't very pleasant either. I made the final arrangements for the funeral. I did text you regarding the day and time, didn't I."

"You did. Come on James, get on with it? You're saying we can rule out Green for being involved in Billy's death, right?"

"Right."

"Then, what is it? I think you have something else on your mind. Are you linking Billy's death to Eve's?"

"Um… I'm not sure."

"I can tell you have a theory, so spill?"

"It's quite a wild one."

"I'm sure I will have heard wilder stories."

"Okay, well here goes, yesterday, Harry, Nicky and I analysed things. We now know that the print found by the police came from Helen's wellingtons."

"Which she has never worn," Philip interrupted.

"Yes. Someone borrowed those wellingtons late afternoon on the Saturday of Sarah's reception shortly before Billy disappeared. A lot of people were in and out of The Manor that day. Helen was there supervising the proceedings and Sarah and her brother Michael were also there.

"I didn't have time today, but come Monday, I intend to start contacting the firms who were working at Moxley Manor on that Saturday."

Philip scrunched his face. "Isn't that interfering with a police enquiry?"

"So what: Harry's away so he can't be harmed. Blackwell has a one track mind. She can't get Becky for Billy's death; however, there's still Eve's. She'll now have to go up to The Manor in an official capacity, and she won't like that one little bit."

"Unless the Miltons happen to be in London."

"True, but she'll still have to interview them, at some point."

"Helen will be interrogated."

"She understands that; she's fine about it." James then laughed. "After speaking to Helen, they'll have to speak to everyone who was at the Manor on that Saturday. My plan is to get to them first."

"She'll find out. Someone is bound to talk."

"It'll be too late then," James joked. "Seriously, I do have a theory. The problem is that some of it comes down to things I've never believed in."

A smile slowly crossed Philip's face, "You have me intrigued," he said.

"Harry and Nicky have read the translated journal; listened to the regression tapes and examined the document signed by the King giving the deeds of Moxley

Manor to the women called Dupton in perpetuity."

"Go on..."

"I'm not sure Harry is altogether with us on this," he said with a shake of his head. "Nicky knew Eve better than Harry, but I can tell he is intrigued. We all agreed that Eve, in her regression sessions, was always searching for something or someone, and frequently spoke of forgive, forgiveness. However, Harry was of the opinion that if there was an element of truth in any of it, which he doubted, Eve was the reincarnation of Celestine Du Pont and Holly was the Cardinal."

Philip frowned, he obviously didn't agree. "What do you think, James?"

"If that were true do you honestly think Eve would leave her precious bees in the care of the Cardinal?"

"No, I do not."

"Neither do I. I think Eve was not Celestine, but Celestine's mother, and that Holly is the reincarnation of Celestine."

Philip was smiling now. "What made you come to that conclusion?"

"The searching and forgiveness words played a part. Also, you did, when you explained to me how so many people, when regressed, believe that they had once been Cleopatra but that they weren't actually Cleopatra; they were part of a crowd, watching her. It fell into place when I remembered Eve saying that, at the burning, people trampled on her feet. If it had been Eve who was being burned at the stake, it would have been impossible for anyone to trample on her feet. I realised that it was a simple case of a mother doing everything possible to protect her child. I think that's also the case in this lifetime. Eve had not only found her daughter, she had also found the Cardinal."

"Have you ever met someone for the first time, James, and had the feeling that you know them? The theory is that you probably have, but in another life-time."

"I've been thinking about that. When Eve met Holly, she realised instinctively who she was. That is why she brought the child into her home, it was to protect her."

Philip was nodding in agreement. "My, my James, you've come a long way. I believe you've been converted. The burning question is – forgive the pun – who is the Cardinal, besides being a rogue tradesman?"

"That's my problem. This morning, Michael Milton phoned and summoned me to The Manor. Sarah wanted to talk to me. I refused. I told him I'd be available here at two if she'd like to call."

"I bet he didn't like that."

"You got it in one. She arrived promptly at two. You should have seen the look on her face, she was livid. She had returned from London to find the auctioneers removing furniture."

"Oh come on now, she knew all about that, she's pulling a fast one."

"True. Since Eve's death, she had assumed that the situation would change. Remember how I told you that at the reception, she'd mentioned to Harry and me that she'd never met Eve, or been to the apiary." Philip nodded. "And remember how I also told you I saw Milton and Blackwell kiss on the path outside the building." James hesitated and lowered his eyes in thought.

Philip nodded again. It appeared to him that James was trying to relive the scene to make sure that what he had heard, he was remembering correctly. It was.

James continued. "As Sarah stormed out of the house I distinctly heard her mumble *'you're just as stubborn'*. I now believe that our conversation was not the first conversation, she'd had on the subject."

"Good God, she lied. She had met Eve."

"That's exactly what I'm thinking," James said with a grin.

"The bitch."

"My sentiments entirely. It's my guess she did go to see Eve, or, maybe they talked on one of Eve's visits to her father. I'm now one hundred-per-cent convinced that they did meet. The conversation she had with me, she'd previously had with Eve, and received the same response. She denied having met Eve, so if she hadn't met her, who could she have been referring to?"

"Actually, I did give her and her brother brief consideration, then I dismissed the thought. Hell James, she's the leader of the opposition. Have you ever heard of a politician being accused of murder?"

"There's always a first time."

"Everyone knows that politicians can't be trusted, in either word or deed, but James – murderers?"

James had a mischievous glint in his eyes. "Are you trying to tell me you never watched, House of Cards?"

Philip nearly choked on a mouthful of brandy. "Do you honestly think she would murder for property, and hope to get away with it?"

"You can answer that better than me."

"What did you make of her brother?"

"Bit of a creep, looks like an orang-utan. I've been told that he's a formidable force. The question is, is he pulling her strings, or is she pulling his?"

"Who knows, according to the press reports, he's determined that his sister will become the next prime minister."

"It's well documented that Sarah has a volatile personality, perhaps Michael has too. It goes with their red hair; it's the Irish in them," James grinned.

"Or Scottish. You're forgetting something, James. The wellingtons were women's so Michael didn't borrow them."

"Ah... but remember Helen telling us that when she knew she was moving into the country she thought she'd need a pair. The only ones she could find were far too big. Wellingtons are cold on the feet. I for one put umpteen pairs of socks on whenever I have to wear mine. That's what Helen thought, if she used plenty of socks, they would fit."

"Makes sense but... Sarah and Michael murderers?" Philip murmured. "In my line of work I hear a lot bizarre stories, but this..." Philip made a clicking noise with his tongue as he pondered. "Let's talk this through. You're thinking that Sarah or Michael murdered Eve, to get their hands on Moxley Manor?"

"I can't think of a better motive. She'd probably boasted about their *'family'* home here in the valley, to a lot of important and influential people, before she was aware of the situation. Her solicitor had been informed. He'd probably casually told her that the lease was up and that he would renew it."

"So, you really think Sarah discussed the matter of the lease with, Eve?"

"I think she must have. When Eve died Sarah assumed that the lease would be renewed. Working on that premise she went ahead and organized a lavish reception for all the bigwigs in the valley and some of her influential Westminster colleagues.

"Today, she arrived from London to discover half of the furniture had gone."

"The furniture didn't belong to The General. It was part of the estate."

"I know that and you know that. Did Sarah know that? I believe there was a lot of assuming on Sarah's part. Nicky dealt with Sarah's solicitors, not her. Sarah apparently left everything to her solicitor. She didn't have the time to be bothered with trivia."

"Okay, so how does that help with Eve's or Billy's murder?"

James shifted in his chair. He didn't want to go down this route but his thoughts wouldn't go away. "Holly used to visit The Manor with Eve and play games with The General; draughts, that sort of things."

Philip nodded.

"After the Miltons began visiting their father, Holly told me that Eve would not take her, at least, not if they were there."

Philip looked intently at James impressed as to how far James had come in taking his favourite subject seriously.

"So... if Eve sensed that one or the other was the

Cardinal, it would explain why she didn't take Holly with her on those visits," James suggested.

"Makes sense. Where do we go from here? We can't go to Blackwell." Philip stared at the colourful Persian rug beneath his feet, trying desperately to stimulate inspiration. "After all these centuries it appears to be coming to a head, I can feel it, and I'm a witness to it. Who needs research when it's happening right before my very eyes? I only wish it hadn't had to be at Eve's expense." His face furrowed in thought. "I'm surprised she never came to discuss the Miltons with me."

"Maybe she wasn't quite sure, maybe she was waiting for a final piece of the puzzle, as we are. I don't know if you've realised that Eve's death, Billy's death and even Dan Green's death, all three died when the Miltons were in residence."

As Philip digested James' words, he took another sip of brandy. "Why kill little Billy? Why kill Dan Green?" he asked.

"I believe that after Eve's death whoever killed her would visit the apiary in the hope of gleaning information as to how the investigation was progressing. On that fateful Saturday, he overheard Billy shouting to Holly that he knew who had killed Eve. Maybe Billy's death was an accident. Whoever it was wanted to know how much the boy knew. The person approached Billy, and Billy not knowing who the person was, became frightened. Then it all went wrong and a simple scuffle landed Billy in the river."

"What about Dan Green?"

"Dan Green was drunk. He knew he'd been found out

about beating Billy, so drunk and full of remorse, he hanged himself. The problem is that I don't believe that scenario for one moment. Green wouldn't have had the guts, and as I've just said, he was drunk. He couldn't have sobered up that quickly.

"I think whoever is responsible for Billy's death decided to use Dan Green as a scapegoat."

"Now that is a thought." Philip took in a deep breath and relaxed his shoulders as he said, "So, we're back to the Miltons?"

James leaned forward, picked up the decanter and topped up his brandy gesturing to Philip to help himself.

"Murder is always easier the second time around. I can see how the suicide scenario would work well for Blackwell. She wants to wrap up the case. Blackwell is in a real predicament. I also wouldn't like to be in Sarah Milton's shoes, she has to return to London and admit to people that her father hadn't owned the property and, in fact, had died penniless."

"What about the press? They'll have a field day." James straightened his legs out in front of him and stretched.

"Can't wait to read the front pages, it'll run for weeks."

James pondered before speaking again. "I made a promise to Holly, that I'd not tell anyone what I am about to tell you. As a doctor I need your assurance that this is treated as patient confidentiality, agreed."

"I'm a psychiatrist. Everything I hear is in confidence."

James reached for a pouf lying idle besides the

fireplace. Pulling it towards him he lifted his legs and rested them on top of it.

"After Billy disappeared Holly told me that she'd woken in the middle of the night…"

"And…"

"Eve was sitting on the end of her bed."

"She what!" Philip shot up from his lounging position. This was more than he could ever have hoped for. Leaning forward, he rested his elbows on the arms of his chair and cupped his chin in his hands. His eyes darted wildly as he waited in anticipation. "Go on, go on…"

"I knew that would get your attention. According to Holly, Eve didn't speak. Holly said she could hear her, *in her head,* those were her exact words. Eve just sat there smiling."

"Yes, yes, go on," Philip urged nodding like one of the *nodding dogs* who sat on the front bench of the opposition party.

"Eve told her that everything would be all right. Holly asked her about Billy and Eve told her that Billy was with her. Remember, that was before I had found his body."

Philip's stomach jiggled beneath his thick green jumper as his head shook from side to side. "I knew it. I knew it and Eve knew it too, she'd known it from the first time they met, and you've just confirmed it; the child has sixth sense. I'll have to talk to her."

"No! Philip I…"

"Don't worry. It's too soon. Plenty of time, I know my job. Did she say anything else?"

"Not really, she said that they were both happy and then she faded."

"Our immediate problem, James, is where do we go from here? If we were to accuse the Miltons, no one will take it seriously. Doors would close. We need proof and the problem is how are we going to get it?"

"God only knows but, I'm telling you now, I have no intentions of letting an innocent child's life be ruined because of someone's thirst for status and power."

"Can you remember where the police searched for the weapon that killed Eve?"

"As far as I can remember they concentrated their efforts on the apiary."

"Let's assume the murderer came from the Manor. Which path would they take?" Philip asked trying to picture the scene.

"The police are certain it was a rock and it went into the river."

"Ah – then the murderer would have to get to the lane, cross over, walk down the bank to throw it into the river. That's a long way to carry a weapon covered in blood. The majority of murderers dump the weapon pretty sharply, which means close to the scene of the crime, particularly if it was covered in blood."

"If the murderer came from The Manor, wouldn't they automatically have gone back the same way they came – weaving through the hives, through the orchard and across the stream?"

"The stream!" Philip's face lit with renewed hope. "I've crossed it many times over the years with Eve. So James, do you think it's in the stream?"

"It's possible. The stream would have been a trickle at the time. Later, it would be a different story; it fills up fast as the water from the hills rushes down to the river. The stepping stones would have been submerged. The police would have taken one look and dismissed the idea."

"A person would have had to wade through deep water, at least twelve feet wide, to get to the other side. If they had dropped the stone into the water, I guess that the police thought it would have been taken out to sea by the force of the water.

"If that person had reached the other side there is only one place they could have gone and that is up to The Manor.

"And, that person would not only have dirty wellingtons but also wet clothing which would be wet way above their knees. Blackwell would have immediately rejected the idea of the murderer escaping that way."

"What about the adjoining woodland, it's thick with shrubbery?"

"The police did a thorough search there. I still suggest we take a closer look at the stream. The water may have gone down, making a white-painted stone visible. If the water hasn't subsided we'll just have to wait a few more days, it's only a matter of time."

Chapter 29 – The Funeral

James felt numb as he stood alongside the hearse watching people parade up the path and into St Mark's church. If anyone had asked him, he could not have described how desolate he felt. He was beyond distraught, unable to believe that he was standing here again, so soon after his wife's funeral. Like his wife, his oldest friend, Eve, was gone forever.

As ridiculous as it sounded, he did think he knew who the murderer was, but he was nowhere near proving it, if ever he could.

As far as Becky and Clare were concerned Blackwell was becoming a nuisance, repeatedly calling, asking the same questions over and over again.

Nicky had told James that she intended to submit a complaint of police harassment, but would wait until after the funeral.

James could hear the organist playing a medley of Eve's favourite hymns, proudly submitted by Holly, he found it comforting.

The organist stopped playing.

There was a quiet lull. It was time.

The music commenced and the organist began to play, *Wind beneath my feet.*

Reverend Arthur Broadbent stood waiting in the centre of the nave. The congregation took to their feet as Eve began her final journey surrounded by her friends.

James, Harry, Philip and Doctor Cobb carried the small coffin. It was entirely covered in an arresting array of late summer wild blooms, intertwined with a variety of herbs, the tools of her trade.

The autumnal display included corn, blackberries, blackthorn with its crimson, gold and purple leaves. Blue Salvia; Dahlia's, Fuchsia and early Chrysanthemums. Ann had carefully chosen her colours and had blended them to create an unparalleled rainbow of delight. She had captured Eve's essence, perfectly.

After placing Eve's coffin on the catafalque James, inconspicuously, glanced around the congregation before taking his seat alongside Nicky, Becky, Holly and Clare. Their faces were expressionless, blank with sad eyes fighting back tears. Becky sat wringing a handkerchief in her hands. James knew it was only a matter of time before it would be needed. Clare frequently gave Becky a comforting pat. This was only the second time Becky had attended a funeral, the first was the funeral of her foster father, Clare's husband.

Doctor Cobb, Philip and Harry took the pew behind where Harry's wife was already seated.

James recognised Felicity from the Bee Association. He was surprised to see Sarah Milton and her brother Michael. He saw the carers, who had taken delivery of the jars of Blue-topped honey the day after Eve died.

Blackwell and Cranmore! What in God's name were they doing here? How dare they come? He bit his bottom lip and swallowed his fury.

The little church was full to capacity; it was standing-room only. He didn't recognise half the people who had come to pay their respects.

After an emotional service, Rev Broadbent thanked everyone for coming. He explained that Eve's remains would be interned in the family mausoleum, witnessed by close friends. He also told the congregation that refreshments would be served in the ballroom of The Fallen Angel, and that they were all welcome.

Reverend Broadbent lowered his head. The organist took it as a sign and, without warning, Henry Purcell's Trumpet, Tune and Air, thundered throughout the building. Eve was going out with a bang.

The Reverend Broadbent, James, Becky, Holly, Philip and Clare, along with Harry and his wife Gillian, followed the coffin, now carried by pallbearers, down the aisle towards the open door and out into brilliant autumnal sunshine.

On reaching the porch James halted the following procession to allow time for Eve to be put into the hearse, which would then drive her around to the East side of the church where she would be placed inside her family's mausoleum.

The atmosphere suddenly changed. A sense of foreboding hung heavy in the air. A deathly silence had descended on the square and the sky had changed colour from clear blue to an eerie watery green.

In the distance an unfathomable, continuous drone could be heard; it appeared to be coming from across the moors to the north. It was soft at first, then it got louder and louder, until it transformed into an ear-shattering hum. The air began to vibrate. From out of nowhere a black mass appeared obliterating the sun, day turned into night.

James stood, his arms outstretched behind him in an effort to restrain the congregation. His eyes remained on Eve. She was halfway down the path being carried towards the low gate and the waiting hearse. Having listened to the strange stories Felicity had told him over the past two weeks he thought he knew what could be happening. Seconds later his thoughts were confirmed.

Billions of Eve's charges swooped in unison. It was an incredible, spectacular sight, the bees moved as gracefully as a synchronized swimmer, swirling over and around Eve's coffin. The column then moved, up and away, changing its shape and hovered in the sky like a huge ball, like a planet.

People were pushing James in an effort to leave the church, he held them back.

"It's the bees! Mummy, it's the bees, they've come back," Holly shrieked jumping up and down in uncontrollable joy. She began to run down the path then suddenly stopped. She stood perfectly still and looked up into the sky at the hovering bees, smiling.

Mothers with little children playing in the park opposite the church, along with people out shopping, began to scream and run for safety.

James yelled to Holly for her to come back inside. Holly had no intentions of obeying. A few rogue bees had entered the porch of the church, then left. People were blindly pushing James in an effort to escape and run, for what they thought to be their lives. He had to make a decision, go and grab Holly, or stop the congregation from leaving; something made him decided to stop the people spilling out through the door and into probable danger.

He yelled for them to get back inside. He heard shrieks and the panic in people's voices. He had to ignore them.

The coffin had almost reached the end of the long drive. People were still desperately trying to leave the church. He again pushed them back this time by using the heavy wooden door. It closed with a resounding bang. Becky began to scream. "Holly's out there. James, she's still out there."

He had momentarily forgotten the child. He reopened the door a fraction and slipped through the narrow gap. "I'll get her," he called over his shoulder.

James looked skywards. The bees were on the move, they appeared to be reassembling. What were they doing? Having formed themselves into the shape of an arrow they then began to descend. Faster and faster, closer and closer they came towards the earth. Once more they swooped and streaked over the coffin. It was like a red-arrows flypast. A flypast of gratitude, a flypast of respect, for the woman who had cared for them all her life, and had so cruelly been taken away from them.

James reached Holly and grabbed her arm but she shook him off. A gust of wind created by the bees caused

James to take a step backwards.

Colony after colony of bees swarmed around them, blotting out the light. Bees blanketed the village square and hovered about fifty feet above the ground as if someone had switched off the sun; thousands of bees all moving in harmony to shade the funeral cortege.

Holly stood calm and still as the bees swirled above them.

"Holly walk slowly back with me," he spoke as calmly as possible.

"I'm fine Uncle James. Go in and keep the door closed. Keep the people inside."

"No, you come here, right this minute." He said urgently, trying not to scare her.

"Uncle James, stop! Go back; you go back. I'm quite safe."

Despite the many theories over the past few weeks, he believed the child.

Instinctively, he knew that she would be safe. If the bees really did have the power of thought and communication, that he was beginning to believe; then they would not harm her, she was their new guardian, although, at this moment she didn't know it.

Daylight returned as quickly as it had gone. The bees vanished leaving behind them an eerie silence.

James half-opened the door and squeezed through the narrow gap into the church. As Becky saw the door opening she wailed, "Holly… Holly…" On seeing that it was James, not Holly, Becky crumpled to the floor and continued to sob. Philip helped her up led her to a pew where she sat shaking with fear.

James spoke urgently to Reverend Broadbent. He told him to explain everything to Harry and Blackwell. Tell them that he would be right outside the door with Holly. What had happened had been unpredictable and James knew that it was quite feasible that the bees could return. Maybe as the hearse carrying Eve left for the mausoleum or, when she was being interned inside the mausoleum. If that were the case, he would be in the best position to grab the child and get her inside to safety.

It was all happening so fast. Loud commanding voices reached him along with protestations and objections from other members of the congregation. A man and a woman were ordering people to get out of their way.

He recognised the woman's authoritarian voice which carried over the cacophony of the alarmed congregation. She was demanding to know what was going on. Someone answered saying, that they didn't have a clue. Another person said it looks like a storm is on its way.

A woman said that she'd had enough of storms. Why was this happening? It must be global warming came the reply.

A young voice contributed to the mumblings by saying that it was a swarm of bees. A man answered in a loud voice, "Bees, what a load of tosh." Feelings of confusion and fear began to ricochet around the inside of the church.

James was still at the main door continuing to hold back the people. Harry had disappeared across to the West side of the church and beckoned Blackwell to follow him. He called H.Q. he wanted as many men as could be mustered. He called the paramedics and informed them that they would need protective clothing.

People were still jostling each other, trying desperately to escape, when Reverend Broadbent's voice boomed through the air. "Will everyone please keep calm? Will you all find a seat?" The congregation fell silent except for a few mutterings. "I have been told that we have been visited by a swarm of bees. As we all know bees can give a very nasty sting. It is not safe for you to go outside, at the moment. As soon as I know anything more, I will inform you. You are quite protected here in God's house, so please; please will you all sit down and be patient."

The Miltons had reached James.

"Sir James, will you open this door and let us out. We have a train to catch. I must be in London by seven," the leader of the opposition insisted.

"I can't let you out for the moment, it's far too risky," James replied.

"Nonsense, what harm can a few bees do? You sound ridiculous," she scoffed. "Sir James, you amaze me, call yourself a Marine, afraid of a few bees." She looked disparagingly at him as she shouldered him out of the way with surprising force. She grabbed the ancient knob and pulled open the heavy door. She pushed past Holly, who was now standing inside the porch and then she began to jog down the path followed by her ever-obedient brother.

James turned to face Becky and mouthed, Holly is fine. Becky nodded and stemmed a choked cry.

Philip was doing his best to console her.

James once again, slipped out of the church, and

joined Holly in the porch.

Holly was standing as still as a statue, staring up into the sky and James realised that nothing he could say would entice her to come back inside the building.

The bemused pall-bearers carrying the coffin had reached the hearse and Eve was now safely ensconced inside. No sign of the bees.

"Holly... please come in now. The bees have gone. Your mother needs you, she's frightened for you."

"I'm fine, honest. I'm not sure that they have gone. Something doesn't feel right. Please Uncle James, you go back inside and don't let anyone come out."

"What doesn't feel right?"

"I don't know; I don't think it's safe. And, Uncle James, please keep still, a sudden movement will spook them."

"Where are they?"

"I don't know."

"Which way did they fly off? I can't see any sign of them."

"I don't know. All I know is that one minute the sky was as black as night and the next minute I was standing here in bright sunlight, and they had gone." Looking out of the corner of his eye James saw that she was smiling. "They were singing, Uncle James."

"Singing, are you sure they were singing?"

"Oh yes, quite sure."

The Miltons were now about ten yards from the gate when, from out of nowhere, the blanket of black descended again and, within seconds, had obliterated both Sarah and her brother Michael.

Ear-piecing screams spiked the air as they tried to fight off the attack. Their movements infuriated the insects even more and they continued to pump their poisonous venom into the two bodies over and over.

As was second nature to James, he made a sudden move forward with the intention of trying to help them. Holly grabbed his arm. "Stand still," the child ordered.

Shocked by the authority in her voice, he did as he was told.

The hum of the bees grew louder and louder obliterating all other noises as they buzzed around Sarah and Michael Milton who were now completely cocooned within the swirling, dark mass.

James stared speechless. It was surreal; it was hard to believe what he was seeing. Holly stood still with a trance-like expression on her face.

"Are they singing now?" James whispered, rather stupidly.

"It doesn't sound like singing."

"What do you think it is?"

"I don't know. I can't see what they're doing."

James knew what they were doing and trying not to sound concerned said, "Holly I think we should go inside, we need to call for a doctor. I think those people may have been stung."

"Maybe."

She turned to face him, unconcerned. "Uncle James, they are so frightened, I can tell.

Those people were the General's children, I saw them once. They shouldn't have run like that. Bees are easily frightened."

At that moment the bees began to form into the shape of another arrow and they took flight. They swarmed over the roof tops of the village and disappeared across the fields in the direction of the apiary. James had managed to turn Holly towards the church door and ushered her inside before she saw the bees leave and the two bodies, crumpled into a defensive foetal position, lying motionless on the path.

Inside the church Holly pushed her way through the people milling around the door. She reached her mother who was quite hysterical; once more tears began to stream down her cheeks. "Thank God. Thank God," she cried as she hugged and rocked her only child. In a booming voice James called for Dr Paul Cobb to come forward.

Paul rose from a pew in the front of the church and waved as he jostled his way through the people blocking the aisle to the main door. James explained the situation. Paul along with Harry, Blackwell and Cranmore went outside without hesitation.

James touched Arthur's arm to get his attention. After a brief conversation the Reverend made his way to the front of the church and standing in the nave he called for everyone's attention. "Members of the congregation the situation we now believe is under control. There were a few bees still flying and we felt that it was best that you stayed indoors for your own safety.

"We think the danger has passed, and it is now perfectly safe for you to leave the Church, however, I'd like to stress caution.

"I suggest we all leave the church in an orderly fashion

by the West door? If you walk down the path and out into the lane, turn right and on reaching the T-junction turn right again and you will see The Fallen Angel. It will be on your left. I repeat, please take care, there may be one or two bees still flying. I don't want anyone to get stung."

People were jabbering ten to the dozen. Slowly, the noise of infernal chattering began to subside as the church emptied of its occupants. James and close friends, along with Reverend Broadbent, followed. Instead of making for the West gate they took the path around the church.

James found it hard to believe what he had witnessed. Strange as it may seem, he actually felt for the bees who had given their lives in retribution for the death of their guardian, Eve.

Holly had found a brush and was inconsolable as she gently pushed to one side the dead or dying bees to make a path for them to walk on. Her face was wet with tears, which she wiped away with the back of her hand before her mother handed her a tissue. "Why mummy? Why...?"

"I can't answer that, sweetheart. I honestly don't know."

"I think they're dying because Eve has died." Her sobs intensified and she spluttered. "Mummy, they knew I was going to take care of them. I told them over and over that I always would."

James overheard Holly, and trying to ignore the sound of crunching bees beneath his feet, he hurried across the verge. The grass verge that was once the colour of green was now black tinged with yellow. He caught up with her. "Not all of the bees Holly. I saw some fly away and they appeared to be going in the direction of the apiary."

Holly stopped crying and her expression changed. Her eyes widened as she stared at him. Although red, they now shone with delight. She began to sniff then blew her nose on yet another tissue. "How many, how many flew away," she gasped.

"Holly, I didn't count them, but there must have been thousands and thousands."

His reply made Holly smile. She began to mumble and it sounded as if she were praying.

Harry picked his way between the ancient, crumbling gravestones, now pockmarked with dead or dying bees. He met up with the little group who had already reached the mausoleum.

The hearse had driven the coffin around the church building and taken it into the entrance on the east side of the property.

They had transferred Eve's embalmed body, dressed in a gown of white silk, and placed it into a sculptured prepared sarcophagus. This was to be her final resting place. The lid was open. Eve looked serene, quite beautiful and very much at peace.

Outside the pall-bearers could be heard whispering as they recounted how the bees had swooped down over the coffin. It was a miracle that not one of them had been stung.

Flickering candles lit the dark, musty mausoleum and eerie shadows danced up and down the walls. Gathered around the sarcophagus, the remaining watchers waited as Reverend Broadbent began by saying a few prayers.

When he had finished he glanced up from his prayer book and nodded. It was the signal for James and Harry to push the heavy carved stone lid of the sarcophagus, closing it for the very last time.

Everyone present began to recite the Lord's Prayer as Holly snuggled in between James and Harry and tried to help; her face ashen as her tiny body shook with emotion. Becky moved forward to stop her daughter, then realised that this was something Holly instinctively felt she must do.

The sarcophagus was now completely secure. Eve, as the last member of the Dupton family, or should it be Du Pont, had been lain to rest. After a final prayer the little group left.

Outside James closed the door, bowed his head, and said a silent good-bye to his life-long friend. Two final prayers were said, by Reverend Broadbent and the short service was over. Later the door would be sealed for all eternity

Harry, who was standing next to James, whispered. "She's an unusual child."

"You can say that again," he replied.

Holly wanted to go to the apiary to see if the bees had found their way home. Clare said she would go with her. As she was a stranger to the area she would feel a little out of place at the reception. Philip offered to drive them saying that he'd be back at The Fallen Angel within fifteen minutes.

Nicky, Becky and Gillian along with the Reverend offered to take charge of receiving their guests at the hotel. Harry and James agreed to meet up with Paul Cobb at the hospital to see how Sarah and Michael Milton were recovering from their ordeal. Walking away Harry leaned closer to his brother and whispered, "Sarah Milton is dead, she suffered an anaphylactic shock and there's little hope for her brother."

Chapter 30 – Michael

James and Harry's footfalls could be heard as they walked across Armstrong's, desert-sand coloured flooring, which was prevalent throughout the hospital. They passed various designated reception areas and the cafeteria. People bustled in all directions and the two escalators were in permanent motion, up and down.

They were told that Dr Paul Cobb had arrived and was in his office. The receptionist phoned through to let him know they were on their way. Harry knocked at the door and without waiting for an invitation walked in. "Any news," he asked, urgently.

Paul waved the two men to a couple of chairs in front of his desk. "Michael Milton is as comfortable as we can make him and his sister is in the morgue. There was nothing anyone could have done. The repeated venom attack was so intense it caused a massive coronary."

"Shit! We'll be inundated with the press when this gets out," Harry groaned.

"I have no doubt about that. There is one consolation. There will be nowhere for them to stay." James replied.

"Huh, they'll bring their own vans. I don't want to

think about it. It'll be chaos."

"I find it hard to believe, or even begin to understand, what has just happened. I've spent the last half-hour searching the internet trying to learn about bee attacks." Paul said.

"And have you...?

"Lots of strange stories but nothing remotely relevant."

"Will Michael survive?" James asked.

Paul shook his head. "It will be a miracle if he does."

James leaned forward, and being unsure how to phrase what he wanted to say, decided to come straight to the point. "Paul, this is vitally important. I know you are not going to like what I'm about to ask you. Before you say anything I want you to consider some things.

"You're going to be on the Board of Eve's holistic centre. Eve admired and trusted your judgment. Remember how she brought your dream of a hospice into reality."

Paul leaned forward and clasped his hands over his ears. "Christ James! Stop it. I didn't think you'd stoop so low. This sounds like blackmail to me."

James laughed. "I'll do what it takes…"

"I know what you are trying to say. The fact is, he's my patient and he's dying. I…"

James interrupted him. "Becky and Holly are also your patients. They need your help to keep out of prison, whether you want to believe it or not, that's where they're headed, and for a very, very long time. I know you feel torn, but Paul, we need you to allow this and we need you to be a witness."

Paul groaned. "Shit! Do you realise what you're asking of me?"

"Yes I do. Give Eve what she would wish for now, the truth. The truth: to enable Holly and Becky to live long and happy lives knowing that they have been completely exonerated. Blackwell is doing her damnedest to have at least one of them convicted. The truth has to be told, Paul."

"Damn you James. I know, I know…" he shook his head and groaned again.

"How long do you think he's got?" Harry asked.

"His systems are shutting down one by one, I'd say no more than twelve hours."

"Does he know his sister is dead?" James' voice demanded a quick answer.

"No."

Harry stood and took over the proceedings. "I'll ask the questions. James you and Paul can say, in all honesty, that you had no idea what it was I intended to say. This is a police matter. These questions are vital to a brutal murder enquiry. I need answers and, you two are witnesses."

"He's sedated; he can hardly move. He can't speak, only grunt. He also can't see. There's not one part of his body that has escaped the onslaught. There's not one inch of his skin, that hasn't been penetrated with venom. He was even stung on his eyeballs. His tongue is so swollen it no longer fits in his mouth, and there's another part of his body that has been repeatedly stung, which, I might add, makes my blood run cold at the thought."

"Shit…" James and Harry spat in unison.

"Just to warn you, so you know, what you are about to see." Paul continued."

Harry groaned, then asked, "What do you mean sedated? Is his brain muddled?"

"No, he is quite lucid."

"I am sorry we have to do this, Paul." James touched his arm in a gesture of understanding and friendship.

"I know."

"Then we must act and act now…"

The three men left Paul's office and walked along the corridor towards the lifts. Paul pressed the call button and they entered the first lift to arrive. He pressed another button on the inside and the lift began to rise. It took them to a private floor.

The door to Michael Milton's room was open and a nurse sat outside at a desk opposite the door. From her position she could see into the room and to the bed where her prostrate patient lay. She stood and followed the men into the room.

Michael's face was like a huge, red-spotted balloon. His eyes had disappeared. His tongue protruded through a slit where his mouth should have been. A sheet was draped over a cage to keep pressure off his tender body.

James took out his mobile phone and switched it to video. He closed the door behind them. The room was light and airy, with a large picture window running the length of one wall. The curtains were of a subtle pink and grey stripe. In the room there were two bucket chairs, upholstered in the same material as the curtains.

Harry walked to the head of the bed and sat in one of

the bucket chairs. James, Paul and the nurse stood back to one side. James adjusted the camera until he had Harry and Michael in the frame. He nodded to Harry. James then began to video the proceedings.

"This is DCI Harry Marchant speaking. With me are Doctor Paul Cobb, Sir James Marchant, Nurse Debra Jennings and Michael Milton. We are at the General Hospital in Meedon Bridge in room G 12. The time is 16.15. The date is the 17th September.

"Michael, can you hear me?"

The reply came by way of a grunt.

"Michael, I am Detective Chief Inspector Maitland. I apologise for disturbing you at this time. I'd like to ask you a few questions. Do you understand?"

Another grunt.

"These questions are of vital importance. As you are unable to speak could you nod for a yes and move your head sideways for a no? Is that something you can do?"

Michael nodded.

"Michael Milton has nodded." Harry said for the sake of the video. Not many things unsettled Harry, he'd had to deal with hundreds of disturbing incidents during his career, but the appearance of the man before him made him feel positively ill. A dead body feels nothing but this man must be in agony. His own body tingled as he thought of what the attack must have been like.

"I want to ask you about Eve Dupton. Do you know to whom I am referring?"

Michael nodded.

"Michael Milton has nodded. Is there anything you

can tell me about her death?"

Michael Milton remained still then shook his head. Michael has indicated, no. Harry asked another question. "Is there anything you can tell me about the death of Billy Bradshaw? Michael has indicated no." Milton remained motionless then Harry saw movement behind his closed lids and so did James and he zoomed in with the camera.

"Is there anything you can tell me about the death of Dan Green?" The movement behind Milton's eyes quickened. He still didn't respond and his body began to quiver. Paul stepped forward. Harry held up his arm to stop him from coming any closer and put a finger to his mouth warning him to keep quiet.

Harry didn't say anything for a moment then said, "Michael you are seriously ill. You have been badly stung by bees. The doctors are doing all they can for you. Unfortunately, your sister Sarah did not survive the attack."

Michael's body began to quiver as he realised his precious sister was dead.

Paul was not happy with this questioning, but reassured himself that he had done everything possible for Milton and he was confident that he was not going to survive. He decided with a clear conscience that he may as well let Harry try to get to the truth.

Michael was making indecipherable noises and began to thrash widely then he suddenly stopped and became calmer.

"I am so sorry about your sister, Michael. I can assure you, Dr Cobb and the hospital staff did all they could."

Tears leaked through slit eyes and trickled over

swollen flesh as they ran down the man's cheeks. Harry pulled a tissue from a box lying on the bedside table and gently dabbed Michael's face and put a fresh clean tissue in the man's hand. Why? He didn't know because he would not be able to lift his hand to use it.

"Am… I di…," Michael managed to utter.

Harry remained silent. His silence told Michael all he needed to know.

Harry was sure now that this would be the turning point in the conversation. "We know that Sarah wanted to extend the lease on Moxley Manor and make it her permanent home."

"Michael Milton has nodded. What happened? Did Sarah visit Eve to discuss the matter?"

"Michael has again nodded. And Eve refused. She explained how she had allowed your father to stay on at the Manor after the lease had expired, because he was terminally ill. When he died, Eve was then able to proceed with her plans to turn the Manor into a Holistic Centre."

Michael nodded. "Ac…unt," he grunted from the back of his throat.

"I can't hear you. Can you repeat that?"

"Ac… id… t…" The sound faded.

"Ah… you're saying that Eve's death was an accident?"

"Michael has nodded. Did they argue and did Sarah hit her with something?"

Michael didn't answer for a second or two then he nodded.

"Michael has nodded to the question that Sarah hit Eve

with something. Do you know what happened to Billy? We found a print from a wellington; the boot came from The Manor. Do you know who borrowed them?"

Michael groaned. It was as if he had given up, he knew he was going to die. His hopes and dreams for Sarah and himself were in ashes. He forced himself to speak. "Scu…ff .le."

Harry glanced at James. James confirmed that he was still filming.

"Billy was riding his bike along the path when you stopped him. He was probably frightened – he didn't know you."

"Uugh…" There was a sickening gurgling sound coming from the back of Michael's throat. Paul stepped forward and held a glass of water and inserted a straw into the slit which was once Michael's mouth.

Michael tried to suck up the liquid. When his throat had been lubricated Harry continued.

"There was a scuffle and Billy fell into the water. Is that what happened, Michael?"

"Michael has nodded. What can you tell me about Dan Green?"

"D…un…k…," he gushed in the hope that the faster he spoke the less pain he would feel.

"We know he was drunk. Did you meet up with him?"

"Michael has nodded. When you realised he was drunk did it give you an idea?"

"Michael has again nodded. What was that idea? Was it to enable you to pin the blame for the two deaths on to him?"

"Again Michael has nodded. Are you telling me that

Dan Green did not commit suicide? That it was you who hoisted him up into the tree and let him drop to his death?"

More tears forced themselves between Michael's slit eyes and he nodded.

"Sar… p …inster…"

"You loved your sister very much, didn't you? You were determined that one day she would become prime minster, so you were not going to allow anything, or anybody, get in the way of that dream?"

Michael has nodded in agreement. "Michael I would just like to clarify a couple of things. From what you have told me am I to believe that you are responsible for the deaths of Billy Bradshaw and Dan Green?"

There was a pause then Michael nodded.

"Michael, was your sister responsible for the death of Eve Dupton?"

Once again tears squeezed from the slits where his eyes used to be and he nodded.

"Thank you Michael. We will leave you to rest, I've no further questions. The time is 16.35. End of recording."

Outside the room Paul and James waited while Harry walked a few yards away to make a call."

"Well…" James asked when he returned.

"I'm seeing him at five."

"Had he heard?"

"Of course he had. As soon as he heard my voice he said, "I'll expect you at five". The entire force is abuzz with what happened. Excuse the pun."

"Right, do you want me to come with you?"

"No thank you big brother," Harry glared at James. "This is police work and I'm perfectly capable of doing my job."

Paul laughed. "You two are a prize pair."

"Will the video be accepted?" Paul asked.

"We don't often get a death-bed confession, never mind having one recorded. It was the only way, and I think we're all in agreement, that there was no duress. A confession was needed, and thanks to you Paul, we got one."

"I suggest we make copies. You have the time Harry, and don't let the original out of your sight."

Paul began to laugh. "Imagine the headline I can see them now, "Leader of the opposition dies in a revenge bee attack." Will anyone ever believe it? It wouldn't surprise me if they fabricated an entirely different story."

"They can't, too many witnesses," Harry replied.

"Not really, Harry. In truth, Holly and I were the only ones who saw what happened, and I don't think Holly completely understood what was going on. I expect the official line will be that she died after suffering a mammoth heart attack."

"At her age? The press won't leave it at that. Also, what can they make up regarding Michael's death?" Paul added.

"I see your point. Her enemies are going to have a field day,' he said pulling a complaining face as he loosened his tie and made a move to leave. "I've got to get out of this suit, it's stifling me but I suppose I had better get over to The Fallen Angel and see if anyone is still there."

Turning to face his elder brother Harry said, "I doubt it. It's a quarter to five." He then emphatically reminded James. "…I don't need you. I don't want you, but you might be able to add some weight to this, after all."

"Ah… are you listening to this, Paul? He can't manage without me."

Harry grunted and as he walked off he said, "I want you there James, as a witness to the proceedings, that's all."

"Harry must seriously be thinking that the Super will try to bury it," Paul quietly said to James.

"It won't be up to the Super, it'll be taken out of our hands. What happens will be a Home Office decision. They'll decide how it's handled. Sorry Paul, gotta go." James hurried to catch up to his brother.

"See you at Eve's at six." Paul called after them as he disappeared back into Michael Milton's room.

Chapter 31 – Suspicion

Superintendent Clive Davenport was a hunched, bear of a man having sat behind a desk for far too long. He was clean shaven. He had grey eyes that sometimes reflected the sky and changed to a brilliant shade of blue. His lips were thin and his nose was broad. Today he looked harassed.

His teak desk was in its customary mess. Harry couldn't understand how he ever found anything.

Clive Davenport knew exactly where everything was.

Evening was fast approaching and the waning sun still warmed the room as its rays filtered through the window pane.

There were no curtains at the window.

An array of framed photographs adorned the walls with him dressed in his finery, recording various police functions.

He sat rubbing his chin with his right hand as he stared at the two men. He groaned. "I've heard some tales in my time. The Leader of the opposition…"

"The press constantly reports on how volatile she is …er, was, sir," Harry reminded him.

"True. How did this come about? Blackwell was convinced that it was …em,"

"Becky or Holly McGrath," James interrupted.

"That's right. What put you on to this, Harry?" Harry explained as quickly and as precisely as possible the order of events and how it was James who had found the clue that changed the direction of the investigation – the wellingtons.

"So the night we were all at Sarah Milton's reception, that was the night you witnessed Milton and Blackwell in a compromising situation, right?"

"That's correct."

"It was also the night the housekeeper told you about the muddy wellingtons …wellingtons she claimed never to have worn since the day she bought them, correct?"

"Yes."

Harry then asked his Superintendent if this was an end to the matter and that Becky and Holly were no longer suspects.

"I think we can safely say that is the case, however, there are still procedures to be followed. I have a feeling that the government would like to supress this story and release their own version of events, but, with a church full of people that could prove difficult."

"Definitely impossible. I've already notified the press in case they began to think along those lines," James said.

"You've done what!"

"I thought the press would like to know that the leader of the opposition had been taken to hospital after being stung by a bee."

"Oh James… Was that all you said?"

"Yes."

Superintendent Davenport shook his head. "I need to get to grips with this bee thing. Where are they now? Are they a danger to the community?"

"I don't think we need to worry about the bees," James jumped in. "If you go to the churchyard you will see the ground covered in thousands, if not millions of corpses, dead bees," he clarified.

"Millions?" The Super raised an eyebrow.

"Yes, I've been informed that it takes about a thousand stings to kill a man and, believe me, more than that stung the Miltons," explained James.

"Good God!"

"A Honey Bee dies after it has stung, Superintendent. The Bees are no longer a threat. You weren't thinking of arresting them were you?"

It was impossible not to laugh.

"You're right about them dying, I had quite forgotten." The Super began to laugh again. "James, you always did have a way to lighten a situation. God only knows how we are going to explain this. It will run forever in the press."

"Who, are driving into the yard as we speak," James remarked.

"Oh shit! Would someone please tell me why we have to live in this era of transparency and accountability? How are we expected to get the job done with Joe public watching our every move?"

Harry glanced at his brother and tried hard to look serious.

"With difficulty, sir."

"You can say that again. Well James, it appears we have you to thank for this, you set the ball rolling in a completely different direction and came up with a winner."

"I think the problem was that Blackwell had two masters and was unable to separate one from the other," James said.

"Superintendent Davenport nodded in agreement. "Not for any longer I'm happy to say."

"Sarah Milton is dead, maybe she will now concentrate on her police work, or ask for a transfer," Harry mused hopeful that the latter would be the final outcome.

"That was not what I was going to say."

"Then what?"

"About an hour ago Blackwell came to see me and she tended her resignation."

"She did what!" Both men chorused.

"She handed me a letter and before I opened it she had left the room. After reading it I followed her. Unfortunately, I was too late and watched her drive out of the yard. Her desk had been stripped of everything that would show she had ever been in this building.

"At the time I found it difficult to comprehend what had made her do such an irrational thing. All she said in her letter was that she was desperate for a complete change. I now know what she meant. Without Sarah Milton she had no reason to be here in the valley."

"She didn't ask for a transfer?"

"No Harry, she's gone, it is as if she was never here."

"I don't think there will be any tears shed tonight, sir."

James drove to The Fallen Angel to enquire how the reception had turned out. Apparently, according to the staff it had been the most exciting day of the year. Accounts of the events at the Church varied tremendously: from one bee to one million bees, from one person being stung to one hundred people being stung.

It was obvious that it was going to be the talk of the valley for some time to come. James expected the majority of the congregation to have given the reception a miss. He had expected them to retreat to the safety of their homes. The exact opposite had happened.

Judging from the staff, the ballroom had been packed to bursting point and the chefs in the kitchen were rushed off their feet rustling up more and more canapés. James was satisfied. He left and made his way to the apiary.

Chapter 32 – The Will

Philip had taken off his jacket and tie. He was helping Becky to put water glasses on the old refectory kitchen table. Nicky was already seated going through some papers. Holly was nowhere to be seen. According to Becky, Clare was in her room, getting out of her Spanx, whatever they were, when James arrived.

"Still waiting for…" He glanced around the room as he took off his jacket and the tie hanging loose around his neck.

"Paul, Harry and Gillian," Becky replied as she handed Philip a couple more glasses, which he promptly put on the table.

Nicky looked up from the papers she was reading. "Are you satisfied with how it went, Dad?"

"Yes I am. It was a beautiful ceremony and a beautiful sunny autumnal day. We couldn't have wished for better, especially after all the rain we've been having lately."

"Except for the time when it went pitch black. We had to put the lights on in the Church." Nicky reminded him. "Anyway, how are the Miltons? Did they get away without being stung? I couldn't believe it when they insisted on leaving. Why is it that politicians think they can walk on water?"

James breathed in deeply he was not looking forward to this. "There's a lot to explain. If you don't mind, it's best we wait until we're all here."

"You're the boss," she chuckled.

The doorbell rang and without anyone answering, in walked Harry and Gillian, both had changed clothes. Harry was out of his uniform and Gillian now wore brown slacks and a bright yellow jumper. Both appeared to be far more relaxed. Paul Cobb followed moments later. "I'm not late am I?" he remarked noticing that he was the last to arrive.

"Right on time. Oh, before we start. Philip, did you order the food?"

"Always one to follow instructions, James. I arranged for enough food to keep us going for a week. We all know that when you start talking, you don't know when to stop. They're delivering promptly at seven," he said with a mischievous gleam in his eyes.

"Good," and true to form James returned the quip. "I couldn't wish for a better valet." He then told everyone to sit. "Right, let's begin,"

Chairs were pulled away from the table, scraping the stone slabs of the farmhouse kitchen floor. Once seated the chairs were jiggled back closer to the table. Glancing around Becky asked, "Where's Holly? Do you want her to be here?"

"Not for the moment. Harry has something to say to you all and then we'll bring her in."

"Over to you, Harry."

Harry began. "Yes… well… as you all know Sarah and Michael Milton insisted on leaving the church despite James' warnings. For a reason that no one will ever be able to explain they were attacked by a swarm of bees."

"They were running, Harry told me, that's what disturbed them," Gillian interrupted.

Harry's eyes moved from his brother, to Philip and on to Nicky, the only people in the room who had an alternative theory, regardless as to how incredulous that theory might be.

Harry continued. "Sarah Milton did not survive the attack." Nicky and Becky gasped. Philip glued his eyes on Harry, anxious to know what was coming next. There were only three people in the room who didn't know what had happened. Gillian had been told when she and Harry went home to change. The others were, Nicky, Becky and Clare. "Michael is still alive and unlikely to survive." Harry glanced at Paul who, by nodding his head, confirmed what Harry had said.

The room fell silent. Not one person sitting around the table knew what to say. Nicky was the first to speak. "This sounds to me that Becky and Holly will still be suspects. "What will happen now?" Her eyes locked onto Harry as she waited to hear what action the police were going to take.

Becky was biting hard on her lip and Philip put his hand over hers.

"Calm down Nicky and listen. After leaving you to play hostess at the reception, your father and I went to the hospital, and there we met up with Paul. It wasn't easy for Paul to agree to our request. Michael was dangerously ill and Paul didn't think he would survive the night. It meant we only had one chance of getting to the truth."

"Oh my God..." Nicky then began to laugh and shaking her head she continued... "I should have had more faith in you Harry, I'm sorry."

"May I please continue dearest niece…"

Nicky gestured a *please go on* with a superior wave of her hand.

"James filmed the interview on his mobile phone; you can all see it later if you wish. The upshot is. Sarah didn't know her father was not the owner of Moxley Manor, as James suspected. We believe, she boasted about her new status as, *lady of The Manor,* and of her expected inheritance to her Westminster colleagues. It must have come as an awful shock when she found out that he died penniless and that The Manor did not belong to him.

"Sarah went to see Eve to persuade her to grant a new lease on the property. As we know, Eve would never have contemplated such a thing. Eve had waited all her life to turn Moxley Manor into a Holistic Centre.

"Most of the country is aware of Sarah's fiery nature. We can only assume that on that day, with such a glowing future ahead of her, she saw that future begin to disappear. It was too much for Sarah to take; her dreams of grandeur had vanished into thin air. Realising that Eve was not going to change her mind Sarah totally lost control.

"She picked up the nearest thing to hand, which we believe was one of the white-painted stones lining the path and, in a split second, Eve was dead.

"After Eve's death Michael came to the apiary, no one there knew him. He blended in, he was just another visitor. He watched and listened. On the night of Sarah's reception, he came in the late afternoon to the apiary."

"Then Sarah must have told Michael what had happened, that she had hit Eve?" Philip interrupted.

"Oh yes, at a guess, I'd say he knew before they were even aware that Eve was dead."

"What about Billy?" Becky reminded Harry.

"I'm coming to that. Knowing how it had rained all Friday night and again in the morning, and also knowing that the land around the apiary would be muddy, Michael borrowed Helen's wellington's."

"Just a minute, I thought they were women's wellingtons." Nicky reminded him.

"Yes and a size seven. Wellingtons are shapeless. They allow for the wearing of umpteen pairs of socks. We found out that Michael took a size eight shoe. They would have been a snug fit but he was only going to wear them for a short while.

"He went to the apiary and overheard Billy shouting that he knew who had killed Eve. He waylaid Billy on the path. Billy must have been frightened not knowing the man. There was a scuffle and Billy ended up in the water."

Becky muttered. "Poor little mite. He was such a lovely boy."

"Last Friday, Sarah went to see James and tried to persuade him into giving her a new lease on the property. James explained how it was not possible. He reiterated the plans for Moxley Manor."

"What I don't understand is why she went ahead with the reception knowing Eve was dead and knowing that the lease would not be renewed. If it was me I'd have scarpered back to London. I doubt she would ever have been considered a suspect," Becky added.

"She didn't come to see me until after the reception. She believed that now Eve was dead the Trustees would have a different viewpoint.

By hosting the reception, I believe her intention was to ingratiate herself with the prominent people in the valley. She had hoped, if needs be, they would put pressure on the Trustees to allow an extension of the lease.

She was assuming that these prominent valley people would be thrilled to have such an illustrious person living in their mist. What a coup for them to have a prime minster resident here in the valley."

"Supercilious bitch! She didn't know the people of this valley. That's the last thing they'd want." Gillian was speaking from experience. She and Harry were living in a barn conversion, amongst those same valley people. Coming into the valley as an outsider when she married Harry, she knew only too well, that you had to earn their friendship and trust, and it didn't matter who you were. It also took a long time.

"What about Dan Green, Dad?"

"It's Harry's case, Nicky."

Harry continued. "As I explained, Sarah went to see James. No doubt she told Michael that James had refused to renew the lease. Michael needed time to think, they both had a lot on their minds and on their consciences. They would have to plan skilfully if they were going to get out of the mess they had got themselves into. Blackwell was working hard at getting Becky or Holly convicted. With Billy's death it had given them another problem.

"Michael went again to The Centre where he witnessed a confrontation between Carol Bradshaw, Dan Green and James. He saw James hand Dan a suitcase and send him on his way. Michael then met up with the drunken man, plied him with more alcohol and somehow got him to the oak tree, next to where Billy went into the water.

"How he did it, I don't know, but somehow he got Dan to stand on a crate. He put the rope around his neck and kicked that box away."

"A crate?"

"Yes Nicky, a crate. We found a broken wooden crate not far from the scene. Perfect, all done, no more problems. Sarah and Michael were now safe.

"Michael was confident that the police would assume that, because Dan Green was guilty of child-abuse, he'd met up with Billy on the path and thrown him in the river. Later, being full of remorse, he hanged himself."

"Neat," Nicky scoffed. "So that's an end to the matter?"

"It sounds like something out of a novel – and to think they wanted to pin it on Holly and me. It makes me so mad…"

"You have every right to be mad." Philip said doing his utmost to console her.

"I don't know what you all think, but I believe we should keep these facts from Holly until she's much older." Becky nodded in agreement.

"Definitely, under no circumstances is this the moment to tell her," Philip emphasised.

Nicky glanced at her watch. "We had better move on, the food will be here in about ten minutes."

"Shall I'll fetch Holly now," Becky asked, she was desperate to know how long she would have before being asked to leave Eve's home.

Where would they go?

Where could they go?

Where would she get another job?

James stood. "I'm nearest, I'll go."

James made his way to the sitting-room

"There you are…" Holly peeped around the high-backed winged chair she was curled up on. He strolled across the room towards her. "Your presence is now required, my lady."

She tried to force a smile but couldn't. "I expect we're going to be told when we have to leave."

There was such sadness in her voice he wanted to hug her. "We'll see. What's the book?" he asked.

"It's one of Eve's."

"Oh …which one?"

"It's a medical book."

"Good grief, can you understand any of it?"

"Not really –well –sort of."

He placed his arms along the back of the chair and leaned over her left shoulder to see what it was she was reading.

The book was open at page one-hundred-and-twenty-seven. James read:

CHAPTER FOURTEEN.

THE HEALING POWER OF CANNABIS.

His blood ran cold in his veins. Saying nothing he held out his hand and took hers. As they reached the dining-room Holly asked, "Do I have to go in there? Isn't this for grown-ups? I don't know anything about Wills."

"Nothing to be frightened of." James opened his eyes wide and nodded as if there was a promise of something good behind the door. He opened it and let Holly walk through into the kitchen and showed her to a chair next to her mother. He glanced towards Harry, who began to speak.

"Becky and Holly I have some good news for you both."

Holly glanced at her mother. Becky shrugged her shoulders implying that she didn't know.

"The police are now satisfied that neither of you are involved, in any way, with the death of Eve, or of little Billy Bradshaw."

"We told you that," Holly snapped. Then shaking her head, she huffed. She was quite bemused as to how long it had taken these silly adults to come to that conclusion.

"I know, I know. The police are obviously not as clever as you. We are extremely sorry for all the distress we have caused you both. Unfortunately, it was necessary for us to get to the truth and anything you may have told us, however small, could have been a great help to us in finding out who the murderer was, and this, we have been able to do."

"Who did it? Who did it?" Holly yelped with glee.

"I'm not at liberty to say for the moment. However, someone may want to speak to you again, only to clarify a few points and to make sure that all our reports are accurate. It's nothing for you to worry about. Your sleepless nights are over." He glanced at Becky as he spoke. Becky smiled as she lowered her head.

Philip placed a comforting arm around her shoulders and whispered, "I told you so."

Regaining composure Becky fumed, "Damn, how I'd like to get my hands on that Blackwell woman."

"I know mum; she's horrible."

"Well, you have nothing to fear from Inspector Blackwell. She has left the police force and also the valley and I doubt we will ever see her again."

"Good riddance." Holly cried clapping her hands. "Can we have a party to celebrate?" Although giggling she knew she had said something naughty.

"Holly!" Becky chastised.

"That's exactly what we're going to do. We're going to celebrate Eve's life after Nicky has explained a couple of things to us, so, over to you, Nicky."

Nicky picked up her folder, opened it and looked at the papers in front of her. "There is not much to tell. I'm just going to reiterate Eve's wishes, which most of you already know. However, this has to be done. I'll not read out all the boring legal jargon. I'll also not read a few paragraphs, which apply solely to my father.

"We all know Eve had been preparing for the day when the lease on Moxley Manor would expire. It was then that the building and land would be returned to the Dupton family. Eve's long-dream of a Holistic centre would then be able to come into fruition. As it was, Eve died. In the event of a premature death Eve arranged for a Trust to be set up and all her assets would become the responsibility of that Trust.

"It was her wish that Sir James Marchant would solely oversee and complete the development of the venture. Eve wanted everything carried out to her precise wishes down to the tiniest of detail. She even designed the indoor swimming pool, the changing rooms, the colour of the robes and towels etc. etc."

Nicky held up two box-files, her arms straining with the weight and said, smiling, "I think you get the picture." Everyone laughed. "With Sir James being solely in control, Eve felt that there would be no disagreement between members of the Trust and, having known him all her life, that Sir James would carry out her wishes to the letter. When the Centre is due to open, the formalities will be put into operation and new trustees will be appointed and you all know who they are. To begin with the Trust will be made up of five members, Sir James, Dr Cross, Dr Cobb, DCI Marchant and me, Nicky Marchant.

"Lastly, Eve asked that her clothes be given to charity." Nicky hesitated. "That's about it. Are we all happy so far with the contents of Eve's Will?"

There was a chorus of an unemotional, "Yes."

"Now, this leaves just one thing… a short while ago Eve added a codicil to her Will."

"What's a codicil?" Holly asked.

"Sush, just listen…" Becky chastised.

Nicky opened another envelope, took out two sheets of paper, and began to read. "I etc. etc. etc. Again, I think we can skip the legal jargon. The codicil states that she wishes, and I quote, *'that my good friends Becky and Holly McGrath, if they should so choose, may occupy Honeycombe Farm for as long as they wish'*."

Becky gasped. In her wildest dreams she had never imagined such a thing and uncontrollable tears spouted from her eyes. "Mummy, mummy does that mean we don't have to leave here. It means I don't have to leave the bees." Holly was almost hysterical as she pushed back her chair and began to race from the room. Philip caught her as she was about to charge past him.

Holly began to struggle. "Let me go, let me go I've got to tell the bees," she cried.

Philip held her tightly. "Just a minute, young lady. Nicky has not finished. I want you to go back and sit down and wait until you hear what else Eve has to say. This is Eve talking and she is talking to you." He held her by the shoulders and stared into her eyes and the child instantly calmed and returned to her chair.

Nicky went on. "*It is my wish that Becky continues to oversee the running of the apiary, and also to continue to work on my research in consultation with my good friend, Dr Philip Cook. If Becky should choose not to accept my wishes I will respect her decision. If that were to be the case, then a manager is to be appointed to oversee the apiary and, that person may live in the property for as long as they hold that position.*"

"I never want to leave," Becky sobbed.

"Now Holly, this concerns you, remember what Philip said, this is Eve talking." Nicky began to read slowly and distinctly pronouncing every word making sure the child fully understood. "*I come to my beloved bees. My bees have been the most precious thing in my life. I would like a wonderful girl called Holly to look after my bees. I know she will love and take of them as I have throughout my life.*

"*If at some future date she chooses to take a different path, then the apiary must continue at all cost, and the bees protected. The trustees will be able to obtain the necessary help from the British Bee Association,*" Nicky slowly closed her folder. "I think that about covers it."

"Mummy, mummy, what does it mean? Has Eve given her bees to me, like a present?" Holly screeched.

"It would appear so, sweetheart." Becky discreetly dabbed away more tears.

"Can I go now? Can I go?" Without waiting for an answer she pushed her chair back from the table and charged towards the door screaming "I'll never leave the bees. I'll never leave the bees."

Nicky burst out laughing. "I remember you telling me Eve said the same thing when she was only six, Dad."

"I know it's strange, very strange," he mused.

It was obvious from the expression on Becky's face she was in a state of euphoria and complete bewilderment. "This is all too much to take in. We don't have to leave, it's wonderful." She began to laugh as she shook her head, "Eve has secured our future, I can't believe it, I just can't believe it."

"She thought the world of you both, Becky." James said.

Becky began to splutter half-laughing half-crying. "I fail to understand Holly. She's only a child and yet she loves those bees. I ask you," she giggled. "Bees of all things. Kittens, puppies, horses, yes, but –bees?"

Clare, who had obviously been listening at the door, came into the room. "All done," she chirruped.

"Yes, and you're not going to believe what's happened. Eve has said Holly and I can live here for as long as we want …and, and," she spluttered. "That's not all; she has given her bees to Holly. I can't take it all in."

"I can, you deserve it. Eve knew exactly what she was doing. She was a clever lady. Where's Holly?"

"Gone to tell the bees. Good grief, listen to me I'm starting to talk like the child."

Clare smiled, and taking charge, said. "Come on, the food will be here at any moment. Will someone please set the dining-room table?"

"I will," Gillian offered.

The women began banging about in the kitchen. "You men can see to the drinks. There's champagne in the fridge and plenty of wine in the rack," Clare called, then continued giving instructions to anyone who was listening.

James had slipped out of the room without anyone noticing. To his left he saw Holly about to jump the chain link fence separating the yard from the apiary. He turned right and raced through the gap between Eve's farmhouse and The Visitors' centre. He then turned sharp left and ran alongside the building stopping short when he came to the end.

Peeking around the corner he saw Holly. She was standing perfectly still, staring ahead. She wore the same transfixed expression on her face he had seen when she was standing outside the church.

Was it possible Holly could communicate with the bees? Was it Holly, knowingly or unknowingly, who instigated the attack? So many inexplicable things had happened over the past few weeks, it was making James look at life from a different perspective. Could Holly be the reincarnation of Celestine Du Pont and Eve the reincarnation of her mother of long ago? The mother who had spent lifetime after lifetime searching for her child in an effort to make her realise, and understand, how she must forgive the injustice that had befallen her all those years ago? Two wrongs don't make a right, as they say in this life-time.

The more James pondered the scenario the more nonsensical it sounded. It was odd however, that the bees only attacked the killers of Eve, little Billy Bradshaw, and Dan Green.

There were plenty of people scurrying for cover, which should by rights, have unnerved the insects even more, and yet no other person was stung.

Did the bees know what they were doing? Are they more intelligent than we humans give them credit for?

What was it Celestine DuPont had screamed as she burned to death at the stake, all those centuries ago? "You will die by a thousand cuts": a thousand stings to be exact.

Holly nodded towards the hives as if saying good-night and, smiling, she began to skip back the way she had come. James turned and raced back the way he had come. He was crossing the cobbled yard, making for the five-bar gate, to open it in readiness for the delivery of their Thai meal, as Holly reached the yard. She was humming as she sidled up to him. Her expression told him that this was to be another secret. He bent his head to her level as she whispered.

"Remember what Eve told me, Uncle James. She told me that everything would be all right." Her face was radiant, her young, fresh skin glowed, her eyes shone and he was given a preview of the beautiful woman she would become. She laughed a laugh he hadn't heard in weeks. Beginning to hum again she practically danced back into the house leaving James mystified.

Again he asked himself the question, could Holly communicate with the bees, and could she have instigated the bee attack?

Was Holly, as the reincarnation of Celestine DuPont, finally carrying out her revenge on the Cardinal, or were the bees simply carrying out their own revenge on the murderer of their guardian, Eve? If the latter proved to be true, then the Cardinal still had to come into Holly's life making this story far from over.

THE END OF BOOK ONE